To those who answer

the call to

move, shoot, and communicate

In 943 AD a terrible plague struck Europe. A medieval chronicler wrote, "it was an *invisibli ignis, carnem ab ossibus separens et consumens*, an invisible fire separated the flesh from the bones and consumed it. *Cum intolerabili cruciati*, with intolerable, excruciating pain, men, women, and children perished... First their toes turned black then their fingers burst open. Their arms and legs convulsed and broke off..., a horrible roar of pain could be heard for miles and an indescribable stench hung for weeks..." They called it holy fire, Saint Anthony's fire, and Saint Vitus's dance. Scientists believe that the grain fungus *Claviceps Purpura*, or one of its deadly cousins, caused the epidemic. It would plague mankind again in the Twentieth Century.

---

*Gas!*

Adrenaline surged through his body. Instinctively he rolled off the bed and wrapped the sheet around his head, seeking cover on the floor. A parachute flare popped in the distance. It hung in the night sky like a miniature artificial sun, lighting up the narrow alpine valley. The intermittent *thunk* of a distant mortar punctuated the deep-throated chugging of a heavy machinegun firing from a squatting helicopter.

*They are pinning us in the village so they can spray us like insects!*

---

He poured three fingers of garlic-flavored vodka in his water glass.

*"Za vashe zdorovoye!"* he said toasting with the image in the mirror. He tossed down the fiery liquid in one gulp.

# Saint
# Anthony's
# Fire

# Larry
# Simmons

## THIS BOOK IS A WORK OF FICTION

Neither the action events nor the characters described in this novel reflect any actual incidents or portray any real persons. The author has endeavored to show the nature of special operations by allusion to historical events and information in the public domain. The names of some public figures have been used in passing to fix the time and locale of the story, but they are not characters in the novel.

 **Simmons International Consulting Group**

Copyright © 2011 by Larry Simmons

All rights reserved, including the right to reproduce this book or portions thereof in any form.

ISBN:  978-0-9838756-5-9

First CreateSpace printing September 2011: www.createspace.com

Cover art by Noah Heller

Printed in the U.S.A.

*Bits and pieces,* he thought. *Bits and pieces come back to me in the dark, their faces staring up at me with that Allah-save-me-look.*

Gurnov grumbled out loud. "There is no Allah you ignorant bastards! God does not live on a planet man has soiled."

Then he thought of his plan, his brilliant, simple plan. *Yeb vas veruyushchii! -- screw you God believers. Ten million dollars and fifty Burmese whores will purge you from my mind.*

---

"They think the Russians are dumping toxins at sea on their way to Johnston Atoll, the kind of stuff they used in Laos and Afghanistan."

"*Huh!*" Sanz exclaimed. "*Yellow Rain?*" he asked.

"You got it. Whatever it is, it's certainly not bee do-do," Julie said.

During the Reagan administration there were disturbing accounts from Hmong tribesmen fleeing Laos that remote villages were being gassed by a *Yellow Rain*. Samples taken by U.S. experts sent to investigate turned out to be bee droppings. The findings seriously discredited the administration's public condemnation of the Soviet Union's use of chemical weapons in Southeast Asia.

Julie stopped under a street lamp and looked up into Lee's eyes.

"Lee, I've got a chance to make a real name for myself in news business."

"Be careful with this one, Honey. It sounds like Saint Anthony's fire."

---

# ------- About the Author -------

*Larry Simmons* *entered the naval service in 1966 and rose through the ranks of the US Navy Seals from seaman to commander. The Seals are a special operations force whose missions include counterterrorism and other high-risk operations. Larry deployed to Vietnam as a member of Seal Team TWO and served in operational billets from Vietnam to commanding officer of Seal Team FIVE in Coronado in 1993. A graduate of Ohio State University, he has a Master of Science in Operations Research from the Naval Postgraduate School in Monterey, California and a Master of Science in Education from National University in San Diego, California. Commander Simmons is a Master Training Specialist and is still teaching men to move, shoot, and communicate. After retiring from the service he served in Saudi Arabia training a maritime special operations force, in Mexico as Regional Director to an organization specializing in kidnap recovery for fortune five hundred companies, and as a consultant on several projects in West Africa and South America. In recent years Larry has been working in the Middle East, as Project Manager for KBR in Iraq and as Country Manager of Falcon Security, the largest nationally owned private security company in Iraq. In 2010, Larry spent a year with the SWAT team in Abu Dhabi. He is currently working in Iraq.*

# Forward

*Tabun, sarin, soman, chloropicrin.* These are not words in a foreign language. They are the cruelest weapons, the poor man's atomic bombs. Only a few oily, sweet-scented drops of VX nerve agent the size of pimples are sufficient to kill a man. Death comes in the cruelest way; sudden muscle spasms, violent jerking motions, slobbering, vomiting, defecating, followed by massive convulsions that result in paralysis and asphyxiation. Choking and blister agents are even more ghastly. Mustard and phosgene burn the eyes and blister the skin in huge ulcerations. The flesh turns black. Victims gasp for air and suffocate in blind confusion.

Then there are awful combinations of chemicals and biotoxins, not to mention the biological monsters that are possible with the new technology of gene splicing. Hundreds of thousands of tons of these terrible agents of death have been produced since mankind began his ghoulish experiment in poison warfare. Tens of thousands died before the superpowers agreed to chemical disarmament, an agreement many believe to be a hodgepodge of half-truths, deception, prevarication, and inveigling. These dogs of war were unleashed long ago and they are not so easily brought to heel.

With regard to the possibility of the human species surviving technological adolescences, the 1990s began with great promise. The United States and the Soviet Union agreed to reduce their arsenals and then the breakup of the Soviet Union accelerated the process. In 1993, a landmark treaty was signed in Paris; the Chemical Weapons Convention, in which most civilized nations agreed to a ban on the use and production of chemical weaponry. But two great questions loom like a pall over a funeral. First, will nations abide by the agreement? Syria? North Korea? Iran? Concerned about Israel's nuclear arsenal, Arab nations want to link chemical disarmament to nuclear disarmament. Compliance is another problem. Some leaders will sign an international accord and then do quite the opposite in secret.

Ridding the world of the poisons of war is much easier said than done. To quote one Russian official, "Destroying chemical weapons is more expensive than making them." It could cost as much a twenty billion dollars to neutralize the arsenal of the former Soviet Union and they do not have the resources. Better to bury, dump at sea or sell arms than to destroy them. Shortly after signing the 1993 Chemical Weapons Convention the Soviet Union shut down its only chemical weapons incinerator plant.

Federal laws prohibit the U.S. Military from transporting chemical weapons about the country or from dumping ageing weapons at sea. Consequently, we must build costly incinerator plants near chemical weapons stockpiles. Working at maximum capacity it will take us years to destroy the sixty million pounds of blister and nerve agents in our arsenals. Unfortunately, the rules for the former Soviet Union are not so well defined, giving rise to the second frightening question: What is happening to these cruelest of weapons? The answer is: They sit rotting like lethal leaking metal coffins monitored by cages of rabbits with tiny pink twitching noses living precarious lives amidst row upon row of deteriorating time bombs. These horrible weapons linger to haunt mankind like ghosts of noxious plasma while rogue nations create the next generation of poison weapons.

The ability of mankind to create carnage is limited

only by the imagination. Those that survived the gas attacks of World War I reported that phosgene smelled like freshly mown hay. It was an odor that struck terror in its victims for the rest of their lives. It is strange how an innocent smell or a startling noise can cause some veteran to relive the horrors of combat in hallucinatory detail. *Bang!* The backfire of an automobile can bring back the crack of a rifle. The odors of freshly moan hay can bring back the terror of a chemical weapons attack.

The source of those living memories is the amygdala, a tiny pea-size tangle of neurons that shackle innocent stimuli to memories of unbearable terror. That kernel of fear is an instrument of survival. Extreme terror causes adrenaline to surge through the veins and instantly stimulates a fight or flight response. The reward for enduring the cold sweat and the pounding heart is the opportunity to live another day. There are other less jolting connections that warn of danger, such as the smell of *plastique* explosives, the glint of a trip-wire, the metallic clack of a rifle bolt sliding home. For some individuals, these mental triggers conjure up images of half-gaping, half-comprehending, sprawled bodies covered in blood.

In this novel Major Alexander Gurnov relives the horrors of his wars. Fear, guilt, and greed drive him to escape his reality and vodka is insufficient to the task. Emotional triggers also compel irrational action, as the young SEAL hero of this novel discovers. To save the one he loves, he violates a direct order and walked among the most deadly weapons known to mankind. Lieutenant Robert Lee Sanz is young, naive, and full of life. He sees the world like most Americans, as just, kind and fair. He doesn't know of the brutality of the world beyond the gentle cradle of the United States of America. Major Gurnov by contrast, has become part of the barbarity that exists in places like Laos, Afghanistan, and Angola. He is hard and smooth on the outside like a hand grenade. But inside, he is all twisted up like a coiled spring ready to explode. His eyes are keen and restless. He continually observes his surroundings like a thief looking over his shoulder for a lawman. At night he watches from a darkened room, unable to sleep. He sits behind the curtain and stares at the world outside, chewing on the fat of guilt and hate and anger. His blood boils and his guts roil as he waits and watches, skulks and stalks, broods and seethes with delusions that drive him mad. And when he does sleep, he sleeps with one eye open so lightly that the softest footfalls in the corridor awaken him. Why? Paranoia is deeply embedded in his nature for good reason. His *amygdala* is hyperactive, a result of carnage wrought and ghosts from his past come to visit.

It takes so little imagination to see yourself under Major Gurnov's cross hairs, going about your daily business, oblivious of a metaphorical barrel lined up on your temple, about to deny you even a fraction of a second to absorb the most important event in your life. Not even the kernel of fear can save you if he unleashes a true weapon of terror, a chemical or biological monster. Criminal, crazy, or fanatic, it doesn't really matter. The question is how do we stop them from joining the ranks of the infamous? Unfortunately, History demands sacrifice and even entire peoples must be sacrificed for us to learn the lessons of the past. Enjoy this trip into the mind of a demented soldier, as a Russian Mafia pirates a ship loaded with chemical weapons bound for destruction on Johnston Atoll.

# Saint Anthony's Fire

*'Tis not easy, brother mine,*

*In a foreign land to live,*

Words from an old Cossack song

# Larry Simmons

# Prologue

A strange calm engulfed the tuna fisher *Westwind*. In doldrums seas she dieseled smoothly north by northeast in a vast empty expanse of flat ocean. Not a whiff of a breeze freshened the stifling air that smothered the pilothouse. Even the vessel's forward speed failed to clear the hot humid air. The helmsman glanced down at the compass, then at the satnav. It was still spitting out near redundant numbers, indicating the vessel was barely making way running into a strong current.

Keo "Poi" Makalapa rolled his eyes and mumbled, *"auwe, auwe,"* a doleful Hawaiian mourn of frustration.

He scanned the ocean in all directions then steadied his course. There were no ships nearby, no lights on the horizon, not even a cloud in the night sky, nothing but stars studding the black velvet of space. Poi eyed the Milky Way and the Grand Mystery above. He envisioned himself as an insignificant speck in a vast limitless universe, his life sustained by an old fishing boat that had seen its best day. The *Westwind* too was an insignificant speck on the broad sea, and the ocean itself insignificant under the inky star studded blackness of the cosmos. Suddenly, he felt alone, completely and utterly alone as if he had a hole in his soul and the essence of his being was rushing out toward the Grand Mystery above. He shook off the thought like a wet dog after a bath.

After a hard night's celebration, his mates were sound asleep. With holds bursting, the *Westwind* was finally homeward bound after months chasing fish about the

Pacific. Poi took a deep drag on his cigarette then wiped the sweat off his brow. The radar was off and so was the single side band radio. To fill the void he flicked a switch and the VHF crackled to life with a burst of white noise and static. In some far off place two fishermen were yakking away on channel sixteen, both with powerful signals.

"Bro, the torpedoes on that little gal were unbelievable, man. When they got to movin' and shakin' she damn near beat me to death."

A squawk of static was followed by a burst of laughter, then, "What a way to go! The old hula-hula, eh bro? Man, I could sure use some of that comfort right now."

"Me too, brother."

He listened to the yammering for a few minutes then switched to twenty-one.

"*Mayday! Mayday! Yacht Sailfish calling. Anyone copy this transmission?*" crackled an excited male voice.

The signal faded in and out so Poi knew the *Sailfish* was beyond his help.

"Vessel calling. This is the United States Coast Guard. Please say again your call sign and coordinates."

"*This is the Sailfish!*" A blast of white noise broke the signal then it faded back in with a barely audible, "*Taking on water!*" followed by silence.

From down below in the bowels of the *Westwind* came a *whoomp* and a groan as a well-worn bilge pump kicked on. The noise startled Poi and caused a sailor's nightmare to course coldly through his veins.

"*Pilikia?* - trouble?" he questioned with a startle. *What if we sink?* he thought. *The life raft is worthless.*

He shook off thoughts of sinking and filled his mind with daydreams of how he was going to spend his earnings when he got home. He was dreaming of an ice-cold beer when he felt it. A slight breeze stroked his sweaty skin. It wafted through the pilothouse ever so gently. He took a deeper breath and something in the air burned his lungs, like hot pepper. It caught in the back of his throat and filled his mouth with a metallic taste. He hawked it up and spit it out, then sucked in another breath that caused a wave of nausea to well up from his innards. Suddenly, his eyes burned and his vision blurred. Then every nerve in his body screamed fire. Excruciating pain overwhelmed his body as if he had been cast into the fires of hell. In spasms, coughing and vomiting, he fouled his pants with uncontrollable bowel movements. Staggering like a man possessed by demons, he tried to make it to the bridge wing. But massive convulsions gripped his legs. Jerking, slobbering, and defecating, he fell to the deck wriggling like a worm in a lethal spray of insecticide. Poi Makalapa retched up a mouthful of blood and died in agony on the steel deck of the *Westwind*.

The seven men sleeping below decks suffered a similar fate. The killer was an old assassin rendered from the grain bins of the Middle Ages. Dipped from an alchemist's cauldron, it was Saint Anthony's Fire intensified by the science of the space age.

# Chapter 1

A dog growled and let out a dusty bark that broke the night silence. It heard something off in the distance beating the air like the wings of a giant flying insect, a whooshing, *thum-thum-thum*-sound, as a helicopter altered course down the valley. Major Alexander Gurnov rolled over in his rack and moaned in his sleep. Instinctively he felt for the Tokarev that lay on the bed beside him. Its closeness gave comfort to his slumber. Feeling the pistol he ignored the dog and pulled the covers up over his head.

The Badakhshan province of Afghanistan was remote, isolated, and desolate. It was a dismal place of dried mud and broken stones unfit for human habitation, and certainly no place for a Russian soldier to die. Gurnov shivered and choked down a reflexive swallow. It was cold in the rugged mountains of the Hindu Kush, cold and dry, so dry his throat was parched. Outside, a cobalt-blue night sky outlined every detail of the landscape in stark relief. The mountains splayed out to the horizon in row after row of jagged barren peaks. To the east lay the Tibetan Himalayas and China, to the south the Khyber Pass and Pakistan. The way north was barred by Tajikistan. In the west the Red Army was on the move, pounding guerrilla positions with artillery and rockets. But in the Hindu Kush they were stalled. There, stonewalls and primitive fortifications speckled the valleys and gorges. Firing points and listening posts capped every dominant crag.

The Mujahideen had learned the weakness of the Soviet Army. They had learned that Russian helicopters were heavily armored on the bottom but had virtually no armor on the top. Using their ancient breech-loading rifles, they shot down at their enemy from high rocky ledges, sending hundreds of soldiers back to the Motherland in body bags. With the strength of Allah and old Lee-Enfield rifles they had wrestled the Russian Bear to a draw. It was the Mujahideen that controlled the Hindu Kush and their successes called for extreme measures to change the tide of battle: Quick, violent, chemical death to exterminate guerrillas in their sanctuaries. Badakhshan was so remote the world couldn't see what the Soviets were doing there. But Alexander Gurnov knew. He was a chemical warfare officer and the horrors of his job were permanently seared into his twisted mind.

The noise from the helicopter grew louder until the panes in the window rattled. Then he heard a noise that caused a bolt of sheer terror to flash through his body, the sound of a metallic cylinder striking the rutted rocky road outside his room, followed by a hissing sound.

*Gas!*

Adrenaline surged through his body. Seeking cover on the floor, he instinctively rolled off the bed and wrapped the sheet around his head. A parachute flare popped in the distance. It hung in the night sky like a miniature artificial sun, lighting up the narrow wadi. The intermittent *thunk* of a distant mortar punctuated the deep-throated chugging of a heavy machinegun firing from a squatting helicopter.

*They are pinning us in the village so they can spray us like insects!*

Mortars and the machineguns didn't scare Alexander Gurnov. Bullets could be avoided. A man could fight

5

back. It was the thought of gas that made his heart race and his temples pound. He had seen the effects of chemical and biological agents up close and personal. Part of his job was battle damage assessment, a military term for examining bodies and buildings when the fighting is done. Like a terrified animal he slithered on his stomach to the back wall of the room.

*There is no escape! I'm trapped!*

A chemical cloud swallowed the building in a yellow-brown haze of lethal fumes, blocking out the light of the parachute flare. Poisonous vapor seeped into the room under the window and around the door like a phantom searching for him. He held his breath as long as he could. When survival compelled him to breathe, he began coughing and choking. His lungs caught fire and his skin turned a sickly yellow. Gasping and retching in uncontrollable bouts of vomiting, he wriggled on the floor in fits of spasms. Scarlet frothy sputum painted his torso. Then blood began to ooze from his eyes, nose, and ears. Death was near. He could feel it. He could see it covering his soul. Then his muscles began to twitch. The spasms grew in intensity from jerking tremors to massive convulsions that racked his entire body. Huge blisters began to appear on his exposed skin and his flesh turned black. Gagging and gurgling in a death moan, he watched the life force leave his body and hover in mid air above him, teasing him with a small prospect of survival.

He was lying on the floor jerking like a dog with a broken back when the nightmare ended. Outside his room an ancient Russian bus rumbled off in a cloud of noxious fumes. Gulping in great gushes of air like a drowning man, Major Alexander Gurnov clutched his face with both hands.

"What the fuck am I doing on this filthy fuckin' floor?" he cursed. *"Goddamn Afghanistan!"*

6

Gurnov knew the answer to his interminable question. For an instant he saw himself in Afghanistan in the back of a helicopter dropping chemical bombs on Mujahideen villagers. As the helicopter gained altitude he envisioned a man running out of a yellow-brown cloud that spread across a narrow rocky gorge. He collapsed in a heap on the ground, writhing in convulsions. Then a child. A little girl child. And another man. And a woman. And another. They looked like bugs sprayed with insecticide, wriggling and convulsing on the barren earth. The images haunted him.

*I'm sweating like a pig. Water. I need water. Damn the Politburo!*

Gurnov got up off the floor and stumbled to a washbowl on the nightstand. He poured in a little water from a pitcher beside the bowl and splashed it on his face. Then he looked at the man staring back at him from the mirror. The dim streetlight filtering in through the closed curtains created haunting shadows around his eyes and nose. His face wasn't ugly, just brutal without appeal, broad browed, heavy cheek-boned, sun-tautened, and thin-lipped with a trace of Mongol around the eyes.

*Gurnov, you son of a drunken whore, when are you going to stop torturing yourself? War is war. Orders are orders. You didn't make the rules. You just followed them.*

"Ah!" he grumbled out loud. "Maybe it was something I ate."

But he knew better.

"If it's the vodka, Gurnov," he said, talking to himself, "you'll have to learn to live with these night terrors. I am not going to give up my juice because a few ghosts come to visit in the night."

He poured himself another glass of water and downed it in one gulp. Looking in the mirror, he mumbled,

7

"These nasty little dreams always tear up your sleep at dawn, Gurnov. So why not wake up at three. Avoid the self-torment, you stupid bastard."

He stared at his drained reflection and thought, *Da! They evade my memory while I am awake. They only invade when I am sleeping, in the early morning hours just before dawn.*

He placed one hand over his stomach and grimaced in pain.

*And they leave me with this sourness in my stomach that I cannot purge.*

He tried to hawk up the sourness but his mouth was too dry. The bottle of vodka next to the washbasin tempted him.

*"Nelzya!* -- not allowed," he grunted. "It's too early for vodka. *Nyet!* Just a small one," he mumbled.

He poured three fingers of garlic-flavored vodka in his water glass and swirled the slivers of garlic around.

*"Za vashe zdorovoye!"* he said toasting with the image in the mirror. He tossed down the fiery liquid in one big gulp.

*Bits and pieces,* he thought. *Bits and pieces come back to me in the dark, their faces staring up at me with that Allah-save-me-look.*

Gurnov grumbled out loud. "There is no Allah you ignorant bastards! God does not live on a planet man has soiled."

Then he thought of his plan, his brilliant, simple plan.

*Yeb vas veruyushchii!* -- *fuck you God believers. Ten million dollars and fifty Burmese whores will purge you from my mind.* He placed his hand over his stomach and suppressed a dry heave. *And remove this sourness from my guts.*

The dog barked again, breaking his train of thought. Down on the street outside his sleazy little room he heard a door slam. He crept over to the window like a soldier on patrol and peeked out from behind the closed curtain. With restless eyes he scanned the wet gloomy streets of Odessa, looking for nothing, looking at everything. Then an engine rumbled to life and a large truck parked on the street began belching diesel fumes. The driver gunned the engine several times and with the grinding of gears and a lurch, drove away. As the truck rumbled off down below, it vibrated his windowpanes like the helicopters in Afghanistan. For an instant the noise heaved him back to a war zone. With trembling hands he went back to the basin and gulped down more vodka. But it was insufficient for the task.

*It will be light soon. I have to see to the rabbits,* he thought.

His ship was sailing in two days and it was his responsibility to ensure that none of the rabbits were dead before departing. Gurnov didn't have to check them personally, he just had to ensure the proper reports were filed before the ship sailed. Enlisted men in protective chemical suits physically checked the ship. Several cages of rabbits were strategically placed in each hold of the *Stashinsky* to act as living sensors. Rabbits couldn't smell nerve gas. That wasn't the objective. They monitored the poisonous cargo by simply being there among the decaying weapons of horror. By drooling, staggering, jerking, and dying they reported leaks. Those that didn't die a horrible chemical death added protein to the ship's meager menu.

Major Alexander Vissarionovich Gurnov was an officer in what was left of the Soviet Chemical Corps. He had learned his trade at Shikhany and Volgograd, and had applied it in Yemen, Laos, Afghanistan, and Angola. He had sprayed, doused, dusted, gassed, and bombed thousands of ill-fated human beings with vile poisons of

9

war beget from the most secret laboratories of the Soviet Union. It was their ghosts that haunted him in the early morning hours after the numbness of the vodka wore off.

With the disintegration of the Soviet Union, Gurnov's prospects in the military were bleak. The Russians and the Americans had signed a secret agreement to destroy their biological and chemical arsenals and with the destruction of CBW, so went his career. And when all the black weapons were gone, so was his means of livelihood. Gurnov's overt assignment was to accompany shipments of deteriorating chemical weapons from Russia to Johnston Atoll in the Pacific. His covert mission was to quietly dispose of terrible top-secret war poisons the Russian Chemical Corps wouldn't admit existed. Plausible denial extended all the way to the Russian President.

Down on the street a bedraggled laborer yelled at someone in a nearby flat.

*"Pozhaluista, Gennady. Bystro!* -- Come, Gennady. Hurry!"

Gurnov jumped, startled by the booming voice. He went back to the window, bottle of vodka in hand, and watched the laborer with hawkish eyes. A teenage boy ran out of a nearby flat and joined the man. Images of emergency decontamination flashed across Gurnov's mind. It was the recollection of an accident that had occurred during the last voyage of the *Stashinsky*. Dead rabbits invaded his thoughts along with soldiers in chemical suits hurriedly hauling an enormous bomb out of the ship's center hold. In the dark of night he ordered them to drop it overboard expecting the great volume of the ocean to dilute the poison. But something had gone terribly wrong. A mycotoxic cloud had drift throughout the night. Weeks later he had learned that a fishing boat had sailed into a pocket of the poison. Reports of the strange deaths had reverberated throughout the South Pacific, inviting the prying eyes of savvy environmentalist and Western news reporters.

A wave of paranoia overcame him. Inside the chemical corps the incident had been blamed on him. He was a decontamination expert and it was his job to ensure that special weapons, that officially didn't exist, were quietly disposed of at sea. He knew his superiors dared not take formal action for fear he would expose what the Russian Army was doing in the dark of night in the vast Pacific. What he feared was informal action.

When the workmen walked off down the street, he pulled a wooden chair up to the window and lit a cigarette, being careful to hide the light of the match. Breathing deeply on the harsh black tobacco he watched the street from behind the closed curtain.

"It wasn't my fault you assholes, you desk-bound pencil-necked assholes."

Then he thought. *They need me because I am the man, a chemical troop. No one knows how to do this.* Then his mind jumped track. *Koshkin and Baranov I can trust. But Markov, nyet. He cannot be trusted.*

After the extortion, Gurnov intended to lay low in Burma under the protection of the drug lord, General Kun Chung. The General ran the opium trade in the Golden Triangle despite the best efforts of the civilized world to stop him. Baranov, Gurnov's spetznaz partner, was the middleman between Chung and Michael Markov, a wealthy Muscovite drug dealer. Markov was the weak link in Gurnov's elaborate plan and as he puffed on his *papiroska* his guts roiled with angst.

*Koshkin was KGB. He knows how to keep secrets. I need him because of his experience as a spy. He knows how the Americans think. He knows their weak-natured spoiled ways. And Baranov. He was spetznaz. He knows how to keep his mouth shut. But Markov, nyet. He's just a whoremonger. A dope dealer. I only need him because of his international banker friends. Twenty-five percent just to launder the fuckin' money. He is a greedy bastard. He has no special training. If not for Baranov, I would have killed the son of a bitch when I came back from Israel. Muscovite Mafioso. Big fancy car. Body guards. Heroin trafficking son of bitch! I know how to get to you, you greedy bastard.*

A new thought crossed his mind. *Cigars. You like Cuban cigars, don't you asshole? I'll get you some Cuban cigars. The best!*

"I have something special for you, Markov," he mumbled out loud, "something that will turn you into a walking hemorrhage, you fucking asshole."

He took another swallow of vodka straight from the bottle and lit another cigarette. Watching the street below, he planned Markov's death in bloody detail.

# Chapter 2

Lieutenant Robert Lee Sanz gazed out over the moonlit Pacific Ocean forty thousand feet below. It was a miniature version of an astronaut's perspective. For a few moments he regretted choosing the SEALs instead of flight school. The aircraft seemed to be suspended in the inky blackness of space immersed in a multitude of stars. On the southern horizon the Milky Way cascaded downward like a splotch of spilled cream. Orion's brilliant belt floated above the equator like a navigational buoy. In an immense expanse of ocean Sanz spotted a faint glow on the horizon.

*Hawaii*, he thought. *I wonder how far it is? Let's see. I used to know a formula. What was it? It's as easy as one, two, three. That's it. The square root of the altitude times one-point-two-three equals the distance to the horizon. The square root of forty thousand is two hundred, times one-point-two-three. She's only two hundred and fifty miles away.*

From the observation seat in the back of the cockpit he watched the aircrew perform their duties in a businesslike manner. They were reserves but Sanz couldn't tell it from their comportment. The crew was well groomed and mature, and the aircraft was clean and well maintained. It didn't have that over-used tired look of an active duty bird. Then he remembered that reserves only flew on weekends. His mind jumped a track and his thoughts returned to Julie Jennings, his fiancée.

*Let's see, at six hundred knots we'll be there in about*

*twenty-five minutes. It'll take a couple of hours to offload and about twenty minutes to get to Pearl. I'll call her from the BOQ at about....*

The latter thought disturbed him. What he had done back in San Diego was against standard operating procedures. He shrugged off his guilt by concentrating on the altimeter. The pilot was beginning a slow descent.

As they neared the volcanic archipelago the scattered islands began to take form. Illuminated by a full moon, they were wrapped in a deep dark Pacific blue and capped with billowing white cumulus clouds that reflected the bright light of a full moon. After thousands of miles of emptiness they were a welcome sight. There wasn't enough fuel for a return trip to San Diego or a diversion to Midway. It was Hawaii or the drink.

Back in the cargo bay the loadmaster checked the pallets to confirm that they were secured for landing. Unlike commercial aircraft that are furnished in light customer-pleasing colors, naked ribs, wiring, and hydraulic plumbing ran along the dreary green bulkheads. The belly of the 141 was like the inside of a narrow olive-drab tunnel that ended in a ramp at the rear. It was filled with gear piled eight feet high wrapped in plastic and covered by nylon webbing. Outside the thin barrier of insulation, powerful engines groaned in the sub-zero frigid air of altitude. The loadmaster finished his inspection and ordered the men of SEAL Team FIVE, Charlie Platoon to resume their seats. Throughout most of the flight the SEALs had sacked out in sleeping bags scattered about the cargo bay. He finished his chores in the rear of the bird then climbed up the steps into the back of the cockpit.

"Lieutenant Sanz," he said, speaking into Sanz's ear so he could hear him over the drone of jet engines, "Would you please take your seat, sir. We'll be landing in a few minutes."

Sanz nodded. "Thank the skipper for the view," he said, as he got up to leave.

The Air Force sergeant acknowledged with a half-salute and carried on with his duties. Back in the cargo bay Sanz joined his men. They were buckled into their seats on the comfort pallet facing toward the rear of the aircraft. Some of the men were leaning awkwardly to one side or the other trying to catch a few more ZZZs, but not Master Chief Tom Blaze. As usual he was reading with a private book light. He looked up as Sanz took his seat.

"They teach you how to fly this bird, L.T.?" he asked, with a wry smile. His Irish face showed the bloodlines of a bruiser.

"No, but they broke out a bottle of Scotch for me, Master," Sanz kidded, with a devilish Dennis Quaid smile. He pushed his camouflage hat back on his head and eyed Blaze with a grin.

Sanz was a handsome man, slim, lithe, muscular, and intelligent. He had the makings of a movie star or a politician. By contrast, Master Chief Tom Blaze was misshapen by war and time. He was a powerfully built man with a pugnacious bulldog expression. But the bright intelligent eyes that peered out from behind his pugilist face exposed another side of his character. Tom Blaze was a genius. He was a connoisseur of scotch whiskey and of a hundred other of life's little pleasures, facts that Sanz used to find common ground. As an officer, the Lieutenant was ultimately accountable for everything and everyone in the platoon including the Master Chief. He had a degree in electrical engineering and a commission in the Navy that gave him rank over all enlisted men, even seasoned warriors like Tom Blaze. But as an E-9, the highest enlisted rank in the Navy, Blaze's stewardship stemmed from years of experience. He smiled at his young officer and went back to his book, knowing full well there was no scotch on Air Force flight 073.

When Sanz felt the landing gear lock into place, he stretched his neck to look out the small porthole next to his seat. The lights of Oahu didn't resolve into a normal grid but lay scattered helter-skelter like diamonds on black velvet. A few linear streaks crisscrossed the scatter.

*Julie is down there*, he thought, as he strained his neck to look toward Diamond Head. *Sound asleep. I wanted to ask her on the beach at Waikiki. Crap! This stupid exercise has ruined everything!*

He was deep in thought thinking of Julie when he heard a hydraulic motor switch on, then an unfamiliar clatter was followed by a hissing sound. Hydraulic fluid began spraying from the overhead.

"*Sergeant!*" Blaze yelled. "*Back here on the double!*"

"*What's wrong?*" Sanz barked.

"Busted hydraulic line," Blaze replied.

Sanz looked around for the aircrew and met the frightened eyes of his platoon. Startled, they were muttering to each other with baited apprehension. Before the sergeant could unbuckle his seat belt and dash back through the cargo bay, the Starlifter took an awkward bank to starboard and lost five hundred feet in altitude. The pilot fought for control using differential engine power to steer the aircraft but they were still listing heavily. Sanz looked out his porthole window. Below he could see the lights of Oahu rushing up at them.

Fortunately for all hands the old sergeant knew his bird. He twisted a few valves to redirect the flow of hydraulic fluid and the line stopped spraying like a ruptured garden hose. When the pilot regained control they were only five hundred feet AGL. Still staring out the window, Sanz saw two military helicopters whiz by. One missed the starboard wing by less than three hundred feet.

*"Damn that was close!"* he exclaimed.

*"No shit!"* Dan Carroll bellowed. He was seated directly behind the Lieutenant on the right side of the aircraft. "A broke dick plane and a near miss, all in two minutes. What else can go wrong?"

"I don't wanna know," Johnson replied. He was the Platoon's load planner, responsive for packing the platoons gear on pallets for military transport. "I just want outta this crate."

"Hell of a way to begin an exercise," Sanz quipped.

"I'll second that motion," Ears Fellars said. Ears was Alpha Squad's point man. He was seated directly behind Master Chief Blaze and his eyes were as big as his ears.

The pilot gained a little altitude and made a huge circle back for a landing. He made several careful maneuvers before entering the approach pattern and was flying on fumes when he dropped the flaps.

Sanz caught a glimpse of Pearl Harbor as the plane floated by on final approach. The responsibility of his mission descended on him like a heavy weight. Just twenty-four hours before Charlie had been the West Coast standby platoon with nothing to do but watch TV and wait for the telephone to ring. Unlike most standby missions, the phone had rung. As the officer in charge of the detachment, he had been the first to receive the call. He had immediately telephoned Lieutenant junior grade Thomas and Master Chief Tom Blaze who initiated the recall of the men. Then he had done something that was completely out of character, something that was gnawing at his guts. He had called his girlfriend in her hotel room in Waikiki. He didn't tell her where he was going. He didn't know at the time. He just called, apologized like a lovesick teenager, and canceled their vacation plans. When the recall went down Charlie only had two more days of standby duty before another platoon took their place. Sanz had signed leave papers and a ticket to Honolulu in his briefcase. He had to let her know he wasn't going to show up. It was the right thing to do. What made his situation worse was that he was planning to ask Julie Jennings to marry him under a starry Hawaiian sky.

Charlie Platoon had been scrambled for a classified joint training exercise under the operational control of JSOC, the Joint Special Operations Command. The troops called the command 'Jay-sock.' It was a headquarters organization, which coordinated counter terrorists forces, the best soldiers, sailors, and airmen the nation could muster. Sanz wasn't told the details of his mission at Team Five, just that it was a hostage rescue mission scheduled to take place in Hawaii. Before the Platoon was fully mustered on the Strand in Coronado he had made a second telephone call to Julie and had committed another violation of the Team's SOP. Only the officer in charge of a platoon could have made such a grievous error for he was the only individual told the nature and location of the mission. Once in isolation all contact with the outside was restricted.

His brief conversation kept replaying inside his head. "Jay-Jay. This is Lee. I can't talk but a sec. I'm not supposed to use the phone. You're not going to believe this, Honey. I'm deploying to Hawaii."

"That's great!" she had replied. "When will you

arrive?"

"I'm not sure yet. The exercise doesn't really get underway for a few weeks. I'll call you when I get to the BOQ."

"Lee, don't get into hot water with your skipper," she had cautioned.

"Julie, there's something I've been wanting to ask you." Sanz had paused for several heartbeats. Finally he said, "I, I love you, Baby."

"I love you too, Lee, and I don't want to see you get into trouble with the Navy. I know how much your job means to you. Remember our agreement?"

"Yeah. I know. It's a working vacation for you."

"Well, I've stumbled onto something really big. Do your job and don't worry about standing me up."

"I'll call you as soon as I can. Gotta go," he had said.

The words kept echoing inside his head. The fifteen men in his platoon depended upon him for leadership. He was the commander, the officer in charge. Moreover, Team FIVE's reputation depended upon Charlie Platoon's performance, and they were working with the best, Team SIX, DELTA, and the FBI Hostage Rescue Team.

*This is only an exercise,* he thought. *Besides, what could go wrong with Master Chief Blaze as the platoon chief? He invented most of the tactics used by SPECOPS. When the exercise starts I'll buckle down to business and we'll kick ass like we did in Monterey.*

Charlie Platoon had received universal praise during the last JSOC exercise. They had been the only unit to execute their part of the mission without a critical error. Sanz looked at his reflection in the porthole window. Blaze was studying his face, using the porthole like a mirror. He turned to meet the Master Chief's eyes.

"This is a dangerous business, L.T. Lieutenant Thomas and I will take care of things for the next few days, but it would be best if you got your woman off your mind before the movin' and shootin' starts," he said, without blinking his eyes. A smear of hydraulic fluid smudged his cheek.

The tone in his voice was fatherly and his countenance was that of a senior officer and not a senior enlisted man. Sanz grinned and looked away, embarrassed that the gnarly Master Chief knew about his preoccupation with Julie.

A shudder run through the airplane as the wheels touched down.

*"Cheated death again!"* Ears Fellars bellowed, loud enough for everyone to hear.

A moment later, the pilot hit the brakes and Sanz felt himself being thrust back against the seat. Abruptly, the pressure eased and the plane rolled gently down the runway. It stopped on the tarmac two hundred yards from the terminal. After several minutes the noise of the engines whined to a stop and loadmaster lowered the ramp. Warm humid air invaded the aircraft.

"God how I love the smell of frangipani in the morning," Blaze commented, in his best Robert Duval impersonation. He stretched in his seat and yawned as if the near disaster they had barely avoided had never happened.

Sanz mused. He admired Blaze but it was in his nature to check things for himself. He sniffed the air and the sweet scent of flowers teased his nostrils.

*Frangipani. The man's got senses like a cat,* Sanz thought. *He can even smell a flower over the stink of engine exhaust. I have to learn to pay attention like that. That's why he's survived all these years.*

In the distance Sanz spotted another 141 barreling down the runway. It taxied toward a restricted area to off load ammunition and other hazardous cargo. Several miles on the other side of the MAC terminal he saw Honolulu International, gleaming with bright lights and busy with 747s. Dressed in camouflage fatigues and jungle boots, the men of Charlie Platoon would have looked out of place among the tourists and businessmen passing through Oahu in flowered shirts. Only a few miles of tarmac separated the two worlds, civilian and military, but they were thousands of miles apart.

The men climbed down out of the 141 with their huge rucksacks slung over their shoulders and walked toward the terminal. Halfway to the building a chief petty officer dressed in khaki waved them over to a waiting navy bus.

"SEAL Team FIVE? Lieutenant Sanz?" he shouted.

"Yeah."

"Good Morning, sir. I'm Chief West, Jay-sock ADVON. Welcome to Hawaii."

"Thanks," Sanz replied.

"Muster your men aboard the bus and we'll take you guys over to Pearl. But leave your load planner and gunner behind to account for your operational gear and weapons. We're staging everything in a hangar over on Ford Island. Isolation begins Thursday morning at oh-six-hundred hours. Until then, all players are restricted to base by order of Lieutenant General Carlson."

"Ooooh!" exclaimed several of the men, with a note of mock concern.

"What about a gear watch?" Blaze growled.

West read Blaze's collar insignia. "We're providing security for the isolation area, Master Chief," he answered. "You don't have to worry about your gear."

Blaze stared at the man with a cold hard read before speaking. "Petty Officer Johnson is our load planner, and our gunner. He's over there with the driver of the K-loader," he continued, pointing toward the ramp of the 141, "making sure none of our gear takes a hike to

21

Kadina. He'll see it all the way to the isolation compound. And Chief West?"

"Yes, Master Chief."

"It wouldn't be good if any of our shit went missing between now and Thursday. *Comprendes?*"

West smiled. The Military Airlift Command was notorious for mixing up cargo pallets. The C-141s transporting Charlie Platoon were going on to Japan as soon as they were repaired, refueled and re-crewed. Blaze wasn't allowing for a screw-up and West knew it. He accepted the veiled threat of personal accountability for Charlie Platoon's gear.

"Outstanding, Master Chief," he said, with respect. "Got you covered. I'll get him over to the BEQ as soon as your gear is accounted for and staged in the hangar."

West gestured toward a female soldier standing on the steps of the bus. She smiled lasciviously at the handsome young SEALs.

"Sergeant Smith will escort you guys over to Pearl and take care of enlisted room assignments. Jay-sock has a block of rooms reserved at the Pearl BEQ. Lieutenants Sanz and Thomas have reservations at the Hickam BOQ."

"Chief West," interrupted Smith, in a soft, sexy voice. "I have the naval officers booked at BOQ Pearl."

BEQ was military-speak for bachelor enlisted quarters. The rooms and facilities weren't quite as nice as the BOQ, the bachelor officer's quarters, which had the feel of a hotel.

"Belay my last, gentlemen," West apologized. "Pearl it is."

Dressed in a camouflage uniform with rolled-up sleeves, Smith was short, round and enthusiastic. She was dark-skinned, heavy-featured, and full-figured underneath her camouflaged BDUs. The men caught that *I'm-*

*available-look* and grinned at each other. Her lively eyes continued to scope them out like a housewife in the meat section of Vons supermarket until she spotted Petty Officer Dan Carroll. Then they twinkled like little stars.

"We got everyone but Johnson, L.T.," Carroll reported. As the platoon's leading petty officer, the LPO, he was the foreman of the platoon, responsible for mustering the men and issuing routine orders.

"Very well," Sanz said. "Let's go."

"*Head 'em up, move 'em out!*" Carroll bellowed, as he circled his hand in the air as if swinging a lasso.

When Charlie Platoon was aboard the bus, Sergeant Smith ordered the driver to proceed then slipped into the seat next to Danny Carroll.

# Chapter 3

Gurnov hated the cold, wet, slushy streets of Russia. Even Odessa, on the Black Sea, was too cold for his liking. To him, snow, wind, and cold were four-letter words of the most obscene kind. Since his first tour of duty in Southeast Asia fighting the Americans, he had had a penchant for what Russian soldiers called Oriental earmuff, two warm silky smooth thighs wrapped around the head. Between voyages of the *Stashinsky*, he and Baranov, his Spetznaz buddy, had visited General Chung and they had made arrangements for an extended stay in the region. The trip had rekindled his preoccupation with the jade gate, the Oriental chasm of delights. Pornographic thoughts tortured him as he watched the gloomy street from behind a dirty curtain. He took a deep drag off his *papiroska*, the taste harsh in his mouth and let his mind wonder, trekking the trails of the Shan countryside.

Burma was a mysterious land of tangled jungles and feuding warlords. More than twenty distinct tribes with names like Akha, Lahu, Mao, and Karen controlled the interior of the country. Most of them were involved one way or another in the opium business. The Shan, Kun Chung's tribe, was the most powerful, making up a state within a state. Kwan Mae village, General Chung's headquarters, was set high atop a ridge that commanded the surrounding terrain. Mortars and machinegun nests, concertina wire and bunkers, controlled all approaches. Thoughts of such fortifications brought comfort to his musings. Then, a youthful feminine voice cried out down the hall and his loins stirred. A tiny voice crying and sighing and singing all at the same time echoed inside his head. He imagined her tight little body undulating beneath him, moaning in pleasure. She was waiting for him in Kwan Mae. He had forgotten here name because it was strange sounding to his tongue. But he hadn't forgotten her lovely young body.

Thoughts of young sexy Oriental girls possessed him. They sashayed around the noisy bars of the Orient like sex goddesses in a fantasy dream. In his mind's eye, he walked down a neon strip through a spiraling sexual galaxy, past street hawkers peddling their wares, past pitchmen pushing flyers advertising pussy ping-pong shows and live sex shows with dildos, past sexy, bikini-clad girls trying to lure him into the throbbing hearts of bars with names like the Pink Pussy, Pussy A-Go-Go, and Erotica.

He took another drag on his cigarette and blew a smoke ring to force his mind from carnal thoughts. Odessa was awakening and she jerked him back to reality with a slamming door down the hallway. Gurnov had a nice stateroom on the Russian ship, the *Bogdan Stashinsky*. But there were men in his charge who wanted to take his place and there were those in the chemical corps that wanted to silence him permanently. When paranoia seized him he often stayed in flophouses, sometimes with a whore.

At night he would sit and watch from behind a darkened window as if eating and talking in adjacent apartments was the material of spies. So many of his habits had the quality of searching for something just missed, something just beyond his reach. Skulking like a coiled viper was deeply embedded in his nature. He didn't really sleep anymore, not since the incident in the

South Pacific, and when he did sleep the lightest steps in the hallway awoke him. And the most innocuous sounds, like the rumbling and hissing of an old bus, could trigger horrible nightmares.

He abandoned his vigil at the window and lay down on the bed. Sleep wouldn't return, he knew that, kept at bay by the apprehension of what lay ahead and the sounds of Odessa stirring to life. Staring in the dim light at the peeling paint on the ceiling, he saw a miniature upside down battlefield with gaunt, ghostly faces that haunted him. He studied every inch of it, every crack, every scab of flaking paint.

Sounds drifted up from the street, hollow metallic clangs which defied identification, rasping coughs, guttural voices, and diesel engines rumbling to life, triggers of horrible nightmares. In the distance he heard the sound of a siren echoing over rooftops with a message of violence. Man's or God's, to Alexander Gurnov it didn't really matter. He was beyond caring. Beyond feeling. Beyond rational thought. Images of torture invaded his mind when he saw the kindly face of a silvery-haired man in the shadows on the ceiling. It was a siren that dug up the coffin full of memories. In hallucinatory detail he relived the one and only day he had spent in the Promised Land.

As the siren drifted away in the distance, it all came back to him in a kaleidoscope of images. Shortly after arriving at Lod airport he had rented a small room, stashed his bag, and went directly to an Arab district to make contact with the Palestinian underground. He displayed the signals Markov had arranged and soon a young Arab no more than twenty-three years old approached and spoke under his breath speaking in the direction of the stonewall of a nearby building.

"Leave this district," he whispered with a thick

accent. "You are being followed."

"But,"

"We will make contact with you when it is safe," he had whispered.

The Arab was gone before Gurnov could respond. Like a tourist he had wondered aimlessly through the streets of Jerusalem. When darkness came he went back to his tiny room and waited for a knock on the door. It came at six in the morning when six burly Russian Jews rushed into his room weapons in hand.

"What is this?" he had demanded.

The response was vicious. They grabbed him from all sides, kicked his feet out from beneath him and searched the room.

"What is this? Am I being arrested?"

Ignoring his demands for explanation, they yanked him to his feet and cuffed his hands behind his back. Wearing only his under shorts they dragged him down to the street and shoved him into the back of a truck. Two men in uniform climbed in after him. They were bull-shouldered and coarse-featured, not unlike himself. To each other they spoke gutter Hebrew. To Gurnov they spoke Russian slang. They hadn't forgotten the language or the hell they had experienced in the Soviet Union.

"Why am I being arrested?" he had demanded.

The biggest one spat in his face and backhanded him with the flat of his hand.

"*Idyot!* This is not Moscow, you Slavic pig!" he had growled like a junkyard dog. Then he mocked Gurnov with a husky laugh, a portent of what was to come.

They rumbled through the streets of Jerusalem using bursts of a siren to clear the way. After a ride straight out of hell the vehicle screeched to a halt at the side door of a stone barrack wrapped in razor wire. Pulling and pushing, the soldiers shoved him into the building and across a large, sterile room. Inside were several young Arabs chained to wooden benches waiting for their turn in the interrogation cell. They stared at him with blank faces and knowing eyes. The soldiers dragged Gurnov down a corridor and shoved him into a grimy cell that reeked of urine and sweat. A single bare light bulb illuminated the dirty brown-stained stonewalls. The only furnishings were two folding metal chairs leaning against the back wall. With his hands still cuffed behind him, he awkwardly unfolded one of the chairs and sat down to wait.

After several hours of contemplating his situation to screams of torture down the hall, the heavy metal bolt on his cell door screeched. Two soldiers marched in, followed by a silvery-haired man in uniform. He had a kindly face reminiscent of David Ben Gurion.

"Picture," he said in fluent Russian.

Gurnov looked confused.

"One way or another, Comrade Gurnov," he cautioned, with a slight shake of his index finger.

Gurnov's bewilderment was taken as resistance. In a blur of motion, one of the soldiers hammered him in the side of the head so hard he saw colored lights. With his hands cuffed there was little he could do to fend off the beating that followed. When they were satisfied they had his undivided attention, they slammed him against the stone wall and took several photographs.

"Thank you for your cooperation, Major Gurnov. Now, please have a seat. I have a few questions you must answer."

The soldiers shoved him down into the metal chair with such force it nearly collapsed. Eyeing him, the interrogator calmly placed the other chair in front of him and sat down. He exhaled heavily and using a clipboard began his interrogation in a businesslike manner.

"Major Gurnov, what is the purpose of your visit to Israel?" he asked pencil in hand.

"I came to visit the holy sites."

The old man smiled. "No jokes, Mr. Gurnov," he said, shaking his finger from side to side. "You are in very serious trouble."

"*For what? I've done nothing. I want to contact my embassy*," Gurnov had yelled.

The old man nodded to his henchmen. The biggest man stepped behind Gurnov's chair and clapped him on both ears with the palms of his hands so hard it nearly ruptured his tympanic membranes. Bells rang inside Gurnov's head and pain seared his brain.

"Now, Mr. Gurnov, why did you go to Katamon yesterday?" the interrogator asked in a loud voice. From experience he knew the Russian would not hear him if he spoke in a normal voice.

Gurnov found himself yelling to make himself heard over the ringing inside his head.

"I was lost."

"Okay, Major Gurnov. Okay. We know you are a big tough Russian soldier. We also know that each man has his breaking point and we will find yours. Of that you can be certain."

He nodded to his assistants and left the room.

Using a length of heavy radiator hose, the bruisers took turns beating him or pounding him with the palms of their hands until he lost consciousness. When Gurnov came to he was alone, left to rethink his precarious situation to the sounds of torture in adjacent cells. Battered and bruised, he struggled to sit up only to slump back against the cold stonewall.

*If this is how they treat Russians, I wouldn't want to be a rag-head,* he thought.

He couldn't understand the language but he thought

he understood one of the Arabs down the hall yelling, *Nazis! Nazis! Nazis!* Soon the entire corridor reverberated with the voices of young Arab men chanting, *Nazis! Nazis! Nazis!* Then he heard a scream and a hissing, gurgling, bleating noise like an animal being slaughtered. It was a sound he knew all too well. It was the sound of death.

"*Allahu Ackbar,*" the Arabs cried out of sync. Then silence fell like a curtain in some macabre play as they muttered prayers to Allah for the departed soul of their comrade.

The old man and his enforcers returned after they had given him several hours to worry. The silver-haired interrogator pulled up his metal chair and asked in a gentle, almost pleading voice.

"Now Major Gurnov, you went directly to Katamon yesterday. Why?"

"I was lost."

"No. No Major. You went to see this man," he said, showing him a picture of an Arab who looked similar to the man who had warned him that he was being followed.

Gurnov's stomach turned over and his eyes bugged out when he saw the photo. The young Arab was seated in a folding metal chair in a sterile room similar to his own. A bloody towel was draped over his chest and his throat was cut nearly to the bone. A hand was holding the head upright so the cameraman could take a picture that was recognizable as a human being. The photo was a fake but it fooled Alexander Gurnov into believing the noise he had heard was the sound of a man being butchered.

"Now, Major, why did you meet with a known Palestinian terrorist?" the old man asked.

Gurnov couldn't tell them what was really on his mind. In the mind game inside his head he remembered his thoughts and he mumbled the words aloud. *"I came here to sell filthy fucking Arab terrorists chemical weapons to kill you stinking, gefilte fish fucking Jews."*

The brutality of the Red Army had taught him to keep his mouth shut. He had just sat there in his chair with his hands cuffed behind his back, mentally preparing himself for the next beating. It was the worst. They worked his joints and his testicles, not enough to break bones or do permanent damage to the body, but enough to sear his brain with lasting memories. An expert palm-hand to the back of his head ended his misery. An hour later he regained consciousness facedown on the floor when the heavy metal bolt rasped open. The ruffians yanked him up off the floor like an inorganic object and shoved him against the wall.

"Mr. Gurnov, I am terribly sorry," the old man had said, without meaning in his words. "It seems we have made an innocent mistake."

One of the soldiers tossed Gurnov's belongings at his feet.

"We have very reliable information," the interrogator continued, "that a Russian soldier fitting your description is planning to supply Palestinian terrorists with chemical weapons to use against the State of Israel. It is most unfortunate, but we thought that you were that despicable criminal."

He had spat out the words like dry cracking concrete.

"Uncuff him," he ordered.

The largest of the men complied with a growl.

"Major Gurnov, I have a ticket for you on our national airlines, compliment of my government for this *unfortunate error.* You may fly out to Istanbul this evening, if you would like?"

Bruised and beaten like a cur dog, Gurnov had nodded agreement without taking his eyes off the kindly face of his tormentor.

"And we hope you will tell *all* of your friends about your pleasant little stay in Israel," the official continued.

The gleam in the old man's eyes told the whole story, as he handed Gurnov his passport and a one-way ticket to Turkey. They wanted the Russian underground to know how efficient Israeli security was at dealing with terrorists and their suppliers.

As the plane lifted off from Lod airport, Gurnov had sworn silently to himself.

*No more deals with filthy rag-heads and their lethal gossip. They can't be trusted. And you Jews*, he thought as he looked out the window with an obsidian stare. *May you all be damned to hell! I arrived on my feet and I leave on my feet, and woe be to the next Jew-bastard I get my hands on!*

Borne on an incredible, almost orgasmic flood of rage, he flew away from the Promised Land with mercenary thoughts of killing in his mind and the seed of his next enterprise bursting inside his head. There were softer targets than Israel, some with a lot more money. Americans. And Major Alexander Vissarionovich Gurnov hated Americans almost as much as he hated Jews.

The sounds of Odessa dragged him back to reality.

"All for naught. *Rien. Nichevo.* Nothing," he mumbled.

*Stupid. I was stupid to deal with those filthy rag-heads,* he thought. *I wonder if it was Markov's big mouth that set the Mossad on to me like a pack of hungry wolves.*

He stared at a scab of peeling paint that reminded him of Markov's twisted smile.

*Yeb vas, Markov. Yeb vas. I'll have something special for you, you loud-mouthed asshole. Something very special. You like Cuban cigars? You are going to get the best Cuban cigars in the whole fucking world. Asshole!*

The first light of day was casting new shadows on the ceiling. In the flaking paint he saw the Hawaiian Islands bathed in the trade winds, isolated, populated, and perfect for his plan. Tokyo would have worked just as well but he didn't harbor ill will against the Japanese the way he felt for the arrogant Americans who received his weapons. The United States had destroyed the Soviet Union, broken its back in an arms race the Russians could not win.

Russian peasant music blared out from some unseen radio that came on too loudly. *Sveshnikov* Choir was singing, *The Broad and Rolling Steppe*. Waves of melancholy rolled over him with images of his youth. His room was too small and too hot, and it smelled of booze and people and fish and cheese and dark Russian tobacco, like his mother's cramped apartment in Moscow. From somewhere down the hallway a gruff voice cursed loudly and shortly the volume of the radio decreased, leaving him with his lost youth in the cold gritty back streets of Moscow.

"Never forget that you are Russian, Gurnov. Wherever you go, whatever you do, you will always be Russian," he mumbled to himself. "You are Alexander Vissarionovich Gurnov, major in the *Red Army*. It is not your fault. You just followed orders."

He felt his damned Russian blood flow in its mad, dark, Asiatic richness. The Russian word *krasny* -- red -- is from the same root as *krasivy* -- beautiful, transforming Red Square to Beautiful Square, and the Red Army into Beautiful Army. Anger boiled in his guts.

"Pathetic. They are pathetic, those who we call the leaders of the Motherland. Khrushchev, Brezhnev,

Andropov, Chernenko, Gorbachev, Yelsin. They do not deserve to stand in Stalin's shadow."

Then he thought, *all but comical, those poor weak-willed vodka soaked bastards. Stalin was vozhd -- a supreme leader. They are clowns. Glasnoz. Peristroika. What a joke. They were unable to understand the social dynamics that tore the empire apart and now they destroy the Motherland. When they are not being fools to the Americanskis, they were being complete idiots to the people of Russka.*

"Tis not easy, brother mine, in a foreign land to live," he mumbled, resigning himself to the fate that lay ahead in Burma. "I must be careful of a *provokatsiya* -- a trap," he said, worried about a trap like the one he had walked into in Israel.


Just after sunrise Gurnov packed his duffel bag and left his tiny room for the last time. He walked to the port district under pewter-gray skies, searching the streets of Odessa for any roving eye out of the ordinary. When he reached the port, the smell of creosote and seaweed assaulted his senses. The odors combined with the rumble of trucks and the clamor of cranes loading and unloading merchants moored all along the pier. But down at the far end there was little activity. The *Stashinsky* was moored in a special berth where access to the ship could be tightly controlled. No one ventured there without a special pass.

The pier watch recognized him, snapped to attention, and saluted as he passed by. All the way down the pier soldiers and sailors stepped aside respectfully and saluted. At the ship's gangway a deep sense of foreboding shuddered through his body. The *Stashinsky*'s black hull reminded him of a coffin. He shrugged off the cold thought of death and walked up the gangway determined to be a rich man in a very poor world.

"*Stoi!* -- stop," the senior enlisted sailor, standing watch on the quarterdeck bellowed.

The duty officer, busy at a dog-eared logbook, turned around to see the reason for the command. His mouth fell open with shock.

"*Idyot!*" he yelled at the sailor. "The Major is ship's company." He saluted Gurnov sharply. "Good morning, Comrade Major Gurnov, sir," he greeted, solicitously. "I am sorry. This sailor is new to the ship. This is his first voyage on the *Stashinsky*," he apologized, nervously. "I'll have him take your bag to your stateroom, sir," he offered.

He vigorously motioned for the sailor to take the Major's bag.

Gurnov eyed the young officer for a few seconds. What he saw was genuine respect for a major in the Russian Army, a hero of the Motherland who handled the deadly poisons of war, the reason the *Stashinsky* existed in her present configuration.

"*Spasibo* -- thank you," he growled. He leered at the sailor as he handed him his bag. Heading for the ship's galley for breakfast he thought, *maybe I will let you live Lieutenant Zhukov. Nyet. No one must survive. No one must know that I survived the explosion.*

# Chapter
# 4

The smell of creosote, diesel fuel, and seaweed hung in the brisk night air as two dark-clad figures crept stealthily from piling to piling underneath the wharf. Here and there shimmering shafts of light, reflecting off the bay, stabbed the open areas between pilings. Like rats in a sewer the two intruders skulked from shadow to shadow, ship to ship. It was a foggy, moonless night and underneath the pier it was as dark as a cave but to the nervous trespassers it seemed as bright as day.

Aided by the noise of stevedores working up on the wharf, they made good time to the last civilian freighter docked alongside the pier. Near its gangway a luminous pool of pewter-gray light reflecting off the bay cast an eerie glow on their gaunt faces. In the underworld beneath the pier they looked at each other and agreed to go on with apprehensive expressions. By day they were port employees, patriots of the Motherland. By night they were environmentalist, also patriots of the Motherland. As port employees they knew the area beyond was restricted and that they were risking their lives. They paddled quickly to the stern of the vessel and paused to observe the no man's land controlled by the military. It was four open berths in length where no ships were allowed to moor when the *Stashinsky* was in port. A motor whaleboat appeared from behind her black hull six hundred yards ahead of them.

"*Back. Back*," the smaller of the two men hushed.

They back paddled a few yards and grabbed onto a

barnacle encrusted piling. Shielded by the freighter tied up alongside the pier, they watched with anxious eyes as the whaleboat puttered slowly toward them with a searchlight shining about under the pier. When it reached the freighter it circled out and disappeared into the fog. The two intruders waited a few minutes then paddle quickly toward the *Stashinsky*. They were near the bow when a booming voice froze them with fear.

*"You there! Come here!"*

A dog barked and adrenaline coursed through their veins. They stopped paddling and listened like deer sniffing the air for a wolf. A beam of a light from a nearby lighthouse illuminated them as it swept by. Then a foghorn sounded. The man in the front of the dinghy nearly fell overboard. His body tensed and he gritted his teeth as he waited for the crack of a rifle. When none came and they were again cloaked in darkness, he breathed a sigh of relief. Up above a gruff sergeant was yelling at a canine patrol. He ordered the corporal to search the apron at the base of the pier a half-mile behind them. Both men breathed a sigh of relief. They waited until all they could hear was the sound of waves lapping against the pilings.

"Let's go," the man in front of the boat whispered.

They paddled quietly past the *Stashinsky*. Twenty-five yards from the end of the wharf they tied the dinghy off to a large pipe running underneath the dock and used it as a footbridge to negotiate the remaining distance to the end of the pier. First one, then the other, climbed up and peeked over the end of the quay, eyes searching for guards. The *Stashinsky* was moored like a ship in quarantine seventy-five yards up the pier. Guards patrolled her weather decks but there were none on the end of the dock. Armed only with video cameras, the two spies scurried to cover and hid in the shadows among spools of rope and pallets of ship's stores. They separated a few yards and began filming the ship.

Up on deck a sailor dressed in a protective chemical suit climbed the ladder to the ship's crane. He dropped the hook and lifted a huge hatch cover off the center hold, then lowered it down on the focsle. A few minutes later a heavily armed convoy of military trucks rumbled down the wharf. Floodlights came on and illuminated the area. Fortunately for the spies they were aimed outward to blind any curious soul looking at the ship from out in the bay.

The first vehicle to roll up was filled with armed troops. They piled out and began dressing out in protective garb. The second vehicle parked directly underneath the crane. It was a large flatbed semi-truck without a load. The two agents signaled each other with gestures of bewilderment. They were expecting weapons to be loaded on board the ship, not off loaded. A few minutes later several semi-trucks rolled down the wharf with APC escorts. The first truck backed up to the flatbed trailer and soldiers dressed in protective chemical suits unlocked the doors. They stepped inside and soon rolled out a pallet containing chemical weapons, which they pushed down the flatbed on rollers like those in the cargo bay of an aircraft. When a pallet was positioned under the ship's crane, the sailor up on deck lowered the hook to pick up the load.

For half an hour the snoops filmed the operation as truck after truck backed up to the flatbed and off loaded its lethal cargo. Then the soldier with the dog appeared. It was too late to sneak back to the end of the pier so they watched anxiously as the German shepherd sniffed the wheel of a vehicle for scent markings of other dogs. Annoyed, the handler yanked the leash and led the animal to the side of the pier where he opened his protective suit and urinated in the bay. It was there that the animal picked up their scent. Ears alert, it led the corporal into the stockpile. Seeing the dog on their trail, both men circled around large shipping containers and tried to sneak back to the dinghy.

"*Stoi!*" the soldier yelled, upon seeing one of the spies.

He let the dog loose, ripped off his mask, and brought his rifle up to shoulder ready. But he checked his fire.

*Stop or I'll shoot!*" he yelled.

Neither of the men stopped. The soldier waited until the dog selected a victim then fired on the other man. He caught the trespasser in the back with a burst from his AK. The impact of the bullets slammed into the man's body and drove him over the edge of the pier. The dog brought the other man down, howling in pain.

From the bridge of the *Stashinsky*, Major Gurnov heard the report of the rifle and saw the commotion down on the dock. He put on his protective mask and rushed down to investigate. When he arrived several of his men were conducting a field interrogation of the survivor.

"What happened?" he demanded.

"Intruders, Major," Lieutenant Romanovsky reported. Dressed in his suit, the Lieutenant's voice was distorted. He extended a high-eight video camera. "They were filming the ship," he explained.

Gurnov eyed the scene. He glanced over the edge of the pier and saw a body floating in the water.

"How many?" he grunted.

"Two as far as we can determine," Romanovsky answered. "I have a dozen men searching the length of the pier."

Gurnov stepped closer to the captive. He was a wiry little man, almost Turkish in appearance, with a shock of wavy black hair and a thick black mustache that covered his upper lip.

Gurnov glanced around for the dog and observed its alertness. Dogs have a superior sense of smell so he knew it was safe to remove his mask.

"How many?" he asked of his captive.

The little man ignored him. He was seated on his buttocks cross-legged with his hands tied behind his back. In a flash Gurnov kicked him in the face, sending him to the pier. Then he stepped on the man's hands with his jackboot and ground his fingers into the pavement.

"*Ahhhhh! God!*" the intruder shrieked in agony.

"God does not live on a planet man has soiled," Gurnov mumbled. "How many?" he grunted, easing off the pressure.

"Just two of us," the prisoner gasped in a faint voice.

"How did you get here?"

"The boat under the pier."

"*Search beneath the pier!*" Gurnov yelled, waving at the soldiers standing around the scene of the incident. "Lieutenant Romanovsky."

"Yes, Major."

"Fish the body out of the water. Take the corpse, this man, and anyone else you find to the airlock in hold number four."

"Major?"

"You heard me *goddammit!*"

"But Major, protocol states that we,"

Gurnov cut him off. "The ship is sailing within the hour, Lieutenant. Put them in the number-four airlock. Is that clear, *schoolboy?*"

"Yes, Major."

"And take the camera to my stateroom."

"Yes, Major."

Gurnov sauntered off in his bulky suit and climbed back up the gangway. On deck, he issued orders to

Captain Dmitriyev, his second in command, then went back to the ship's bridge to join the Captain. From inside they watched the final stages of the loading operation. Gurnov waited until the hatch cover was lowered on the center hold before taking his leave. While Captain Shvachko got his ship underway, Gurnov made his way to the number four airlock.


In the presence of Lieutenant Romanovsky, the demanding Major conducted a field interrogation. Still wearing his protective chemical suit he questioned the prisoner.

"Who do you work for?" he grunted like an alien from outer space. The MOP equipment not only distorted his voice but it exaggerated his size. The horrified prisoner, chained to the bulkhead like a pirate in a dungeon, blurted out the first thing that came to his mind.

"*Pravda*," he lied. "I am a newspaper reporter."

"I don't think so," Gurnov grunted. "Drop his trousers."

"*Major?*" Romanovsky gasped, shocked by the order.

Gurnov shook his finger in the Lieutenant's face.

"*If you question my orders one more time, schoolboy,*" he yelled, "*I'll have you shot and thrown overboard with this asshole.* Now drop his pants. I want to see his cock."

The baffled officer complied without further protest.

"I thought so," Gurnov growled, upon seeing the man's penis. "*Jew!* You work for the Mossad."

"No," the little man pleaded. "I am Russian."

"Your cock is bobbed like a kraut sausage. You're a fuckin' Jewish spy."

"*No! I'm Russian. I'm not a spy.*"

"Then why were you filming a classified military operation? *Huh?*"

"*Greenpeace*," the little man blurted. "You are poisoning the sea. What you are doing is criminal. Our people, the Russian people, must eat the fish of the sea and you are poisoning them. *You are poisoning the food we eat!*"

"*What?*" Gurnov exploded. "I know what you are. You're a fuckin' Jewish spy selling out the Motherland."

The ship rolled gently to one side as a tug took up a strain. The *Stashinsky* was underway.

"I'm going to visit you every day, *clipped-dick*. And everyday I'm going to cut off one of your fingers. And when they are all gone, I'm going to blow out your fucking brains and feed you to the sharks. *You fucking Jewish spy!*" he screamed, like a mad man.

Romanovsky watched in horror as Gurnov took out his knife and, with the man screaming at the top of his lungs, severed a pinky finger like sawing off a piece of jerky.

"I'll be back, Jew boy," he said, tossing the man's bloody finger on the deck. "Seal the lock," he ordered. With the little man groaning in agony he glared at Romanovsky before turning to leave.

# Chapter 5

Julie Jennings lay on her back in the sand, eyes closed against the morning sun. At her feet the restless Pacific Ocean whispered in morning calm. Big waves were breaking out on the reef offshore but on the beach near the Hawaiian Hilton they were only a foot high. If paradise consisted solely of beauty then she had found magnificent perfection. But Julie saw none of it. Her body responded to every tactile sensation, to the coolness of the water, to the freshness of the sea breeze, to the texture of the sand, but not her mind. She tried to put it out of her thoughts. She just couldn't, not after she had seen the bodies.

Today was not like her first day in Hawaii when she had plunged into the cool surf with clear vision and a simple story to tell. Life had become more complicated. Lee was coming in from San Diego and the people that had agreed to speak with her on camera were giving her the cold shoulder. Local news reporters had clammed up. Her interviews had all been cancelled. Even the coroner, who had shown her the bodies of the fishermen and allowed her cameraman to film his morgue, had changed his mind about an on-camera interview. If a tsunami had surged up onto the beach and boiled over her, her mind would have continued with her thoughts undisturbed.

*This is not a new disease*, she thought. *It can't be. Maybe there was an accident and they were exposed to sulfuric acid fumes from the ship's batteries. That would account for the blisters but not the subcutaneous hemorrhaging.*

Julie closed her eyes tightly and rubbed them, as though she could rub away the images, the black and blistered bodies of eight fishermen. She lay still, perfectly and desperately still, trying to focus her thoughts. But there was no erasing it. She had spent too many hours examining autopsy reports that had mysteriously appeared under her door.

"Miss Jennings?"

She held up her hand to shield her eyes from sun.

"Dr. Robbins," she exclaimed, surprised by his appearance.

Robbins had been one of the doctors she had met at the coroner's office, the one who had hardly spoken a word.

"I called your room and when there wasn't an answer, I thought that you might be on the beach," he said, staring out to sea as if she wasn't there.

Julie sat up and looked at him.

"Since all my interviews have been cancelled, Dr. Robbins, I have nothing better to do," she said with a hint of annoyance.

"Please don't look at me, Ms. Jennings. I would just as soon not be seen with you."

"Why?"

"Since your arrival, Dr. Chang has come under very strict orders. The governor is afraid of public hysteria. They're afraid the media will start a panic before they can determine the cause of death."

"Hummm," Julie mumbled under her breath.

"There are all sorts of rumors floating about the Islands, Ms. Jennings, from alien encounters to secret government experiments. Is there some place we can talk privately? I think I'm being followed."

"Followed? Why? Why would anyone be following

you?" Julie asked. She stared up at him for explanation.

"I happened to mention my findings to a newspaper reporter. My comments didn't set well with my colleagues or the governor's staff.

"I see. How about the breakfast bar?" she proposed.

"No," he replied emphatically, aghast that she should suggest such a public place.

"Okay. Then meet me in my room," she offered, with a cautious eye.

"No tape recorder and no camera, Ms. Jennings. I'll talk to you, but strictly off the record. Agreed?"

"Sure."

"Room number six twelve, Rainbow Tower?" he asked.

"Yes."

"I'll meet you there in twenty minutes," he said.

He was lost in the beach crowd before Julie could gather up her belongs.




Twenty minutes later when Dr. Robbins showed up she wasted no time in getting down to business. Having a strange man in her room under unusual circumstances was unnerving so she had visited Gordon Forbes, her cameraman, and asked him to sit on his balcony and listen for a scream. Gordon had her room key and was only two doors away. With her balcony door open she felt reasonably safe. Besides, Robbins was a frail, colorless little man who possessed the demeanor of a mortician. He wore thick spectacles and slicked his hair down with a heavy coat of Alberto VO5. She could smell it when he entered her room.

"How long have you worked for the coroner, Dr. Robbins?" she asked, notebook in hand.

"Oh, I don't work for the coroner's office. I'm a toxicologist. I was called in as a consultant because of my expertise in naturally occurring toxins."

"Poisons?"

"There are some very nasty poisons in this world, Ms. Jennings," he said, as if surprised by her response.

"Please call my Julie."

"Certainly. My name is John." He looked at her note pad. "This interview is strictly off the record. Agreed?"

"Yes, of course," Julie said, as she put down her pad and pencil.

"As I was saying, I'm a specialist in natural poisons."

Julie couldn't resist asking the obvious question. "Natural as versus manmade?"

"Yes. Toxins may be classified as natural or synthetic. My expertise is in naturally occurring poisons such as snake venoms, amphibian and mollusk secretions, plant compounds, that sort of thing. Most people have heard of curare, a plant extract used by South American Indians on their blowgun darts. But they also use betrachotoxin from frogs for the same purpose as well as other toxins."

"Do you mind if I write some of this down? I'm not familiar with betatoxin."

"Betrachotoxin," he corrected. "You can find the information at the library. Look for a book entitled, *Nature's Super Poisons* by John Robbins," he smiled.

Julie wrote down the title of the book.

"You might also look up Project M.K. Naomi. You'll find it very interesting."

"I've never heard of it," Julie said, scribbling down the words.

"It was a secret CIA project which produced poison weapons. The Soviets did the same thing. Do a subject search on Soviet sabotage weapons. Also look up Saint

Anthony's Fire and Saint Vitus's Dance. The information will add depth to your documentary."

"I'll do that," Julie replied. "Thanks."

"There are many naturally occurring toxins, Ms. Jennings. Some newts, for example, produce tetrodotoxin. Did you know the U2 pilot, Gary Francis Powers, had saxitoxin on his person when he was shot down over the Soviet Union? It is derived from certain species of mollusks."

"No. I didn't know that."

"He didn't use it of course, much to the dismay of the Eisenhower administration. Here in Hawaii we have a type of soft-bodied invertebrate coral related to the sea anemone, a coelenterate called limu-make-o-hana, which produces one of the deadliest toxins on earth," Robbins continued in a rambling professorial tone.

"Do you think those fishermen died from ingesting the limu-hana?" Julie asked.

"Limu-make-o-hana," he corrected. "No. No they did not. But it's only fair to say that everyone else involved in this investigation believes that they died from ingesting some unknown naturally occurring toxin."

"Contaminated food would appear to be the most likely cause of death. Botulism?" Julie pressed.

Two days after meeting with the coroner someone had slipped a copy of the autopsy report under her door. The preliminary findings suggested food poisoning as the most like cause of death. "Your line of reasoning is exactly the same as Dr. Chang's."

Chang was the coroner of Oahu.

"I did a thorough search for *clostridium botulinum* bacteria and the full spectrum of *fusaria*, as well as a number of other possible candidates. There were none to be found in the ship's food containers or garbage."

*He's been on the boat. I wonder where it is?* Julie

thought. "Where is the *Westwind*, John?" she asked.

"It's in quarantine in a small harbor over on Lanai."

"Ah huh. I see. So you were asked by the coroner's office to examine the ship for sources of poison?"

"Yes. Me, and others."

"Were you present at the autopsies?" she pressed.

"Yes."

"What do you think killed those men?"

Robbins took a breath and exhaled slowly.

"I was consulted because Dr. Chang suspects *fusaria* or *ergot*."

"Fussara?"

"*Fusaria*," Robbins corrected. "There are a variety of chemically related, biologically active fungal metabolites produced by fungi. Fungal toxins have accounted for hundreds of thousands of human lives over the ages. Look up Saint Anthony's Fire and Saint Vitus's Dance at the library and you'll understand Dr. Chang's reasoning. Generally, poisoning occurs when people ingest bread or other foods contaminated with *fusaria*."

"The autopsy report mentions trico-tricotha-tricothecene residue," Julie said, mispronouncing the toxin.

"Ahhh. So Dr. Chang let you see the autopsy report?" he asked, surprised by her statement.

"I didn't say that, Dr. Robbins."

"But you have seen it?" he asked, with a bewildered expression on his face.

Julie didn't want to lie to the man so she looked him square in the eye and answered, "Yes. I have." *He's not the one who slipped it under my door*, she thought, as she studied his face for clues.

Robbins was an intellectual egghead and his facial features gave away his inner feelings. He was surprised she had seen the preliminary report.

"I see," he muttered. "Then I'm not alone."

"Alone in what?" she asked.

He thought for a second and said, "I found trichothecene residue in all the bodies. That's a metabolite produced by *fusaria*."

"I'm confused," Julie frowned. "I thought you said…,"

"The trichothecene I found was synthetic."

"How do you know that, Dr. Robbins?" Julie asked, suspiciously.

"Because of the presence of both right and left hand molecules," Robbins explained. "There is no question in my mind. Those men were killed by a synthetic nerve toxin combined with other chemicals, probably a hemorrhagic agent and a blistering agent."

Julie's mouth fell open. *Nerve gas. Greenpeace is right*, she thought.

In a meeting with representatives from the environmental organization, Greenpeace, it had been suggested to her that the Russians were dumping chemical weapons at sea and that the fishermen had sailed into a pocket of nerve gas. She had agreed to join them on one of their ships to trail the suspected vessel on its next voyage from Odessa, Russia on the Black Sea to Johnston Atoll in the Pacific.

"But the others disagree?" she asked.

"Dr. Chang is convinced there is a rational explanation for my findings or that I made an error in my analysis. I did not," Robbins said emphatically.

"Could someone, say, a criminal or a crazy, cook up such a toxic brew, say, someone who has a beef with the company that owns the fishing boat?"

Robbins shook his head. "No. The synthetic is too sophisticated to be produced by anyone without a state of the art laboratory."

"Like who?"

"I don't know. I doubt that I could concoct such a poison without tremendous resources at my disposal."

*Greenpeace is right*, she thought. *It's the Russians.* "So that's why I've been shut out," she said. "I've been asking too many questions about Johnston Atoll?"

"Johnston Atoll?" Robbins asked, with a befuddled expression. "The Wildlife Sanctuary?"

"There's a chemical incinerator plant there," Julie explained.

About eight hundred miles from Oahu on an isolated, speck of an island in mid-Pacific, the U.S. Military dismantled and destroyed chemical weapons by the ton. The atoll was so remote few people knew of its existence.

"Oh. I didn't know that," Robbins said, with a furrowed brow. "Surely you don't...,"

Julie cut him off. "No. No, I don't. Not at all."

A concerned expression filled Robbins's face.

"The *Westwind* was discovered more than a thousand miles from Johnston Atoll. The island couldn't possibly be a contributing cause."

"I agree," Julie said. "So why the hush-hush?"

"Dr. Chang was ordered by the governor to avoid all news media to prevent public hysteria. No offense intended but you know how some of those people are. Alien encounters. Flesh eating bacteria. I mentioned to one reporter that I had found a possible synthetic agent and he wrote an article suggesting the U.S. Government was conducting secret nerve gas experiments. The gag order *is* necessary, Julie. We are trapped on these islands, you know."

"Nice place to be trapped," she smiled. Julie stared at him studying his face for clues. Her gaze made him nervous.

"I've seen some of your documentaries, Ms. Jennings,

and well, the quality of your work is a cut above the rest of the vultures in the news business. Before I go I want to wish you the very best on this new project. I sincerely hope that I have been of some assistance."

*The man's serious*, she thought. *He really likes my work.*

"Thank you, John," she replied. "I'll be sure to buy a copy of your book. Say! When the heat is off, would you be willing to do an on-camera interview?"

"Uh. Ah. Perhaps," he said, shyly. "I'm basically a very private person."

"We could show your book," she teased. "And we could rehearse the questions and answers before we turn on the camera." She watched his eyes closely. "I'll let you review the interview and the parts you don't like, I'll cut out."

He nodded his head in hesitant agreement.

"Do you have a business card?" she asked.

"Why yes," he replied, taking out his wallet.

He removed a card and handed it to her.

"I must go now," he said. "Good day, Ms. Jennings. And best of luck to you."

"Thanks, John. Thank you very much. I'll be in touch."

He bowed like an English gentleman and left the room.

As soon as the door closed she called Gordon Forbes on the phone.

"Forbes," he grunted hurriedly, like a worried elder brother.

"He's gone, Gordy."

"How did it go?" he asked, anxious to find out what Robbins had told her.

"Quite well, actually. When the heat's off, I think he'll do an on-camera interview."

"Great. So don't keep me in suspense. What did he have to say?" Forbes asked anxiously.

"He thinks they were killed by a synthetic nerve agent," Julie said.

"Ooooh," Forbes gasped. "I smell government cover up. Is he the one who slipped the autopsy report under your door?"

"I don't think so. I think we have another friend in the coroner's office."

"Actually, Jay-Jay, we have a lot of friends here in Hawaii, people who don't want to see this thing covered up. My buds are right about this, you know," he said, referring to Greenpeace.

"Looks like it," she agreed.

Forbes was a charter member of Greenpeace and it was his connections with the organization that had led to Julie's involvement.

"They're the reason we're on to this story and not CNN or ABC."

Julie was silent so Forbes dropped the subject.

"What's the plan of the day, Boss?" he asked.

"You and Fred catch a plane to Lanai. The *Westwind* is quarantined there."

"Where?"

"I don't know Gordy. He didn't say. Grab some footage of the boat and the security around it."

"But where?"

"Lanai! There can't be that many places to stash a boat. It has *Westwind* painted on the stern. Find it," she implored.

Forbes was silent for a few seconds as he thought over the assignment. "No worries. Lanai is not all that big. I'll find her."

"Meet me back here in a week?" she said.

"Roger, as your SEAL pup would say. What are you

going to do?" Forbes asked.

"I'm going to the library. I have a new angle to research."

"I thought your stud muffin was coming to town?" Forbes asked, with a resentful tone.

"He is. Sometime this weekend."

"You tell that swashbuckler you've got to have your beauty rest. Gotta look good on camera, you know. Tah-tah," he said.

"Bring me my key, you lecher."

"Sure thing, Boss, as soon as the hula dancer leaves my room," he kidded.


As Julie spoke with Forbes on the telephone, Robbins waited for an elevator down the hallway. He paid little attention to the tall gentleman who joined him.

"Good day," the man said, in a peculiar English accent.

Robbins responded pleasantly. "Good morning," he said solemnly, lost in thought. The shy doctor ignored the stranger and watched the elevator lights.

When the lift arrived the man glanced up and down the hallway as if looking for someone.

"My wife," he said, holding the automatic door open for Robbins. "She's always late," he complained.

Seeing the elevator was empty, the man waited for Robbins to enter before pushing the hold button.

"Dr. Robbins?" he asked to confirm Robbins's identity.

Surprised to hear his name, the frail toxicologist looked the man directly in the eyes for the first time.

"Yes?" he answered, expecting to see an FBI badge in the man's hand.

What he saw was an aluminum cylinder that appeared from out of the man's pocket. Dressed like a well to do tourist the stranger's movements didn't appear threatening, nor did the small cylinder that he held in his hand. It looked like an expensive cigar holder. The gentleman held the canister at arms length as if offering Robbins a cigar. Before Robbins could decline with a shake of his head a clear mist sprayed him directly in the face. Caught off guard, the toxicologist never knew what hit him. He collapsed on the elevator floor writhing in convulsions. His face turned blue and his eyes bugged out as he gasped for breath. When the elevator doors opened at the ground floor people rushed to his aid. But it was too late. Robbins was dead.

Nickoli Koshkin passed Gordon Forbes in the hallway as he walked calmly toward the stairs at the end of the hall. He walked down six floors and joined the crowd in the lobby. From a distance he watched the confusion as hotel security and medical personnel tried to fathom the problem. He waited until an ambulance took Robbins away, face covered by a sheet, before leaving the posh resort.

# Chapter
# 6

"Where you go?" she demanded in broken English.

Baranov couldn't speak the Shan language and Mae Lee couldn't speak Russian but pigeon English and sex adequately bridged the gap between their two distant worlds.

"India," he lied.

Yuri Baranov stuck a grimy pair of wooden chopsticks into a deep bowl of chicken noodle soup and poked away the chopped green chilies and leaves of coriander to get at the gray bits of bird at the bottom. He fished out a large piece of meat and chewed it. It was tough and gristly. He looked at Mae Lee and frowned. Ignoring the worry lines on her face, he went back to fishing in his noodle soup.

"Why you go there? Why you go leave me? When you come back?" she persisted with a sad face.

Mae Lee was a voluptuous little thing. Like most Shan women, she was light-skinned and more Chinese featured than Thai. But she was tall, and being taller than most Shan men she was an outcast. Baranov had no idea that her height was the reason General Kun Chung had given her to him. To Yuri she was a little sex goddess. To Chung she was a freak.

He held up three fingers. "Three weeks," he growled, mouth full of food.

He wasn't about to tell her that he was going to Hawaii even if she was a gift from the General, not that she would have known where in the world Hawaii was.

He spit out what remained of the stringy free-ranged chicken and slurped up a knot of noodles.

"When you leave?" she demanded.

"In a couple of hours."

She pouted and pretended to cry. "You no come bak me," she whimpered like a little schoolgirl.

"I come bak," he grumbled.

But still she pouted. He exhaled heavily, abandoned his chopsticks and stood up.

"I vill come bak," he repeated, in a softer tone. "Three weeks. I come bak."

Baranov was a huge barrel of man, over six feet tall and built like a linebacker. He had closely cropped hair and a tough, unfriendly face. He gathered her in his arms like a child and hugged her. To the Shan Mae Lee was too tall. To Baranov she was tiny. She felt light and slender and smelled like the freshest and most delicate of spring flowers. They stood there in the light of the oil lamp with tendrils of joss smoke wafting in the air.

"You make promise?" she pleaded.

"*Da.*"

"You promise you come bak?"

"*Da.* Three weeks."

She pulled away and looked up at him with warm eyes, lips parted, inviting. She knew how to penetrate his tough Cossack exterior. He kissed her tenderly, feeling the rose petal softness of her young lips. Then their tongues touched, ever so gently before their mouths closed on each other. The kiss ignited a blaze deep down inside Yuri Baranov that surprised him. She sensed the heat of his loins and pressed her sensuous little body tighter against him. Kissing him more passionately and digging her fingernails into the heavy muscles of his back, she stoked the flame inside the big Russian into a roaring fire.

She pulled away from the kiss, panting slightly, and made the slightest little movement with her shoulders. Her batik sarong slipped down her back to the floor revealing all of the delights of the Orient. Mae Lee didn't own panties or a bra. They weren't necessary in Shan territory. Her delicate fingers carefully unbuttoned his shirt and searched out his belt buckle. Helping herself to the contents of his pants, she softly stroked him, while kissing his chest and nipples.

"You come bak?" she pleaded, between kisses. "You come bak me?"

"*Da*," he grunted.

In moments they were both naked, lips barely touching, his throbbing male member pressed against her firm soft-skinned tummy. He scooped her up in his arms like a small child and carried her to the bed they had shared for the past six months. Nothing had to be said. No words were necessary. Failing death Yuri Baranov would return to the Golden Triangle. But Mae Lee wasn't sure that he would return so she set out to ensure that he would come back to her when his business was done.

He gently placed her on the bed and lay down beside her. Caressing her hair he looked into her eyes before their lips met as delicately as before, tongues touching, teasing. When he ran his hand up her tummy to a firm apple-size breast, its nipple small and hard, she inhaled quickly in little gushes of pleasure. Slowly, ever so slowly, he traced the curve of her body with the tip of his tongue until he circled her dark areola several times before taking the nipple into his mouth. Her breath deepened and she began to coo in soft little sighs as he sucked and nibbled on it. Greedily, she pushed him over to the other breast, and then back again. Slipping his hand down her slender waist, he gently probed her silky mound of jet-black hair.

"Oh Yuri. I loves you," she sighed, legs parting, opening herself up to his touch. The best porno star in Hollywood couldn't have done a better job of acting.

When his fingers found her wet vagina, she sucked in her breath in little gushes of pleasure. Teasing her, he toyed with her clitoris until he could feel the tension in her body, and see, even in the dim light of the oil lamp, a flush spread over her youthful landscape. She looked up at him with wide imploring eyes and guided his pulsating phallus into the chasm of delights. Their eyes locked as she took him inside, deeper and deeper into the smoothest, warmest world Yuri Baranov had ever known. He was far from the wet slushy streets of Moscow and happy to be a mercenary.

For a half-hour their bodies entwined oblivious to the world outside their thatch hooch, their moans and sighs of ecstasy drifting out into the jungle. When he exploded, she rolled over on top of him and covered him with wet kisses and tears.

"You come bak," she sobbed. "You no leave me, Yuri?" she begged.

After making love to a Russian no self-respecting Shan would have anything to do with her. Without Yuri Baranov for support she was doomed to the life of a common whore with a neighboring tribe. He looked into her brown almond-shaped eyes.

"I come bak, Mae Lee. I promise. Tell your sister I bring Alex bak."

She hugged him with glee and snuggled into his arms like a little kitten.


Baranov was dressed in civilian clothes when the General's battered World War II jeep screeched to a halt outside his hooch. Without speaking, he kissed Mae Lee goodbye, grabbed his backpack, pistol, AK assault rifle, and ambled out the door. The driver, a wiry little man about the same vintage as the jeep, motioned for him to get in with a wave of his scrawny hand. Baranov glanced back at Mae Lee standing in the doorway. She was just a slender little figure silhouetted by the light of the oil lamp. For a few seconds he wondered if he would ever see her again. He was beginning a mission that had no certain outcome.

"You come bak?" she begged.

*"Da!"* he growled, tired of hearing her beg. He climbed in the jeep and it lurched off down the dirt road.

Footpaths that linked village to field to village crisscrossed the Golden Triangle. The few roads that existed were little more than elephant walks used to pack opium and rice to market. As they bounced along, the jeep's orange headlights illuminated the thick jungle foliage on each side of the track. Yuri noticed that pachyderms had recently chewed the undergrowth. Fresh brown cannonball size piles of dung littered the way.

For twenty minutes the jeep wheezed and smoked down the trail. Near the Salween River gorge they came upon several *mahouts* driving overburdened elephants loaded with wooden boxes. Men with torches led the elephants off the pathway so the jeep could pass. Baranov eyed the cargo as they squeezed by. Boxes of explosives, detonation cord, and blasting caps were precariously swinging and jostling with each step of the huge beasts.

*All in one big pile waiting to go boom,* he thought. *But not here. When I say go boom.*

He considered the exchange they were about to make with General Chung.

*What is Chung going to do with a shit-load of chemical weapons?* Then he thought. *He'll take over the whole damn country. If employed properly with Gurnov's help they will scare the shit out of the Rangoonese.* A vision popped into his head, a vision of power in a country ruled by Chung.

*A villa in Rangoon would be nice. Mae Lee would like that. Maybe we can get a house on a beautiful white sandy beach with palm trees all around.*

As Baranov mused about his future in a foreign land, the jeep choked and grumbled down the trail for another ten minutes, making little better time than the elephants. Near the river, the driver stomped on the brakes, jammed the gearshift in reverse, and backed up under a huge banyan tree. He switched off the engine and turned on the yellow beam of a worn out flashlight.

"We go," the driver yapped.

Collecting his backpack and rifle, Baranov followed the old man into a double-canopied Tarzanesque jungle. They hiked down a narrow elephant walk that led to the river through a stand of huge fig and banyan trees tangled with roots, vines, and dangling lanais. Bright splotches of moonbeam slashed through the canopy, jabbing pillars of silver light into the jungle floor. Behind them, from time to time, Baranov could hear the *mahouts* and their elephants struggling down the trail.

Using the dim flashlight sparingly, they descended a twisting switchback too steep for the smoky old jeep to negotiate. From time to time Baranov caught sight of the river and a native village down below. It was almost nine o'clock when they reached the river valley. The kampong that lay ahead was silent. Here and there the light of a flickering oil-wicked lamp seeped through the bamboo slats of stilted huts built out over the river. Near the village they walked through a stand of tall teak trees and low growing bananas. Fifty meters from the first hooch, Baranov heard the unmistakable clack of a receiver sliding home. In a heartbeat he dropped to the ground, rolled to the cover of the nearest tree, and brought his AK up to shoulder ready.

The old man chuckled then cut loose with a string of spitfire curses that the Russian couldn't understand. He had learned a few words in the Shan language but not the malediction the old man was spewing out. The sentry lit an oil-fired torch and led them to a string of teakwood pirogues lined up along the riverbank. Baranov spotted Lee Chung seated up on one of the stilt platforms built out over the river. He climbed up a notched log that served as steps and saluted, not a real military salute, but a courtesy salute for the General's son.

Lee Chung was dressed in native clothing, bare-chested, and was seated Buddha style. It was the first time Baranov had seen him in anything other than green military fatigues. He was lean but strong, with a clean-cut handsomely chiseled face that betrayed no emotion. In the orange light of a burning torch, his narrow eyes revealed a hint of excitement. He motioned for Baranov to sit and went about the business of preparing his evening chew. He made a cud by folding a heart-shaped *bai plu* leaf around an *areca nut*, tobacco, and lime, then offered it, along with a glass of beer, to Baranov. Yuri accepted the offerings.

"*Spasibo*," he said, bowing his head slightly from his crossed leg posture.

Lee Chung smiled revealing blackened teeth and red stained gums. He made another chaw for himself, then pressed it into the side of his cheek, and began chewing, open mouth. Almost immediately the bitter astringent went to work. Both men began spitting red jets of saliva into the river below. In minutes the Russian's face and lips were numb.

Baranov noticed that Lee Chung wasn't wearing the

gold jewelry he usually wore. But he said nothing. The trip along the western coast of Thailand to Malaysia was dangerous. Pirates controlled the Andaman Sea. Even the first leg of their journey, down the Salween River to the Burmese port of Moulmein, was two hundred miles. Once out of Shan territory, they would be vulnerable to attack. Dressed as river people they stood less chance of drawing attention to themselves.

General Chung often hired Malaysian pirates to ferry heroin out to passing freighters. Using his contacts he had hired a large boogie to ferry the party to Langkawi Island, some six hundred miles south of Burma to rendezvous with the *Stashinsky*. In preparation for the exchange, he had sent his eldest son ahead to oversee the transfer at Moulmein.

Baranov and Lee Chung drank beer and chatted until the elephants arrived. In keeping with his spetznaz training, Yuri excused himself so he could conduct a final inventory. Although he had thoroughly checked the shipment in the General's armory, it had been out of his sight for several days and thus required a second look. Each component was necessary to construct the massive bomb he intended to create. He waded in the water, moving from pirogue to pirogue, checking boxes off the list he had prepared. When all the boxes were accounted for to Baranov's satisfaction, Lee Chung gave orders to shove off.

In a long train, the ten boats motored south with the current, their long shaft engines chugging away steadily in the darkness. Baranov watched the orange oil-lamp lights of the village disappear behind them. He settled down in the bow of the boat, making himself comfortable. The surface of the river was as smooth as glass and the sleek long hulls of the pirogues cut easily though the water. Silver moonlight danced on their wakes and illuminated the river but it was insufficient to see anything on the riverbanks. A black-green wall of jungle loomed up from the river. Soon he fell asleep, lulled by the constant beat of the diesel engine in his boat. Several times during the night he was awakened when the engine stopped. Clutching his assault rifle, he watched the banks with night eyes as the swift current quickly carried them silently past sleeping government outposts.

In the morning he awoke to the stillness and beauty of Chinese watercolor scenery. On the far bank, splayed against a clean aquamarine sky, jagged calcium karsts jutted sharp fingers three hundred feet high. Some forgotten sea that had once submerged the entire region from Burma to China had created the formation. The Salween had cut deeply into the soft sedimentary rock creating surreal, thickly jungled cliffs hanging over bare jagged spires pocked with caves.

The far bank was controlled by the Rangoon government, the near bank by a rival tribe. As the boats rounded a bend in the river, a cliff face caught his eye. It looked different. Experience had taught him to closely examine the unusual. Part way up the cliff he spotted a cave and in it a government outpost, protected by sandbags. The post had a superior command of the river that made it possible for a handful of men to control access.

They were running an hour behind schedule and first light had caught them in the open. Using the early morning mist, Lee Chung tried to slip past the outpost by floating along silently. Baranov was enjoying the beauty of the morning when a .50 caliber machinegun opened up from the mouth of the cave. The blast echoed off the walls of the gorge, startling animals and birds that complained loudly. It stopped just as suddenly then cut loose with another burst that chopped into the water directly in front of the lead pirogue. A soldier appeared on the bank down below the cliff. He yelled at them and waved them over with a red flag.

Lee Chung shouted orders and the boatmen started their engines but instead of making for the bank they made a run down river. From the near bank, another heavy caliber weapon cut loose, firing in the direction of the cave. The friendly fire sent the soldier with the flag scurrying for cover in the jungle. The two weapons exchanged fire sending green tracers flying over the heads of the river men. The monsoons had ended, but the river was still swollen from the rains and the late summers melt from the Himalayan ice cap. Assisted by the fast moving river and the friendly automatic weapon, the boats raced past the checkpoint.

Throughout the day they pressed on past fishing villages and small boats working the river. Fifty miles north of the Sea of Andaman, they made landfall in a thickly jungled area up a small tributary. There they refuel at a native village and ate well, complements of General Chung's advance party.

At last light they pressed on. Near Kyaikto the Salween opened up to form a wide body of water several miles across. Keeping to mid channel, the squadron separated like a fleet of fishing boats until they passed the ferry terminals linking the road from Bangkok to Rangoon. Then they regrouped for the final leg of the journey.

It was three in the morning when they reached their objective. Junks, boogies, dhows, and sampans of all sizes were tied up at piers, moored along the bank, and anchored out in the river. With efficiency borne of experience, Lee Chung led his men directly to a large boogie. It was moored alongside a pier with two other seagoing sailing vessels. He banged twice on the hull and six half-naked Malays in raggedy sarongs appeared on deck. They yawned and went to work helping the Shan unload the pirogues.

Lee Chung dispatched his boats as soon as they were unloaded and made himself comfortable in the captain's small cabin at the stern of the ship. He and Baranov were settling in when a Malay sailor beckoned them on deck. Phuong Chung, the General's eldest son, presented them with a spy, bound and gagged.

The older brother was short and stocky, developing that lumpy look that comes from drinking too much rice wine. He lit a cigar-sized cheroot and spat out a nasty sounding string of orders. Three Shan henchmen dragged the poor retch over to the center hold and tossed him below deck headfirst. Baranov couldn't understand the ensuing conversation but from the look on their faces he could tell they were agitated about something.

"What's going on?" he asked.

Phuong ignored him and climbed up on the bamboo pier. He walked down the wharf and climbed down onto the deck of the adjacent boogie.

"What the hell is going on," Baranov demanded.

"That man spy on us," Lee Chung explained. "We go. Quickly."

"Then let's go," Baranov agreed.

The two brothers had a few words bow to stern as sailors shoved the vessels away from the pier. With Lee in command of one ship and Phuong the other, they maneuvered out into the river under diesel power, then chugged down current at full speed. When they reached the river's mouth, Phuong turned west and headed for a rendezvous with a passing freighter to drop off a load of heroin. Lee continued south.

Clear of the harbor, the captain ordered sails aloft and the vessel took to the breeze like a Yankee Clipper, straining and listing sharply to port. The sun was above the horizon and it wasn't until they reached international waters that Baranov finally relaxed, knowing they had successfully evaded Burmese gunboats. Keeping land in sight on the eastern horizon, they sailed due south toward the Straits of Malacca.

After a breakfast of tea and rice, Lee Chung ordered his men to bring the informant up on deck for interrogation. Using a combination of water torture and joint manipulation, two of his goons beat the man half to death. When they were satisfied they had wrung all useful information out of him, Lee Chung plunged an eight-inch blade into his belly and disembowelled him with one quick downward thrust. The man's eyes were wide with pain and fear at the sight of his exposed intestines. He screamed and wailed with horrible groans that later haunted the ship's crew for days. Flopping and wriggling on the deck like a fish out of water, arms bound tightly behind his back, the tortured soul begged for death. Chung grunted at one of his enforcers and the thug slit the man's throat, ending the shrieks of terror. Hot sticky red blood pumped out onto the deck as the body quivered in death spasms.

The Shan weighed the corpse down and tossed it overboard. Seeing the expression on Baranov's face, Lee Chung explained.

"Rangoonese. He work for puppet government. No problem," he said shaking his head.

Baranov glanced down at the bloody deck, then back at Lee Chung.

"Guts attract crabs," Chung explained. "No body to find."

He grinned, showing his betel nut stained teeth.

Baranov hunched up his shoulders and lifted both palms in the air in a gesture of no big deal. "I like crab!"

he roared.

The sun glinted off his gold-capped front tooth.

But there was evidence. When Phuong Chung pulled back into port later that evening, an old man with a Nikon camera shot several pictures of the vessel to go along with the pictures he had taken during the night. He had no idea what was in the wooden boxes the Shan had loaded aboard the other vessel and neither did the analyst back at headquarters in Rangoon. But he knew the Shan were up to something atypical. And from time to time he took a little money on the side from American CIA informants. Even in the Golden Triangle secrecy was difficult to maintain.

# Chapter
# 7

A few hours after Sanz checked into the BOQ, Lieutenant Thomas, Master Chief Blaze, and Petty Officer Carroll mustered in his room. The enlisted men of Charlie Platoon called them the *top four* because they made the major decisions. Charlie was composed of two officers and fourteen enlisted men, configured to operate as a platoon, as two squads, or as four four-man fire teams. When the platoon operated as squads, Sanz paired up with Petty Officer Carroll and six others to form Alpha Squad. That way Thomas, the junior officer, had the benefit of Blaze's experience with him in Bravo Squad. When they operated in four-man fire teams, the *top four* were the fire team leaders.

The men of Charlie Platoon were all experts in explosives, weaponry, diving, parachuting, and small unit tactics. In addition, each man was also a specialist in a focused area such as communications, combat medicine, boat handling, and the other skills necessary to survival in the world of special operations. Carroll's specialty was intelligence and his grapevine was rapidly expanding. Sergeant Smith had provided him with real-time information on Exercise *Freedom Express*. Sporting a grin, he reported the latest information to the group.

"What else did that little gal do for ya, Dan," Blaze asked, when Carroll had finished his briefing.

"Nothing yet, Master," Carroll grinned. "But I'm working on it."

Sanz approved an easy schedule for the days before

isolation would restrict them to Ford Island. When the meeting broke up, Blaze stayed behind. When they were alone, he took several frangipani leis out of his briefcase and handed them to Sanz.

"Give these to Ms. Jennings when you see her," he said, in a fatherly voice. "This sort of thing is real important to a woman."

"Thanks, Master. Where did you get these?" he asked, surprised by the Master Chief's resourcefulness.

"Ah, some old gal was selling them outside the Chief's Club. She guaranteed me success if I placed them around the neck of any woman. Seeing as how she was referring to me and her, and a fifty dollar bill, I avoided the trouble and I'll pass 'em on to you."

"Fantastic," Sanz said, then sniffed the fragrant flowers.

"You know, she really did us right in that SEAL documentary. Told it like it is without all the B.S." Blaze slapped Sanz on the back like a favorite son. "She's a real fine woman and for the life of me I can't understand what she sees in an ugly cuss like you."

"Master?" Sanz said, in a serious tone.

"Yeah?"

"Thanks for understanding."

Blaze winked and left the room.

As soon as he was clear of the building, Sanz dashed down the breezeway and called the Hawaiian Hilton. But there was no answer in Julie's room. All afternoon he kept dialing the hotel over and over. By early evening he was beginning to get worried.

*I shouldn't be doing this,* he thought, as he sneaked down the breezeway for the sixth time. He was feeling like a criminal slinking around a tourist hotel. *It violates the spirit of the exercise.*

Not expecting an answer, he dialed the number and

asked for room six twelve.

"Hello," Julie answered.

"Hi, Baby. It's me."

"Oh, hi honey," she said, in a tired voice. "When did you get in?"

"Early this morning."

"Great."

"I'm here at Pearl Harbor," Sanz said, excited to hear her voice. "Can you meet me at the Visitor's Center at the main gate in an hour? It's right down Nimitz Highway, H-1 to the Pearl Harbor exit."

"Lee?"

"Yes."

"Oh, nothing Sweetheart. I'll tell you all about it when I get there," she said, with reservation in her voice.

Sanz didn't want Thomas to see him using the public phone in the breezeway so he kept the conversation short.

"I'll see you in an hour then. I'll be waiting at the main gate."

"Lee?"

"Yeah."

After a long pause she said, "I love you."

"I love you too, Baby, more than anything in the whole world. And I can't wait to get my arms around you," he said unctuously.

"I'll be there in forty-five minutes, Webfoot. Don't make me wait," she warned.

"Not a chance," he said. "See ya."

There was something in the tone of her voice that troubled him. He shrugged it off as he walked down the breezeway to his room. He tried to read but couldn't, all the while seeing Julie naked on his bed. So he watched TV until just before six-thirty, then ran the short distance to the main gate. He was waiting in the parking lot when she drove up. As soon as she stopped the car he jumped into the passenger seat like a springbok in heat. Their arms entangled and their lips touched in a long kiss.

"Oh, Lee, I've missed you so much," she said when the embraced ended.

Julie had only been in Hawaii for two weeks but they greeted each other like two young lovers who hadn't seen one another for months. When the welcome ended, he put the leis Tom Blaze had given him around her neck.

"Why thank you," she smiled, pleased by the gesture. "I haven't been laid in Hawaii yet."

"I can do better than flowers on a string," he grinned.

"Show me, Webfoot."

He reached for the door handle and jumped out of the car. Julie grabbed her purse and they headed for the BOQ hand in hand. Along the way she broke the bad news.

"Lee, I've got to go to Malaysia," she said.

"What? Why?"

Sanz stopped on the sidewalk and stared into her eyes. The light from a streetlamp illuminated her face but failed to expose the apprehension she felt inside. Julie Jennings wasn't a beautiful sexy-looking woman like Marilyn Monroe and she didn't have that *look* of a Diane Sawyer or a Katie Couric. Her chances of becoming a talking head on a prime time news broadcast were slim. She was a six on a ten-point scale and she knew it. Her breasts were too small and her legs were too thin. But underneath her light summer cotton dress was a woman possessed of true grit and determination, and a fiery passion for life. Her eyes told the whole story. They were a book in themselves, flecked with Irish green. Warm, bright, and intelligent, they hinted of the passion Sanz knew and loved. They drew him in like liquid pools of pure curiosity. Her eyes were like two sparkling jewels that hypnotized him.

"I didn't want to tell you on the phone, Honey," she whispered, "but do you remember that incident I told you about, about those fishermen who died from a mysterious disease?"

"Yeah. What's Malaysia got to do with that? I thought they were here in Hawaiian."

"The autopsies were conducted here. Malaysia just happens to be a great location to get some professional footage of a Russian ship." Apprehension crossed her face as she looked up at him. "Lee, I believe the U.S. Government is covering something up. I think those fishermen died from a manmade biotoxin."

Sanz frowned. "Poison?"

"A super poison made from a plant or an animal."

"Julie, I'm not following you," Sanz fretted. "What's poison got to do with a Russian ship and the U.S. Government?"

"It's a long story."

"I've got time. Tell me about."

"Do you know anything about a CIA project code named M. K. Naomi?" she asked.

"No. No I don't," Sanz answered, taking her hand.

As they strolled slowly toward the BOQ she explained.

"*M. K. Naomi* was top secret developmental program that produced super poisons for the CIA. If it was poisonous, CIA scientist made a suicide pill out of it or a top secret James Bond weapon to assassinate bad guys. They experimented with all types of snake venom, ricin from castor beans, saxitoxin from mollusks, poisons from frogs and puffer fish, you name it and they experimented with it. I'm surprised you SEALs don't know more about such things. M. K. Naomi was made public several years ago."

"Julie, what's this got to do with those fishermen?"

72

Lee asked, wondering what she was leading up to. He was getting more concerned by the second.

"Well, if our government did it, you can bet that the Soviets did it too. The societies of Eastern Europe and Russia are steeped in witchcraft and alchemy. There is always a grain of truth in folklore, you know."

"Yeah. I'll buy that," he agreed.

"Russia, in particular, has been plagued throughout the ages by ghastly fungal poisons like *ergot* and *fusaria*. Do you know anything about such poisons?"

"No. And now you definitely have my attention. What the hell is *ergot*?" he asked.

"It's a nasty hemorrhagic killer found in spoiled wheat or rye. In the nineteen forties thousands of Russians died from eating bread made from poorly wintered grain. Minutes after ingesting contaminated food the victims began to complain that their mouths were on fire. Huge rashes appeared on their bodies that eventually turned their skin black. The worst afflicted bled from every opening in their body. It doesn't take much imagination to envision the Russian military turning such a killer into a weapon. In fact, it's in keeping with their wolfs bane culture. The fishermen died from such a poison."

"I'm still not making the connection between the fishermen and Malaysia."

"Greenpeace has been spying on a Russian ship that they think is transporting weapons to Johnston Atoll. It's supposed to transit the Malacca Straits soon."

"Greenpeace," Sanz gasped. "You can't trust those flakes."

"They have video of a ship loading in Russia and offloading at Johnston Atoll. I've seen it."

"Johnston Atoll? Doesn't ring a bell," Lee confessed.

"It's a tiny speck of an island about eight hundred

miles southwest from here. The only thing on the island is a giant chemical incinerator plant operated by the U.S. Government.

"You think the U.S. Government is responsible for the death of those fishermen?" he asked, incredulously. "Is that what those whackos are telling you? Julie, that's ludicrous. *No! Don't tell me?* It's that wacky cameraman of yours, isn't it? *He's a certified nut case.*"

"No. Gordy is not the source of this one, Lee," she grinned, as she thought about the verbal wrestling matches they always got into. "By the way, he thinks you're Attila the Hun reincarnated." Then her face turned serious again. "Lee, I wouldn't have anything without Greenpeace," she argued. "No one in the U.S. Government will talk to me."

"Why?"

"I've been asking too many pointed questions and somebody doesn't like it. They are covering something up."

"Have you asked the right people to grant you a tour of the island? Maybe I can help," Sanz reasoned.

"Yes, I have. Access denied. The Pentagon and the State Department are stonewalling me. And now Hawaiian State officials are shunning me. The coroner cancelled an interview that was approved before I left San Diego."

"Humm. Did he get a good look at Forbes? He might have cancelled because of his ponytail and earring, or maybe he overheard Saxon rambling about some crazy conspiracy."

Saxon was her sound and light man. She ignored the remarks.

"So far Greenpeace, and one of the doctors who participated in the autopsies, are my only sources of information. Someone, I don't know who, slipped a copy of the autopsies under my door, complete with pictures of the bodies."

"At your hotel?"

"Yeah. It found it inside the morning paper."

"Why?" Sanz asked.

"Why what?"

"Why would Greenpeace be feeding you information?" he asked.

"I don't know that it was Greenpeace, Lee," she replied with a worried expression.

"I tell you why, Julie. Credibility," he suggested. "Their crazy environmental stunts have soiled their reputation."

"Maybe you've got those people all wrong. Besides, the reason is irrelevant."

"If you're not careful they'll ruin your credibility too," Sanz warned. "I would hate to see you on the evening news in a rubber boat running back and forth in front of a Russian ship."

"Lee, they think there is a secret agreement between Russia and the U.S., that we are helping them destroy chemical weapons at Johnston Atoll."

"That doesn't add up to murder and a cover up."

"I'm not suggesting the fishermen were murdered. And neither are they."

"*Aaah!* An accident? So you think the U.S. Government is covering up an accident?"

"They think the Russians are dumping toxins at sea on their way to Johnston Atoll, the kind of stuff they used in Laos and Afghanistan."

"*Hummm!*" Sanz exclaimed. "Now I'm getting the picture. *Yellow Rain*?" he asked.

"You got it. Whatever it is, it certainly isn't bee do-do," Julie exclaimed.

During the Reagan administration there were

disturbing accounts from Hmong tribesmen fleeing Laos that remote villages were being gassed by a *Yellow Rain*. Samples taken by U.S. experts sent to investigate turned out to be bee droppings. The findings seriously discredited the administration's public condemnation of the Soviet Union's use of chemical weapons in Southeast Asia.

Julie stopped under a street lamp and looked up into Lee's eyes.

"Lee, I've got a real story here, a chance to make a name for myself. I know you've been looking forward to spending some time together, and I don't want to disappoint you, but I've got to follow this story to the bitter end."

She often used him as a sounding board. In fact, he was the reason her SEAL documentary had received so much acclaim. They had met in Coronado when Sanz was assigned as her escort officer for a news story about the U.S. Navy SEALs. At the time she had been an assistant producer at KUSI. Subsequently she had quit her job and produced a SEAL documentary for Discovery Channel. It had received great reviews. Now she was struggling as an independent to make a name for herself as a producer and a reporter. Sanz was astute enough to know that this story had Nightline, Sixty Minutes, and Frontline written all over it. He studied the seriousness of her expression.

"I understand, Honey. I only have a few days off anyway and then all I'll see of Hawaii is the inside of an aircraft hangar."

"Then let's make the best of it," she suggested, snuggling up against him.

He wrapped his arms around her and held her tight. The warm muskiness of her body intoxicated him.

"Be careful with this one, Julie. It sounds like Saint

Anthony's Fire." Then he whispered in her ear. "Let's go up to my room and talk about it."

"No," she said emphatically. "Let's go up to your room and I'll make you forget about it."

"Promise?"

"Bet your swim fins on it, Webfoot," she said.

They took the stairs up to the fourth floor and sneaked down the breezeway to Lee's room. When the door closed behind them he wrapped his arms around her and pulled her close. For moments they stood in the dark while the heat of passion built to an ancient fire.

"Lee, I love you," she murmured. "I've loved you since the day I first saw you on the beach at Coronado."

"I love you too, Julie. I wanted to ask you in some beautiful place, but something tells me this can't wait. Will you marry me?"

"Yes, Lee. Oh yes. I thought you'd never ask," she gasped, with a sigh of relief.

Moments later they were naked on the bed. He pressed his mouth to her lips and kissed her tenderly for endless time. Later when she was moaning beneath him and the power of her clutching loins were drawing him in, deeper and deeper, as if vacuuming up his soul, he marveled at the beauty of life. He had to force his mind to clear so he could hear her sweet love song. "Oh, Lee I love you. I love you, I love you," she quivered, as she reached the peak of orgasm.

Passion embroiled them. It was a bond they both intended to last for a lifetime. Later, they lay together, raw and silent, yet communicating their renewed commitment through lips and fingers. Reality slowly returned with the muffled sounds of Pearl Harbor bustling with nightlife.

Sanz got up, turned on the TV, and while listening to the news, made a pot of coffee. When it was brewed he poured two cups, gave one to Julie, and asked the question that was burning in the back of his head.

"How did you get involved with this story, Jay-Jay? Was it that hippie cameraman of yours?"

"No. I received an anonymous fax from someone here in Hawaii."

"Someone in Greenpeace?"

"Maybe."

"Then the connection is Forbes?"

"Maybe. He's a charter member of the organization but he doesn't know any more about this than I do. Gordy levels with me about everything. I think the seniors in the organization trust me because of Gordon."

"So what was in the fax?"

"It was two newspaper clippings. One about the fishermen here in Hawaii and the other was on the Skull Valley incident in Utah. I was intrigued by the words scribbled on the cover sheet; *they'll cover this one up too, so* I did some research."

"Now it's beginning to sound like Fred Saxon," Sanz mused. "Skull Valley?"

"Yeah. In March nineteen sixty-eight, more than six thousand sheep mysteriously died in Skull Valley, Utah. That's about twenty miles from the Dugway Proving Grounds. The Army denied responsibility for more than a year but when the necropsies turned up VX residues, they officially admitted that they had been spraying nerve gas from an airplane and that a valve had stuck open causing a toxic cloud to drift halfway to Salt Lake City."

"Nerve gas testing? In the United States?" Sanz exclaimed, incredulously.

"Yes. It's hard to believe. What do you know about chemical and biological weaponry, Webfoot?" she asked.

He grinned his best Dennis Quaid smile and acknowledged his ignorance with a shrug. "Bugs and gases? Raid! I don't know squat, Jay-Jay," he admitted, "but enough to know that I don't want to be on the receiving end."

"In the last few weeks I've spent hours poring over the subject. When we first planned our vacation I thought this was going to be a simple news segment I could sell to KUSI. Lee, this is huge. Most people think that chemical warfare begins and ends in World War I with the doughboys dying in trenches. But it doesn't. Secret programs have carried on man's ghoulish research in poison warfare. Millions and millions of tons of toxins have been produced. There is so much it will take years for us to destroy our stockpile. Did you know that just a few miles from Denver there's a gigantic chemical arsenal?"

"Yes. That I do know. The Rocky Mountain Arsenal," Sanz answered.

"It's not very far from downtown Denver. We store the most horrible weapons known to mankind there. Sarin, soman, tabun, VX, mustard and God only knows what else. It's in all kinds of weapons from bombs to artillery shells stored right on the flight path to Stapleton International. Can you imagine what would happen if a big jumbo jet crashed into one of those warehouses? The place is overflowing with leaking caskets filled with VX. Do you know what VX is, Lee?"

"No. No, I don't," he confessed. "But as usual, you've done your homework."

"VX is the devil in liquid form. One drop the size of a freckle is enough to kill a person. It causes its victims to spasm, to jerk and twitch all over. They slobber, vomit, and defecate, and finally collapse in massive convulsions that result in asphyxiation. It's a horrible way to die Lee. Absolutely ghastly."

"I can imagine," he said, with a sour face.

"Then there are vesicants that burn the skin. Even Hitler wouldn't use them. Did you know he had a huge stockpile of vesicants? Hitler, *Hitler* of all people, actually refused his general's permission to use them?"

"I don't remember that from history class."

"The Russians use combinations of agents that blister and cause massive hemorrhaging. God only knows what they developed in their secret black programs. The autopsies of those fishermen are strikingly similar to reports smuggled out of Laos."

"So you think they are dumping black weapons at sea?"

"Like us, they produced thousands of tons of sarin and soman, and mustard and phosgene. And like us, many of their weapons are old and leaking. Did you know that the U.S. Army has officially admitted to more than a thousand leaks in U.S. arsenals?"

"No."

"I can only imagine what's going on inside Russia. Unlike us, they don't have the resources nor the means to destroy their war poisons. They only had one chemical incinerator plant and it stopped working years ago. It makes sense that we are helping them destroy their weapons. And it also makes sense that they are dumping the stuff they say *doesn't exist*."

"Like Yellow Rain?" Sanz asked, giving into the logic of her reasoning.

"If they are dumping super poisons in the ocean I'm going to catch 'em on camera even if I have to follow them all over the Pacific Ocean in the company of environmental extremists."

Sanz saw the determination written on her face.

The anchorman on the TV grabbed their attention as he reported the death of a man at the Hawaiian Hilton. The unidentified individual had apparently succumbed to another mysterious Polynesian illness. The news producer was milking the incident for all it was worth, interviewing people who entered the elevator to assist the man.

"That's your hotel," Lee said. "You'd better stay here tonight."

"I wouldn't have it any other way, Webfoot," she grinned.

She reached for his hand and pulled him over to the bed.

# Chapter 8

Vladimir Nickolaevich Koshkin eased into a lawn chair and surveyed the harbor with his binoculars. From a vantage point high in the hills of Pacific Palisades he could see the urban sprawl that flowed along H-1 from Honolulu to Makakilo.

*There*, he thought, focusing on Hospital Point. *I'll take Yong-Sook for a walk along the channel so I can get precise GPS coordinates.*

For months he had been observing Pearl Harbor, counting ships, submarines, and airplanes. Sometimes he used a telescope to zero in on details. In his former life as a spy such information was considered crucial. From his terrace he could see Ford Island in Pearl Harbor, the submarine base, Hickam Air Force Base, and Honolulu International. A 747 jumbo jet sailed across his view momentarily grabbing his attention. He followed it to touch down. It never ceased to amaze him how anything so monstrous could fly, let alone soar halfway around the planet.

"Singapore Airlines," he said out loud, recognizing the paint scheme.

*Save me a seat*, he thought.

He had purchased tickets on the plush carrier for subsequent days around the arrival of the *Stashinsky*. Buying tickets in advance and paying cash ensured that he had several escape plans available if anything went wrong.

*I wonder if the NRO and the CIA are watching the*

*ship*, he thought. *Alex and Yuri should rendezvous soon. That could draw attention to the ship.*

Turning his attention back to the activity on Ford Island, he thought, *What kind of unit is that? They operate like spetznaz.*

Helicopters had been landing and taking off all day, ferrying soldiers dressed in black. The unusual troop movements unnerved him.

"Special operations," he mumbled.

*I should book passage on a few freighters,* he thought, thinking of another E&E plan. Then his mind jumped track. *It wouldn't matter if they had a satellite bolted to her main mast. By the time they figure out she's not going to make port of call at Johnston Atoll she'll be anchored here. One simple wire transfer to Estonia and the money will disappear. And so will I.*

Koshkin's career with the KGB, the *Komitet Gosudarstvennoy Bezopasnosti*, had begun when he was twenty years old. At the time he had stood a straight six feet tall, weighed a muscular 180 pounds, had wavy chestnut hair, hazel eyes, and a handsome face. Now his hair was graying and he was less than six feet. Women still found him attractive, not raving, fall down, swooning good-looking, but attractive. At forty-eight Nickoli Koshkin simply blended into society, neither ugly nor handsome, remarkable nor inconspicuous. He was a submerged man that people rarely remembered after his passing especially if he didn't draw attention to himself.

Koshkin had grown up on a *kolkhoz*, a collective farm, the inhabitants of which lived in clusters of one and two room log huts spaced along an arc drawn through the potato fields of the Ukraine. His parent's lived in a hovel with a dirt floor and no plumbing or electricity, and what little heat there was came from a wood burning stove. In the winter the family of seven had huddled together for warmth in squalid conditions impossible for Westerners to understand. But the cold windy Steppes of his youth were a far cry from the island paradise of Hawaii. He liked life that way.

*I live as I must live, son,* Koshkin's father had told him many times. *You must live as you can. Our society is controlled by a small and powerful group of men. You can achieve a worthwhile existence only by becoming closer to them. It is not enough to stand outside the fence or break your back on a collective farm. You must get inside and the KGB is your key. You must work hard my son, and study long, and never say anything against the State or its leaders.*

And so he had studied hard and worked long, and after several applications, was finally accepted into the secret brotherhood of spies. After only six months of field training in a school outside Moscow, he was assigned as a low-level apparatchik to the strategic Red Sea port of Hodeida in Yemen. In those days the squalid little colony of six hundred Russians lived in an abject state of siege in fear of the natives and of virulent native diseases for which their doctor had no cures. One disease caused death by means of a consuming fever that the doctor told him "Burns up the brain. It's an excellent candidate for the Chamber." It would be years until Koshkin found out what the doctor was talking about or what went on inside the Chamber. Not long after he began his assignment, he got a hint.

In the streets of Hodeida, he recoiled at the sight of amputees, victims of the ancient Yemeni practice of cutting off the hand of a thief. Criminals were caged and pilloried in the marketplace where passersby could stone and spit on them. To his revulsion, the Yemeni openly relieved themselves on the streets, using stones in lieu of toilet paper. The practice caused a latrine stench to permeate the stagnant air that hovered above 100 degrees in miserably consistent 96 percent humidity. He accepted the dangers posed by volatile and unpredictable tribesmen who spent their days chewing *qat*, a narcotic coca-like leaf gown to the exclusion of all other crops. Working the filthy streets of Hodeida with informants that were a cut below the natives he considered loathsome, Koshkin came to view the Yemeni peoples as subhuman.

The Soviet government had bought control of Yemen through President Abdullah al Sallal. Sallal was afraid to openly deal with the Russians, fearful of the reaction of powerful tribes that surrounded his weak government. So the KGB acquired a house in Hodeida for secret meetings. Koshkin's job entailed managing security for Ambassador Rakhmatov during his meetings with President Sallal or members of his government. His hard work and diligence soon ingratiated him with the Ambassador who entrusted him with increasingly sensitive missions. One of those missions would change his life.

His first encounter with Alexander Gurnov and Yuri Baranov had come in Yemen. They were both young like himself, and members of the *Glavnoye Razvedyvatelnoye Upravlleniye*, the GRU, the KGB's Armed Forces Directorate. A year into his assignment, Ambassador Rakhmatov's daughter was kidnapped and raped by the son of a powerful sheik who was visiting from the mountains above the city. The teen eventually let the girl go when he grew tired of molesting her but that was just the beginning of the nightmare. An enraged Rakhmatov demanded the head of the perpetrator and when Sallal failed to deliver, either because he was unwilling or unable, Rakhmatov contacted the Center and requested special assistance. The KGB assigned Gurnov and

Baranov.

Things were not going well in Yemen and the rape of an Ambassador's daughter clearly showed the disrespect that the Yemeni had for the Russians. Baranov, then a soldier in the *spetznaz* and an agent of the GRU, and Gurnov, a specialist trained in poison warfare, were given orders to avenge the crime and to send a signal to the Yemeni people.

Koshkin put down his binoculars, finished his vodka, and lit a cigarette. He took a deep drag and lay back in the chase lounge thinking of his youth in Yemen.

*The three Cossacks*, he thought. His lips formed into a smile. *What a trio.*

Then their first mission came back to him in bloody detail, wiping the smile off his face. He heard Gurnov's voice echo through the years. *When I'm through with these assholes they'll be walking hemorrhages.*

They had gone down to the beach for a late evening swim and a few drinks to discuss the plan when he was given a hint of what went on inside the Chamber.

"But how, Alex? How will you do it?" Koshkin had asked.

Gurnov had lifted one palm defiantly in the air and shook his head no. He was drunk and his eyes were blurry.

"Secret weapon, Comrade," he had smiled. Then he had laughed maniacally. The laugh haunted him through the ages as if the three of them were still on the beach in Yemen. "You have no need to know, Nickoli."

Baranov's voice boomed from the past like a tape recording.

"I will get the filthy bastards to come to me. Trust me," he had bragged.

"What am I supposed to tell the Ambassador, Yuri?" Koshkin had asked.

"Nothing."

"What?" Koshkin had blared. "He'll have my head and he will send your asses back to Moscow."

Gurnov had growled at him like a junkyard dog. "Tell him we are going to kill every goddamn one of the sons-of-bitches, and anyone else who gets in the way."

Thinking of what they had eventually done to the Yemeni sent a chill down his spine. He took another drag off his cigarette and closed his eyes, reliving their evening swim in the Red Sea.

There on the beach in Yemen, Koshkin had gulped down more vodka than he could handle. They all drank too much in those days. He had tried repeatedly to get the men to tell him the details of their plan but they wouldn't confide in him. But as the bash wore on and the men became more inebriated, he got a glimpse of their assassination plan. It was Baranov who eventually hinted at the method of delivery.

"Okay. Since you're a fuckin' Cossack like us, I'll tell you this much," Baranov had slurred. He picked up his vodka glass, stared at the clear liquid, swirled it around and said, "Arabs covet the forbidden, Nickoli. Never forget that. It is their biggest weakness. They can't handle the forbidden."

"What are you babbling about?" Koshkin had complained.

"We're going to invite them down to my camp. I'll give them knives and bullets and trinkets until they all come down. And I will teach them how to fight their enemies. To celebrate their success, I'll have a party and I will use alcohol to pickle their brains. It's the forbidden, Nickoli. It turns them to putty," he had grinned.

Baranov had been working in the Middle East off and on for more than three years and he was confident in his understanding of the natives.

"But their religion forbids it, Yuri," Koshkin had protested. "The Ambassador is going to have my ass."

"No he won't.... I'll use the subtle art of diplomacy. Rakhmatov will understand. I'll sit them down around my campfire and there will bottles and food. But I will only give them soda while we drink whiskey. I'll tell them lies. I'll tell them what fine warriors they are, and then I'll mention how relaxing it is to have a drink of whiskey when the fighting is done. I'll suggest to them, subtly of course, that the customs of warriors takes precedence over society and that it is permissible for *real warriors* to drink whiskey together on special occasions. I've done it before. Once an Arab starts drinking, he cannot stop. When they are drunk, Alex will do his thing."

"And what will you do, Alex? I have to tell the Ambassador the details of what you're going to do or he is going to fire me, and send us all back to Moscow."

Ambassador Rakhmatov was demanding action and Koshkin's head and career were on the line.

"Fuck the Ambassador. Even Yuri doesn't have the clearance to know what I'm going to do. Tell Rakhmatov I'm going to turn them into bloody fucking corpses. Tell him they will beg for death before they die."

Several Chinese girls had walked down to the beach for an evening swim. It was so hot and sticky in Yemen. Their appearance ended all serious conversation. They had walked by the intoxicated Russians without looking or speaking despite catcalls and lewd gestures. The women had waded into the water fully clothed and splashed in the warm surf. Soaked to the skin their clothing clung to their slim bodies outlining every feminine detail. The three Cossacks had watched them hungrily, drinking and smoking at their picnic table. In detail the rape that followed replayed inside Koshkin's head as if it had happened only yesterday.

"Nice ass, but no tits," Gurnov exclaimed, leering at the girls. It came back to him in vivid detail…. "Nickoli, you ever get any chink pussy?"

"*Nyet*," he had replied, appalled by the question. "Forbidden, Comrades. The yellows are sub humans like the Arabs and the niggers. Sub humans the lot. The only thing worse are those mongrel Americans. Mixed breed shits," he had said vehemently, as if spitting out the words.

"They look good to me, man," Baranov bellowed. "My philosophy is simple. Kill the men and fuck the women. Yellow, black, or white, makes no difference to me."

Gurnov had belly laughed. "I can live with that doctrine, Yuri. I see we have a lot to teach poor Nickoli from the *kolkhoz*."

"Forbidden, Comrades," Koshkin had repeated. "Only a wall separates the Chinese compound from ours but it might as well be the Red Sea. Sometimes we wish it was the Red Sea. At night, they climb up on the wall, bang on tin pans, blow bugles, and shout curses at us to disrupt our sleep."

"Shout back at them," Gurnov had blurted.

"And fuck some of their women," Baranov had laughed. "That'll make them sleep at night. And you too."

Gurnov had guffawed.

"Soviet policy prohibits any response," Koshkin had explained.

"Fuck policy, and the women," Gurnov roared, slurring his words.

"My friends, I'm beginning to see why we don't have any respect in this land," Baranov snarled. "I think I'll go patch things up, eh?" he said, tottering to his feet. "I'm going to ask the tall one for a little comfort. Want some, Gurnov?"

"Yeah!"

Staggering down the beach, with Koshkin protesting, Baranov had boasted of his newly acquired mastery of *samooborrona bez oruzhiya,* sambo for short. It was a unique Russian form of karate. Near the water's edge he demonstrated a technique by tossing Gurnov and Koshkin in the sea near the Chinese girls. Grappling in the edge of the hot surf, he plunged in and grabbed the tallest of the girls. Pulling her close with one arm, he clutched her by the crotch with his free hand, and underwater began massaging her privates. When the girl screamed, he smothered the sound with his mouth, bending her back with his powerful body until her head was just above the water. Gurnov and Koshkin grabbed the other two girls.

It all came back to him in a blur of bittersweet memories. Underwater he had pulled up the girl's dress, pushed aside her underwear, and thrust himself inside her. She was the forbidden. Thoughts of the rape excited him. The danger. The excitement. That had been his first taste of Oriental women. They had become an obsession that he couldn't get over.

When they were done, Baranov had bellowed out a laugh. "Comrades," he had shouted, "Let's have a drink. We have just improved Sino-Soviet relations."

They let the girls go, laughing to tears watching the frightened women streak up the beach dripping with water and squabbling like hens in a language they couldn't understand. Koshkin had expected trouble from the Chinese community but none came either because the girls failed to report the matter or the Chinese were waiting to see what the Russians did to even the score for the Rakhmatov affair. They didn't have long to wait.

True to their word, the two assassins lured 60 Yemeni

males down from their highland village. With Gurnov's assistance, Baranov fed them well and taught them weaponry and tactics. At the end of the training course they got them snot-sucking drunk and packed them on their camels for the long ride back into the mountains. Two days later the Yemeni became deathly ill. Hideous brown splotches and black and blue swellings disfigured their bodies. Their hair and teeth fell out, and a sticky secretion oozed from their eye sockets. Then blood began to seep through their pores. Before dying from the strange malady, they suffered immensely, which pleased the Ambassador to no end.

Two weeks after the party, a neighboring tribe, cousins in blood, decided to make war on Baranov's training camp for giving their brethren the strange Russian disease. Hearing word of the attack through his informants in Hodeida, Koshkin had warned his fellow Cossacks. He had even helped Gurnov intercept the Yemeni.

As the tribesmen patrolled down through a rocky gorge on their way to Baranov's camp, a lone Ilyushin aircraft flew up from the valley floor. Gurnov dropped a single drum of chemicals from the plane. It didn't explode like a five hundred-pound bomb sending a shower of metal and rocks hurling through the air. In fact it didn't make much noise at all. It just issued forth a dirty brown, sweet smelling cloud that engulfed the Yemeni. They foamed at mouth like rabid dogs, vomited, bled from the nose, and died in the rocky ravine. Four hours later even their camels were dead.

Ambassador Rakhmatov was pleased with the results of the mission and soon thereafter Koshkin, Baranov, and Gurnov were promoted. Through his new friends Koshkin had learned the true meaning of Soviet intelligence. *Center* meant Moscow. Everyone knew that. To *swim* meant to travel. *Illness* indicated arrest. A *wet affair* was an assassination. A cover story was called a *legend,* a *shoe,* a passport, a *cobbler,* a technician who forged false documents. They termed a radio transmitter, a *music box,* and other arms of the Soviet, as *neighbors.* Women were call *sperm dumps* and high-level officials were called *suits.* They could speak in a language all their own. Throughout the years they had remained close *neighbors* and brother Cossacks.

Koshkin later learned that the special bureau within the KGB that had assigned Gurnov was called the *Kamera,* or Chamber. It was actually a laboratory whose mission was to invent undetectable means of exterminating human beings. The Chamber specialized in poisons for which there were no known antidotes, and devices that killed efficiently while making death appear to be the result of natural causes. Alexander Gurnov was a rising star within the poison warfare community. Vodka would be his millstone.

Earning his way up the ranks of the KGB, Koshkin had excelled, attaining the rank of colonel in the secret organization. He was posted to the United Nations in New York, to the Russian Embassy in Washington, D. C, to the consulate in Los Angeles, California, and several other plush assignments. He learned to speak English smoothly and fluently and that propelled his career. His ethics mattered not to the KGB.

No nation in the history of mankind had ever practiced espionage so massively and as aggressively as did the Soviet Union. For decades, they systematically stole the scientific, industrial, and military inventions of other nations. They relied upon the KGB, and men like Nickoli Koshkin, to find foreigners who could be recruited to provide the crucial intelligence necessary to sustain subversion in both emerging and advanced nations. To Koshkin, espionage represented opportunity. It caused him neither feelings of guilt nor pleasure. Like many Ukrainians of his generation and class, he never acquired a sense of personal identity with the Soviet Union nor any allegiance to it. He thought of it simply as a *kolkhoz*, a collective. When it fell apart, he had turned to the new endeavor of private industrial espionage.

For a brief moment he felt guilty for assassinating Dr. Robbins. It was a different chemical agent from that which had killed the fishermen. Its use was intended to mislead the scientific investigation. The KGB called it *maskirovka,* a concept of deception, camouflage, and subterfuge all rolled into one modus operandi. Nickoli Koshkin was a master at *maskirovka.*

*The man was getting too close*, he thought. *It had to be done*.

Koshkin stubbed out his cigarette butt and went inside. It was a simple house the KGB had once rented to keep an eye on Pearl Harbor. He poured himself a drink and lit another cigarette before dialing a number in Moscow. The phone rang just a few short blocks from Lubyanka prison.

"Markov Consulting International," answered a huge bodyguard.

"Michael?" Koshkin asked. He could hear chatter in the background.

"One moment," said the Mafioso on the other end of the line.

He put his hand over the receiver and looked at his boss who was engaged on another line. He nodded a couple of time and Markov cut short his conversation. Seated behind his large imported teakwood desk, compliments of Yuri Baranov, he coordinated ten deals a day, mostly drugs and money laundering.

"*Da,*" he growled into the receiver.

"Michael, Nickoli, here. How are things going?" Koshkin asked.

"Outstanding. And how is business going on your end?" Markov replied.

"Great, just great. The shipment is in transit. Are the accounts ready for transfer?"

"*Da.*"

The Mafioso looked at his henchmen and grinned. He took a drag off his cigar and blew a smoke ring.

"I anticipate that we will make a deal in about two weeks, so it is of utmost importance that things go well on your end. My partner was very disappointed with the Israeli transaction."

"Nickoli, business is business. I can't be held responsible for the actions of Jewish merchants. You know that," Markov argued.

"Alex can be, how shall I say this Michael, lethal when crossed, especially when drinking. Your percentage is very high for the level of risk you are taking in this venture. If anything should go wrong on your end things could turn out very badly for you," Koshkin warned.

"Is that a threat, Nickoli? Are you threatening me?" Markov asked.

"No. Of course I'm not threatening you. I am just telling you that our business associate is a very dangerous man. Everyone knows the bankers in Estonia are less than honest. With so many hands involved, unforeseen things can happen. For your health I hope nothing goes wrong on your end."

"Don't worry. Baranov and I have done many deals. Ask him," Markov insisted.

Markov was a big man in the troubled back streets of Moscow, one of the biggest movers and shakers in the drug business. But he was not beyond the reach of the three Cossacks.

"*Da. Da.* I know that you and Yuri have done business before. But your deal with Alex did not go so well, my friend. He is pissed and if anything goes wrong with this deal, well, you know that the *Kamera* is very close to your office and it is a place near and dear to his heart. Alex thinks you screwed him on the Israeli venture. If one *ruble* goes missing, one stinking *kopec,* I wouldn't want to be in your shoes, Michael."

A shiver ran down Markov's spine. He had heard rumors and stories.

"There will be no problems on my end," Markov insisted. "Nickoli. Believe me. I understand. Tell Alex I am very sorry that things turned out so badly. I'll make it up to him. I'm working with an Iranian who has contacts at the highest level. The big guys want to do business with us," Markov said, with more bravado than he felt.

"Good. Perhaps later we can talk more about the possibilities. For now, *do svidaniya*," Koshkin said.

He hung up the phone before Markov could continue the conversation.

Russia and its neighboring states were awash in illegal money. Bribery was commonplace, murder and extortion the norm, and racketeering was a way of life. The average pay for a policeman was less than three hundred dollars a month, pocket change for *boyevik* Mafioso like Markov. There were no laws against money laundering, fraud, or organized crime. With the development of computer and communications technologies, financiers with homes in Paris and Luxembourg could shell game a billion dollars around the globe in seconds. And with encrypted faxes and cellular telephones their illegal activities were all but impossible to trace. Markov felt secure in Moscow, but not from

Alexander Gurnov.

Koshkin went back outside and resumed his surveillance of the military bases. It was a spy's habit to watch planes and ships come and go. A few minutes later he heard his lady friend, Yong-Sook, enter the house. She was a Korean beauty he had met in a little club down town. Less than half his age, she was happy not to be working the streets to pay off her bondage. He finished his drink and counted the helicopters at Ford Island, then the transport planes at the military terminal. He was watching a 747 float by when his binoculars went dark. He put them aside as Yong-Sook placed a fresh drink on the table and sank down in a chase lounge opposite him. Leaning back she bent both legs at the knee and shot him a prefect beaver. While inside making the drinks she had removed her panties. She smiled when he took notice.

Sleek and lean and beautiful beyond belief, she beamed at him with mysterious almond shaped eyes. He followed the path from her toes to the jade gate. Her tan legs flowed up from bare feet, ankles strong but delicate, calves curvaceous and full. The inner parts of her thighs were lithe and firm with a slightly yellow tone to her silky smooth skin. The sexy curves ended brusquely in a pert black satin triangle that beckoned him like a Siren's song.

"Next week I want you to go to Korea," he said, staring at the chasm of delights.

"Why?" she asked, in a soft sexy little voice thick with accent.

"Vacation."

"I take vacation with you in Korea?" she asked happily.

"First, you must go alone. I have business to attend to here."

She pouted and pushed out her bottom lip.

"I want you to rent us a little love nest down on Cheju do?"

A smile brightened her face. "You come Korea?"

"Oh, I'm going to come *a lot* in Korea," Koshkin grinned.

Yong-Sook did not understand the sexual innuendo.

"Don't worry, my pet. I'll be along in a few weeks and then we'll have a nice time on Cheju. When it gets too cold we'll go to Rio. You ever been to Rio?" he asked, knowing she had never been anywhere but Korea and Hawaii.

"No. Where Rio?"

"I'll show you a picture when we go to Honolulu to buy your ticket. You'll love it there. The women dance around half-naked and sunbathe without their tops."

She was excited. She wiggled out of her chair, slinked over, and knelt down beside him. She had a tight little belly on a long slender waist, and higher, barely concealed by her top swelled two proud and protruding little apple-size breasts. Koshkin's glandular cheering section was throbbing with excitement. She glanced down at him and smiled. Placing her lips on his pants directly over his bulging shaft, she blew her hot breath through the cloth of his pants, driving him wild with excitement.

"You, my little Tigress, are worth every penny I paid that old mama-san."

He had bought her out of bondage for two thousand dollars. She smiled and handed him his drink. They clinked glasses.

"Korea," she said. "*We-hi-oh!*"

"Rio," he replied. "*Salute!*"

After gulping down the fiery liquid, she looked down at his hungry member and said, "Let's go inside. I make him happy."

He smiled and she pulled him up out of his chair and led him directly to the bedroom. Undressing first, she combed her long black flowing hair with her fingers so it surrounded her face. It framed two mysterious eyes and a gleaming white smile braced by two tiny dimples. She helped him undress and urged him onto the bed on his stomach. For a while she kneaded his back with her delicate little hands, doing marvelous things to his muscles. Then she gently rolled him over, and kissed him, letting the nipples of her breasts just touch his skin, sending tiny electric shocks of excitement through his body.

"You like?" she whispered, nibbling on his ear.

"*Da*," he exhaled in pleasure. "I like."

She planted a moist kiss on his lips and he felt his whole body responding with a hum, as if some powerful motor inside him had just switched on and was revving up to speed. He wanted her. He wanted her so badly he would have given away his share of the fifty millions dollars. Truth in fact, she was the reason he had decided to throw in with Gurnov and Baranov. He needed the money to continue their costly relationship.

He tried to pull her up onto him but she resisted and began working her tongue down his body. She toyed with his nipples, and circled his belly button. Finally, she slid down and knelt between his legs. Carefully studying the look on his face, she stroked him gently. Her silver bracelets jingled fast then slowly as his body tensed near orgasm. Keeping him on the edge of excitement with finely tuned caress and hot breath and tongue, she teased him until he could take no more.

"Please, Yong-Sook. Please," he begged. "You're torturing me. I want you. I love you, Baby. I love you so much I would do anything for you."

She smiled coyly and slithered up his body mounting

him like a horse.

"You good man, Nicki," she whispered sweetly. "You good man for me."

Raising herself up on her knees, and straddling his body, she gently lowered her wet chasm of delights down onto his throbbing gland, slowly engulfing him. Then he saw something new in her eyes, something he hadn't seen before, something that hadn't been there before. She paused for just a second, taking all of him into her body.

"You come Korea?" she pleaded. "You no leave me? You come Cheju with me?" she begged.

"I'm not going to let you go, Tigress. Never," he said. He thought, *Maybe it's true what they say about Oriental women. They don't care so much about a man's age.*

Yong-Sook picked up the pace. Her head pitched forward, then back, tossing her long black hair down her back. With grinding hips and delicate teasing moves she drove him to orgasm. As he came she gasped and stiffened, her whole body rocking in ridged, spasmodic waves, her voice crying and sighing and singing all at the same time.

"Oh Nicki, oooh Nicki. I loves you, Nicki. I loves you."

Koshkin had found heaven in the West with a woman of a yellow race he had once considered to be a subhuman. He had to go through with the deal. It had to work. There was no way he was going to lose his Korean sex goddess. No way.

At eight o'clock they drove to the airport and bought a one-way ticket to Seoul, Korea, and then on to Honolulu for dinner. Afterwards, they strolled the Korean alley where many of her countrymen made a living selling celadon, cloisonné, and counterfeit goods imported from the Orient. Later, walking through the mall near Waikiki,

Koshkin selected the perfect location to plant the first chemical bomb. After a leisurely evening in paradise they went home and made love again.

# Chapter 9

As the ferry passed the Arizona Memorial on Battleship Row, General Carlson put down a batch of intelligence reports and looked out from the backseat of his sedan. He noticed the slight sheen of oil on the surface beneath the crescent shaped monument.

*Arizona's tears*, he thought, remembering the plaque he had seen at the visitor's center on the other side of the bay. The persistent leaking of oil from the engine room of the *Arizona* was poetically described as the ship's tears weeping for its fallen crew. He had forgotten that since his last visit to Hawaii.

Carlson was early for a speech he was to give to the men and women of Exercise *Freedom Express*. To occupy his time he had stopped at the visitor center to pay his respects to those who had died during the attack on Pearl Harbor. As the ferry passed the Arizona he gave a half salute. With respect duly rendered, he picked up his reports and thumbed through them. He briefly scanned a sanitized message. It reported the attempted sale of chemical weaponry by a Russian Army major to Palestinian terrorists. With all that was happening in the world the incident was too minor to warrant his full attention. Corruption was running rampant in Russia. Several messages reported seizures of weapons being sold on the black market. Nuclear, biological, and chemical warfare technologies were for sale to the highest bidder and there was little the United States could do to stem the flow.

*The face of warfare is changing,* he thought. *It's only a matter of time until a weapon of mass destruction ends up in the hands of a terrorist.*

He thought about his Special Operations Command and the brave men and women in his charge. Their job was to rush to the scene of an incident to deal with the problem.

*Counter terrorism,* he thought, *is just ambulance chasing. The evil genie is out of the bottle and sooner or later one of the rogue states will put a weapon of mass destruction in the hands of crazy kids willing to commit suicide. I wonder if it will be a nuke in the trunk of a Mercedes or a sack of anthrax scattered from the top of the Empire State Building. God Almighty, Our Father in Heaven, how do we put an end to this madness?* he silently prayed. *How do we stop this insanity?*

Carlson took his awesome responsibility personally. As Commander in Chief of the U.S. Special Operations Command his job was to plan for, and when directed by the President of the United States, conduct selected special operations. In his mind's eye he saw wafer-sized plates of plutonium the size of cookies slipping quietly past a customs agent in remote Kazakhstan. He could see secret programs growing at an accelerated pace in Pakistan, India, Libya, Syria, Iraq, Iran, North Korea, and China. He had recently directed *Operation Sapphire,* an airlift mission in which the United States military had flown into Kazakhstan at the request of Russians to help them confiscate tons of enriched uranium. Efforts by Iranian agents to buy nuclear materials had drawn attention to a huge stockpile of yellow cake that had been neglected by the crumbling Soviet bureaucracy. Only swift intervention had prevented the Iranians from acquiring tons of yellow cake, the first step in processing uranium into weapons grade material. Plutonium was quite another matter. It only took a few kilograms to make a bomb and the Russians had tons of the metal. Moreover, the scientists responsible for weapons grade material were underpaid, if paid at all.

*Opportunity makes a thief,* he thought, remembering the words of a Russian general he had met at a conference in Poland. *If temptation is there day after day and you are struggling to survive, sooner or later it will get you. That is human nature. We need help now, General Carlson. Tomorrow will be too late.*

Carlson pondered the problem. He was aware that General Alexander Lebed had reported his findings on the control of nuclear weapons to President Yeltsin. The report was shocking, especially his analysis of terrorist style weapons. Of 184 suitcase bombs, one-kiloton nuclear devices disguised as large suitcases, Lebed had only been able to account for 34. The others were lost by inventory. Thousands of nuclear warheads were unaccounted for. Tens of thousands of weapons were managed by military personnel who were underpaid, and hungry. When Yeltsin refused to accept Lebed's analysis of the situation, someone had leaked the substance of the report to the West.

*Desperate men do desperate things,* he thought. *The unsettled state of social and economic life in Russia is truly a world problem given the awesome technology they possess. People in such conditions will use any means to get their hands on a large sum of money so they can disappear to spend their lives in Hawaii or Brighten Beach, anywhere but Russia. They need help establishing and maintaining security at strategic facilities and somehow I have to convince Congress and the President to be proactive in helping them before it's too late. If one of those suitcase nukes gets into the wrong hands, a hundred thousand people will be at risk.*

In his mind's eye he saw a blinding white flash. *But it's not if. It's when and where? Tel Aviv? New York? LA?* Then he thought, *if Lebed is right, it's already too late.*

As Carlson's ferry pulled up to the dock, he looked off in the distance at the weather worn aircraft hangar that served as command central for Exercise *Freedom Express.* It looked like just another derelict left over from World War II. But inside he knew that the activity was thoroughly modern, and frenetic. Army, Navy, and Air Force units had staked out territory like hungry settlers, converting the huge building into a small city of tangled streets and makeshift encampments. Soldiers, sailors, and airmen were working diligently on boats, helicopters, and sophisticated operational equipment, waiting for his command to strike an unknown enemy.

"Phillips, find a place to park," Carlson ordered. "I want to take a walk along Battleship Row. Alone."

"Yes, sir."

Major Phillips turned his attention to the driver of the sedan.

"Park over there, corporal," he ordered, pointing out a good location to stop the car.


As Carlson walked alone down what was left of Battleship Row, a leatherneck army colonel with close-cropped hair stepped up to a microphone at the rear of the old hangar. He was a tall man, older than most in special operations, and he wore a camouflaged uniform taken straight off the hanger. His hair, once dark, was now salt and pepper and cut so short it looked like the bristles on an old brush. An E-9 sergeant standing beside him yelled attention in a voice that sounded like a foghorn. For thirty seconds there was a stir of activity as everyone stopped what they were doing and positioned themselves to listen.

"Good morning, ladies and gentlemen. Welcome to Exercise *Freedom Express,*" the Colonel said. The PA system screeched and the sergeant jumped to adjust it.

Lee Sanz looked around at Tom Blaze. The gnarly Master Chief had seen the Colonel approaching the general's podium and he had quietly placed Charlie Platoon at parade rest. They were assigned the least desirable space in the building, a corner near the open hangar doors.

"At ten hundred hours General Carlson will be here to formally commence the exercise," the bird Colonel bellowed. "Before he arrives, Lieutenant Colonel Houston will form you up and go over the administrative and housekeeping aspects of the exercise. While he's doing that I'd like the senior officer and senior enlisted man from each unit to muster in the briefing theater. Thank you for your attention."

He turned around and walked off like a man who was late for an important meeting. Houston immediately began shouting orders over the PA, directing the position of each unit. DELTA was assigned front and center.

"Mike, Dandy Dan, you've got it," Sanz said, speaking to Lieutenant junior grade Thomas and Petty Officer Dan Carroll.

Sanz motioned with a nod of his head for Blaze to follow him to the back of the hangar where several large maintenance spaces had been converted into a Tactical Operations Center and a briefing theater. As they walked along several of the SEALs in a sister encampment kidded them.

"Hey, *lookey here.* If it ain't the glory boys from Hollywood," an East Coast comrade grinned. "How are you doin', Master Chief? You too, Lieutenant?"

"High speed, shallow draft, Petty Officer Leon," Blaze replied, jovially. "Always on target." Blaze sighted down his finger like aiming a pistol.

As they walked by another sailor commented. "That's because you guys always get the easy *Hollywood* targets. Try takin' down an underway ship at night," he said in a surly tone.

Blaze stopped and turned around to face the young petty officer."

"Petty Officer Jarvis?"

"Yes, Master Chief," the sailor gulped nervously.

"You got a problem?"

"No, no Master Chief."

"Did I detect a slight tone of derision in your voice, Petty Officer Jarvis?"

"No. No Master Chief."

Jarvis didn't know what derision was, but he was smart enough to know that he didn't want any from Master Chief Blaze.

"Well, I think I did and I believe I know what's eatin' you. Maybe you're sore because of the bruising you guys took up in Monterey. Your doin'. Not ours. So let me explain a few facts of life that you may have overlooked, Petty Officer Jarvis. I was taking down underway ships, *at night*, before you got out of high school." Blaze stared at the group with a hard expression. "I suggest you concentrate on team work, gents, Jay-sock team work. We are one team, with separate targets. You win some, and you lose some, so don't get hung up on the past. Carry on and charge with finesse," he grinned.

"You bet, Master Chief," Jarvis replied, sheepishly.

"We're gonna kick some ass this time, Master," another sailor said.

"I have no doubts about it. I put most of you through

BUD/S. You wouldn't be here if I didn't have the utmost confidence in your potential to do great things."

BUD/S was the acronym for Basic Underwater Demolition SEAL training, the SEAL basic training course located in Coronado, California. Blaze had taught there for years and had put many of the rank and file through the course.

Blaze winked at Sanz as they walked on toward the back of the hangar to join a crowd of people queued up to enter the restricted area. Soldiers guarding the doors were checking badges for access authorization. Sergeant Smith smiled salaciously at Sanz as she checked his badge. He ignored her hungry eyes and glanced over at Blaze. The Master Chief winked and pushed his cheek out with his tongue.

"Dandy Dan will get some of that," he whispered.

Inside, the briefing room was furnished with row after row of neatly arranged folding metal chairs placed in front of plywood map boards and a projector screen. As Sanz selected two seats he whispered to Blaze.

"We sure travel heavy, Master. Too damn heavy," he said, referring to the tons of equipment and material that had been flown to Hawaii for the exercise.

"It's the tank mentality, Lieutenant. Amass such an overwhelming force that the enemy gives up from fear. Trouble is, terrorists don't play by the old rules of correlation of forces and centers of gravity," Blaze continued.

"We don't need all this stuff to take down a ship," Sanz argued.

"That's not what this is about, L.T. This is a show, a big show for the VIPs who pay the bills. You know the Army. They couldn't function without formal briefings. That's about all a general does, you know, is travel from one briefing to another listening to homogenized bullshit filtered by slick talking colonels. If it wasn't for their intelligence reports, and a few well-placed straight shootin' sergeants, they'd be as baffled as us snake eaters," Blaze explained, cutting his eyes over at Colonel Ardison. "That's one of the good ones. He has the makings of a fine general."

Ardison was bucking for brigadier. He was a seasoned warrior who deserved promotion. Intelligent, hard working, and dedicated to God and country, he was a leader who paid attention to the smallest detail even the placement of chairs in the briefing theater.

"He reminds me of General Carlson. The old man will ask a technical question of a buck sergeant in Fort Bragg in the morning and the same damn question from a major in another part of the country in the afternoon, usually about communications, or logistics, or intel, and woe be to the poor son of bitch who tries to bullshit him," Blaze smiled.

When everyone was seated and quiet, Ardison spoke.

"Gentlemen, *Freedom Express* is the largest counter terrorism exercise ever conducted by Jay-sock. It consists of a controller staff of more than five hundred people orchestrating the activities of more than three thousand players. The terrorists, our opposition force, are composed of more than a hundred experienced soldiers drawn from the ranks of Special Forces Group ONE and SEAL Team THREE, the best damned soldiers and sailors this nation has to offer." He qualified his statement with a smile. "Present company excluded, of course."

His audience of seasoned warriors grumbled agreement with a jumble of, *here-heres*.

"Our targets will not be known to us until the OPFOR attacks them. Moreover, we won't know our specific missions until our political leaders determine how best to handle the situation. This is a free play exercise, gentlemen. I stress *free play*. War games of this type follow a set pattern. First, the attack, then negotiators get a crack at resolving the incident with words. But all the words in the world won't solve this one."

Ardison looked over his troops.

"The tangos, our brethren in arms, *will* become frustrated with negotiations and they *will* kill hostages, one by one. *Go-no-go* will be determined by the situation and orders issued by civilian authority. You'll be briefed on the chain of military and civilian command in a few minutes, but first, I have a video from the CINCPAC PAO to show you. I haven't seen it yet but I have been told the locals are on to us. Take this as a lesson in OPSEC."

OPSEC was military term for operational security. Ardison pointed at two soldiers in the corner. They quickly rolled out a television hooked up to a VCR and worked the machines like a crew-served M-60 machinegun. While one soldier turned on the TV and adjusted the volume, the other controlled the VCR. A local news anchorman's face filled the television screen.

"Good morning, paradise. Welcome to *Morning Addition*. Today's topic is military operations. Question? What were those noisy airplanes doing circling low over Oahu early Saturday morning? Were they the ghosts of Pearl Harbor or part of a large military training exercise? That's what a government spokesman told Action Five news. But then he added that the exercise was secret and that he couldn't talk about it. Whatever they were doing it caused a ruckus. At three A.M., police dispatchers were inundated with hundreds of questions and complaints. Here to answer for the military is Captain Michael Bowers from the office of the Commander in Chief, Pacific Command. Captain Bowers, welcome to *Morning Addition*."

"Thank you, Tom. It's a pleasure to be here," said an immaculately dressed naval officer in a crisp white uniform. The camera focused tight on his face then back on the reporter.

"Now, Captain, rumor has it that those aircraft were part of a large military exercise taking place here in Hawaii. Should the viewers be prepared for more early morning activities?"

"No, Tom. Those aircraft were part of a routine training exercise designed to enhance unit skills and improve coordination among the services. There will be no further operations over land that will disturb the public."

Bowers practiced response humored the reporter. The anchorman smiled and attacked.

"Captain Bowers, I have a reliable source at CINCPAC who told me that in two weeks the U.S. Military will begin the largest special operations exercise ever conducted in Hawaiian waters. Were those aircraft part of some larger mission?"

The camera focused tight on Captain Bower. He was trapped and his facial featured showed it. "We have several military exercises planned for the coming quarter, Tom," Bowers answered, flatly.

"Captain, I have a reliable source at American-Hawaii Lines that told me the *SS Independence* will be attacked by mock terrorists. Will the military be ordered to rescue the vessel?"

"*Ambush!*" Ardison yelled. "So much for the secrecy of the SEAL mission."

A grumble of astonishment passed through the

briefing room.

Bowers was trapped. He cleared his throat before speaking.

"Tom, it is our policy not to discuss the conduct of future training exercises. However, I will say that it is not unusual for civilian vessels to participate in exercises of this nature."

"Ah, come on, Captain Bowers. We're proud of our boys in uniform. We're behind them one hundred percent, unless we lose too much sleep of course." He grinned at the camera. "Captain, the public has a right to know about these kinds of maneuvers. It's taxpayer money you're spending and my guess is the *Independence* didn't come cheap."

Bowers decided to limit the damage by tossing in a little bureaucratic double talk.

"We are testing a contingency plan. One of the objectives is to determine the interoperability of disparate stateside units."

"By disparate units you mean the Army's top secret DELTA Force and the Navy's SEAL Teams?" the reporter asked. "The ones stationed out on Ford Island?" He smiled.

Several of the men in the briefing theater called the reporter dirty names.

"The only delta we know of Tom, is an airline," the colonel in charge of DELTA commented from the audience. Some of the men chuckled.

"That's ah, that's ah, not exactly the issue, Tom," the polished public affairs officer replied. "This exercise is designed to test the ability of the Pacific Command to support the Department of Justice with forces from the continental United States in the event a crime is perpetrated upon a U.S. flagged commercial vessel," Bowers stammered.

What are we talking about here, captain? Piracy? Hijacking? Terrorism?" the seasoned reporter asked, pressing the attack. "Break it down for us."

"Well, all of the above," Bowers said, reluctantly.

Bowers was extremely uncomfortable and it showed on his face. The reporter pressed his assault.

"I've been told by the FBI that they will board the *Independence* to investigate criminal activities under the jurisdiction of the Department of Justice. Is that true?"

Bowers smiled, relieved that one of the leaks was obviously the Federal Bureau of Investigation.

"That is correct, Tom. The legal framework for such cooperation was established several years ago. Congress passed anti terrorism legislation giving federal agents authority to investigate terrorist acts against U.S. citizens outside the territory of the United States. A realistic scenario, the details of which are not known to us in advance, will challenge the Pacific Command in the coming weeks. FBI agents from our local office may," Bowers paused before saying, "will, be assigned to interview witnesses, victims, and captured terrorists should a mock incident occur on a U.S. flagged ship and should our forces be ordered by civilian authority to seize the vessel."

"You bet your liberal ass we'll take her down, *Tom*," a salty Master Chief from SEAL Team SIX commented for the back of the audience.

"I see," said the newsman. "Captain, who are these terrorists? I mean, I know they are U.S. soldiers and sailors, but who are they supposed to be. Palestinian terrorists? Domestic terrorists?"

"*Turn it off!*" Ardison shouted, shaking his head. "I've heard enough of this bullshit."

One of the enlisted technicians scrambled to shut off the machine. Ardison walked back to the podium and frowned before addressing his men.

"Gentlemen, *Freedom Express* is a joint military and civilian exercise designed to test CONPLAN oh-seven-thousand. Like you, I am just a player. I don't know what the targets will be, but I do know the *Independence,* an eight hundred foot passenger ship is the centerpiece of the exercise. The management is suspending tourist operations for a couple of weeks to refurbish some of the ship's cabins and they made her available to us for a song and a dance. The bottom line is, the OPFOR will seize her and several other targets in this AO to test our ability to respond to the various hostage situations and to the decisions of our political leaders. The President is playing in this exercise, gents."

"God," groaned a soldier in the back of the room, "are we in deep shit, or what?"

"*Enough! I'll hear no more insubordination!*" Ardison yelled, with an angry tone.

He glared at the crowd of seasoned troops for a half a minute before continuing.

"It's easy to guess what the SEAL's primary mission will be, the *SS Independence.* Captain Watson?" he said, looking at a sharp SEAL officer dressed in a fresh camouflage uniform. "Do you have everything you need to take down a ship of that size?"

Handsome, blond, and in outstanding physical condition, the SEAL officer looked too young to be the same rank as the gnarly old Colonel.

"Yes, sir. We're ready for any contingency," he answered in a confident voice.

"DELTA?"

"Yes, sir," grunted a young clean-cut Army colonel.

He too was the same rank as Ardison, and like Captain Watson, junior in seniority but not in rank.

"Your missions are TBD," Ardison said.

TBD was military slang for *to be determined*.

"They'll be on dry land somewhere here on Oahu."

"We're ready," Colonel Boyd insisted, with confidence.

"That's a lot of territory, John. As this thing heats up I want you to keep your gear staged on the birds."

Ardison knew the helicopters would be staged from a carrier offshore. Anything left behind when the units transferred to sea would be beyond reach or too embarrassing to transship.

"Roger. Will do," Boyd replied.

"SEAL Team FIVE?"

"Here, sir," Sanz said.

Unlike the other two senior officers, Lee stood up at attention.

"Lieutenant Sanz, I'm told by my spies on the controller staff that the OPFOR will seize a second, smaller vessel that you'll have to take down simultaneous with the other missions. Are your men and gear ready for such action?"

"Yes, sir."

"Very well then."

As Lee resumed his seat, Ardison looked hard at him, then at Blaze. The tension in his face seemed to ease when his eyes met the Master Chief's.

"Gentlemen, the tangos will be able to communicate between targets. You see the problem?" he said, looking directly at Blaze, then at Watson and Boyd. "This is the most ambitious and the most difficult exercise we've ever conducted. One mistake by any player could jeopardize the success of the whole mission. And since the entire chain of command is playing, all the way up to and including the President of the United States, we are on a very short string and under a very powerful microscope. *We have to communicate!* We have to take all of the targets down at the same time. I repeat. We have to take all the targets down simultaneously. There are no Army targets here. No Air Force targets. No Navy targets. No SIX, no FIVE, no DELTA. Got that?"

The crowd responded with a jumble of *here-here*s, *yes-sir*s, and *amen*s.

"Now, I want you and your men looking good when General Carlson arrives." Ardison looked at his watch. "He'll be here in about half an hour. So let's get down to business."

After the briefing, as Blaze and Sanz walked back to their section of the hangar, the Master Chief opined his disquiet.

"You know, L.T., we're going to get the hardest mission."

"How do you figure that, Master? Even Colonel Ardison doesn't know the targets yet," Sanz challenged.

"Oh yes he does. He knows."

"Why do you think we are going to get the hardest target?"

"Simple. The *Independence* is not going to be underway. She's too big. It costs a lot of money to move a ship like that around. And you heard what he said. We got her for a song and a dance. Redneck civilians are going to be working on her. DELTA is going to get some target like the MAC terminal or the admiral's residence, something on a base that Uncle Sam owns. And we are going to get a smaller, less important, highly maneuverable, hard to find, underway mother."

"I got the picture. Underway, at night."

"Bingo. There is no way they're going to spend this kind of money and not do a night underway ship boarding operation," Blaze continued.

Sanz swallowed hard. Charlie Platoon was facing the most difficult military operation in the JSOC inventory.

"*Jesus!*" Sanz exclaimed.

"Now don't start praying on me, Lieutenant. Makes me nervous," Blaze grinned.

"I hope we're not being set up. The guys in SIX and DELTA are still rankled over the Monterey op," Sanz opined.

"No way. Too much involved here for anyone to monkey around. We got it because we're damned good and Ardison knows it. He's bucking for general. The man needs success and we're going to give it to him, aren't we, sir?"

Blaze smiled that devious Tom Blaze smile that filled Sanz with confidence.

"You bet we are. Show time." He high-fived with the salty Master Chief.

"Even if we have to cheat," Blaze continued. "Now, where the hell is Dan Carroll? We need some intel."

"Like what?"

"Like who's gonna be riding that small, highly maneuverable underway mother."

"Sergeant Smith?" Sanz asked.

"You're learning fast, Lieutenant. Now back to work."


The young corporal standing guard at the checkpoint shifted uneasily at his post. Sweat stained his crisp battle dress uniform and doubt furrowed his brow. The major standing in his face was getting angrier by the second.

"Corporal, do you know who is in that car?" he asked.

"Yes, sir."

The staff car waiting at his gate was flying a red pennant with four white stars. Sweat trickled down his forehead from underneath his camouflaged doggy hat.

"You will open that gate, Corporal, or you will find your ass in the North Carolina boondocks with a hundred pound ruck on your back. Is that clear?"

Major Phillips looked more like a Hollywood actor than a general's aide. He was wearing a class "A" uniform right off the hanger, a belt holding a .45 caliber pistol, and Oakley sunglasses that reflected the corporal's image.

"Sorry, sir, but no one is allowed access to the isolation area unless they are on this list."

"General Carlson is in that car, *son*. He's the reason you're here. Everyone in that damn hangar works for him," Phillips said, pointing out at the airfield. Grass and weeds were growing up through the tarmac. *"That includes you!"* he yelled.

"Sir, I don't have a problem with the General, sir. His name is on my list. It's you, you and the, the driver I, I can't let in, sir," stuttered the young soldier.

"Corporal, generals don't drive themselves. You know that. *You will open that gate!"* yelled Phillips, shaking his finger in the lad's face, "or…,"

"Sir, yes, *sir!* But only for the General, sir," said the frightened guard holding his ground. He placed a shaky hand on the pistol strapped to his side. He wasn't sure if this was a security test or a simple screw up in paperwork.

The major did an about face, returned to the sedan, and spoke briefly to General Carlson. The young corporal felt sweat drip down his body as the General got out and walked slowly toward him. He popped a snappy salute and held his breath for an ass chewing.

"So, Corporal, I understand there is a problem with the access list?" Carlson said. He spoke with a deep North Carolina accent.

"Sir, yes sir. My orders are specific, sir. No one is to be allowed into the isolation area unless they are on the access list, sir." He swallowed hard. "Sir, your name is on the list sir, but not the major's and not the driver's."

"I see," Carlson grinned. "You're doing one hell of a job, Corporal. Keep up the good work." Carlson slapped the soldier on shoulder and turned to face the major. "Major Phillips," he snapped.

"Yes, General."

"See that this man is advanced one pay grade. I'll drive myself out to the hangar."

"Yes, sir," Phillips replied, with angry eyes. He cut a vicious glare at the young soldier.

The corporal saluted as Carlson drove through the checkpoint. He was afraid to look at the Major.

The aircraft mechanics working on the helicopters parked on the tarmac were the first to spot the General, but it was too late to sound the alarm. He drove the sedan into the mouth of the open hangar and got out amidst the beehive of activity.

"*Aten-hut!*" Blaze bellowed, loud enough to bring the activity inside the building to a halt.

Carlson waved his hand with a gesture of no. "*Carry on! Carry on!*" he said. Seeing Blaze, he walked over to the SEALs as Sanz saluted for all his men. Carlson returned the salute.

"Hello, Tom. Good to see you again, you salty old dog," Carlson said, with a bright smile. He ignored everyone except the Master Chief and shook his hand vigorously.

"How's your hammer hanging, General?" Blaze asked.

"Better than the last time we met. That was a hell of a fracas down in Bolivia, wasn't it?"

"Made my dick hard, General," Blaze grinned, with a backhanded Aussie salute. "Let's go do it again."

Carlson smiled, then his face turned serious. "How's this one going, Master?" he asked, referring to *Freedom Express*.

"Best damn exercise I've ever been on, sir. Gear's all here. The men are trained and ready to go. Colonel Ardison has it all in one sock, sir. I think you ought to make him a general."

Carlson chuckled. "Maybe I'll do that, if *Freedom Express* lives up to promise. And maybe I'll make an officer out of you yet."

"Oh no, General. Don't do that," Blaze gasped. "I'm having too much fun. Besides, making me a J.O. would be a step backwards at my age."

Carlson ignored the response.

"What do you think about working off a sub?" he asked.

"A submarine? In, in this exercise?" Blaze stammered, taken aback.

"Ah huh. I see. You haven't been brief yet. Forget my last. You'll hear about it soon enough. I wouldn't have taken this on, Tom, if you hadn't been the senior NCO." NCO was army talk for non-commissioned officer. Blaze stared at the General. "I have utmost confidence that you will make us proud."

Blaze gulped hard. "General, let me introduce the finest officer I've ever had the pleasure of working for," he said, gesturing at Lee Sanz.

Carlson extended his hand and eyed Sanz like a fine

racehorse.

"That's one hell of an endorsement coming from the finest Master Chief in the United States Navy," he said, pumping Sanz's hand firmly. "Please to meet you, Lieutenant. Your team did a hell of a fine job up in Monterey. Matter of fact, outstanding would be a more apt description."

"Thank you, General."

"I've got an even bigger challenge for you this time," Carlson hinted.

"We can handle it," Sanz replied.

"We've got a lot of people watching and a lot at stake," Carlson cautioned.

He glanced at the back of the hangar. Colonel Ardison was rushing around like a busy fire ant. As he scrambled around he pointed at lieutenant colonels and commanders, making a rotating sign with his finger, directing them to muster the men in formation in front of the podium.

"Excuse me, gents. Duty calls. Have a great day," Carlson said.

Sanz saluted as the General walked off. When he dropped the salute he stared at Blaze, mouth open.

"Submarine?" he gulped. "In a CT exercise?"

The Master Chief hunched up his shoulders and shook his head in dismay. "I wouldn't bet against it."

The operational phase of Exercise *Freedom Express* was underway. Across the Pacific, so was the Russian ship the *Bogdan Stashinsky*.

# Chapter 10

The Mekong River is called *The River of the Third Eye*, an allusion to the Third Eye of Wisdom in the forehead of the Buddha. It is also called *The River of Many Tears*. It is born high in the high Himalayas just north of Lhasa, Tibet not far from the birthplace of the Brahmaputra, the Irrawaddy, the Salween, the Yangtze, and the Yellow. The others turn north or south or east and unite people in their great fertile valleys, but not the Mekong. It divides people. It runs along the borders of China and Burma, Laos and Thailand, Cambodia and Vietnam, and by the time it flows into the South China Sea it has accumulated many tears. Tears bequeath wisdom, and the Mekong, river of many tears, leaves a lasting impression on all those who cross her.

Gurnov looked out through the open cargo door of the Ilyushin transport and studied the earth below. At sunset, the Mekong River looked like a ribbon of filigree flowing down through the blackening hills of Laos. It lay peaceful and gentle on the land. He took a deep breath and relaxed in the cool air of altitude. But his respite was short-lived. The pilot banked hard to the right over the *Plane of Jars* and dropped nearly fifteen thousand feet in a steep dive. He swooped in low over the jungle at tree top level and headed up a deep gorge on the Vang Vieng side of the Phu Bia Mountains. Near his target he put the aircraft in a hard climb to clear the mountain peak and passed directly over a large Hmong village at two thousand feet.

Gurnov pushed the experimental sack of chemicals out of the cargo door and watched it fall five hundred feet before exploding into a blue-colored cloud of gas that filled the gorge. It quickly engulfed the village, catching more than fifty people in the open returning from the surrounding poppy fields. They fell to the ground, knocked unconscious by the experimental incapacitant. The gas wasn't designed to kill, just to knock its victims out for twelve to fifteen hours.

The pilot cleared the mountains and made a second pass up another gorge. At just the right moment Gurnov pushed out a second bag of chemicals, disguised as a fifty kilo sack of rice. He watched it fall toward the earth and explode five hundred feet above the ground, sending out a yellow-brown cloud that covered the village. With mission complete, the special team returned to base without a thought to the consequences of their actions. It was easy to kill from long distance, to drop a bomb from high altitude, or push a button on a console far out at sea. But it is quite a different matter to look death square in the eye, up close and personal. Gurnov couldn't see the consequences of his actions, just *The River of the Third Eye* reflecting the last light of day.

Near a small town deep in Laos, the Ilyushin landed on a dirt airstrip in a swirling cloud of dust. The town was little more than an intersection of unpaved roads filled with a throng of bucolic peasants. Dreaming of a woman and a cold beer, he grabbed a pedicab and headed for the hotel that served as headquarters. Moving through the twilight of this strange Oriental landscape that bellowed its existence to the surrounding emptiness, he was suspended in time without a thought, without remorse for what he had just done to his fellow man. As the three-wheeler bounced down the dusty road thronged with people, he eyed the Chinese-style storefronts that lined both sides of the road. They were so different from those in the Motherland, with their gaping, open shops at ground level and crowded living quarters up above. He wondered what his life would have been like if he had been born in such a place instead of the cold gritty streets of Moscow.

Laotian music blared from a loudspeaker as he burst through the door of a small hotel like a gunfighter in a wild western town. He sauntered past little low-bowing Oriental girls who catered to his every whim. A strong smell of shrimp paste, fish sauce, lemon grass, and burnt garlic overwhelmed his senses, as he pushed aside the pink plastic curtains that covered the entrance to the noisy bistro in the back. They were the odors of the Orient, the ones that repelled mosquitoes in the muggy heat of the tropics. With carnal thoughts in his mind, he took a seat at the bar and ordered a Singha beer. He liked Thai beer the best. It had more kick. And then there was Mekong Whiskey, and Mekong dreams of more than one woman in bed with him at the same time.

Gurnov drank with the pilots, laughing and joking with tiny bar girls dressed in sexy batik sarongs, until he was blitzed. He suppressed the image that was haunting him by making love to his favorite Laotian whore. Sleep finally came when exhaustion closed down his mind. But it didn't last.

He returned to the Phu Bia Mountains with a Russian scientist to check the results of the ghoulish experiments. As the helo flew low over rice paddies and jungle, and into the mountains, he tried to stop the torment. It was there that *The Third Eye of Wisdom* began to haunt him.

At ground zero all animal life was dead; people, dogs,

chickens, pigs, water buffalos, even insects. The villagers' skin had turned black and blood was oozing from their eyes, noses and mouths.

*I have become a killer,* he thought, gaping at the horrible nature of the destruction he had wrought. *Nyet. I am not a mass murderer of innocent people. I am a soldier! I am just doing my duty!*

At the outer edge of the kill zone those that weren't dead were groping for air, like fish out of water, mouths silently moving, eyes vacant as if staring at the beyond. Appalled by the gruesome scene, he turned for the waiting helicopter.

*Damn the Politburo. What have we done?*

Only the highest levels of the Soviet government could authorize the experimental use of chemical and biological agents, and only the head of the Party could approve such a mission.

Empathy compelled him to stop and examine a child no more than seven years old. She was a miniature version of the whore he had spent the night with. Her face was gaunt and ravaged with sickness, her eyes were sickly yellow and huge with despair, and her jerking movements were pointless, as if searching for something that was beyond her understanding. Slobbering and gagging in a pitiful death moan, she clutched his leg with one bony arm. With blood oozing from her nose, she looked up at him, begging with huge brown Oriental eyes.

*She is going to die*, he thought.

The weight of what he and his nation were doing in the remote Laotian Mountains was almost more than he could bear. As he stared into her vacant eyes, he slowly unholstered his Tokarev pistol.

*She's going to die,* he thought, *in slow misery. She only got a small dose of the mycotoxin.*

She stared up at him as he aimed the pistol, unable to comprehend what was about to happen. Gurnov squeezed the trigger as an act of mercy, as an act of humanity, but the weapon refused to fire. He pulled the trigger again, and still the pistol wouldn't fire. Over and over he pulled the trigger and all the while the little girl kept staring up at him with empty dilated eyes. Then, a third eye, *The Third Eye of Wisdom*, appeared in the center of her forehead, and as if by magic the bullet in the chamber of the Tokarev exploded. The sound caused air to rush into his lungs in a gasp of astonishment. He sat bolt upright in his rack to find himself in the darkness on the *Stashinsky*, shaking all over, gasping for breath, and trembling with the fear of ghosts that come in the night.

*I didn't pull the trigger. The goddamned gun just went off! It just exploded!*

Gurnov got out of bed but sank back down on the side of his rack full of anguish, haunted by his past.

"I had to do it," he mumbled.

For a long time he sat in the darkness listening to the sounds of the ship creaking and the sea lashing the hull. The *Stashinsky* rolled from side to side and pitched up and down in an angry sea as she sailed relentlessly eastward toward death row for another lethal load of manmade poisons.

With trembling hands he switched on his reading light. His heart pumped at the sight of the Tokarev. It was lying beside him on the bed like a coiled rattler, the same pistol that had ended the child's life. He had kept it all these years. It wasn't a pretty weapon, not like the classic and functional lines of a P-38 or Browning High Power. It had excessive Cyrillic engravings on the grip and the flanks, the mark of an officer in the Soviet Red Army. The Reds had copied the design directly from Colt, but they had left off the safety. Who needs a safety anyway, so the saying went, if all guns are always loaded. Gurnov remembered the almost rifle-sized cartridge of the Tokarev. In his mind's eye he saw the child's head explode over and over again from the impact of the heavy bullet, like a video image skipping and replaying over and over in his mind. He could see the bullet smash into *The Third Eye of Wisdom* and brain matter spatter against his pant leg. He couldn't get it out of his mind. Then he realized he wasn't breathing and gulped in air like a drowning man. With trembling hands he grabbed the vodka concealed beside his bed and took a large swallow straight from the bottle. But the vodka didn't help. Nothing helped. It only blurred the image playing inside his head. It couldn't erase the past. Nothing could.

*You had to do it, Gurnov. She was in misery. When are you going to stop torturing yourself, you son of a drunken whore? It happened more than twenty years ago at the beginning of your illustrious career. War is war, Gurnov. Orders are orders. You did as you were told to do. You just followed orders, you Cossack bastard.*

The thoughts ran through his head like a mantra, blotting out the image of *The Third Eye.*

*Knock, knock, knock.* Gurnov jumped. His torment ended with rapping on his door.

"*Kto tam?* - who is it?" he demanded.

"Captain Dmitriyev, sir," came a reply from the passageway.

"Wait," Gurnov commanded.

He hid the bottle of vodka under his rack and put on his clothes. Before shouting at the closed door, he lit a cigarette. "*Pozhaluista!* - come," he ordered.

Captain Dmitriyev, his second in command, opened the stateroom door and stepped smartly into the room. He saluted before speaking.

"*Prostite* - excuse me, major. I am sorry to disturb

you, but I saw your light was on."

Gurnov nodded as he eyed Dmitriyev with suspicion. "Report," he ordered, gruffly.

"Sir, the rabbits in holds number four and five are dead," he reported, in a businesslike manner.

Dmitriyev was typically Slavic in appearance. He was a handsome, slim young man with faintly Turkish features, a small, neatly trimmed mustache, dark-brown wavy hair pushed back under his hat and a perpetual swarthy expression on his face. His blue eyes and pleasant mouth looked manly but arrogant. With his report of bad news his brow furrowed with concern.

"When was this discovered?" Gurnov exploded.

The intensity of Gurnov's reaction caused the color to drain out of the young captain's face. He swallowed hard before answering subserviently.

"About five hours ago, sir."

Gurnov scowled as he acted out the part he had planned so meticulously.

"Why wasn't I informed immediately?" he demanded.

He didn't like Dmitriyev and he didn't trust him. He didn't trust anyone in the chemical corps. By this point in his career he should have been a senior colonel or a general but he had been passed over for men like Dmitriyev who had a formal schoolhouse education.

"I didn't wake you, sir, because the ocean is shallow and there are many ships nearby. We are in the Straits of Malacca."

"I know very well where we are, *Captain!*" Gurnov snapped. "What is the nature of the problem?"

Dmitriyev stared at Gurnov with his mouth open. Hold number four was off limits to all hands without special authorization from Gurnov himself. He answered the question cautiously, ignoring the problem in hold number four.

"Hold number five is full of VR-55 containers from Azkaban. If the major recalls, they were lost by inventory and left in the Karakum desert for more than twenty years. They were in very poor condition when we retrieved them, sir."

"Yes," Gurnov growled. "I recall that they were staged by schoolboys, *who never served a day in Afghanistan,* and forgotten by those morons in the supply corps."

The way he said the word *schoolboys* was clearly intended to be contemptuous of the military, in general, and men who had formal education, in particular. Dmitriyev ignored the insult.

"I suspect a drum of mixed soman is leaking, sir," he continued. "Perhaps one of the plastic bags has a small hole in it"

*How right you are, young Captain Dmitriyev,* Gurnov thought. *And you would shit your pants if you knew I put the hole in the bag.*

The Soviet Union had produced large quantities of the nerve agent soman. VR-55 was a thickened form of the oily substance designed to persist on the battlefield for weeks. In his mind's eye Gurnov saw a procession of Mujahideen insurgents patrolling down a narrow footpath in their dingy gray turbans. Shouldering their ancient Enfield rifles like farm tools, they crept through a lethal patch of broken stones spread with jellied soman. It stuck to their feet and soaked through their baggy pantaloons. When the chemical contacted the skin, they began to writhe and squirm like earthworms wriggling in a bath of insecticide. He saw the face of a white bearded Afghan, his nose gnarled like an old tree stump. As the old Muslim vomited and fouled his clothes, he mumbled a final prayer to Allah.

*Allah Ackbar!*

"Yeb vas veruyushchii," -- fuck you God believer, Gurnov mumbled.

Dmitriyev thought that Gurnov was cursing him. His reply shook Gurnov out of his flashback.

"Major?"

"*Yes!*" snapped the tortured warrior. "What do you want?"

"Sir, I was saying that I believe hold number five is contaminated with soman vapors."

"What else could it be, Captain?" Gurnov demanded.

Dmitriyev's face went blank. He was thinking, *I wonder if he knows about the incapacitant mixed in with the soman containers? Probably not. There is only one small pallet.*

VR-55 was thicker than bunker oil, and unlike non persistent chemical agents such as sarin and mustard, it didn't instantly release fumes. It killed by contact and slowly poisoned its surroundings. The incapacitant the Afghans called Blue-X was not designed to kill. Blue-X was what the Americans called a *riot control agent* and it shouldn't have been on board the *Stashinsky*. It was a highly non persistent agent that gave off volatile fumes. Dmitriyev began to wonder if the chemicals in hold number five were compatible with one another. His greatest fear was a rupture of hold number four caused by an explosion resulting from leaking incompatible chemicals in an adjacent hold.

"I tested the AGV and the TMS to ensure that they are ready for use. As soon as we are in deep water sir, I will dump the soman and decontaminate hold number five," Dmitriyev said, ignoring the problem in hold number four. He watched Gurnov's face for reaction.

The shipment from the Karakum desert was in such bad shape that they had made plans to dump it in the Indian Ocean. But the environmentalist had trailed them too closely and the seas had been too rough. Captain Dmitriyev was anticipating a dump in the Pacific Ocean in deep water. The AGV-3 was a personnel decontamination unit adapted to the *Stashinsky*. It consisted of three chambers in which soldiers could scrub down their chemical suits with detergents designed to break down chemical poisons and kill biological agents. The TMS-65 was a larger unit designed to decontaminate vehicles. It had been specially configured with hoses and a vacuum unit to decontaminate and de-water compartments within the ship.

"Very well. We will decontaminate tonight," Gurnov ordered.

A look of utter shock crossed Dmitriyev's face. "But Major? It is almost daylight. We cannot drop the soman overboard in these waters," Dmitriyev protested.

"As you were, Captain Dmitriyev. We will decontaminate this ship tonight, *tonight* as in twelve hours from now," Gurnov growled, without blinking his eyes.

"As you wish Major," Dmitriyev replied, studying Gurnov's face for clues.

Dmitriyev was a graduate of the Kalinin Military Chemical School and the Moscow Academy for Chemical Defense, but unlike his boss he had no practical battlefield experience with the poisons of war. But he had a secret mission. He was supposed to observe Gurnov closely and report any aberrant behavior to the captain of the ship. What he was witnessing was clearly aberrant behavior.

"I will be down in half an hour. Have a suit prepared so I can inspect the holds personally," Gurnov continued.

"Major?" questioned the young captain.

"Both you and Lieutenant Romanovsky need to have your hearing checked. I said, *have a suit prepared so I can inspect holds number four and five.*"

"Yes, sir."

Dmitriyev was thoroughly baffled by the order. Hold operations were generally relegated to junior enlisted men.

*Perhaps he's worried about an explosion that would rupture the holds*, Dmitriyev thought, trying to make sense of Gurnov's order. The super poisons, he only knew by rumor, were secured in hold number four in the middle of the ship.

In the *Stashinsky's* belly there were tons of agents contained in barrels, steel canisters, down loaded bombs, old rocket warheads, deactivated land mines, defused artillery shells, and decrepit cluster bomblets. They were segregated by type of munitions and by type of poison; persistent, semi-persistent, and non persistent. Some weapons were filled with asphyxiating chemicals such as phosgene, diphosgene, and chloropicrin. Some contained blood poisons such as, tabun, soman, sarin, cyanogen chloride, and hydrocyanic acid. Others held lethal vesicants like mustard and trichlorotriethylamine. Then, there were the top-secret super poisons in hold number four, the ones that never finished a voyage. A leaking barrel of thickened soman was only a minor complication that could easily be handle under the right circumstances; maneuver room for the ship and darkness to conceal their actions. The problem was the ship's location and course. The *Stashinsky* was sailing through a narrow shipping channel between Sumatra and Malaysia.

"Sir, the prevailing wind is to the east. We will have to change course toward land to decon," Dmitriyev informed.

"Captain Dmitriyev, you will see to the men and the equipment. I will tell the captain of this vessel what we must do to complete our mission successfully. Is that clear?"

"Yes, sir."

*He is worried about those environmentalists,* Dmitriyev thought.

The Greenpeace organization had eight ships and they had taken it upon themselves to watch the *Stashinsky* when she was underway. Shortly after passing through the Bosporus, the *MV Sirius*, had fallen in behind them and had followed them down through the Suez Canal and most of the way across the Indian Ocean. As they neared the Straits of Malacca, she turned about to follow a Japanese vessel known to transport plutonium.

During their last voyage through the Straits of Malacca, the *MV Greenpeace*, a former Royal Dutch Navy ship with an on board helicopter, had picked them up near Singapore and had followed them all the way to Johnston Atoll, forcing them to alter their dumping plans. The deep sea, belonging to no one and to everyone, was being monitored by a worldwide environmental organization and they were making the home of the leviathan, the burial ground for atomic reactors and toxic wastes, more difficult to use in private.

The *Stashinsky* had been specially fitted with seven hermetically sealed holds, each with entry compartments that acted like diver's air locks. The small rooms allowed soldiers in protective suits to enter the large holds without contaminating the entire vessel. Each hold was fitted with separate pressure, temperature and gas monitoring gages, and an exhaust system that vented to the top of the stack where hot fumes from the ship's boilers carried the poisonous fumes aloft. The living sensors, the rabbits, could be seen from outside the holds by means of viewing ports. Dead rabbits were sure sign of contamination but, since the holds were sealed and monitored by gages, it wasn't a problem that couldn't wait until they were in deeper water.

To decontaminate, the ship had to maintain a course that resulted in relative wind, which blew away from the vessel. The men had to vent the hold, bag or remove the leaking weapon, spray down the area with detergents, vacuumed up the residue, and jettison it overboard, a process that took several hours. Previously, they had only conducted such operations in remote areas of the ocean in deep water.

As part of his education, Dmitriyev had toured the facilities of the former Soviet chemical industry. He had visited the Bandyuzhsky chlorine works on the Kama River, the Chapayevsk plant near Kuibyshev, factories in Azkaban, Khibinogorsk, Beresniki, Karaganda and many other strategic facilities. But he had never been briefed on the black programs that produced the super poisons. Officially they didn't exist. Only Gurnov knew what was really in hold number four. The Captain of the *Stashinsky* would do anything he recommended to protect and ultimately rid his ship of its contents.

Like Gurnov, Dmitriyev was part of the *Stashinsky's* top-secret dumping mission, but he didn't know the specifications of the weapons they were disposing of at sea. Just rumors. He concluded that Gurnov's behavior was in keeping with the situation and his strange personality, and he began to worry that he should have awakened him when he had first learned of the dead rabbits.

"I am sorry, sir. I should have awakened the major earlier," he said, turning to leave. He paused outside the door and saluted before scurrying down the passageway like an obsequious servant.

When the door closed, Gurnov looked at himself in the mirror and smiled. "Perfect."

Gurnov shaved and put on a fresh uniform before walking up to the bridge. Outside the confines of the ship the pungent sea breeze smelled good. So he stopped at the railing to watch the dawn sun slowly claw its way over the horizon. It touched the tops of the waves with pale gold and shadowed the troughs in a silvery gray. On the narrow afterdeck, he paused again under a flapping Russian flag badly soiled by salt spray and worn by the wind. He gave it a lazy salute.

*Yesterday is but a memory. Tomorrow is but a dream. Now, is only the pain of the moment. Damn you Gorbachev and your peristroka! And damn the Politburo for what they have done to you! Glasnosts! What a joke.*

For a few moments he stood motionless on the steel deck chewing over the past, watching the white caps.

*I'm a soldier and I don't want to die at sea,* he thought.

Mentally, he recited a soldier's poem.

> *Soldier, soldier,*
> *Everyone must die.*
> *So die for your county,*
> *Die with your boots on and your head held high.*
> *Neither water nor fire,*
> *Comfort you in your last hour.*
> *In the earth is your end,*
> *Russian soil is your friend.*

"What country?" he grumbled. "They've destroyed it, the stupid bastards."

Boiling with a flash of anger, Gurnov trotted up three steep ladders to the bridge and opened the hatch with a screech. The men on duty looked sleepy but they scrambled to alertness at his abrupt appearance. Dressed in his major's uniform Gurnov looked impressive, compared to the sloppy sailors who manned the vessel. The officer of the deck, Lieutenant Zhukov, was leaning against a gyroscope repeater wedged between the bulkhead and the device when Gurnov barged onto the bridge. He straightened up and saluted.

"Good morning, Major Gurnov."

Gurnov returned the salute as he walked briskly to the chart table. "Where are we located?" he demanded.

"Here, Comrade Major," the quartermaster said, pointing to a location west of Penang, Malaysia. Gurnov picked up the dividers and ticked off the distance to shore in both directions. Malaysia was one hundred and twenty miles due east, Sumatra a hundred miles to the southwest.

"What is our speed?" Gurnov asked.

"Eighteen knots, sir," reported the OOD.

"True wind?"

"Almost due east, sir," the quartermaster reported.

"Has there been any sign of those pesky green ships?" he asked, referring to the Greenpeace organization. All the environmental ships were painted green. They flew distinctive rainbow colors and had a white dove of peace with an olive branch painted on their bows.

"No, sir. Not since the *Sirius* turned about yesterday evening," Zhukov answered.

Gurnov eyed the OOD meanly. "Is the Captain awake?" he asked.

"Yes, sir. He is taking breakfast in his cabin," Zhukov reported.

*"Spasibo,"* Gurnov said, thanking the men.

He walked through a hatch in the center of the bridge, down one deck to the Captain's quarters, and knocked twice.

"Enter," came a gruff voice from inside the cabin.

Gurnov opened the door and stepped inside. From

his galley table Captain Shvachko eyed him with a serious look of concern. He was eating *tkhum-dulma*, breaded boiled eggs.

"A visit from you at this hour always means trouble, Major Gurnov," Shvachko said as he forked one of the eggs.

He was years younger than Gurnov and two grades higher, but he didn't pull rank when they were alone. He feared the contents of hold number four. He had heard rumors.

"Tea?" he asked pleasantly, gesturing with his hand for Gurnov to have a seat at his small table. On it was a plate of doughy buns and some jars of jam.

"Yes, please," Gurnov said, taking a seat.

The Captain's quarters enjoyed a Czar's touch with a kingly desk, handsome red furnishings, and a steward dressed in a snowy white coat. The steward drew the major a cup of tea from a silver samovar and added heated milk and sugar while Gurnov helped himself to a pastry. When the orderly had finished his duties, Shvachko signaled for him to leave the stateroom by lifting his chin and nodding his head. They waited until the door closed before discussing the problem in the belly of the ship.



Later, as Gurnov walked forward along a main deck astir with working sailors in shabby dungaree uniforms, he felt the ship come about. He paused at the rail, holding his brown-green combination hat with its bright red trim in his hand to keep it from flying overboard. With the sun low on the horizon to starboard, the *Stashinsky* steadied on a new course northeast toward Langkawi Island.

*Baranov, you sneaky spetznaz bastard, you'd better be there,* he thought.

Gurnov took in the sea breeze for a few moments before heading down to the holds of the ship. He failed to notice the tiny helicopter hidden by the glare of the sun. But the pilot saw the *Stashinsky*. He was low on fuel so he marked her change of course and headed toward Penang.

# Chapter 11

Malaysia forms the southern most tip of Asia. Separating the South China Sea from the Indian Ocean, it is a long, slender peninsular country that juts south by southeast from the mainland almost to the equator. The Malaysians believe that their country has the shape of a dragon's head sticking up out of the sea, its bony crown facing China, its soft vulnerable throat exposed to Indonesia across the narrow Straits of Malacca. Much of the world's seaborne traffic passes through the straits, which bottlenecks between Kuala Lumpur and Singapore to less than one hundred miles. It has always been a land of water people. To this day pirates prey upon unwary merchantmen, swooping in on the unprepared in their wooden sailing vessels called *boogies*. The word *bogeyman* originates from Malaysian pirates and their beautiful sailing vessels.

Julie Jennings stared out at the sleek prow of a bogey standing proud in Penang harbor near the *MV Greenpeace*. The bogey looked so graceful and exotic compared to the bull nosed hulk of the Dutch-built deep-sea salvage tug. It reminded her of a New England schooner, free and at one with the wind and sea. While she was admiring the bogey a small helicopter appeared and circled the *Greenpeace*. She watched it land on the stern of the steel ship and shut down its rotors. From shore she could just make out tiny figures rushing about on the afterdeck.

*I wonder if they've spotted the Stashinsky*, she

thought, as she took in the beauty of the morning.

The trip from Hawaii to Penang had been exhausting and her mind was dull from jet lag. Day was night and night was day and her body and soul was still back in Hawaii with Lee Sanz.

"Hey, Jay-Jay, listen to this," Gordon Forbes said.

Julie yawned and looked around at him with tired eyes. He was seated on a wooden camera box, reading from a stack of papers he had downloaded from the Internet. He had packed the information in one of his equipment boxes and hadn't been able to get to it until they reached Penang. Forbes was a Southern California environmentalist true to soul with a whale tail charm strung around his neck on a leather cord and a tiny earring in his left earlobe. He was bald down the center of his head and he wore his hair too long on the sides and in the back.

"Chemical weapons have been stored on Johnston Island since nineteen seventy-one. They include rockets, projectiles, mines, mortars, and one-ton containers filled with nerve and mustard agents. Before destruction operations began in nineteen ninety, JACADS stored about seven percent of the total U.S. stockpile."

JACADS was an acronym for Johnston Atoll Chemical Agent Disposal System.

"I don't believe that," Fred Saxon commented. "It's too remote and too small to have that much shit on it."

Saxon was short, pudgy, and out of shape. He looked like the straight man in a bad situation comedy and he relished the role of devil's advocate. This was his kind of job, uncovering some deep dark nefarious government secret.

"More than two million pounds of nerve and mustard agent have already been destroyed, and get this, according to this source JACADS has already disposed of all of its M-fifty-five rockets and one class of mustard filled projectiles. They are supposed to shut down the facility and dismantle it when all of the munitions have been destroyed."

"Bullshit. If that's so, why are ships still offloading containers there?" Saxon interjected.

"I don't know, Fred. For Christ's sake, I'm just reading what's on this poop sheet, man," Forbes complained.

"Classic government subterfuge," Saxon replied. "Say one thing and do another. I'll bet there are Russians stationed on that island."

"Listen to this. Public Law *one hundred-four hundred fifty-six*, requires the demonstration of safety and effectiveness of said facility. Tests were conducted in four phases called operational verification testing, OVT."

"OVT my ass," Saxon blurted out. "That's just government B.S., Gordon. What's so hard about burning chemicals at high temperature?"

"Doing it without getting killed, shit for brains." Forbes snapped. He continued reading from his stack of papers. "From nineteen ninety to nineteen ninety-three the Army successfully demonstrated to regulators that JACADS could safely dispose of any type of munitions or agent."

He looked up to see if Julie was listening before reading another page.

"Several organizations and agencies have oversight responsibility. The Senate Armed Services Committee, the Senate Readiness Subcommittee, the House National Security Committee, the House Military Readiness Subcommittee, the House Appropriations...,"

"Enough Gordon, enough. We get the picture," Saxon interrupted. "Everybody's in charge and nobody's in charge, and they're burning Russian weapons without taxpayer approval."

"Why won't any of those agencies talk to us?" Julie asked.

"Because we're on to something big, that's why," Forbes replied. "They're up to something on that island, something secret that they don't want the public to know about."

"They are probably into gene splicing and all kinds of nefarious shit," Saxon alleged excitedly.

"Fred."

"Yeah, Gordy."

"Dude! You can't use words like *nefarious* and *shit* in the same sentence. It just doesn't work," Forbes criticized. "Julie's pet SEAL will think you're a nerd."

"Screw you, Gordon."

"Not on your life, pudgy. You'll have to settle for another man."

"*Screw you*, Gordon."

"You, my corpulent friend, are running out of shit complected nefarious vocabulary," Forbes chuckled.

Saxon gave Forbes a dirty look and shook his head in exasperation.

"It's what happens between here and there that worries me, guys," Julie said, more to interrupt the meaningless chit chat than to engage the conversation. "The immensity of the ocean is a cloak for the unscrupulous. Unfortunately, the birthplace of life on earth, the home of the leviathan, is now the burial ground for atomic reactors and toxic waste."

"Saxon, write that down. Write that down, man! We've got to get her saying that on camera with that Russian ship in the background, hopefully dumping something overboard."

"Yeah. Like what, man," Saxon asked, "a vile of botulism?"

"Anything, man. Garbage. It doesn't matter."

"Yeah, yeah. Keep going, Julie. Gordy's right. You're on a role," Saxon encouraged.

"Cut the crap, guys. I'm too tired to think." She pointed at the *MV Greenpeace* and shook her finger. "All I want to do is climb into to a bunk on board that ship and sleep for two days."

"Awh, no sleep, Julie? I keep telling you to lose that oversexed, fascist boyfriend of yours," Forbes kidded.

"Gordon, you mean fabulous boyfriend. He asked me to marry him, you know," Julie smiled.

"*What?* What did you say?" Saxon stammered.

Julie grinned. "I said yes, of course."

"Bad move. Real bad move. He's going to give you a social disease."

"Gordon!" Julie snapped.

"Yeap. You're gonna get establishmentitis; kids, dog, and a little house in suburbia. You won't be worth a shit to mankind when you're barefoot and pregnant."

"*Look!* I told you they got our message," Saxon said, pointing at the ship. "They are launching a boat."

The crane on the *Greenpeace* lowered a rubber Zodiac boat into the sea. A tiny figure climbed down the side of the ship and shortly the Zodiac was zipping across the harbor toward them at top speed. While they waited Forbes continued reading his Internet reports.

"Hey get this. In nineteen twenty-six, Johnston Atoll was placed under the auspices of the Department of Agriculture as a breeding ground and refuge for native birds. Today, it's managed by the U.S. Fish and Wildlife Service as a national wildlife refuge."

"Bingo," Saxon barked. "There's the connection. Someone on the island in Fish and Game is a tree-hugger."

"Yeah. That's how Greenpeace found out that the

Russians are making regular deposits there," Forbes agreed.

"Guano deposits," Saxon added.

"Fred, man, that's not funny," Forbes snarled and then continued reading out loud from his Internet reports.

"JACADS uses a highly trained work force and automated mechanical demilitarization equipment." He looked at Saxon. *"That what it said,"* he declared, "and a state of the art incineration system to dispose of chemical munitions while protecting workers, the peoples of the Pacific, and the environment."

"Oh yeah," Saxon sassed. "Peoples of the Pacific? Tell that to those dead fishermen."

"I believe it," Julie interjected.

"Believe what?" Forbes asked.

"That JACADS is safe and state of the art."

"Then why are we beating this dead dog?" Saxon asked.

"JACADS is not the issue, Fred. The U.S. Government has put a lot of money into JACADS, and similar systems, and you can bet that they all work with the efficiency of a nuclear power plant. This is a story about the poisons of war and what happens to them when they reach their shelf life. This is the story about the defilement of the oceans, about toxins slowly spreading around the globe in huge subsurface currents. It is a fact that the U.S. Army dumped chemical weapons at sea until a storm of protest made them stop. We know proof-positive that the U.S. Navy dumped spent reactor cores at sea until they were forced to stop by court order. But the Russians are under no such constraints or public scrutiny. The sailors doing the dumping probably don't know what they're throwing overboard. Even if they did, they don't care nor understand the consequences of their actions. Most people think the ocean is too immense to be polluted by a few reactors or a thousand shiploads of toxic chemicals. Even many educated people don't realize that there are enormous subsurface currents circulating from ocean to ocean, pole to pole. How do we explain all that in a documentary that is less than an hour in length? How do we show people, not just Americans, but people all over the world, that the planet is being defiled by secret war poisons?"

"Fred, did you get that. Write that down man! We've got to catch them in the act, Julie. We've got to have a smoking gun to make this thing work. We've gotta get it on tape with you in the foreground talking about it, and we can't do that without my buds in Greenpeace," Forbes cautioned.

"And so, here we are, dependent upon environmentalists extraordinaire, who have a reputation for extremism," she said, watching the Zodiac close the distance. "Gordon?" she said, turning to look him in the eye.

"Yeah."

"I know you are a charter member of the organization and that you trust them implicitly. But I'm not, and I don't. I don't want these people seeing our script. I'm not spending my life savings to make this documentary to resurrect the credibility of extremists or to increase their public contributions."

"They are not so extreme, Julie," Forbes argued.

"Whatever, Gordon. They have an agenda that may or may not conform to ours. We're here to expose an international crime against humanity, not make Greenpeace look good in the eye of your camera."

"Sure thing, Boss. Sure thing. I understand your concerns." He thought about her statement for a few seconds and said, "I'm in this thing with you one hundred percent, Julie. I'll keep our cards close to the vest. You can count on it."

"Thanks, Gordy."

"Me too," Saxon added. Then he began to rattle off what was on his mind. "Julie, Gordon and I have been working over your rough draft and it fits perfectly with the footage we have so far. But there is nothing in it about ocean currents spreading pollution all around the world. We've got to get you down to Scripts to interview some oceanographers. I'll ah, I'll *carefully* query the scientists on the ship about ocean circulation and cut that angle into your dialogue."

"Good idea, Fred," Julie agreed. "Right on target."

Forbes added to the team spirit of the moment. "When I get back to Santa Barbara, I'll cut in selected shots of the autopsy photos, the newspaper reports, etcetera, and I'll contact Will Limon about doing the voice over between the talking heads."

"That's great," Julie said. "Now all we need is a smoking gun."

"We'll get it," Forbes mumbled, watching the Z-bird close the shore. "And not at the expense of a credibility train wreck."

He opened up one of his wooden boxes and took out his $50,000 Sony video camera. Panning the area, he focused tight on Julie looking out at the harbor with the ships in the background. He held the shot for a few moments and then closed the focus to show the *MV Greenpeace* and the speeding rubber boat headed toward them. He repeated the shot over and over until the Zodiac closed the shore. He dropped the camera down to a knee-level perspective as the boat ran up on shore on a two foot wave.

The coxswain drove the boat right up on the sand in front of them. He bounded out like a cowboy jumping off a bronco and abandoned his craft. He had long brown hair braided into a ponytail that slithered halfway down his back. Sporting several earrings, worn out jeans with holes, and a tie-dyed tee shirt, he had the appearance of the quintessential hippie right out of the sixties, until he spoke.

"Miss Jennings?" he asked, with a heavy Australian accent.

"Yes," Julie replied, extending her hand.

"I'm Lance Noble," he said, shaking her hand. "I'll take you out to the ship." He glanced around at the pile of gear on the beach. "All of this too?"

"Tools of the trade, sport," Forbes said, reading the man's face through his camera lens. He turned off the camera and extended his hand. "Gordon Forbes," he said. "I'm the camera bug."

Noble shook his hand and then Saxon's.

"Fred Saxon. Script writer, sound and light."

"Please to meet you blokes. We may have to make two trips," he said, looking at all the gear, "and we must hurry. The chopper spotted the *Stashinsky* just after dawn this morning."

"Great," Julie exclaimed, excitedly.

"Not so great, Ms. Jennings," Noble replied. "She changed course. Turned about in a busy shipping channel. We have to hurry to catch up. As we speak, the captain is making preparation to get underway."

"Let's go," Forbes bellowed as he began hurriedly packing up his expensive camera. He took out a small high-eight to film the ship at water level during their approach and hung it around his neck. Grabbing a camera box he said in a terrible English accent, "Let's go, mate. We'll make it in one trip."

Noble chuckled. "We'll have to work on that accent, *mate*. It's a bit too British for me, sport."

Out in the harbor, the helicopter lifted off the deck

and flew off in a westerly direction.

"He'll head west for a few miles and then north along the coast," informed Noble.

"What's north?" Julie asked, as she lugged her bag toward the rubber boat.

"Malaysia, Thailand, Burma. There's no way for the *Stashinsky* to get to the Pacific Ocean without sailing through the Straits or *all the way* back around Sumatra."

"Would they do that?" Julie asked.

"No. We don't think so. Our ship, the *Sirius,* followed them across the Indian Ocean. They took a direct course down through the Straits."

"Did they dump anything in the Indian Ocean?" Saxon asked.

"No. The *Sirius* stayed right on top of her until they entered the Straits. She was halfway through the passage when the helicopter saw her change course."

Julie mused. "Would they dare dump toxins so close to land?"

Noble loaded a wooden box in the boat. "Not likely. Too shallow and too much traffic. They probably spotted the helo and are trying to evade us. During her last voyage we picked her up here off Penang and followed her all the way to Johnston Atoll, and back to the Indian Ocean where the *Sirius* took over surveillance. As soon as you're aboard, we're going to head northwest. The helo will spot her, or one of our merchant friends," Noble said, confidently.

"Then let's shake a leg, *mate*," Forbes groused, grabbing one of his shipping cases.

"That's *mate,* as in pieces of *eight, mate*," Noble smiled.

"*Okay, mate. Shrimp on the barbie, dingo, and kangaroo*," Forbes kidded.

"That's *roo, mate*. We Aussies leave off the *kanga,*"

Noble corrected.

"Didgeridoo and buckaroo too, mate," Forbes joked, moving gear as fast as he could.

"Oh, gawd! I can see this is going to be a hell of a pleasure cruise," Saxon said, sarcastically.

With Julie in the bow of the overloaded boat, the three men pulled the Zodiac out into the bay and turned it about.

"*Anchor's away, mate,*" Forbes shouted for effect.

Noble started the engine and slowly motored seaward.

"Gordon," Saxon snapped. "You're getting on my nerves, man."

"Pudgy, you're just sore because I said that you'd have to settle for another man."

"Screw you Forbes!"

"Nebber-happin', buckaroo," he replied, as the boat picked up speed.

# Chapter
# 12

Military and civilian VIPs passed through the old hangar on Ford Island like cars in a subway station. Each entourage received a formal presentation, followed by a JSOC capabilities video showing Special Operations Forces in action. The video was composed of dramatic footage of high-speed boats, helicopters, and special aircraft infiltrating men dressed in black from head to toe. In a swirl of action, with silenced weapons blazing, the black-clad warriors blasted their way into buildings and buses and airplanes, scaled the sides of ships, and slid down ropes onto rooftops to rescue wide-eyed hostages from sinister looking terrorists.

After the video dignitaries were invited into the hangar to view equipment displays and to speak with enlisted men dressed in full battle gear. Such dog and pony shows were a great source of annoyance for the troops. Most of them didn't realize that such demonstrations were necessary for the survival of the SOF program. Political leaders had to be convinced by seeing and touching, and by taxpayer funded business trips to exotic locations like Hawaii.

Exercise *Freedom Express* was following a well-defined script that slowly built in intensity to the pointy end of the spear, a rescue mission. By far the most difficult part of the exercise was the planning and logistics phase which was hidden by the glitz of prop wash, the flash of stun grenades, and by armed men swiftly maneuvering inside the dark confines of a kill house.

For General Carlson, it was like building a dragster, months and months of effort for a six-second payoff roaring down an asphalt strip. But unlike a drag strip where spectators watch the show, assault operations were performed at night. Videotape was the best he could do to show the congressmen and important staffers what the United States of America was getting for its investment in the SOF program. The denouement of *Freedom Express*, the exciting part of the exercise, the very reason the organization existed, was still days away and it would take place under cover of darkness.

The glue that held the exercise together was the controller staff. Headed by an army lieutenant colonel, the controllers orchestrated the war game, coordinating the actions of the players, the rescuers and the terrorists, as well as the timing of events. The rescue force and the controller staff had set up headquarters in separate buildings on Ford Island. The opposition force had established its command center across the harbor at Hickam Air Force Base. General Carlson visited all three headquarters and received formal briefings at each location. When he was satisfied with safety and control, and the timing of VIP visits, he gave the order to commence operations.

Following the approved agenda, the controllers simply sent an electronic message to the OPFOR ordering them to seize their targets. Dressed in civilian clothes, soldiers from Special Forces Group ONE and sailors from SEAL Team THREE moved onto the *SS Independence*, into the Hickam Air Force Base air terminal, which they re-designated as Honolulu International, and aboard a small inter-island cargo vessel, the *MV Alliance*. The *Independence* sailed from Honolulu Harbor and tied up pier side at Pearl Harbor where ship's work continued. For exercise purposes it was constructively located at sea outside the twelve-mile limit. Using the smaller ship as a mobile command center, terrorist leaders steamed around the Hawaiian Islands, using the ship's radio to make demands according to the war game MSEL, the Master Scenario Events List.

Calling themselves the ATF, for Action Through Force, they demanded the release of twenty-four terrorists held in a Middle Eastern prison and one hundred million dollars in U.S. currency. They gave the President three days to meet their demands at which time they threatened to kill hostages, one every hour on the hour until all three hundred people were dead.

Their demands set in motion a number of messages from the White House and the Pentagon, establishing the chains of command and activating Contingency Plan zero seven thousand. Logistically, the men and equipment were already in place. As Commander in Chief of the Special Operations Command, General Carlson assumed his duties, *planning, and conducting selected special operations, if directed by the President or the Secretary of Defense.* With everything on track and under control, he turned his attention to a deluge of VIPs.

*"Ah-ten-hut!"*

Lieutenant Sanz and the other warriors in the briefing theater stood at attention as General Carlson, the senior member of the House Armed Services Committee, and several other congressmen and staffers entered the room.

"Please, take your seats, gentlemen," Carlson said gently.

Sanz couldn't help but admire the professional atmosphere Colonel Ardison had created. If not for the old aircraft hangar and the rough-cut map boards, the briefing could have been in the Pentagon. When everyone was seated in the cushioned chairs in front of the podium, he put the men at ease and opened up with a well-rehearsed greeting like a TV anchorman. He introduced the leaders of the three assault units, the personnel on his staff, and gave a brief overview of the exercise. When the introduction was complete, he turned the floor over to his intelligence officer. As the major took the stand a slide appeared on the center screen.

"Gentlemen, at oh-five hundred on the thirteenth of October, members of the ATF seized the *SS Independence*, the *MV Alliance,* and the control tower at Honolulu International airport," he said, like a reporter in a war zone.

As he spoke, pictures appeared of the two ships and the terminal tower. With photos, maps, satellite imagery, and aerial photography he smoothly painted a terrible picture like a weatherman describing a force five hurricane headed for land. He continued with a barrage of mock facts as if they were the real thing and concluded his briefing with the terrorist's demands.

Playing the part of master of ceremonies, Ardison introduced several other briefers who ran down everything from the chain of command to the disposition of assets in the Pacific Theater. When the visitors were thoroughly saturated with minutia, he showed them a videotape of SOF in action. When it was over he spoke directly at the senior congressman but used an inclusive term.

"Gentlemen, are there any questions?"

"Very impressive. Very, impressive indeed," said Congressman Dirk, the senior member of the committee.

Several of the VIPs mouthed agreement.

The portly congressman cleared his throat and in his most sonorous voice asked, "As I understand it Colonel Ardison, under CONPLAN oh-seven thousand, the CIA is required to activate local intelligence operatives to acquire critical information for mission planning. Does the CIA have a player cell within exercise *Freedom Express* and if so, are they providing you with realistic information?"

*Damn*, Sanz thought, *this guy has memorized the CONPLAN*. He wondered how the seasoned Colonel would respond.

Ardison was caught off guard by the nature and specificity of the question. He looked at Carlson. The General nodded and Ardison replied like a polished anchorman on the six o'clock news.

"Sir, with regard to your first question, the Central Intelligence Agency does have a cell playing in this exercise. We have established electronic liaison with that cell which is based in Langley, Virginia and to date they have provided us with information on ATF leadership, organization, and their past activities. In addition, they have provided us with detailed drawings of the vessels and the tower facilities. With regard to your second question sir, I cannot comment on the quality, quantity, and sensibility of the information since all intelligence in this exercise is fictitious."

Carlson spoke up. "Gentlemen, good intelligence, the availability of airlift, third country access, and communications connectivity are the major problems we face in such crises. By far the hardest nut to crack is figuring out who the terrorists are and what they really want. Hard *intel* is a function of the area of concern and the assets we have at our disposal in that area at the time of the crisis. Factors such as satellite coverage and the existence of agent networks within the area enter into the equation. The CIA player cell in *Freedom Express* is providing artificial information in accordance with the exercise MSEL."

Carlson spoke the acronym MSEL, as measle, but it

didn't throw off the congressman. He knew that General Carlson's staff had provided the CIA with the information they were sending to JSOC. It was part of the game. He was focused on bigger targets: Interoperability and connectivity. He nodded his head in understanding before pressing the issue.

"General, I have a fair understand of our intelligence deficiencies. Let me rephrase my question. Do you believe there is sufficient connectivity and cooperation among the various agencies of the intelligence community to provide you with the information you need, provided it is available somewhere within the intelligence system?"

"Yes sir. I do," Carlson nodded. "We have made great strides since Desert One."

Sanz was in awe. He had never been privy to such high level discussions that went on in the Pentagon on a daily basis. But he was conversant in the problems that faced the SOF community. In 1980, a hastily assembled U.S. task force had attempted to rescue American hostages held in Tehran, Iran. The operation had ended in complete disaster at an Iranian desert assembly site code named, Desert One. Internationally, the failure had given the U.S. a black eye. Since Desert One there had been other problems such as the inability to get forces to an aircraft hijacking in Malta, political problems with the apprehension of the hijackers of the Italian cruise ship, *Achille Lauro*, and men killed in action in Grenada and Panama. Many of the problems were attributed to poor communications and a lack of coordination.

"Good. I'm pleased to hear that we've solved the coordination problem." Dirk eyed Carlson before looking back at Ardison. "Colonel Ardison, one of the briefers stated that you have a Beechcraft two-hundred conducting surveillance on the targets. Was that correct?" Dirk asked.

He knew the answers to the questions because he had voted on the bill that allocated funds for the aircraft. His posturing was for the committee. He wanted their support in procuring more cargo aircraft for the Air Force, aircraft that would be built in his district.

"Yes, sir. That's correct. It's a special configured airplane outfitted with advanced electronic detection equipment designed to pick up any radio transmission sent between terrorist cells and possible collaborators outside the target areas."

"I see. I take it the choice of aircraft has to do with maintaining the element of surprise, I mean non-military and that sort of thing?" Dirk pressed.

"Yes, sir. Exactly."

"Very well. I'll tell you what's troubling me. The terrorists only struck yesterday and already you have all these men and this special equipment at your disposal. Is that realistic? I mean, how on earth do you get such a small, unique aircraft to the scene of a crisis before the war is over? I'm a private pilot and I have a fair idea of how long it would take to ferry a Beech halfway around the world. If you would please, conceptually walk me through this thing."

Carlson smiled. The congressman was focusing on the major problem facing U.S. CINCSOC, getting to the scene of a crisis in a timely manner and the connectivity of assets once they were deployed overseas. He knew he had an ally in Dirk. The congressman was reiterating the information he had passed along while they were playing golf in D.C.

"Excellent question, Congressman Dirk. Excellent," Carlson interjected. He nodded at Ardison to continue.

Sanz picked up on the head and eye signals between the men. As a junior officer his job was to keep his mouth shut and his ears open, and speak only if spoken to.

"Sir," Ardison continued, "our equipment is configured for rapid airlift anywhere in the world. Most of our equipment breaks down to standard sizes for quick deployment by C-141. The helicopters, the Beech, and some of the larger COMM suites require C-5 transport."

"And are those aircraft readily available for your use?" Dirk asked.

"No sir. We are dependent on the U.S. Air Force and on their transportation priorities," Ardison replied.

"That doesn't answer my question," Dirk said in a booming voice. He turned to look at Carlson.

Carlson answered. "Gentlemen," he said, getting up out of his chair. "There is a great deal of artificiality built into exercise *Freedom Express*." His brow furrowed. "For one thing, U.S. CINCSOC is providing the terrorists, the hostages, the controllers, and the assault units. So logistically, this is a much bigger challenge than a real world operation where I would only have to deploy a strike force. But having said that I hasten to add that Congressman Dirk's question cuts right to the quick of a serious problem we face in today's military. We *don't* have sufficient lift in the inventory to provide for all contingencies."

Dirk smiled approvingly.

Carlson continued. "Getting the right men and equipment to the scene of a crisis, and then providing them with hard intelligence to work with is a very, very difficult assignment, especially if the incident is on the opposite side of the planet. And once we get there, we cannot afford another failure like Desert One."

He gave each VIP a hard look.

"Terrorism is the new face of warfare. It is the challenge of our time. The lessons of history are clear.

Vietnam drained our confidence. Desert One stained our reputation. The bombing of the U.S. Marines in Beirut made us feel impotent. Losses in Grenada and Panama obscured our successes. We must learn from the past. If we are to remain a great nation we must meet this new challenge square on. As you will see from the success of exercise *Freedom Express* we have built, in the Special Operations Command, the finest special warfare capability in the world. Today, we *can indeed* conduct special operations anywhere, anytime, and anyplace in the world. No other nation can make that claim. But SPECOPS is only a tool, an instrument of political will and resolve. Counter terrorism is purely reactive. We are ready to meet this new challenge, as we have known it from past incidents. However, I caution you, gentlemen. We had better damn well get a handle on the trade in the technology of weapons of mass destruction, because there will be little SOF can do once the genie is out of the bottle."

"By that I assume you mean a nuclear weapon in the hands of terrorists?" Dirk asked, in an annoyed voice. Carlson had strayed from the theme they had agreed upon, more cargo aircraft for the Air Force.

"Yes, sir. Nuclear, biological, and chemical," Carlson said gravely.

Sanz mouth fell open at the word, *chemical*. Julie was tailing a Russian vessel loaded with deadly chemical weaponry. His mind focused like a laser.

Dirk thought for a few seconds and asked, "Let's assume for the moment that we have an incident such as that portrayed in *Freedom Express* and that the terrorists do not possess a weapon of mass destruction. How do you propose to conduct such an operation to minimize the loss of life?"

"For that question, I'll resume my seat and allow my

experts to lay it out for you in detail," Carlson replied. He sat down in his chair and nodded at Ardison.

Ardison pointed at the back of the briefing theater and three slides appeared on the boards depicting the three targets for *Freedom Express*. The tower at Hickam Air Force Base materialized on the center screen. The slide on the right showed the SEALs boarding the *Independence* from boats and helicopters. The one on the left screen showed SEAL Team FIVE boarding the *Alliance* from sea by means of a submarine. A military artist had prepared the drawings as cut-a-ways showing huddled hostages inside the buildings and ships. Fixed wing aircraft were dropping parachutists and providing gunship cover. Helicopters were hovering over the targets with black figures sliding down ropes. The artist had used a non-dimensional approach showing different types of aircraft aloft and a carrier supporting the operation from offshore. Ardison step by step walked them through the assault phase of the mission.

"Gentlemen, these three slides graphically show our approach to this mission. Using our Beechcraft, we have determined that the six terrorists aboard the *MV Alliance* are the leaders of the BATF organization." Ardison misspoke. Like many in the special operations community, he detested the Bureau of Alcohol, Firearms, and Tobacco for their actions at Waco, Texas against the Branch Dividians.

"They have established radio communications between the *Alliance*, the *Independence,* and the tower, and they are in constant contact with one another. We must therefore take down all three targets simultaneously. The first step in such a crisis is to negotiate, negotiate, negotiate, stall for time, and try to work out a peaceful solution. However, when negotiations fail, and for this exercise we know that negotiations will fail, when the terrorists begin killing hostages, we anticipate that we will be ordered to use force to rescue the hostages. In any such crises we would utilize all assets at our disposal. For example, we would use F-14 interceptors operating from the nearest land base or carrier to control the air space. At the first opportunity we would airdrop Army Rangers into the area at night by C-130 to surround buildings, control lines of communications, and seize the nearest airfield. In exercise *Freedom Express* we will employ Army Rangers but not here in Hawaii. To save money we will infiltrate our Rangers using MT1X square parachutes into a drop zone near a remote airfield in Fort Campbell, Kentucky. That airfield will be constructively considered to be Honolulu International. As you can see on the slide, using Blackhawks and 53's we will ferry medics and other specialty personnel with surveillance equipment to preplanned sites. At H-hour, when given final authorization by civilian authority, we will send in sharpshooters aboard 500MD helicopters equipped with infrared sensors and silenced tail rotors. They will take station around the targets, and will shoot any terrorist who threatens the assault force. All players will use simunitions or wear MILES gear so we can accurately score the success of the operation."

"Colonel, is that MILES gear the army laser tag stuff?" a staffer interrupted.

"Precisely," Ardison replied. He watched with amusement as the man wrote a note on his pad.

"Using Blackhawks and 53's, DELTA and SEAL assault units will fast rope into their respective targets. SEAL Team FIVE will attempt a first, a clandestine underway ship boarding of the *MV Alliance* using a submarine as an infiltration platform. With the element of surprise we intend to assault the targets simultaneously. After we have seized control of the

159

targets, the FBI Hostage Rescue Team will assume their duties as representatives of the Department of Justice to conduct a thorough investigation of the incident."

"Most ambitious," Dirk commented. "Could this operation be done, say, off the coast of Lebanon?"

"Yes, given sufficient time to establish an FOB in the AO," Ardison replied.

Carlson expounded on the issue. "With the problems of third country access we must plan for the worst case and that is an operation conducted from a carrier at sea. Such operations are very difficult but they obviate the major problem we face, and that is, getting third county permission to stage military operations from their soil. Many of our allies fear reprisals and are reluctant to give us access. Of course, we must have the airlift to deploy overseas, a base to work from, or an airfield to transship men and equipment out to a carrier. I believe we can put a complete package overseas, Blackhawks, HH-53s, 500MDs, boats, men and equipment, in five days."

"In five days a lot of people could be dead," a staffer blurted out.

"True," Carlson responded. "But we do not have the budget to forward deploy a ready force to every theater and we must consider the fact that all our C-5s could be deployed overseas when the balloon goes up. In that case we would have to wait for their return to Fort Bragg before deploying to the scene of an incident."

Dirk smiled. Carlson was back on message.

"What about the Marines? They are already forward deployed," asked another staffer. "Why not assign Marines deployed on amphibious ships the Jay-SOC mission? They are already deployed to the Pacific and the Mediterranean."

Carlson looked at the man. *Jarhead*, he thought. *Simper fi*, he said under his breath. "The Marines don't have the special training and equipment necessary to conduct counter terrorist operations. They are a young force, mostly nineteen-year old kids with M-16's and a gung ho attitude. Now don't get me wrong by that statement. They are some of the best troops in the world and they would take this job on in a heartbeat. They're just not trained for this mission nor do I believe we should dilute their busy training schedule with SPECOPS. They have too much on their plate as it is."

"Do you maintain a package in a ready status to deploy?" a congressman asked.

"Yes," Ardison answered. "Two hour standby."

"And are the aircraft usually available for deployment?" he continued.

"No," Carlson said, loudly. "We do not have enough C-5's and 141's to tie them up idling on the runway. That's not an option, gentlemen."

"Then we'll have to see that more aircraft are made available," Dirk said.

He looked from person to person in the delegation meeting their eyes.

"Can you conduct such an operation without losses, without the loss of innocent life?" a staffer asked.

"No. I cannot guarantee one hundred percent success in any such operation," Carlson answered, honestly. "This is a very dangerous business."

Dirk thought for a few seconds and asked, "Now let's assume for the moment that the terrorists in question possess a weapon of mass destruction. How do you propose to conduct such an operation to minimize the loss of innocent life?"

Carlson gave the congressman a hard look.

"There is no easy answer to that question, Congressman Dirk. If a group of fanatics gets hold of a nuke the loss of life could be staggering. We don't have an easy remote method of neutralizing such a weapon. There is no magic electromagnetic pulse that will defuse a nuclear weapon."

"What about biological and chemical weapons?" a staffer asked.

"We have a team of specialists at our disposal who are trained in biological and chemical warfare," Ardison added. "However, we only have one unit and its capabilities are extremely limited."

"By limited, what do you mean?" the man pressed.

"I mean they possess the protective gear to enter a contaminated area but not the means of cleaning up a massive spill or neutralizing a biological cloud. Thousands of people could be threatened and there is little we could do to prevent or limit the effect."

"I see," Dirk said. "And I see the reason for the General's forceful statement that, *we had better get a handle on the trade in weapons of mass destruction.* What can we do, General Carlson?"

"The first thing we need to do is to help the Russians help themselves. The greatest danger is nuclear proliferation. Chemical agents concern me but as we saw in the Tokyo subway attack their effects are limited by comparison to the threat posed by biological agents and atomics. Any way we approach the problem of nuclear and biological proliferation, we also address the problems of chemical weaponry proliferation. The key is to keep the genie in the bottle."

"What about the Lebed report?" asked a staffer, referring to a report of missing nuclear weapons by Russian presidential hopeful, General Alexander Lebed.

"I know General Lebed personally," Carlson said. "If he says that more than a hundred nuclear weapons are missing, then you can bet your life's savings that they are. Sooner or later one will surface in a blinding white flash.

The intelligence community better get on this problem."

For a minute there was silence. The troops stared at one another with puzzled expressions. Sanz was wondering what they were talking about when Congressman Dirk added. "This issue requires further discussion but not in this form."

"Agreed," Carlson grunted.

Sanz was astounded by the gravity of the problem facing the nation. From the gist of the conversation he correctly concluded that the Russians were unable to account for more than a hundred nuclear weapons disguised as suitcases. As he listened to the political posturing he thought about the Russian ship Julie intended to film. It was loaded with toxic chemicals bound for a small atoll not a thousand miles from where they were seated. He doubted that anyone in the room knew of its existence.

Then he thought, *Yellow Rain? I wonder if it really exists.*

The dialogue went on for a few more minutes. Finally Colonel Ardison concluded the briefing and the Sergeant Major called the men to attention while the VIPs departed the briefing theater.

Sanz was troubled by what he had heard and by the thought of Julie filming a Russian vessel suspected of committing crimes against humanity. He left the briefing theater with an anxious mind. He was nearly back to his corner of the hangar when more trouble assaulted him. At first he failed to notice an Army Major eyeing him with a mean expression written all over his face. Deep in thought, he fished his pants pockets for the key to his footlocker. When the man started shouting it didn't immediately dawn on him that the soldier was yelling at him. His thoughts were so preoccupied with Julie that he had to take a double take for the scene to register in his mind.

*"Lieutenant! Yes you, goddammit! Don't walk away from me when I'm talking to you."*

Sanz was dumbfounded by the verbal attack. He stopped and looked at the Major with a puzzled expression on his face. The Major was dressed in a starched battle dress uniform complete with spit-shined boots that reflected the dim light of the aircraft hangar like a mirror. Under his hat his head was peeled down to white walls and his face was as clean-shaven as a boiled egg. Sanz recognized him as one of the officers that had taken a verbal bruising during the Monterey operation.

"I'm sorry, Major Verduchi," he said. "I didn't know you were talking to me".

"Get your hands out of your goddamned pockets," Verduchi roared. "What are you doing, Hollywood? Playing with yourself?"

A group of soldiers standing nearby chuckled at the remark. The Major had an overbite and his buckteeth gave him a sort of horse-faced appearance.

"I was just looking for my key," Lee explained.

"You heard what I said," Verduchi snapped. "I don't want to hear your sorry-assed excuses."

Lee held up his hand with a key in it then glanced around. A dozen soldiers were gathered up to watch the Major dress down the Hollywood Lieutenant. Sanz realized what was taking place. A flash of anger surged through his body. In a physical confrontation he knew he could take the man out in a few heartbeats. But to do so meant court martial.

*"Stand at attention!"* the Major yelled.

"What?"

*"You heard me, goddammit!"*

Sanz took several quick steps toward the Major with a body posture that looked like a physical attack but he stopped short of touching the man. His actions caused Verduchi to flinch and brace himself for a punch. Lee stood at ease directly in front of the soldier. Eye to eye at less than a foot Lee stared at Verduchi with cold thoughts of beating him to death.

"Do you have a problem with me, Major?" he asked in a threatening tone.

"I have a problem with any officer who sets a bad example for enlisted men. Officers don't walk around with their hands in their pockets."

"Major I suggest you look in the mirror. An officer doesn't dress down another officer in front of enlisted men *for any reason*," Sanz growled.

"Are you threatening me, Lieutenant Sanz?" the bulldog Major asked.

Lee stared at him.

"Yeah. One up one down," Lee said. "I'll take you on anytime."

It was an old saw that the Major understood. A soldier could take on a superior one rank above and hold his own if he had a good reason. Sanz was an 0-3, Verduchi an 0-4. Moreover, Sanz was a unit commander with responsibilities that far exceeded the rank of a lieutenant.

"Let's take this up with Colonel Boyd," he pressed.

Boyd was Verduchi's boss. The soldier studied Lee's face.

"You'd like to slug me, wouldn't you, *Hollywood?*"

"*Yeah!*" Sanz yelled, right in the Major's face. "But I wouldn't touch your cunt-ass with used Kotex, not unless you touch me first," he whispered. "That would be assault, wouldn't it Major. Why don't you assault me with more than words, *Spit shine!* C'mon. Take your best shot."

The soldier stared at Lee without blinking all the

while biting the inside of his lip with a menacing snarl. He weighed the consequences of explaining his actions in front of his Colonel. Knowing that Sanz attended higher-level briefings with his boss, he decided to press the attack at a later date.

"Carry on, *Lieutenant Hollywood*," he said with disdain.

"Sure thing, *Major Verduchi*. And I'll do so without fucking up *Freedom Express*, like you did *Operation Fastback*."

Sanz glared at him waiting for a response. When none came he did an about face but spun one heel around so that it scraped the toe of the Major's spit-shined boots.

"Sorry about that," he said with his back turned toward the Major. "Maybe you could *order* one of your men to buff them up for you."

Lee looked at the soldiers watching the heated exchange of words. He studied their faces for clues hoping the Major would shove him in the back or hit him with his fist. He knew he could take the man under any circumstance but he needed a good excuse to beat the crap out of a major and he needed witnesses. He braced for a blow in the back of the head. When none came he walked away.

As he passed the enlisted soldiers he said, "They make much better movies in Hollywood, gents. Get a life."

# Chapter 13

Julie woke slowly, gradually struggling up a spiral of consciousness, fitting together a puzzle of unfamiliar sounds and strange sensations. She had been dreaming of Lee when her body heaved softly, as if she were lying on a gigantic swing that had momentarily left her weightless. Half asleep she realized that it was a sea swell, transmitting its motion through the ship, through the mattress of her bunk, and into her body. She came awake in a dark cabin to the sound of a ventilator blowing cool air.

*The Greenpeace,* she thought.

She tried to recall how she had come to be in the bunk, but it was all a blur, like looking through the fog of a dreary day. Then she recalled a frightening climb up the side of the ship on a tiny chain ladder, then a crane hoisting up the rubber boat with their equipment.

It was still light outside. Somehow she knew that it was still day time even though no light of the sun penetrated the cabin. For her it was both morning and evening all at the same time. Her body clock told her it was dark but in Southeast Asia it was late afternoon.

Then she remembered the captain, heavy set and bearded like a Yankee skipper. Captain Murphy had been businesslike but cordial as he got the ship underway. With heavy eyes she had watched Penang grow smaller and smaller as the *MV Greenpeace* sailed westward toward the last known position of the *Bogdan Stashinsky.*

Recognizing the signs of exhaustion, Murphy had assigned her his best stateroom, fed her a big breakfast, and returned to his duties. Then she remembered that Fred and Gordon had been bunked below decks in a space that was more of a passageway than a stateroom.

*Fred will be grumbling in the morning,* she thought, *and Gordon will have talked Lance Noble out of his stateroom. What am I thinking? It's not morning. I've got to get out of this bed. It's evening.*

She felt around in the darkness and turned on the bed lamp to illuminate the small stateroom. It was Spartan, cramped, and colorless but it had all the amenities a sailor needed. It even had its own bathroom, consisting of a small commode, shower, and sink, built into a space smaller than a closet. It was a luxury few aboard the ship enjoyed. Julie glanced at her watch.

*Wow. I've been out for almost five hours. So much for acclimating. I'll never get to sleep tonight.*

She climbed out of the bunk and shuffled to the bathroom, still dressed in the jeans and the cotton blouse she had worn from Hawaii. Flipping on the bathroom light, she had a fright. Her eyes were puffy and her hair was a mess. She quickly undressed and took a shower, relishing the warm water. Outside the skin of the ship it was hot and humid but inside it was cool and dry. She quickly put on fresh clothes, combed her hair, and made herself presentable. Still trying to shake the lethargy of jet lag, she headed for the galley for a cup of tea. As she staggered down the companionway, unaccustomed to the motion of the vessel, her stomach turned over.

*Oh no, Julie,* she thought. *You are not going to get seasick in front of these people. That's not a part of the plan.*

She willed herself not to get sick, even if it meant taking Dramamine. The smell of over-brewed coffee led her to the galley. She opened the door to cameras and sound equipment set up for an interview. Fred and Gordon were talking with a couple of men she took to be scientists by their dress and grooming.

"Hey, Julie. Have a good nap?" Gordon asked cheerfully.

"Yeah. Never felt better," she replied, without meaning in her words.

Everyone seemed to stare at her as she walked toward the counter for a cup of tea.

"How do pilots do it?" she asked. "My body tells me it's three in the morning."

"It is three in the morning, *somewhere*," Fred quipped.

The older bearded man, seated across the table from Forbes, smiled pleasantly and nodded his head in agreement.

Saxon pushed his pudgy body away from the table and hurried over to the counter. As he drew himself another cup of coffee, he whispered. "Shake the cobwebs, Jay-Jay, and get your tush over there. The guy with the beard is a professor of oceanography. He's out here collecting data for a report on global warming, which he says may produce a thermohaline collapse."

"A thermo-*what*?"

"Here," he said, handing her several note cards with questions scribbled down on them.

"Fred, I can't do an interview now. I feel like crap. I'm half asleep for Pete's sake."

"No whimpering, Jay-Jay. What would your SEAL boyfriend say?"

"He'd say you're a damn work-a-holic. I thought I was the boss of this outfit?"

"You are sweet cheeks and don't you forget it. Now, get your buns over there and impress the man with a perspicacious question."

"Fred, one of these days you're going to choke on a ten-dollar word. Can't this wait until tomorrow?"

"No. He's leaving the ship as soon as the helo is available to take him back to Georgetown. He was supposed to go ashore this morning but the captain sent the helo out lookin' for the Ruskies."

"Have they located the Russians yet?"

"No joy. Change frequencies, Julie. Back to the professor. He's studying the salinity of oceanic currents flowing through the Malacca Straits. Recall that little discourse of yours on the birthplace of life and home of the leviathan? Well he's the man. We have some good stuff on tape. But you know Gordo. He's got to shoot the same thing from five different directions. We can work magic with the footage back at the studio, but it won't mean crap without your pretty face in there for few questions. Grace us with a few *preguntas*. Okay?"

Julie nodded agreement. Saxon plopped a half-dozen sugar cubes in his cup then hurried back to his equipment. Julie finished making herself a cup of tea then joined the men at the center galley table.

Saxon introduced her. "Julie, this is Professor Vernon Taubes and his associate Doctor Robert Wilson. Gentlemen, this is Julie Jennings, the reporter we've been telling you about."

Julie shook the professor's hand. "I am very pleased to meet you, Professor Taubes."

"The pleasure is mine," Taubes replied. "I sincerely wish you the best with your documentary."

As Julie shook Doctor Wilson's hand she gave Fred Saxon a hard look, as if to ask, *what have you two been telling these people?*

Gordon's face was hidden behind his camera but it didn't dampen his enthusiasm for his work. "Professor," he said, adjusting his lens to focus on the bearded man's face, "would you please explain to Julie that *thermohalogen* stuff you were telling us about."

"Certainly, Mister Forbes," he replied, ignoring the error.

"Miss Jennings, I was just explaining to your associates,"

"Cut. Cut," Forbes interrupted. "Professor, would you explain it as if you and Julie were the only two people in the room? And Professor, please don't look at the camera. Just pretend it's not here."

"Certainly, Mister Forbes. Certainly. I think I can do that."

Like most people he was bothered by the presence of the camera and Forbes's penchant for perfection was making matters worse. Taubes cleared his throat nervously.

"Professor?" Julie asked, taking control. She paused a long beat so Forbes could focus the camera on her face. "Are the oceans of the world static or do they actively interact with one another?" She looked the Professor directly in the eyes to take his mind off the camera.

"Actually Ms. Jennings, it is one body of water in circulation. The best way to explain interaction within this body of water is to imagine the journey of a hypothetical molecule as it travels around the globe. Oceanographers call this journey, thermohaline circulation, because the heat of the sun drives it. In Greek, *therme* means heat. *Hal* may be loosely translated as salt or sea. Thermohaline, or heat-salt circulation, spreads solar energy from the tropics to the poles by means of enormous oceanic currents."

"In effect, what you are describing are invisible rivers of water flowing around the world from ocean to ocean?" Julie asked, leading the professor.

"Exactly, Ms. Jennings. Cold water is denser than warm water. It sinks at the poles and flows subsurface toward the equator causing the warmer waters of the tropics to be pulled north. This creates enormous gyres. The best-known example is the Gulf Stream. Off the Atlantic Coast of the United States the warm water of the tropics flows north all the way to Europe, keeping it relatively warm and habitable. Europe would be covered in snow for a great part of the year if not for the Gulf Stream."

"I see. Professor, what is El Niño?" Julie asked.

"Aaaah. *El Niño* is an excellent example of heat pooling and oceanic circulation. Generally, strong trade winds blow from east to west along the equator across the Pacific. This pushes the water and heat westward away from the Pacific Coast of the Americas. But occasionally the winds die off and the warmer waters flow back toward the Pacific Seaboard. This pattern significantly affects weather in the Americas."

"So what you are describing is somewhat like a pot of boiling water?" Julie asked.

"Exactly. Imagine our hypothetical molecule of seawater sinking near Iceland. It joins billions of other cold sinking molecules that gain speed as they sink deeper. They ride along the bottom near the mid-oceanic ridge all the way from the North Atlantic to the South Atlantic where they encounter the Antarctic circumpolar current. For hundreds of years, perhaps thousands, our molecule circles the Antarctic continent until it is finally gets caught up in a current that carries it out into the Pacific. There it rises to the surface and is perhaps caught up in El Niño. It is pushed and buffeted by storms, heated by the sun, and cooled by Arctic winds. For years it languishes in the Pacific. But eventually it travels back up through the Malacca Straits and out into the Indian

Ocean. There it gets caught in powerful eddies generated by the Antarctic circumpolar current. It goes round and round for years until it passes near the Horn of Africa. There it gets caught in a current that carries it back into the Atlantic and northward in the Gulf Stream along the East Coast of the United States. And from there it makes its way back to Iceland where it joins cold sinking water and begins its journey again."

"Fascinating. How long does such a journey take, Professor?" Julie asked.

"No one knows for sure, Ms. Jennings. Perhaps thousands of years. Evidence suggests that thermohaline circulation has existed for eons. I study foraminifera."

He eyed Julie for sign of understanding before continuing.

"Foraminifera are microscopic creatures that float in the sea. When they die they rain to the bottom and become entombed in the mud. By analyzing sediment cores for changes in foraminifera we are able to determine changes in the earth's climate tens of thousands of years ago. My specific area of interest is thermohaline collapse. I believe that manmade parasol gases are inducing climatic changes that are influencing thermohaline circulation. A major change in circulation could precipitate another ice age."

Julie quickly redirected the Professor before he could begin a dissertation on global warming. "Professor, if toxic substances such as those found in a nuclear reactor or chemical weapons were dumped into the Pacific, could those toxins flow into the Indian Ocean, and the Atlantic? Specifically, could they get into the food chain?"

"Most assuredly, Ms. Jennings," Taubes replied. "The oceans make up seventy percent of the earth's surface. They are interconnected by thermohaline driven currents.  As you suggested, imagine the oceans as a pot of boiling water and it becomes clear.  Any substance dumped into the pot will eventually circumnavigate the space."

"I see.  But what about deep water such as the Challenger Deep in the Marianas Trench?  What if poisons were dumped in an ocean trench?  Do currents flow that deep?"

"Yes Ms. Jennings, they most assuredly do. Anything man dumps into the sea will eventually finds its way back to mankind."

Julie continued the interview, asking the same questions over and over from several different points of view until the cook ran them off to prepare the galley for dinner.

While Gordon and Fred put away their equipment, Julie took a walk on deck.  The wind, the smell of ocean, the spray, and the movement of the ship were invigorating.

*No wonder Lee loves the sea*, she thought.  *A person can think out here.  The ocean has a way of putting you at ease and on edge at the same time.  It's so beautiful and yet so humbling.  One mistake and....*  She shook off the thought of the ship sinking.  *I can understand why they say a captain is married to his ship.  Anything other than total commitment would be disastrous.*

The *MV Greenpeace* was small in comparison to the huge freighters plying the straits.  But it seemed big to Julie.  She walked about the rolling deck until she found a bollard large enough to sit on.  Hanging her arms over the railing, she watched a flying fish sail over the waves and plop back in the sea, frightened by the passage of the vessel. The sun was still well above the horizon but it was low enough to reflect harshly off the water. She shielded her eyes with her hand and counted the ships around them.

"Jeez!" she muttered when she hit twenty. *This is a busy place*, she thought. *Maybe the Russians have slipped by us.*

She imagined the Russian ship running a parallel course beside one of the huge oil tankers steaming through the Straits. Then she thought about Lee for a few minutes, considering his dangerous profession. That is the beauty of the open sea. It forces the mind to wonder. A cloud covered the sun and a shiver went down her spine. It was a deep feeling that ran to the core of her existence, a feeling she couldn't understand. The weather was beautiful, not ominous. The scattered billowing clouds created a blotch of dappled sunlight on the surface of the sea. She didn't know if the emotion was fear for Lee or for herself.

"Something is going to happen," she muttered. "Something terrible."

*I wonder if they spotted the Russians. Maybe they are dumping chemicals in the Straits. Maybe Greenpeace has been putting too much pressure on them and they are dumping in shallow water.*

In her mind's eye she visualized a black freighter steaming along in the darkness with sailors rolling barrels of toxic waste over board. For a half hour she mused and stewed, running over in her mind different ways of telling the story on film. The sun was low on the horizon when Fred and Gordon sneaked up behind her and interrupted her thoughts.

"Hey Julie, it's almost dinnertime," Forbes said. "It wouldn't be good to keep Captain Blackbeard waiting. He might hang us from the yardarm."

Julie stuck her thoughts in the closet and left the sea to the sea.

"I don't feel like dinner, more like pancakes and eggs."

"How about sardines and beer, and a nasty Cuban cigar," Forbes suggested.

"You bastard," Saxon choked.  He leaned over the rail and dry heaved.

Forbes laughed.  "Would you believe he's already eaten a fist full of Dramamine?  Look at him feeding the fish.  I wish I had my camera," he chuckled.

"Gordon, sometimes you can be such an insensitive mug," Julie said, with a smile that Saxon couldn't see because of his involuntary convulsions.

She motioned for Forbes to help her.  They grabbed Saxon by his arms and held him so he wouldn't fall over board.

Whenever the *Greenpeace* was steaming routinely on the open sea, there were two settings in the mess.  The younger men, engineers and first lieutenant, juniors, thirds and seconds, the radio officer, and those whose watches began at eight, dined at seven o'clock.  The captain, the senior officers, and guests dined at six.  Dinner was not a formal affair like a ship of the line but Julie, Gordon, and Fred waited for the Captain by standing behind their assigned chair.  Captain Murphy entered the mess just as the ship's bell chimed.

"Please have a seat, lady and gentlemen," he said.

His mannerism, though informal, emitted authority, an absolute necessity for command at sea.

"So, Ms. Jennings, how was your nap?" he asked, before Julie was seated.

"Just fine, Captain," she said, scooting up to the table. "But I slept too long. I'm afraid I'll be up all night tossing and turning."

"Try a bit of my brandy after dinner. It helps, doesn't it, Professor?"

"It certainly does, Captain. And a fine brandy it is."

A Filipino waiter began serving them. Fred took one look at the curry and excused himself.

"Captain Murphy," he said with a burp that he covered with one hand, "would you please excuse me, sir," he gurgled. He placed his hand over his mouth and waddled out of the galley on unsettled sea legs.

"Ralph is calling," Forbes quipped.

Murphy watched him leave. "Anymore landlubbers?" he asked with a grin. He looked directly at Professor Taubes.

"Just as I get accustomed to the motion of the ship, it's time for me to leave," Taubes declared.

"Speaking of leaving, Professor, I'm afraid we'll have to delay your departure for a few more days."

"Oh?"

"We've been unable to locate the *Stashinsky* and I need the helicopter aloft for the search." "But Captain Murphy, I have reservations for tomorrow and appointments to keep at the university," Taubes expressed with great concern.

"See Lance Noble after dinner, Professor. He'll establish a radio link so you can rearrange your schedule," Murphy replied, with finality.

"But, Captain,"

"I am sorry, Professor. Right now my number one priority is finding the *Stashinsky* and I need the helicopter to do that. As soon as we are back within range of Penang, I'll put you ashore."

"Very well," Taubes replied, with an edge to his

voice.

"Captain," Forbes asked, "will the helo be flying tonight?"

"No Gordon. It's too dangerous. Too many squalls. She's inbound as we speak. But don't worry. We'll find her in the morning."

Julie looked at Forbes wondering why the Captain had used his first name and had addressed her as Ms. Jennings.

"Captain, would it be possible for Julie and me to accompany the bird. I'd like to get some shots of the all ships in the Straits and the morning light works well for my camera."

Murphy looked at Julie and answered Forbes's question.

"It's okay by me Ms. Jennings, but you'll have to get up by three-thirty," he cautioned. He watched her face for clues as to what she thought about getting up so early in the morning.

"I doubt that I'll sleep a wink tonight, Captain," Julie said, and smiled pleasantly.

"Brandy, Ms. Jennings. Brandy will turn you about."

"Speaking of turning about, do you think the *Stashinsky* has turned back?" Julie asked.

"Noooo. They probably spotted the helo and are taking evasive action. My guess is they'll slip in with a group of freighters and try to get past us in a squall. They won't go around Sumatra. Too far. Too costly."

He took a big shovel full of rice and curry and munched on it.

"Do you think they would dump toxins overboard in the Straits?" Julie queried.

Murphy took a sip of water before answering.

"I wouldn't put anything past the Neanderthals, Ms. Jennings. They are an ignorant lot, you know. We've seen them dumping in deep water."

"If you've seen them dumping, why didn't you film them?" Gordon questioned, confused by the Captain's revelation.

"We did film them, Gordon," he said with a growl. "From a distance. You can't make out did dilly."

"May I see the video? Maybe I can enhance it," Forbes suggested.

"What's ours, is yours, Gordon. I told you that and I meant it. It's for a same cause. But you're wasting your time with our video. The man who took the footage wasn't a professional like you and his equipment was second rate. We were too far away and it was dusk. In my binoculars I could see what they were doing. I thought we had them dead to rights. I was absolutely livid when I saw the film. Nothing but a dark shape on a horizon bobbing up and down."

"Captain, to make this documentary credible we've got to catch them in the act. Your helo is the best platform for the job, especially at night. I brought along a night vision camera with a telescopic lens," Forbes said.

"You are welcome to go on every flight. Whirly will be thrilled at the opportunity of dangling you from a rope again. All I require is a copy of your footage for our records."

Julie looked at Forbes and he hunched up his shoulders in a gesture of *no problem*. "Easy to make a copy, Boss," he said, in a pleading voice.

"I don't have a problem with sharing our aerial footage, Gordon," she said. "This is a give and take world." She looked at Murphy. "Thank you for your hospitality Captain Murphy, and for the opportunity of doing something positive for mankind."

"I would rather think of it as something positive for the environment, Ms. Jennings. At my ripe old age I have come to dislike many aspects of mankind."

"Captain Murphy, there is something that is troubling me," Julie said.

"Shoot," Murphy replied.

"If the Russians are shipping chemicals to Johnston Atoll for destruction, why are they dumping them at sea?"

*How's he going to answer this one*, she thought. She had come to believe that the Russians were dumping toxins that they wouldn't or couldn't admit existed, toxins cooked up in top-secret laboratories. What she wanted to know was Murphy's thoughts on the matter.

"That is a good question, Ms. Jennings," Murphy replied.

"Julie," she smiled.

"Julie it is," he beamed, like a Yankee skipper at the helm. Then his expression turned serious.

"Julie, just for sake of argument, suppose your government secretly agreed to help the Russians dispose of few million tons of deadly nerve gas. A good place to do that in secret would be Johnston Atoll. You'll concede that that is a possibility, wouldn't you?"

Julie nodded.

"Five hundred thousand tons is about the limit of the JACADS facility," Murphy stated, stroking his beard. "I think we'd all agree that such a deal would be in the best interest of the United States and for that matter, mankind. But knowing your government, I would be willing to bet that there are prerequisites, perhaps safety conditions placed on the material that they will accept. I mean, the blokes on the island are not going to accept rockets dripping with mustard, are they?"

Julie nodded agreement.

"The Russians produced some *six hundred million* tons of nerve gas. And they have little if any capability of disposing of it. They can't sell that much to terrorists. They can't give that much away to rogue states. They can't turn it into commercial products. So what can they do with it, Julie? Bury it? Dump it in the ocean? They have millions of rusty barrels full of the stuff, leaking rockets, deteriorating land mines, and God only knows what else. It only stands to reason that to save face they will deliver the agreed amount to Johnston Atoll and dump every drop they can in route."

"It's the *'what else'* that most concerns me, Captain Murphy," Julie said.

He stared at her with a knowing eye. "Yes. Dead rabbits, Ms. Jennings."

"Rabbits?" Julie questioned, taken off guard.

She glanced at Forbes. His mouth was open. He too was all ears.

"From time to time we've come across rabbit carcasses in the *Stashinsky's* wake."

"I don't understand," Julie said, staring at the weather worn Captain's face.

"The Russians use rabbits as living sensors to monitor chemical storage area," Murphy explained. "Knowing that, as well as the poor diet on board the vessel, we sent a few carcasses off for analysis."

"Diet?" Taubes asked. "I'm not making the connection."

"Professor, the food on board Russian ships is not so good. If the rabbits were edible they would have been consumed by the ship's crew."

"Oh. I see."

"And necropsies?" Julie asked.

"The unknown, Ms. Jennings. Killer unknown. Our scientists were unable to identify the causative agent of death." He searched Julie's face for several seconds. "We intend to expose an international crime against humanity and we believe you are just the person to do the job. We have thoroughly reviewed your work and we have the utmost confidence and trust in Gordon. You are very good at what you do young lady and I pledge to you our full support in this important endeavor."

Murphy had recently received a telefax from the *Sirius* informing him about a body that they had recovered in the wake of the *Stashinsky* just before the ship entered the Straits of Malacca. The corpse had no digits and the skull was ruptured so badly that the victim was beyond recognition. Greenpeace strongly suspected that they had recovered one of their two missing members, men who had gone missing while on a mission to film the *Stashinsky* being loaded in Odessa. Murphy didn't think it prudent to mention the report over dinner.

"Thank you for the compliment, Captain," Julie said. "Thank you very much."

In the distance came the steady beat of rotors. It caught Murphy's attention first. He cocked his head to one side and listened.

"There she is," he said.

The sound slowly built in intensity until the helicopter flew by. Then the telephone beside his chair rang and he picked it up.

"Murphy here," he said.

He nodded his head to the voice on the other end of the line.

"Bring her in and tie her down for the night. Prepare for launch at oh-four thirty. Two pax," he ordered, then hung up.

He looked at Julie. "Still no sign of the Ruskies."

Julie studied the captain's face. He was chewing over his options. He picked up the phone and ordered a course change, then turned his attention back to his guest.

"Ramon," Murphy said to the steward.

"*Si*, Captain," the Filipino replied.

"Brandy, please."

Murphy got up from the table and motioned for Julie to follow him to a private corner of the wardroom.

# Chapter 14

The *Bogdan Stashinsky* was a patch-painted freighter named after a KGB hero who had won the *Order of the Red Banner* for assassinating enemies of state with a poisonous gas weapon. Painted black and capped in brown with red piping, she was a relic in the day of roll on, roll off container ships. But she could still part the waves at more than thirty knots.

Running into the wind, Captain Shvachko maneuvered her north across the shipping lane, anxiously eyeing the procession of ships plying the Straits. Tankers and bulk carriers, grain and ore ships predominated, riding tall against the horizon. There were small freighters sprouting vast deck cranes and huge modern container ships stacked high with rectangular steel boxes. As the *Stashinsky* neared the Malay coast boogies graced the sea with tall sails and sleek prows. But there was no sign of the green painted ships of the environmentalist, nor their helicopter. The cavalcade of merchants became monotonous in their black and grey anonymity. As night began to fall the waters of the Straits turned a dark gray.

"All ahead one third," Shvachko ordered as they neared the coast.

"All ahead one third aye," repeated the seaman at the engine console.

"Extinguish bridge lights. Darken ship," Shvachko ordered.

The OOD repeated the order. Over the ship's intercom a seaman passed the word on the one-MC to darken ship. All over the vessel hatches were closed and red lights were turned on. The OOD physically checked the running lights by walking to each side of the bridge wings and looking at them. Red for port. Green for starboard. Satisfied the ship was lighted in accordance with international convention he reported to the captain.

"Sir, the ship is darkened."

"Very well," Shvachko grunted.

As the thickening night moved closer to the ship, the crew operated by dim red light that spared their night vision. When the gray interlude between day and night was over, the sky, the land, and the sea merged at indistinct places. The flashing lights of buoys, village lights on the distance coast, and ships in the channel gave off sharp pricks of red, green, and white in a black moonless void as the *Stashinsky* sailed relentlessly northward toward the lee of Langkawi Island.

At 2200 hours Shvachko ordered, "Extinguish running lights."

"Pardon me, Captain," the OOD exclaimed, not believing he had heard the order correctly.

"*I said, extinguish the running lights*," Shvachko boomed.

"Aye, aye, Captain," the nervous officer replied.

He could tell by the tone of the Captain's voice that he didn't want to be questioned. The OOD complied and the ship was suddenly invisible to the outside world.

"Left full rudder, steady on course two six zero," Shvachko ordered.

The helmsman repeated the order and turned the ship to port. Shvachko held the new course for hours steaming in darkness toward the western shoals of Langkawi. The time passed quickly as the crew located buoys, visually and on radar, and took bearings of known landmarks. Shvachko himself put his face in the radarscope on numerous occasions to check the ship's position relative to the land and the sea going traffic out in the Straits. At 2300 hours he ordered the crew to make preparations to anchor. The OOD and the bridge crew were totally baffled but they dared not question the Captain's orders. The *Stashinsky* had a secret mission and they all knew what it was. Orders were issued to be followed, not questioned.

"Stop engines," he ordered.

"Stop engines, aye," the seaman on watch repeated.

For a few minutes the *Stashinsky* plowed through the sea from momentum while Shvachko checked the fathometer for the depth of the water under the keel, the radar for position, and the ship's direction relative to the wind. When he was sure it was shallow enough and they were alone on the sea, he gave the order to let loose the anchor. The ship vibrated as a heavy chain ran out. It sent a shiver through the ship. In his stateroom Gurnov felt the rumble of the anchor chain and checked his watch; 23:45.

He smiled. "Baranov, you sneaky son of a whore, you'd better be on time," he mumbled.

He buckled on his pistol belt, checked his Tokarev, and holstered his weapon like a gunslinger. His hands were shaking so he took several deep breaths to calm himself. This was the moment, the moment he had planned in excruciating detail. To steady his nerves, he took a big swig of vodka straight from the bottle and sang a verse from *Wonderland*, Vladimir Vysotsky famous ballad. He put out of his mind the fact that Vysotsky had killed himself with heavy drink at age forty-two.

*There is much unclear in this strange land,*
*You can get confused and lost,*
*It even makes you feel creepy all over,*
*If you imagine what can happen.*

Gurnov checked the contents of the nylon tote bag he had prepared for the occasion. He took out a western handheld GPS unit the size of a pack of cigars and checked to see that it was working. He couldn't get a fix from inside his stateroom but he determined that the battery was up and the unit was functioning properly. Then he took out a radio smaller than a clay brick and checked its frequency setting and battery level. In the bottom of the bag there were several canisters of Blue-X the size of kitchen fire extinguishers. His gas mask lay on top of them. He had counted the exterior hatches on the *Stashinsky*. Bound in a bundle by a rubber band was more than enough heavy nylon zipcuffs to secure every opening on the ship twice and cutter-pliers to remove them when the siege was over. Satisfied with his inventory, he sang another verse from *Wonderland* as he re-packed his bag.

*Suddenly, a precipice, you need to jump,*
*Will you be a coward, or will you leap bravely?*
*Ah? Eh? Just so, my friend,*
*That's the main point.*

He took another gulp of vodka and put the bottle in his bag, a welcome aboard gesture for Baranov.

"Okay. Time to go Gurnov. Do not delay. You will leap bravely, you son of a drunken whore," he sang. "*Da!* Of course you will, you Cossack bastard."

With hands shaking, he picked up the bag, stepped out of his stateroom and walked forward toward the main deck. Quietly and carefully he maneuvered around the light locker, which baffled the red light of the passageway, and opened the watertight hatch. Like a soldier on patrol he carefully checked the main deck forward. It was empty. The sea and anchor detail had already gone below decks. He closed the hatch behind him and worked his way to a ladder that climbed to the

02 level. As he walked up the steps he looked up at the bridge wings above. The deck was dark and there was no moon so he knew no one could see him. When he reached the ships main air intakes he stopped and searched the vessel for any sailor that might be taking in the night air. There was always a sailor or soldier on the stern of the ship taking in the breeze or grabbing a smoke in the lee of the vessel. There was no one on the foredeck so he took out his radio and the GPS, and turned them on.

"Alpha Charlie, this is Whiskey November," he whispered in English, just in case the frequency was being monitored.

He repeated the call several times and was beginning to get nervous when his radio crackled to life.

"Whiskey November this is Alpha Charlie, over," Baranov reported in poor English.

He sounded like a German, *Viskey Novemver.* The volume was set so high Gurnov nearly dropped the radio on the deck. He quickly turned down the volume and scanned the deck around him. Whispering into the radio, he read the coordinates off his GPS in reverse order. It was a simple code he and Baranov had agreed upon. A few minutes later his radio crackled again.

"Whiskey November?"

"Roger," Gurnov replied.

"Four hours."

"Roger, out," was Gurnov's only reply.

*Damn it! He is way behind schedule. I have to change the time of the briefing.*

He had ordered Captain Dmitriyev to assemble the men in the galley at 2400 hundred hours. He had to delay the meeting. He didn't want the men anywhere near their protective chemical gear when he gassed the ship. He quickly trekked back to his cabin, stashed his bag, and went to Dmitriyev's room. He knocked hard on the door and tried to open it. It was locked and there was no answer from inside.

"Shit," he grumbled.

Gurnov walked briskly to the galley and peeked inside. The room was filled with gray and brown-green uniforms with bright red trim. Two of the junior officers were watching several soldiers play cards. Others were drinking tea and chatting in small groups. A thick haze of cigarette smoke hung in the air like a cloud on a rainy day.

*Not much circulation of air in the galley*, he thought. *I should toss a canister into this space.* Then he thought. *Nyet. They could never reach their chemical gear without passing out.*

Gurnov looked for Captain Dmitriyev but he wasn't in the galley. As he turned to leave he met the captain coming down the passageway.

"Ah! Major Gurnov. I am glad that I found you. I was just up on the bridge checking the wind. Captain Shvachko is asking for you."

"What does he want?" Gurnov growled.

"He is concerned that we are too close to land. There are native fishermen nearby. He wants to know if you want to move the ship farther to sea."

"No!" Gurnov barked.

Dmitriyev's brow furrowed.

"He said that the winds and seas are calm and that he can maintain station without anchoring."

Gurnov's mind was racing. He had to make a move.

"Very well. Are all of the men assembled in the galley?"

"Yes, Major. They are awaiting your instructions."

"Very well. Wait for me in the galley."

"Major?"

"Yes."

"I have confidence the men can perform to your expectations while the ship is underway. I suggest..."

"I will make this decision," Gurnov snapped, cutting him off.

"Yes, Major."

Dmitriyev eyed him suspiciously. He saw the pistol strapped to his hip and nervously avoided his eyes. Gurnov waited until Dmitriyev stepped into the galley before hurrying down the passageway. He dashed into his room to retrieve his bag and as he turned to leave came face to face with Dmitriyev standing in the passageway.

"Major. I-I forgot to tell you. Captain Shvachko said that there has been no sighting of the environmentalists."

Dmitriyev looked at the bag in Gurnov's hand and then down at the pistol strapped to his belt. Gurnov suspected that the information about the environmentalists was just a pretext for Dmitriyev to follow him about the ship.

"Very well. Please come in. There is something I must tell you," Gurnov said with a hint of intrigue.

A look of concern flashed across the young Captain's face as he stepped into the stateroom. He was expecting to learn a deep dark secret about hold number four.

"Close the door please."

Dmitriyev shut the door behind him and turned to see Gurnov placing the bag on his bed. He unzipped it.

"There is something you should see," he said, stepping back. "Look," he ordered, pointing at the bag.

Compelled by curiosity Dmitriyev walked to the bed passing Gurnov who took a position near the door. Dmitriyev carefully opened the bag and peeked inside. A look of disbelief and confusion furrowed his brow. When he turned to Gurnov for explanation, his expression turned to shock. He was staring down the barrel of a

Tokarev pistol.

"But, Major. I-I don't understand," he stammered.

"Simple young Captain Dmitriyev. It is time to leap bravely from the precipice."

"But I-I..."

Gurnov squeezed the trigger and the Tokarev exploded with a boom. The heavy projectile struck Dmitriyev square in the chest, shattering his sternum and knocking him back onto Gurnov's rack. The body jerked in spasms and slumped to the deck. The report of the pistol, contained within the steel confines of his stateroom, caused Gurnov's ears to ring. He quickly opened his door and checked the passageway. Taking a silencer out of his pocket, he screwed it onto the barrel of the pistol, all the while glancing up and down the passageway. When no one appeared he dashed to his rack and grabbed his bag of supplies. Locking his stateroom door behind him, he raced against time.

Slipping out on the main deck, he moved quickly from hatch to hatch in a route that he had rehearsed ten times in the dark. At each of the watertight doors he ziptied the hatch closed, sealing the crew inside the skin of the ship. When he reached the stern on the 01 level he came upon a sailor, foot up on the railing enjoying a cigarette. The noise of the ship's generators, engines, and ventilation system masked his footsteps so he stood still against a bulkhead scanning the poop deck to ensure there was no one else on deck. Inching closer, he maneuvered to within five feet before taking a shot. The noise of the pistol sounded more like a man spitting up phlegm than a weapon discharging. When the bullet met the bone it sounded like a baseball bat smacking against a side of beef. The weight of the heavy projectile shattered a rib and knocked the breath out of the man. But it didn't kill him. He crumpled to the deck gasping, clawing at the entrance wound. He looked up at Gurnov with crazed eyes begging for explanation. Gurnov fired a second shot that struck the sailor in the head ending his life. To temporarily conceal the body, he dragged the corpse to a recess in the ship's bulkhead. He dared not shove it overboard for fear it would wash ashore and draw unwanted attention to his passage of the Straits.

Gurnov's route led him all around the weather decks of the vessel with exception of the bridge on the 04 level. It eventually took him back to the ship's fresh air intakes on the 02 level forward of the bridge. There he took out two canisters of Blue-X and initiated them. A cloud of incapacitant invaded the ship sucked up by the ventilation system. When they were exhausted he took out two more canisters and fired them off. In his mind's eye he could see his men and the ship's crew scrambling for breath. He could see them gasping and retching and scratching the deck, fear bugging out their eyes, thinking that the gas was lethal. He thought he heard men clawing at a nearby hatch trying to get free but it was only his imagination. The gas caught the crew that wasn't on watch sound asleep in their racks. Some passed out in their beds. Others rolled out off their racks and crawled along the deck retching and vomiting before succumbing to the gas. The soldiers in the galley ran out of the space at the first sign of the incapacitant but it was too late. Some held their breath and crawled along the deck on all fours trying to reach their protective gear. But their equipment was too far away.

*The bridge,* he thought. *I have to take the bridge.*

Gurnov jumped as the ship's alarm exploded with the signal to abandon ship. He knew that the bridge hatches would be open on both sides of the vessel and that the bridge crew would escape the gas. Sweating from fear and pumped up on adrenaline he raced up two decks on the starboard side of the ship. Men were choking and gasping on the bridge wing. Vomit covered the deck. He could see Shvachko and several men bent over on the port bridge wing, sick and groggy from the incapacitant.

Gurnov put on his gas mask, stepped around the sailors and entered the bridge. Men were lying on the deck, unconscious. Several were piled up in the ladder way leading from below decks. The dim red light illuminating the bridge created a surreal scene through the ports of his gas mask. No one was conscious on the bridge so he closed the starboard hatch and ziptied it from inside, locking the crew out of the ship. He turned off the abandon ship alarm and patrolled through the haze to the port hatch, pistol in hand. Shvachko, now on his feet, saw the pistol come to bear but there was nothing he could do. His eyes bulged out as Gurnov fired. Shvachko died not knowing the identity of his killer. The huge bullet slammed into his chest and hammered his body back against the bulkhead of the bridge wing. As he slumped to the deck, blood smeared the cold steel at his back.

Selectively, Gurnov shot all of the officers on the port bridge wing. He let the enlisted men live. Leaving them retching and gasping for breath, he locked them out and walked back through the bridge to the starboard hatch, reloading on the move. Using his cutter pliers, he cut the ziptie and opened the hatch. Standing in the hatchway he identified the officers from enlisted. There were two. The sailors were all on their knees bent double from nausea. He shot the first officer in back of the head. Then he aimed the weapon at the second man. He paused when he recognized the young lieutenant who had welcomed him on board the day the ship departed Odessa.

"*Da*. You I will let live, young Lieutenant Zhukov,"

he mumbled. "For the time being."

Gurnov stepped out of the hatch, walked up wind, and removed his mask.

"*Lieutenant! Lieutenant Zhukov!*" he yelled.

The young officer looked up at him with uncomprehending eyes. Mucous was streaming from his nose. His eyes were so watery he couldn't see. Salivating like a rabid dog, he couldn't answer.

"*Lieutenant Zhukov! There has been an accident!*" Gurnov yelled.

He pulled the young officer to his feet and began ushering him to the ladder that led down to the 03 level. The sailor staggered and fell to his knees several times.

"*Take a deep breath!*"

The man coughed and began retching again.

"Easy. Easy. Take another breath. That's right. And another."

Gurnov helped him to the ladder way and down to the foredeck on the windward side of the ship. Still in a daze the sailor slumped to the deck. Gurnov ziptied his hands behind his back and his feet together and returned to the windward side of the bridge where he counted the living. Then he walked around the bridge and counted those on the port side.

*Seven. Ah, good. An easy number to handle,* he thought.

He helped those who could move down the ladder and cuffed them alongside Zhukov. The others he dragged down the steps. None of the sailors were alert enough to resist. When all seven were secure, he entered the ship and began clearing the interior, working his way down from the bridge. One by one he dragged the unconscious crew to pre-selected compartments and locked them inside, selecting out the ones he needed to sail the vessel. It took an hour just to clear the 02 and 03 levels. When he was satisfied he controlled the ship, he opened enough hatches to clear the air, which he knew would take hours if not days to complete. Exhausted, he rigged several containers of Blue-X to the ship's ventilators and untied Lieutenant Zhukov and four of the men trussed up on deck. Threatening them with his pistol, he told them that deadly chemicals were rigged to the ventilators and that he would release the gas with a radio-firing device if they misbehaved. Confident he was in command, he ordered Lieutenant Zhukov and his men to lower the accommodation ladder.

# Chapter 15

Clouds lay up against the mountains in the center of Oahu bathing them in scattered showers. Below the ceiling, the foothills were ablaze with thousands of lights as people went about their business oblivious to events, which were about to threaten their lives. Around Ford Island, Pearl Harbor bustled with activity, unaware that JSOC was about to launch the operational phase of exercise *Freedom Express.*

Fully dressed for combat, the men sat on the tarmac outside the hangar lined up in stick order. They chatted quietly, or nodded sleepily, as they waited for the helicopters.

"Here comes the General," Dan Carroll hushed.

The others ignored the comment and continued their private conversations. Shortly, the wheels of an aircraft screeched as a C-12 touched down and hurled past them. At the end of the runway it turned around. The pilot revved the engines, varied the pitch of the propellers, and taxied toward the hangar. He jostled to a stop at the side of the hangar and shut down the engines with a cough. The black clad warriors watched silently. Momentarily the hatch popped open and several men climbed out of the aircraft. They all recognized General Carlson by his profile. Accompanied by Colonel Ardison and several VIPs, he marched up to the formation. In the dark, to the sound of crickets chirping, he addressed them in his most sonorous voice.

"Warriors of Jay-sock," he bugled. "The devil is in

the details. And in the business of special operations, details overlooked, spell disaster and death. That's why we train, and train, and train!"

He walked among them reciting battles past.

"*Dragon Rough,* nineteen sixty-three. Belgian paratroopers freed a group of hostages held by Simba rebels in Stanleyville, Congo. *Son Tay*, nineteen seventy. U.S. Special Operations Forces attempted to free POWs from a prison camp near Hanoi, Vietnam. *Tang Island, Cambodia*, nineteen seventy-five. The crew of the merchant ship *Mayaguez* was hijacked by Cambodian thugs. U.S. forces seized the ship and rescued thirty-nine crewmen. *Entebbe, Uganda,* nineteen seventy-six. Israeli commandos rescued one hundred and five people held hostage at an airport terminal. Nineteen seventy-seven, *Mogadishu, Somalia*. Twenty-eight GSG9 commandos stormed a hijacked aircraft. Three terrorists were killed. One commando, one stewardess, and four passengers were wounded."

He paused, but kept walking slowly among the ranks. He circled around behind one stick and walked down another row.

"Gents, terrorism is undeclared warfare. When U.S. diplomats in Tehran were seized and held hostage on the fourth of November, nineteen seventy-nine by Islamic militants, an illegal act was committed against all citizens of the United States of America. The government of Iran was obligated under international law to protect foreign diplomats. Instead, the G.O.I. not only acquiesced to the taking of hostages, but demanded ransom for their safe return. It has happened over and over again. It has happened since the disaster at Desert ONE and it will happen again in the future. *Beirut, nineteen eighty-three! Malta, nineteen eighty-five!* The *Achille Lauro, nineteen eighty-five!* Terrorism is the new face of warfare and we must be prepared to fight it. I know you are prepared for this new challenge to freedom. During exercise *Freedom Express* we are going to prove it to our political leaders in Washington," he said loudly.

He was thinking, *Dear God, what would I order them to do if the enemy had a nuclear weapon?*

"We have our critics. The faultfinders will always have something to say from the comfort of their easy chairs. If we are going to be damned because we dare to attempt the rescue of innocent people who are threatened with torture and death, then let it be so, because we know in our hearts that we have done everything humanly possible to mitigate the loss of innocent lives. Sally forth with confidence gentlemen, defiant, with honor and dignity, knowing that you are the best in the world. Good hunting and remember, think safety."

Carlson walked to a waiting sedan to the applause and cheers of his men. His next stop was controller headquarters, then on to the *Independence* to watch the assault with a group of dignitaries.

When the applause died away the men began talking quietly amongst themselves.

"The General sure do talk pretty, don't he?" said Petty Officer Johnson, Charlie Platoon's gunners mate.

His nickname was Three Fingers. He'd lost two making field expedient explosives.

Dan Carroll leaned back on one elbow. "He gets paid for talkin' pretty. We get paid to kick ass. *And I like my job.*"

"I sure hope this isn't another cluster fuck," Shifty King added.

Shifty's primary job was taking care of the platoon's scuba gear. He was a little more relaxed than usual because the operation they were about to conduct didn't require locking out of a submarine underwater with scuba. The platoon was geared for a surface launch. "That op up in Monterey was as screwed up as a whore's nightmare," he continued in his southern drawl.

Lee Sanz, Mike Thomas, and Tom Blaze listened to the men jabber about nothing, while thinking about the mission ahead.

"Master Chief, what went wrong up in Monterey?" Carroll asked.

"Communications," Blaze replied, reluctant to get into a conversation.

"We've heard that excuse, Master Chief," Shifty King pleaded. "What exactly does it mean?"

"It means someone changed the plan at the last minute and not all the players got the word," Blaze explained. "It's that simple."

"Shit. That's exactly what happened down in Grenada and Panama," Three Fingers cursed. "Got some pretty damned good men kilt to. Why would he do that?"

"Who?" Carroll asked.

"Colonel Ardison," Three Fingers answered. "He knows what happens when you go changin' things at the last minute."

"He was told to do it," Lieutenant Junior Grade Thomas said.

"By who?" they all asked.

"Whoever the political guy was who was playing the part of the President," Blaze answered. That instills one hell of a lot of confidence in me knowing some politico asshole is in charge of my life," Johnson added, facetiously.

"If you want my opinion, that's what happens every time, even on all them good ops the General was talkin' about," Johnson said.

"Good ops? You call Malta and the *Achille Lauro* good ops? An opinion is like an asshole, asshole," Shifty

King jeered. "Everybody's got one and there ain't nobody wants yours, Four Fingers minus one."

"Screw you," Johnson sassed.

"You can't even mix a little black powder without blowing yourself up," King snickered.

"It wasn't black powder, shit for brains," Johnson argued.

"There's always a politician in charge of military ops," Carroll argued.

"Not if somethin' goes wrong," Johnson joked. "Then it's the General's fault."

"That's true," Shorty Moore agreed.

"You know what's unfuckin' believable?" Carroll asked. He answered his own question. "That we ever get so many armed men, *any* place, *any* time, without shootin' the shit out of ourselves or snaggin' a wire."

Special Operations Forces often infiltrated by means of helicopters flying at low level. One small mistake in route planning or navigation could result in an aircraft flying into an electric power line. Since night vision goggles limited pilot visibility, all hands acted as lookouts. The cry of *Wire!* on a dark night struck terror in the hearts of all commandos and was instantly followed by a yank on the cyclic which was guaranteed to stressed the chopper to its limits.

"Don't go talkin' that kind of trash, Dandy," Fellars objected. His nickname was Ears, because he had huge ears that stuck out from the sides of his head at near right angles. "I've had too many close wires in my time."

"We don't need so many people to kill a few tangos," Shorty Moore said. He was six foot four and built like a fullback. "The more people involved the more chance of a screw up."

"Master Chief?" Shifty King asked.

"Yeah," Blaze growled, letting them know he was

annoyed by the banter.

"Why the hell are we infilling by submarine? It don't make any damn sense to me."

"Cause everyone wants to play in special operations nowadays. Simple as that, Shifty. Besides, it's not such a bad way to go. Good food, good place to sleep and someone to watch out for our butts if things go bad," Blaze answered.

"Well it doesn't make a lot of tactical sense to me," Shifty argued. "Subs are too slow."

Blaze ignored him.

"They're a lot faster than you think," Carroll informed. "I was workin' off a flattop last year during Colonel Blitz and I saw an SSN out run the carrier underwater."

"How do you know that, if it was underwater, shit for brains?" Johnson demanded.

"Cause they tracked it in CIC, Five Fingers minus two. I watched 'em do it. The carrier was doing forty-five knots and the sub walked away from us."

"Underwater?" Shifty asked, incredulously.

"That's what I said, *Drifty*. You hard of hearing?" Carroll growled. In the distance, came the steady beat of rotors. "Listen," he hushed. "Here they come."

The sound slowly built in intensity and a squadron of five choppers appeared in the west. The flight grew in size and the noise from the engines and the rotors rose in volume until it overwhelmed all other sounds. A lone ground crewman walked out on to the tarmac twenty-five meters in front of them, illuminated his signal batons, and began directing the lead pilot to his landing spot. The rest of the aircraft followed in trail formation, two on each side in a staggered V.

Along with the helicopters came a windstorm. The rotors grabbed everything on the tarmac and blew it up

201

into the air. Dust, sand, and debris swirled around the commandos, blinding them, as the helicopters hovered before making their final descent to earth. A scrap of paper caught up in the rotor wash, swirled past Charlie Platoon, clearly showing the pattern of the artificial windstorm. When all of the big HH-53s had landed, the noise abated to the turning of engines at minimum throttle and the wind died off.

Without a word, the first line of grunts moved out to board their assigned helicopter. Sanz and his men, encumbered by the weight of weapons, motors, gasoline, and heavy Zodiac boats, struggled to the trail bird on their right. They loaded their equipment through the ramp at the rear of the bird, and while the flight crew strapped it down, buckled themselves in the troop seats, which lined both sides of the cargo bay. Lee Sanz signaled to the ground crew and to the flight crew when all his men and equipment were on board then strapped himself into the troop seat next to Master Chief Blaze.

Each man carried a Heckler-Koch MP-5 modified with a silencer. A nine-millimeter pistol was strapped to their legs in a hard plastic Safariland holster. They wore black pants, boots, long sleeved shirts, and their hands were blackened with camouflage paint. In their pockets they carried black ski masks to cover their faces. Stun grenades and knifes hung from their belts.

The engine and rotor noise increased, and the helicopters lifted off the ground. They hovered briefly in formation at one hundred feet then slowly pitched forward. The sortie began a slow climb, gaining speed and altitude as they thundered down the runway. They cleared Ford Island at five hundred feet, banked to the left, and circled back toward the ocean.

The flight out to the *USS Enterprise* was less than thirty minutes. Halfway there, Charlie Platoon's helicopter split off and made for the *USS Aspro*, SSN 648 standing off from the carrier fifty miles to the north.

The big helicopter skimmed over the surface of the sea at a hundred knots following a flight plan that took them to a precise coordinate eighty miles from land. Rendezvous at sea, especially at night used to be a near impossible task. But with the advent of the Global Positioning System, GPS, both the helo and the sub navigated to a precise point on the globe. In total darkness the crew of the helicopter located the black bullet shaped vessel bobbing on the open sea and hovered fifty feet above it.

The SEALs tossed out a thick nylon rope and slid down to the after deck of the sub one at a time. Then the flight crew lowered their equipment down by winch. The entire operations took less than ten minutes. Lee Sanz watched as the helo cycloned off, leaving them with the quiet sound of waves washing against the hull of the submarine.

Once on board, the enlisted SEALs operated with precision. With the help of the sub's crew, they quickly stored their equipment. The motors, weapons, and ammunition were lowered into the aft escape trunk and sealed inside the chamber. They stored their fuel bladders in a line locker adjacent to the trunk and tied them down. The Zodiac boats, tightly bundled into long cigar shapes, were loaded through the main hatch, and stored in the passageway forward of engineering. As soon as the gear was properly secured, they mustered on the mess deck to raid the ship's galley.

Sanz, Thomas, Blaze and Carroll joined the captain and senior members of the crew in the officer's wardroom. Only the submarine's tiny kitchen, which served both officers and enlisted men, separated the two spaces. Seated in the wardroom, they could hear the platoon gabbing with the crew. While the SEALs ate everything the cook set before them for MIDRATS, the submariners, enthralled by the SEAL mystic, gathered around them for show and tell.

"Welcome aboard the *Aspro*," the captain greeted, as he barged through the door. He held the rank of commander but on board the *Aspro* it may as well have been God.

"Thank you, Captain Kilian," Sanz replied.

They introduced each other's crew and while they were shaking hands the phone at the head of the table rang.

"Excuse me," Kilian said, picking up the red phone. "Captain here," he answered. "Yes. Thanks. All ahead two thirds, two hundred feet," he ordered, then hung up the phone. "The target vessel is about seventy-five miles west of us," he reported, "on an easterly course. I'll have you to a launch position is less than two hours."

Momentarily the sub shuddered as the screws churned the sea. The vessel took a down angle. The furnishings began to creak as the *Aspro* picked up speed with depth. The angle was uncomfortable for the SEALs. Ignoring the list of the ship the navigator laid a chart on the table and pointed out the course and speed of the *MV Alliance*, the currents, winds and weather. As the *USS Aspro* flew underwater toward the enemy vessel, they discussed launch coordinates, launch procedures, rendezvous signals, and emergency procedures to be used in case the SEALs failed to board and seize the merchant at the appointed time.

Except for Master Chief Blaze, every operator in Charlie Platoon had been against using a submarine for an infiltration platform. Blaze knew the submarine force was in troubled waters. The U.S. Military was under tremendous pressure to cut the budget and that meant the loss of men and machines. Without the Soviets for an archenemy, the SSNs needed operational assignments to maintain their viability and numbers. In the remote Pacific, helicopters were in short supply. Every aircraft capable of conducting special operations was needed for the big show, the assaults on the *Independence* and Hickam Field. The *USS Aspro* made up for the shortage while giving the submarine force a new mission.

In Tom Blaze's crafty mind he saw opportunity. He read General Carlson's signal flags and made up his mind to make it work. Launching from the deck of the *USS Aspro* at night was his kind of operations. It was crafty, cunning, the unexpected, and that was his definition of real special operations. Contrary to popular belief, fast attack submarines had tremendous speed underwater, far exceeding any merchant vessel. Low in profile, they could surface and close a ship to within a few miles and still be invisible to a merchantman's radar. With sea swells on a moonless night for cover, he knew his Zodiac boats would be invisible to man and electronic device. He had left nothing to chance. He had even called in an old favor to ensure the success of the mission.

# Chapter 16

The *Greenpeace* pitched and shuddered in an angry sea shaken bow to stern by a rogue wave. Outside, a rainsquall lashed the side of the ship. Julie rolled onto her back and stared into the darkness. Her mouth was dry and sour. The brandy had worn off at two-thirty and for half an hour she had tossed and turned. Her thoughts were aimless ranging from San Diego to Odessa. Then the image of a blackened corpse flashed through her mind.

*Dr. Robbins doesn't know the Russians are transporting chemical weapons to Johnston Atoll*, she thought. *If he didn't consider dumping as a possible cause of death then neither did the coroner's office.*

She had no idea that Robbins was dead. The news reports she had seen in Hawaii hadn't disclosed the name of the man who had died in the lobby of the Hilton.

After dinner, over several glasses of brandy, Captain Murphy had confided in her. He had made it very clear that he was convinced that the Russians were responsible for the death of the fishermen. Using a chart, he showed her the course the *Stashinsky* had sailed across the Pacific during her last voyage to Johnston Atoll. Over the plot line, he had drawn the *Westwind's* track and the location where the Coast Guard had recovered the bodies. When combined with currents and prevailing winds it appeared that the two vessels had crossed paths in space but not time. The *Westwind* had crossed the *Stashinsky's* track a mere four hours after her passing.

Before resuming his duties on the bridge, Murphy had given her a book on the history of chemical warfare and an article on a Russian assassin named Bogdan Stashinsky. Before retiring she had thumbed through the history book then read the article on the spy. It had tortured her brief alcohol induced sleep.

*I wonder why they named the ship after a defector*, she thought. *It's got to be some sort of bureaucratic double entendre.*

The *Stashinsky* was named after a KGB agent, a Ukrainian born and raised in the village of Borshovity. In his teens, Bogdan Stashinsky had been arrested for riding a train without a ticket and when the police interrogated him, he had snitched on his parents who were members of the Ukrainian nationalist movement. The information was his passport to enlistment in the KGB. At first he served in the *spetzgruppa*, an organization formed to intimidate Ukrainian workers. After his apprenticeship he was sent to Poland where he worked as a conduit to Ukrainian decedents. By 1957 he had proven himself and was given an assassination assignment.

The KGB provided the weapon. A Department 13 officer supplied him with a metal tube about seven inches long and half an inch in diameter, and explained that it contained a glass ampoule filled with prussic acid. When fired, a spring detonated a small charge that crushed the ampoule causing the poison to spray forth as a vapor. At first Stashinsky didn't trust the weapon so he tried it on a dog. When this experiment was successful he decided to kill two people for the KGB. Armed with this special weapon, disguised as a cigar container, he entered the newspaper building of the *Suchasny Ukraina.* Stashinsky climbed the stairs just ahead of his target, Lev Rebet, a Ukrainian intellectual and literary figure that was writing anti-Soviet articles the KGB disliked. At the first floor landing he did an about face and descended the stairs, meeting Rebet coming up. Using a newspaper to cover the weapon, he sprayed the poison directly into the man's face.

Prussic acid is a colorless and odorless poison which, when inhaled as a vapor, causes coronary thrombosis. Death comes in as little as two minutes and leaves no trace to be found at autopsy. Rebet died in the stairwell, not knowing his killer. Stashinsky caught Stefan Bandera fumbling with his keys at his apartment door. The angry fanatical cold war combatant tried to leap out of the way when he saw the canister appear from behind the newspaper, but he too was caught full in the face by the poisonous mist. He died in the hallway outside his apartment.

Under the specific direction of the Presidium of the Supreme Soviet, Stashinsky was decorated with the *Order of the Red Banner* for his extraordinary services to the KGB. But living in austere Moscow was not to the liking of his German wife whom he had married while on assignment in East Germany. When they found electronic bugging devices in their Moscow apartment, she convinced him to defect to West Germany. There he told all. The day after his defection, Soviet forces began erecting the Berlin Wall. They claimed that West German agents had tortured Stashinsky into making statements that were untrue. The Soviets never admitted culpability for the death of the two Ukrainian decedents.

Julie flipped on her reading light and swung her tan legs over the side of the small bed, still thinking about Stashinsky and the ship named after him.

"Where are you, you black assassin?" she mumbled, wondering if she would have her first encounter with the *Bogdan Stashinsky* with the morning light.

She ambled across the deck to the bathroom and turned on the shower.

The smell of coffee brewing led her to the galley. The cook was up by three and bacon was sizzling on the grill by half past the hour. The odors roused the ship slowly to life. Julie drew herself a strong cup of coffee and joined Forbes for breakfast.

"Sleep well?" he asked, as she sat down with a tray filled with scrambled eggs, sausage, and toast.

"A few winks, thanks to the Captain's brandy," she replied, with a yawn. "How about you?" she asked, making small talk.

"Not much. Sleeping in a hallway is not my idea of a pleasure cruise," Forbes grumbled.

He took a sip of his coffee and for a while they ate in silence. It was Forbes who broke the morning calm.

"Last night after you went to bed, I spent some time on the bridge," he said.

"So you're the reason we ran aground last night, huh?" Julie kidded.

Forbes ignored her levity. "I had a long chat with Murphy," he said.

"Oh. What did he have to say?"

"He likes you. He said that you're a real smart bird."

"I suppose that's a compliment?" Julie said, facetiously.

"You bet." He eyed her and whispered, "They have spies in Odessa and one on Johnston Atoll."

Julie met his serious expression. "Oh," she whispered. "What else did he tell you?"

"You are right about JACADS. It is squeaky clean. The inside guy has been providing them with pictures of the whole enchilada, the munitions they're burning, aircraft on the runway, ships that dock, the whole damn thing. Nothing on that island caused the death of those fishermen."

"Gordy, I believe the Russians are dumping something, a poison Western science is unfamiliar with," Julie conceded.

"According to the spies in Odessa, some of the shipments were loaded at night under heavy security."

"The black weapons," Julie suggested. "The stuff that doesn't officially exist."

"Exactly. Murphy thinks they're going to do a big dump this time. They've had the *Stashinsky* under constant surveillance for months." He gave her a hard look. "I don't want to alarm you but a few days ago the *Sirius* recovered a body from the *Stashinsky's* wake. They are not sure but they think it is one of their guys from Odessa."

"Oh?" Julie exclaimed with a hint of fear in her eyes.

"The corpse had no fingers and the skull was bashed in.

"My God," Julie gasped. She pondered the thought. "That adds a new dimension if the body can be positively identified. Gordon, I've been thinking about this all night," she said, in a businesslike manner. "I believe the best way to approach this film is to work from the general to the specific, a sort of historical expose followed by a *what-if*. We'll start with the killing ground of Ypres with soft music that builds in intensity, something like Mussorgsky's *Pictures at an Exhibition*. The voice-over will talk about the early history of poison weapons. Then we'll shatter the calm with flashes of those poor fishermen and brief images of the boat, the bodies, the newspaper articles, and the *Stashinsky* underway across the Pacific. You up for a trip to Belgium?"

"You bet, if you're paying the freight," Forbes grinned.

"We'll dredge up some archival footage of doughboys fighting in World War I, then cut in a few shots showing mustard and phosgene victims interspersed with the peaceful rolling green hills of Ypres where all that human tragedy took place. Next we'll cut to the talking heads, men who know what went on inside I.G. Farben and the other big companies that produced chemical weapons. We'll chase the historical angle from blister agents, to nerve agents, to binary weapons, and on to modern day bio-engineering."

"Sounds like a plan," Forbes agreed.

"Then, using aerial shots of the Rocky Mountain Arsenal, Muscle Shoals, Pine Bluff, and other U.S. depots, we'll graphically show the tonnage of toxins that we have produced since mankind began his ghoulish experiment with poison weapons. Then we'll ask the big unanswered question, what's happening to these cruelest of weapons, the poor man's atomic bomb? An expert answers. We're destroying them. We're burning them. We're abiding by international agreement. Enter JACADS footage, a pristine facility operating at max capacity to rid the world of these leaking coffins of death. Now the next big question, what are the Russians, the Brits, the French, and others doing with their aging weapons? An expert answers. We don't really know what's going on inside the former Soviet Union."

"Flash," Forbes added. "An image of the *Stashinsky* being loaded in Odessa."

"Exactly."

"I think I can enhance a snippet of the Greenpeace video," Forbes informed.

"Great. We can add it to what we get. Would you believe the *Stashinsky* is named after a KGB assassin who killed his victims with a chemical weapon?"

Forbes shook his head. "Nah," he exclaimed incredulously. "That would take too much brass."

"The Russians have never been known for subtlety. Believe it. Stashinsky received a medal and a ship named after him for murdering his fellow countrymen."

Forbes eyed her with a frown.

Julie continued. "Last week I read an article about a top secret CIA project code named M. K. Naomi. It produced chemical and biological poisons made from snake venom, plant extracts, frogs and such. We'll use a talking head to flesh out project Naomi then ask the question, what were the Russians doing while we produced poison weapons? You see what I'm getting at?"

"Yeah. A parallel," Forbes replied.

"Enter Dr. Robbins. We'll get him to talk about his book, project Naomi, and an East German military manual entitled, *Chemical Agents and Defense Against Chemical Agents*. It has a list of similar sabotage poisons developed by the Soviets. Off and on, we'll show the *Stashinsky* relentlessly sailing eastward toward Johnston Atoll. With a little luck we'll film her dumping at sea."

"The smoking gun," Forbes said.

"Yeah. I heard what you said to Fred," Julie said in an accusatory voice.

"What? What?" Forbes asked, perplexed by the tone of her statement.

"Remember, it doesn't matter what it is, a vial of botulin, garbage, anything will do? I can't do it, Gordy. I just can't. We've got to catch them in the act, and we have to be able to identify what they're throwing overboard or I can't use it," she said, seriously.

"You are such a straight arrow, you know that? You expect me to film an illegal dumping operation at night and be able to identify exactly what they're throwing

212

overboard?" Forbes asked, incredulously.

"Yes. Integrity calls," Julie insisted, with a gravely serious expression on her face.

Forbes grinned. "You got the right guy. The best."

"And I know it." Julie smiled.

"Have I told you about my new toy?" Forbes asked, with a gleam in his eyes.

"No."

"Well, it's all digital, sees in the dark, and it has a focal length that would cause an astronomer to have an orgasm." He grinned devilishly.

"This I've got to see."

"Eat your grub, *mona mi,* and I'll show you some real magic."

After breakfast they walked out on deck carrying Forbes's expensive digital camera. The rain had stopped and the ship was rolling back and forth in wallowing seas. It was still dark but the sky in the east was beginning to turn slightly yellow. Forbes leaned up against the railing and hoisted the camera to his shoulder. He adjusted it to near zero light conditions and said, "Here. Have a look."

Julie put her eye up to the rubber cup shrouding the lens. "Wow," she exclaimed. "This is amazing."

The camera turned night to day. Back on the stern of the ship she could clearly see men preparing the helicopter for takeoff.

"You ain't seen nothin' yet. Keep the image centered on the pilot's face," he said.

Inside the bubbled cockpit of the helicopter the pilot was busy checking out his machine. Forbes pushed a button and the camera zoomed in until the man's face disappeared. She found herself looking at the pupil of the man's eye, then his nose, and finally the stubble on his chin.

"This is truly amazing," Julie raved.

"It gets better than that. Whirly's too close for max zoom. When we get airborne I'll show you what she'll do."

Forbes took the camera and sighted in on the flight deck.

"We'd better get going. It's almost time for liftoff," he said.

They walked aft along the port side of the ship to the flight deck and reported to the crew chief. He assigned a crewman to assist them with their life jackets while he briefed them on emergency ditching procedures. The aircraft was rigged with pontoons so it could land on the water. But it wasn't designed to float in heavy swells. After the briefing, Julie was first to climb into the tiny cockpit. It was too small for three people so the crew had removed the passenger side door to make room for Forbes and his camera.

Julie took the pilot to be a U.S. Marine right off the *Kitty Hawk* until he spoke with an Australian accent. Speaking loudly over the sound of engine noise, he welcomed them both aboard. He put on his headset and explained the communication systems to Julie.

"If you want to talk, Ms. Jennings, push this button," he said, pointing to a switch on the cord leading up to her headset.

Julie pushed the button and said, "Please call me Julie."

"Certainly. My name is William Overton," he said. "But my friends all call me Whirly. Goes with the job."

It was first light by the time Whirly revved up the engine and turned the rotors. Forbes adjusted the harness to act as a safety belt and put one foot down on the pontoon. Standing with one leg on the float, he leaned further out, testing the equipment.

"Are you ready, Gordo?" Overton asked.

"Yeah," Forbes grunted, busy with his equipment.

Overton flipped a switch and spoke into his radio mike. "Greenpeace, Greenpeace, this is Little Bird. Ready for launch," he reported.

"PERGRA. Have a good flight Little Bird," Captain Murphy answered from the ship's bridge.

The noise of the turbine increased and the chopper rose straight up off the deck to a height of a hundred feet before Overton nosed her forward and picked up speed. Julie's stomach turned with anxiety. A few minutes into the flight she settled down and began to breathe easy.

"What's the plan, Whirly?" Forbes asked, wind blowing the hair on the sides of his otherwise bald head.

"We're going to run up along the Malaysian coast to Langkawi Island, then hang a left and fly across the straits. When we can see land clearly we'll double back down the Sumatra side and meet the ship for a refuel. If we haven't found her by then we'll head out the other direction."

"Can they get by us?" Julie asked.

"No, not even in this weather," Overton bragged. "We can almost see across the straits. Captain Murphy's got the *Sirius* hove to in the mouth of the strait, Indian Ocean side, just in case they try to out fox us by sailing around Java."

Overton turned his attention to the ships down below. With binoculars he studied each vessel. A half-hour into the flight, he pushed his mike button and said, "Julie,

Gordon and I have made a few flights together. He ever talk about it?"

"No," Julie replied.

"I can feel a whale of a story coming on," Forbes grumbled. "Julie, Whirly stretches the truth a bit for dramatic effect."

Overton chuckled. "Not one bit, Julie. And I've got the best part on film to prove it."

"Ahh," Forbes complained.

"It happened down near the Antarctic," Whirly said, sounding like a man reading a children's book out loud.

"Here we go again," Forbes protested.

Julie smiled at Whirly, anxious to hear the tale. The wind whirling inside the cockpit was invigorating and the motion of the helicopter through the sky was exciting.

"You see, we were shadowing this Japanese whaler that we suspected was taking endangered animals. So we sneaked up on her from behind an iceberg, popped up to five hundred feet, and caught the blokes dead to rights draggin' in a sperm. Gordo got so excited he climbed out on the pontoon to film these dingoes and well, as you might guess it was cold and slippery. He keeps yelling for me to get closer, waving his hand like a referee in a rugby match. So I circled the ship at a hundred feet letting him shoot her from every angle. Still he keeps yelling *closer, closer*. Hell, I damn near rested a pontoon on the whale's rail. The long and the short of the story is, Gordo fell off."

Overton chuckled at the thought.

"Jeez, Gordon. What happened?" Julie asked.

"I got the shot that convicted the bastards in a Japanese court. That's what happened," Forbes answered.

"Sure, Gordo, sure. Now for the rest of the story. You see, the safety belt catches him but old Gordy here

216

was hanging upside down beneath this bird like a rag doll. He couldn't climb back up without letting go of his camera and you know he wasn't about to do that."

"Jeez," Julie exclaimed, face alight. "What did you do?" she asked.

"He scared the shit out of me," Forbes griped. "He took off like a bat out of hell with me hanging upside down."

"And?" Julie pressed.

"He landed on the iceberg and I climbed back in. No big deal," Forbes explained.

"Yeah. He climbed back in alright, with eyes as big saucers, and pants wet from you know what," Overton chuckled. "His hands were shaking so badly I had to buckle up his seat beat."

"Now you've stretched the truth too far, Whirly, right in front of my boss. I wasn't shaking cause I was scared, Julie. I was freezing my ass off," Forbes argued.

"Yeah, yeah, yeah. We got us a hangin' danglin' cameraman, Julie. The real deal. But he tells me that you're the real pro. Is that right?" Overton asked.

"I like to think of myself as a professional," Julie answered, in a confident tone. "But the proof is in the product and the product takes team work, and right now, without you, we'd be back on the *Greenpeace* drinking coffee."

"Well thank you for including me in your team, Julie. Will I get to see my name in the credits?" he asked.

"You see what kind of people we're dealing with, Julie," Forbes said. "The next thing you know, he'll be sending us a bill for five hundred bucks an hour, and a request for royalties."

Overton chuckled. For several minutes he and Forbes chatted about old times. Julie eventually tuned them out and took in the experience. They were flying north at about a thousand feet paralleling the coast of Malaysia. Gray squalls and yellow sunlight blotched the sea below from horizon to horizon. To the east in the distance she could just make out a white line of sand chasing the shoreline, broken by harbors, rivers, and mangroves. Off to the left, the traffic in the straits was heavy in both directions. From time to time Overton used his binoculars to get a better look at a merchant ship that had the general profile of the *Stashinsky*. Several times he changed course to avoid low-lying clouds drenching the sea with heavy rains.

"This is sure easier than chasing whalers," Forbes said. "At least it's not ten degrees below zero."

"You bet. I love this kind of flying," Overton replied. "This is better than sex."

"There you go again stretching the truth, my man," Forbes corrected.

Gurnov was in complete control of the *Stashinsky* when Baranov sailed up in a sleek Malay boogie. He bellowed up at Gurnov in a booming voice that carried across the waves.

"*Privet!*"-- Greetings.

His gold tooth flashed like a glint of gold off an onion dome church roof in Moscow. "Come aboard," Gurnov yelled, from the deck above.

Malay sailors secured the wooden vessel to the accommodation ladder rigged down the side of the ship. Baranov stepped over, AK in hand, and walked cautiously up the steps, eyes scanning the deck above like radar. They had spoken several times on the radio but Baranov was a cautious man, always wary of a trap. Senses alive, he sniffed the air. The *Stashinsky* gave off a peculiar odor and in the dim light her black hull reminded him of a coffin.

When he was close enough to see Gurnov's face at the top of the gangway, he asked, "Any problems?"

Gurnov held up a radio fire device so Baranov could see it.

"No. As long as I have this the crew will do exactly what I tell them to do."

"It won't work inside the ship, *Zakuski*," Baranov stated matter of factly.

*Zakuski* was the Russian term for assorted platters of sliced salami and fish, chopped vegetables, and globs of caviar smothering halves of boiled eggs. It was a term of endearment owing from Gurnov's love of gorging himself at cocktail parties.

"I know that. And you know that. But they don't," Gurnov grinned, maniacally.

"*Krasivy obshchestvennaya rabota, Alex* - Beautiful social work, Alex," Baranov smiled, flashing his gold tooth.

"You are late," the nervous major growled.

Baranov walked up and they gave each other a traditional bear hug with slaps on the back.

"Danger comes in large measure from inside one's own head, old chum," the spetznaz warrior said. His voice had a deep resonance.

"The environmentalists have been following me and they have a helicopter," Gurnov explained. "I wanted to load the explosive under the cover of darkness and sneak by them in a squall."

"You have the weapons General Chung wants?" Baranov asked.

"Yes, of course, and a few special ones for us. Your woman had better not fuck with that box or Shan territory will be uninhabited when we get there," he warned.

Gurnov gestured at a stack of wooden boxes staged near the accommodation ladder. One of the crates was addressed to Baranov and Mae Lee. It contained black weapons.

"She knows what to do," Baranov snarled. "Let's make the exchange and be gone, you Cossack bastard. We have money to extort from candy-assed Americans," Baranov bellowed.

Gurnov held up his hand. "First, as I promised, you son of a drunken whore." He reached in his bag, took out his bottle of vodka, and tossed it to the big man.

"Ha, ha," Baranov chucked. "I too am a man of my word."

"*Ahoy! Down below. Bring me my bottle!*" he yelled.

One of the Shan disappeared into the captain's cabin. When he reappeared he was holding a bottle of Mekong Whiskey. Lee Chung took it from his goon and climbed the accommodation ladder, weapon in hand. When he reached the Russians, he handed the bottle to Baranov and eyed Gurnov suspiciously.

"It is good to see you again, Lee Chung," Gurnov said.

As a gift, Gurnov extended Captain Dmitriyev's pistol. Chung grinned and accepted the gift. "Alex, my friend, Lee Chung will bless this barter and we will be on our way."

After toasts straight from the bottles, Chung inspected the chemical weapons and agreed to the exchange. He walked to the side of the ship and shouted down at his men. Like deck coolies they scrambled to unload the boogie. They opened the hatch and began hauling out wooden crates like army ants on patrol. When several of the boxes were stacked on the deck, Malay sailors shouldered them, and carried them up the accommodation ladder.

Nearing his turning point Overton eased the cyclic forward, banked to the right, and dropped three hundred feet in altitude to avoid a squall line. On the other side of the clouds he spotted a ship anchored in the lee of Langkawi Island. Focusing his binoculars he eyed the dark form in the early morning light.

"Bingo," he yelled, and pointed at the *Stashinsky*.

"We've found her?" Forbes asked, squinting his eyes to see the ship.

"She's not underway. She's anchored," Overton exclaimed.

Forbes began to ready his camera like an excited teenager. Julie strained her eyes to see then borrowed Overton's binoculars.

The *Stashinsky* looked like a lot of the freighters she had seen plying the straits. It had a bull nose, a clear foredeck and an after superstructure that rose up several decks to the pilothouse at the stern. Tied up alongside, Julie could just make out a native sailing vessel.

"*Greenpeace, Greenpeace*, this is Little Bird, Little Bird, over," Overton called, trying to raise Captain Murphy on the radio.

He repeated the call several times as they closed the distance to the *Stashinsky*.

"Damn. It must be the weather," he complained, giving up.

Overton buzzed by the Russian ship at five hundred feet then doubled back. When he closed her the second time he hovered at a hundred feet just off her starboard bow. Forbes, already out on the pontoon, focused his camera and zoomed in. What he saw in his lens baffled him. Native coolies were carrying boxes up and down an accommodation ladder. He panned the camera to the deck of the boogie and zoomed in for a tight shot.

"*We've got 'em, Julie!*" he yelled. "*They're off loading*

*weapon! Closer, Whirly! Closer!"*

Waving his hand like a director on a motion picture set, he directed Overton to fly lower and closer. He shot the deck of ship, the deck of the boogie, and the coolies running up and down the accommodation ladder carrying boxes in both directions. Then he signaled for Overton to turn so he could shoot Julie inside the cockpit with the ship in the background through the bubble canopy of the helicopter.

*"Say something profound, Julie!"* he shouted. *"Anything! Just move your lips. We'll fit the words later."*

"This is Julie Jennings reporting from Southeast Asia. We are in the Straits of Malacca, just off the coast of Malaysia in a helicopter provided by the environmental organization, Greenpeace. Out there," she said, glancing and pointing at the vessel, then looking back into the camera, "is the Russian freighter the *Bogdan Stashinsky*. We believe she is transporting aging chemical weapons to an American incinerator plant located on Johnston Atoll near Hawaii. Yesterday the ship inexplicably changed course and is now off loading what appears to be boxes containing chemical weapons."

*"Beautiful!"* Forbes yelled from the pontoon. *"Just beautiful. Now closer, Whirly. Closer!"*

As Forbes filmed the ship, Overton hovered about, moving around to different angles and in and out so closely his pontoons nearly touched the railing of the freighter. Through his lens, Gordon saw a big man with an AK assault rifle standing on deck. They all saw him shoulder the weapon. Forbes hung on tight as Whirly took evasive action. But it was too late. Baranov emptied a thirty round magazine into the engine and transmission of the helicopter. He knew exactly where to aim to bring down the fragile bird.

The engine was the first to go with a loud bang. Overton was pulling back on the cyclic and increasing throttle when it exploded. Debris shot out in all directions, whirling through the air like buzz saws. Out of instinct he pushed the cyclic forward and crash landed on the deck of the *Stashinsky* a mere twenty feet below. The blades struck the ship's rigging and shattered like matchsticks, sending a shower of missiles careening off the weather decks. A large section slammed into a group of coolies cutting the men in half. The helicopter pitched on its side and tore itself apart.

The force of the impact was so great it knocked Julie unconscious and killed Overton who was on the bottom side of the crash. Cushioned by Julie and the pilot, Forbes, camera still in hand, staggered out of the shattered cockpit. He pulled Julie out and rushed back for Overton. He was pulling Whirly's lifeless body clear of the wreckage when Baranov planted a front thrusting kick into his back. The force of the blow sent him to the deck.

Baranov and Chung began shouting orders in pigeon English, Shan, and Malaysian. Down below the coolies shoved the boogie away from the side of the ship. When the boat was clear a horde of men heaved the helicopter to the railing. Pushing and shoving and prying with everything at hand they bulldozed the small aircraft over the side. It landed in the water with a *swoosh* and refused to go down. Seeing the machine floating upside down from a pontoon that hadn't ruptured, Baranov pumped a thirty round magazine into it, sending the helo to a watery grave. Then he yelled at the men on the boogie to bring the boat back alongside.

While Baranov directed the exchange of cargo, Gurnov, with the aid of Lieutenant Zhukov, plotted a course and prepared the ship to get underway. Three hours later they were running with merchants heading south through the Straits of Malacca. Later that night, while Captain Murphy searched for his missing helicopter, the *Stashinsky* slipped by him at full speed in the company of several oil tankers.

# Chapter
# 17

The *USS Aspro* was steaming along at five knots twenty-five miles ahead of the *Alliance*, when Captain Kilian ordered, "Up periscope." He grasped the control handles as the scope rose from below decks, and flipped them down. Peering at the world above, he turned in a full circle, checking the surface of the sea for traffic. There was none. The submarine's sensors had already fixed the location of all the ships in his general vicinity and the quartermaster had plotted them on his chart, confirming the positions provided by JSOC satellite imagery. Submerged at sixty feet, the *Aspro* was invisible to the world above.

Kilian listened as his radioman made contact with the *Tactical Operations Center* on Ford Island. With his masts up out of the water coordination was easy. Steaming at two hundred feet, command, control, and communications took on new dimensions for JSOC. This was the first exercise the submarine community had conducted with the Special Operations Command and Kilian was unaccustomed to such high level attention. The Pentagon, the FBI, and even the CIA were actively involved. Individuals in Washington, D.C. were playing the part of the National Command Authority. Someone in the White House was playing the part of the President of the United States.

"Delta Tango Oscar, Delta Tango Oscar, this is Delta Tango Charlie, Delta Tango Charlie, over?" the sub's radioman queried.

Delta Tango Oscar was JSOC's call sign. The signal bounced off a satellite in orbit twenty-two thousand miles up in space and back down to Ford Island a mere eighty miles away. Satellite communications provided reliable, secure, communications in all weather conditions. Every time the sub made radio contact a satellite down link provided them with the latest weather and battlefield intelligence, including satellite imagery of the *Alliance*.

At Ford Island, the TOC was buzzing like a beehive, directing airplanes, helicopters, ships, and a submarine, while keeping the chain of command informed all the way up to the White House. Terrorists on board the *Alliance* had given the President an ultimatum: Release ten of their comrades held in prisons or they would begin killing hostages in two hours. Following the ultimatum, a surveillance aircraft circling the Hawaiian Islands had intercepted a signal from the *Alliance* to the *Independence*, instructing them to kill ten hostages in two hours. The SIGINT intelligence was immediately sent to CINCPAC, the Pentagon, and the NCA. H-hour was fast approaching. Anticipating an order to take the targets by force, Colonel Ardison maneuvered his units into assault positions.

"Delta Tango Charlie, this is Delta Tango Oscar, roger over?" the radioman on Ford Island replied.

"Delta Tango Oscar, be advised we are at L.P.," the submarine reported.

The fact that the sub was in a launch position eased Ardison's mind. While the U-boat was underwater steaming they had been out of radio contact.

"Roger, Delta Tango Charlie. Good copy. Delta Tango Oscar out," the JSOC operator replied.

Ardison nodded at his radio operator signaling him that he understood the transmission clearly. The soldier made an entry in his log and continued his vigil.

L.P. was short talk for launch point for SEAL Team FIVE, Charlie Platoon. It was a shifting position determined from navigation fixes on the *Alliance* provided by an E-2 Hawkeye aircraft circling aloft. The *Alliance* was steaming at six knots between Lanai and Oahu, randomly changing course from time to time. Aloft with the tracker, F-14 interceptors maintained a constant protective envelope around the battle forces. CAP wasn't needed but was exercised.

"Rangers to final assault positions," Ardison ordered. "Turn up the helos."

An army lieutenant colonel and a navy commander rogered the orders and saw them through to completion, tracking every movement on a control board. In Fort Campbell, Kentucky, Ranger units sprung into action creeping up to their final assault positions surrounding the airfield. It was in the middle of nowhere and thousands of miles away from Oahu, but it constructively played the part without the cost of moving a Ranger battalion all the way to the Hawaiian Islands. On the carrier, ship's crew began preparations to launch helicopters that would ferry the DELTA force to the Hickam Field and SEAL Team SIX to the *Independence* moored in the bay at Pearl Harbor.

The assault force was divided into three units; Red, White, and Blue. Ardison's job was to hit all three targets at the same time. Task Force Red, responsible for the tower at Hickam, constructively played as Honolulu International, consisted of two 500MD helicopters, three Blackhawks, one HH-53, and thirty assault troops. Task Forces White, responsible for seizing the *SS Independence*, comprised two 500MD helicopters, three Blackhawks, two HH-53s, two SOC boats, and fifty assault troops. Task Force Blue, the *USS Aspro* and SEAL Team FIVE Platoon Charlie, was tasked with boarding and seizing control of the *Alliance*. The plan included radio jamming to sever the communications links amongst the terrorists.

Charlie Platoon's L.P. had changed three times in the last two hours as the *Alliance* changed course to rattle the battle force. Each time, pumped up on coffee and adrenaline, Ardison had adjusted the assault plan. The *sine qua non* for success in special operations was the element of surprise, an element that was almost impossible to achieve given the circumstances. Tactically, the rescue plan made extensive use of maneuver to bring several types of forces to bear in the objective areas from several different points of origin. Even destroyers were employed to shadow and pressure the terrorists on the *Alliance* into specific sea-lanes. Timing the approach of two separate flights of helicopters and two fleets of small boats to three different targets was a complicated task, made more difficult by the fact that the *Alliance* was underway. Ardison drew himself another cup of coffee and paced the floor, listening to the radio chatter from five different sources. He stopped and looked at his map board, mentally measuring the distance from the *Aspro* to the *Alliance*.

"Launch SEAL Team FIVE," he ordered.

"Delta Tango Charlie, Delta Tango Charlie, this is Delta Tango Oscar, over?" his radioman queried.

The sound of man's voice echoed through the attack center on the submarine eighty miles to the south.

"This is Delta Tango Charlie, roger over," the submarine answered.

"Delta Tango Charlie, launch Task Force Blue."

"Good copy. I repeat. Launch Task Force Blue. Delta Tango Charlie, out," the sub's radioman acknowledged.

The attack center was dark and crowded with men monitoring and controlling every vital function of the war machine. The orange-red glow of banks of instrument lights illuminated the cramped space. A dozen men sat in the dark flying the multimillion-dollar marvel just below the surface making way at five knots.

Kilian looked at Sanz. "Well, Lieutenant. We got you here. Good luck."

"Thanks Captain," Sanz replied.

Lee turned and walked briskly out of the attack center.

The space wasn't separated from the rest of the ship. Located directly beneath the sail it was only ten paces forward of the main ladder leading to the aft weather deck. Charlie Platoon was stacked in the passageway below the main hatch ready to go. Sanz joined Thomas and Blaze standing outside Kilian's stateroom.

"Standby for launch," he said.

Several of the men bellowed, "Hoo Yah," the SEAL battle cry.

They all heard Kilian order, "*Surface!*"

Sanz, Blaze, and Thomas stepped into the Captain's stateroom to watch the CCTV monitor. In the Attack Center, Kilian pointed his periscope aft and flipped on the video system. For several minute the monitors in the galley, the wardroom, and his stateroom, showed nothing but water and dark sky in black and white. Then the sub slowly rose up out of the sea and the aft deck was awash with frothy white crested waves. When the vessel was fully surfaced, Kilian ordered the first lieutenant to open the main hatch.

"XO, you have the CON," he ordered. He couldn't resist going out on deck. As the ship's master, it was his call.

"Aye, aye, sir. XO has the CON."

The quartermaster repeated the order and logged it. Before Kilian could walk the ten paces from the attack center to his stateroom, men were scrambling up the ladder and out on to the wet slippery deck. He joined Sanz, Thomas, and Blaze, and watched the action on deck.

"I wish I could go on this raid," he said, with an envious smile. "Do you guys actually get paid for this?"

He looked at Sanz and winked. Something about special operations excited him. The operations he had conducted in his career were at the opposite end of the spectrum from counter terrorist missions.

"Captain, we've got an extra gun," Blaze suggested, facetiously. "How are you at scaling the side of an underway ship?"

The Master Chief's face and hands were blackened. His eyes bore through his mask with fierceness.

"Oh no, Master Chief, I'll stick with the wishin' and leave the shootin' to you guys," Kilian replied.

Out in the passageway the men were struggling to push and pull a heavy Zodiac boat up the ladder.

"*Goddammit Three Fingers, put some ass in to it!*" Carroll shouted, his voice carrying through the stateroom's open door. Blaze peeked out.

"*I'm pushin'! I'm pushin! It's hung up over here,*" Johnson complained.

Shorty Moore put his linebacker shoulder on the bottom of the boat and gave it a mighty shove. His huge frame and powerful legs pushed the boat up the ladder three feet. The Zodiac was rolled into the shape of cigar just tight enough to fit through a hatch that was designed large enough to load torpedoes down into the sub. Up on deck, Shifty King, Ears Fellars, and Monty Montgomery were heaving on nylon ropes. With Shorty's added strength, it slid through the hatch like a mother seal giving birth to a pup.

Ears, Shifty, and Monty, pulled it out on deck and drug it out of the way for the second boat. Like a drill team they reached back down the hatch for the lines attached to the second boat. When both inflatables were on deck, the SEALs and the sub's crew worked like a machine. They retrieved the motors, weapons, and ammunition from the escape trunk, and the fuel bladders from the external line locker. Using ship's air from a hose fed out from the escape trunk, they inflated the boats and installed the floorboards and motors. When the inflatables were seaworthy, they eased them over the side, holding them fast by the bowlines. Two at a time the commandos climbed down the slippery curve of sub's hull to the bobbing Zodiacs, using lines held fast by the deck crew.

When Sanz was seated in his Z-bird, he looked back at Kilian standing on the deck of his submarine.

He gave him a salute and said, "We'll be back for dinner, Captain."

"Steak and baked potato. Don't be late," he joked.

Submariners prided themselves on feeding well.

In less than seven minutes from the time the hatch opened the Z-birds were underway. Dry deck launch operations were routinely accomplished in less than fifteen minutes from the time the ship surfaced to the time she slipped back beneath the waves. Much depended upon the proficiency of the sub's crew. Kilian's men were well trained. The *Aspro* slipped beneath the surface in less than fourteen minutes.

"Com check," Sanz ordered, as they motored slowly into the inky blackness of the Pacific.

As 'Ketchup' Ketchem, the platoon's radioman, established a satellite link with JSOC, Sanz called Thomas on his inner squad radio.

Two, this is One. You copy," he whispered.

There was a hiccup of static in his ear, then, "I copy. Read you Lima Charlie. How you, me, over?" Thomas queried. His boat was lying off ten yards.

"Read you same, out," Sanz answered.

"Ketchup?"

"Yes, sir?'

"We got com?" Sanz asked, referring to a SATCOM link with the TOC.

"Yes, sir. Five by."

"Two this is One, you got com?" Sanz asked.

Thomas answered in a hushed voice. "Roger."

The throat mike around his neck picked up his voice even in a whisper and transferred it to the earpiece in Sanz's right ear.

"I copy. Waypoint one." Sanz looked at his GPS. "I read course one one five degrees."

"Roger that," Thomas replied. "Read same. Out."

The boats slowly motored toward their first waypoint guided by the GPS. The *Alliance* was headed directly at them and they were on a constant bearing and a decreasing range.

Back on board the *Aspro*, Captain Kilian watched them through his periscope. The tiny rubber boats rose up out of the sea and disappeared as they crossed wave crests and plunged into troughs. He was surprised when he lost sight of them at one mile. Even his sensitive sonar array lost track of their engine noise at 1500 yards.

*The SEALs are a silent option*, he thought.

When Sanz reached his first waypoint he reported his progress to the TOC.

"Delta Tango Oscar, Delta Tango Oscar, this is Delta

Charlie Five, Delta Charlie Five. Waypoint one, over?" Ketchup whispered into the receiver.

"Roger Charlie Five. Proceed to waypoint two," the radio operator at the TOC ordered.

With Charlie Platoon in position, and gambling that the President would authorize an assault, Colonel Ardison ordered the carrier to launch helicopters. While Charlie Platoon silently motored along toward their second waypoint, activity on board the carrier grew frenetic. Men scrambled about the deck loading in reverse order. Task Force 160 pilots fired up their aircraft while ship's crew untethered the helicopters from the deck. When all hands were accounted for and strapped in, they thundered off the deck one at a time directed by controllers inside the ship's flight center. The helicopters gathered in two formations like swarms of angry bees and flew off for land, flying just above the surface of the sea.

The smaller 500MDs led the way, carrying sharp shooters strapped into external seats rigged outside the canopy of the aircraft. Skimming just above the surface at one hundred knots, the gunners had an E-ticket ride money couldn't buy. Hovering above their targets like menacing bumblebees, their job was to provide surgical firepower while the larger HH-53 helicopters disgorged their troops. Using thick nylon ropes the assault force could slide down like firemen on a pole and storm the terrorists in a lightning surprise attack using stun grenades and machineguns. As the helicopters flew toward a loiter point, ground troops surrounded the air terminal. They slowly crept up to their final assault positions. At sea a fleet of SOC boats, vectored by an aircraft circling aloft, sped toward the *Independence*.

When the President gave the order to take the targets by force, Ardison breathed a sigh of relief. Recovering, refueling, and repositioning such a complex assault force presented a large number of problems, not the least of which was crew exhaustion. He calculated a *Time on Target* that was within the operational constraints of SEAL Team FIVE and issued the order to attack. TOT was less than fifteen minutes from the time the terrorists had stated that they would begin killing hostages. Watching the three task forces from aloft, an E-2 Hawkeye controlled their approach, changing the speed and the direction of each unit so that they reached their targets at the precise time.

The boats were like big black insects swimming quietly, half in, half out of the water. The men of Charlie Platoon were at low profile, leaning forward on the rubber tubes as they closed the *Alliance*. The seas rolled up beneath them, lifted them briefly then hid them in deep troughs of inky blackness. Just inches above the surface, they were invisible to radar and the sharp eyes of lookouts stationed on the ship.

Sanz looked up at the night sky. He identified Orion's belt floating above the equator. It reminded him of the time he and Julie had spent a night in the Mojave Desert. Far from the lights of the nearest town the heavens above had been ablaze with stars.

*I wonder where she is*, he thought.

Her words came back to him. They were lying on their backs looking up at Orion.

"I can't get over how different the colors are," she had said about the stars in the sky. "What's the red one called?"

"Rigel," he had replied. "No. I stand corrected. Betelgeuse. Reverse the letters. Rigel is blue. Betelgeuse is red," he had said.

"You lay corrected, Webfoot," she had kidded. "You're on your back."

He had guided her finger across the diamond of Orion

naming the stars.

"What's the orange one called?"

"Aldebaran."

"Boy are you up on this stuff," she had said.

"Celestial NAV. Mandatory subject for naval officers."

"Okay. The brightest one?"

"Sirius. And that's Vega. And that's Capella, the goat. See her kids?"

"Yes."

Lee could almost feel her kisses, hot and wet. They had made love all night underneath a desert moon. That was the first time. He hungered for her touch.

On the horizon, a sliver of moon appeared, and ahead of them the *Alliance*, steamed directly at them at six knots.

"Boss, they want us to speed up a knot," Ketchup whispered.

"What?" Sanz asked.

"Tracker just called. They want us to speed up a knot," he repeated.

"Send them a rog," Sanz ordered.

Sanz ordered his coxswain to pick up a knot and passed the word to Thomas in the other boat. There was no exact science to measuring the speed of the rubber boat over the sea. The coxswains modestly increased the revolutions of their engines and waited for the next order.

*Concentrate*, Sanz thought. *I have to concentrate on this mission.*

At a thousand meters, he called Thomas.

"Two this is One," he whispered.

"Go," Thomas replied.

"Peel left," he ordered.

"Roger."

They split up and circled out to form a heart shape in

the ocean, coming in on both beams of the ship. With the *Alliance's* forward motion they closed on the quarters. As the lights on the ship resolved, Sanz realized that anyone on deck would be blind to their approach. A man standing in a light can't see into the darkness that surrounds him.

"Two, this is One, over," he whispered.

"Roger, One," Thomas answered.

"See anything?"

"There are two men on the stern of the ship starboard side."

"Roger, out."

Sanz scanned the stern with his scope but the lights on the ship were too bright. So he used a thermal imager. The wind was blowing in his direction and the heat of the vessel's open hatchways and stacks obscured the image.

"Two, this is One. Where are the men located?" Sanz asked.

"They are moving. One man just went inside. The other is on the stern 01 level just to the starboard of the beam."

"Roger. Can you close the ship undetected?"

"Yes."

"Then let's do it," Sanz ordered.

The two Zodiacs approached on the outside of the wake, coming in on the quarters, so that they were not directly behind the ship where the sailor was standing. With silenced weapons at the ready, they closed the vessel. Sanz whispered distance estimates to Thomas until he made contact with the *Alliance* under the curve of her hull. The bowman attached a large magnet on the side of the ship and with a rope held on to it to control the bow of the Zodiac. The coxswain matched the course and speed of the *Alliance*. Using a magnetic ladder laid up against the side of the ship, Ears Fellars began his climb at precisely H-Hour minus two minutes, just slightly ahead of TOT for the other units.

With the rubber boat bobbing beneath, Ears climbed up and slid silently on deck. Hiding in the shadows, weapon at the ready, he covered his teammates. Sanz was the second man in Alpha to climb on board. When both boarding parties were on deck, Sanz on the port, Thomas on starboard, the coxswains steered away at right angles maintaining a constant bearing and increasing range. They circled around and followed in the wake of the ship looking for strobe lights with their NVGs. If the boarding parties bailed out, the plan called for jumping overboard and lighting off infrared strobe lights to aid in recovery.

Following routes they had planned and rehearsed on a similar vessel, they maneuvered quickly up and down both sides of the ship in four fire teams. Sanz patrolled forward toward a ladder that led up to the bridge on the port side. Carroll and his two men moved aft. On the starboard side, Thomas and three men moved aft and up a deck. Blaze and his two men patrolled forward on the main deck 01 level opposite from Lieutenant Sanz.

As Blaze sneaked by an open hatch, a man in the shadows reached out and pulled him close. He pointed forward and held up three fingers. Then he pointed to starboard and held up two fingers, then portside and held up one. Blaze nodded and the sailor rubbed a splotch of simunition paint on his chest. He took up a comfortable position on the deck and pretended to be a dead man.

Blaze had served in every team in the SEALs and he had friends all over the community. Knowing the deck was stacked against them, he had made a deal. He cheated. Half of the terrorists on board the *Alliance* were from SEAL Team THREE. The sailor had just told him the locations of the army terrorists.

"One this is Three," Blaze whispered, as he eased forward in dark. The motion of the ship, the wind, and the sound of the waves masked his movements.

"Go," Sanz whispered.

"One down, five to go. There are two terrorists just forward of your position on the main deck forward."

"Roger," Sanz replied. He thought, *How the hell does he know that?*

Blaze was on the opposite side of the ship with the foredeck of superstructure between them.

Sanz placed one hand on Fellars' shoulder. He gave the hand signal for enemy, held up two fingers, and pointed forward. Ears nodded acknowledgement and crept cautiously ahead, silenced MP-5 at the ready. They were falling behind schedule. The helos would be buzzing all around the other two targets by now and they knew that the terrorists would alert those on the *Alliance* that they were under attack. To prevent such a disaster, Colonel Ardison had commenced communications jamming operations.

Moving quickly the SEALs struck the vital areas of the ship. As Carroll's element rounded the stern, he shot a smoker with two rounds center chest. The silenced MP-5 spat out a paint round that splattered a splotch of red on the man's camouflage uniform. He was wearing eye protection and a white armband.

"One, this is Four, over."

"Go."

"I just popped one. Four to go," he reported.

"Roger," Sanz acknowledged.

Sanz, Thomas, Blaze, and Carroll were maintaining inner platoon communications. Just forward of the superstructure portside, Sanz and his fire team sneaked up behind two army sergeants dressed in camouflage uniforms with white armbands. They appeared like ninjas out of the dark. Ears startled one of the men by nudging him with the can of his MP-5.

"*Goddammit!*" he gasped. "I nearly pissed my pants, shitbird."

"Shut the fuck up, sarg," Fellars hushed, "or I'll pop you in the dick with one of these," he said, threatening to shoot the sergeant with a simunition round.

The paint rounds were capable of a causing a nasty sting or putting out an eye. The soldiers had taken off their face shields to smoke at the worst possible time. They threw down their cigarettes and ground them out on deck then quickly put on their eye protection.

"Too late, asshole," Fellars growled. "You're dead. You got it?"

"No argument here, buddy. Man, you guys are good. I didn't see shit. Did you?" asked the senior of the two soldiers.

They had been expecting a helicopter assault with plenty of warning to put on their protective gear.

"How'd you guys get aboard the ship," the other soldier asked, excitedly.

"If you don't zip up your lip, sarg, I'm gonna empty this cannon on your crotch."

Fellars dropped the weapon down to waist level. The sergeant dropped both hands down to cover his privates and grinned. "Okay. Okay. We're dead."

"This is One," Sanz whispered into his mic. "Four down. Two more to go."

"This is Two, roger."

"This is Three, roger."

"This is Four, that's a big rog," Carrol **Bogdan** acknowledged.

On the opposite side of the ship from Sanz, Blaze took an army sergeant prisoner.

"One, this is Three. One POW. One to go," he

239

reported.

"Good copy," Sanz replied.

Moving quickly, the four elements barged through the superstructure of the ship like tanks on maneuver prepared to shoot anyone wearing a white armband. As they scrambled about the *Alliance*, four controllers from the JSOC staff fell in behind them, listing every little fault for the debriefing. When the take down was over and Charlie controlled the vessel, the list of errors exceeded two pages of grief and indigestion despite the fact that they had eliminated five of the six terrorists before the controllers even knew they were on board the ship. The men of Charlie platoon steeled themselves for a negative after action review.

# Chapter 18

Julie woke with a throbbing pain inside her skull and a dull ached in her shoulder and arm. She forced her mind to focus on her immediate circumstances. She was on a ship and it was vibrating with speed. With her eyes closed she listened to the creaking of furniture as the vessel rolled from side to side and pitched fore and aft in huge waves. She could hear an almost inaudible *woosh* of water rushing alongside the hull.

The *Stashinsky* was making top speed driving into wind whipped squalls of rain. It shuddered and shook as it plowed into big combers. Julie tried to open her eyes and found that she couldn't, not quite. She could see but her sight was restricted due to swelling around her eyes and nose. Her head was pounding but she was able to move, if barely.

The ship rolled heavily to port into a big swell, then back to starboard. The motion caused her to move in the bunk, shifting her body weight to one side. She winced and gasped in pain.

*A broken rib*, she thought.

Julie opened her eyes and looked around the cabin. It was a nice room, manly and important. Then she became aware of something bulky around her wrist and arm. She felt it with her free hand. A magazine was rolled up around her forearm and tied in place with strips of cloth.

*"Gordon!"* she cried out.

"Ah, you awake from the dead," came a voice from the other side of the stateroom.

Forbes forced himself up from the makeshift pallet he had made on the deck.

"Damn," he grimaced. "Every bone in my body is sore," he said, as he shuffled across the room.

"Whirly?" she asked, as Forbes sat down on the bed beside her.

"He's dead, Julie, at least I think he is," Forbes said, sadly. "How are you?"

"I'm alive. That's about all I can say," she answered.

"You had me worried last night, little lady," Forbes joked, with his best John Wayne imitation. He was trying to make light of their dire situation.

"How long have I been out?" she asked.

"A couple of days," he replied. "The least you have is a concussion. I put a splint on your arm just in case, but I don't think it's broken."

"Cracked ribs," Julie murmured.

"What?"

"I can't breathe deep. I think my ribs are broken," she complained, breathing in shallow gasps. "Where are we?"

"You don't want to know."

"The *Stashinsky?*"

"Yeah. Somewhere just below the bridge. I can hear people walking about up above. Last night I heard men talking loudly in the room across the hall," he whispered.

"What are they going to do with us, Gordon?"

"I don't know, but if they were going to kill us, they would have done it by now."

"What happened to Whirly?" Julie asked.

"I pulled him out of the helicopter after I got you out. His skull was caved in. I was trying to help him when the lights went out. When I came to we were locked in here."

He checked the bruise on her face and head.

"Want something to eat? We're on a bread and water

diet, you know."

"No. My face is too sore," she groaned.

"Stop whining. You've got to drink, *Little Bit*. Here, I'll help you."

Julie whimpered in pain when he raised her head up off the mattress far enough to drink a little water from a cup he had placed near the bed. She lay back down and took several shallow breaths.

"Better?"

"Yes. Thanks."

Forbes tore off a small piece of black bread and put it to her lips.

"Here. Don't even try to chew it. It's as hard as a rock. Just hold it in your mouth until it melts. You need nourishment, Julie. Gotta do it," he insisted.

Julie complied despite the pain. Forbes pulled up a chair and watched over her. When she swallowed the bread, he gave her more water and then more bread.

"You did a first rate job splinting my arm," Julie said, exploring her body for damage.

She touched her face with her fingers. Her eye was puffy and swollen.

"Doc Forbes at you service, Boss. Don't worry. There is no permanent damage to that pretty face but you're going to have a shiner for a couple of weeks."

"Thanks, Gordy. Thanks for taking care of me," she said.

"Wait till you get my bill," Forbes joked. "I don't come cheap, you know."

His levity released some of her anxiety. He fed her more bread and water. Just as suddenly as she had come to she fell back into a restless sleep.

It was oddly quiet in the cabin as he listened to her short shallow puffs of breath. The sounds of the ship haunted him, the creaks and strains of a vessel heading into harms way.

*We are in deep kim chi, Little Bit*, he thought, *deep deep kim chi*.

No one knew they were aboard the Russian ship. Overton had failed to make radio contact with the *Greenpeace* before they went down. For all Captain Murphy knew the helicopter had run into foul weather or had mechanical trouble and had set down for repair. A maelstrom of rain pummeling the skin of the ship muted the sound of the sea. It made him drowsy. He needed rest too. The impact of the crash had strained his back and neck muscles. It hurt just to breathe. He waddled back to his pallet and drifted off to sleep.

The next morning there was a noise at the door as someone in the companionway unlocked it. It creaked open and a steward came in carrying tea and pastries, followed by a major in a Russian Army uniform. The soldier was packing a large pistol strapped to his leg and by the look on his face Forbes knew he was not the kind of man to lock horns with. Clean-shaven, neat in appearance, and fit, he was the epitome of the Russian military. The man was in his late forties and his face had taken on a brutal countenance, stern and unforgiving. Like a beaten dog the steward placed the food on a small counter and left the room.

The major gave them a hard look, waved his hand, and said, "Eat. Drink. Be my guest."

"What are you going to do with us?" Forbes asked.

"Depends," Gurnov grunted, eyeing Julie. "She is not so well, eh?"

"Concussion. Broken ribs. She'll be okay in a few days," Forbes replied. He glared at the major. "Depends on what?" he demanded.

"Please, my English is not so good. Speak slowly," Gurnov ordered.

"What are you going to do with us?" Forbes asked, speaking slowly and distinctively.

Hearing the conversation brought Julie to consciousness. She opened her eyes and sat up on the side of the bed with a struggle that nearly caused her to pass out. Forbes went to her and sat on the edge of the bed. The Russian eyed them both without pity.

"What does, *Green pies*, mean?" Gurnov growled.

"Green peas?" Forbes asked. "Food! In what context?"

"Context?"

"How are the words used?" Forbes asked.

Gurnov took a slip of paper out of his pocket and read the words in stilted, broken English. "Off da coast of Malaysia in helo-copter provide by Green piss."

"You've been watchin' video, my man. It means the environmental organization called Greenpeace let us use their bird," Gordon answered.

"Bird?"

"Helicopter."

"So you are not environmentalist?" Gurnov asked, cautiously, mispronouncing the words.

"No. CIA," Forbes joked.

A look of shock crossed Gurnov's face. His hand went down for his pistol.

"No. No. No. We are not CIA," Julie groaned. "He's joking. We're independent filmmakers."

Gurnov eyed her cautiously. "Joking. He joking... Independent means you work for nobody? *Da?*"

"*Da*," Forbes mocked.

"Yes," Julie replied.

"Who knows you are here?" Gurnov demanded in a

stern voice.

His face took on a brutal expression. He would have thrown them overboard with the helicopter but he needed intelligence. He had to know who was behind the filming of the *Stashinsky*. He wanted to know if they were part of the environmental organization or from the American government. He and Baranov had viewed the videotape several times in the captain's stateroom and had argued about what they should do. Tokyo was closer and perhaps an easier target. Then it came to him. Filmmakers could be useful. They could provide visual evidence that would frighten the Americans into quick action.

"*Greenpeace* knows we are here," Julie answered.

"You are the boss, no?"

She nodded.

"Why you spying on me?" Gurnov demanded.

"Because you are dumping poisons in the sea," Julie answered.

Gurnov sneered and did an about face. She had unwittingly answered his most burning question. No one knew they were on board the *Stashinsky*. Captain Murphy had frantically passed the word from ship to ship to keep an eye out for his missing helicopter. Gurnov had monitored the transmission. The *Greenpeace* was almost a thousand miles behind them still searching for her missing bird. He opened the stateroom door stepped into the companionway and picked up Forbes's camera. Crossing the room, he handed it to Gordon and stepped back.

"Does it work?" he asked.

Forbes pressed a few buttons and looked through the viewfinder. "Yes."

"Then I will let you live. You vill make film," he said, shaking his finger at Julie like a pistol.

"What kind of film?" she asked, defiantly.

"Make film of dis ship? I want you to tell President of United States de people in Hawaii are in big troubles, very big troubles, if he not do what I say."

"What are you going to do?" Julie asked.

"I will let you live to make film," he said shaking his finger at her, "but if you make troubles, I vill throw you overboard," he growled like a cur dog. "I only need cameraman," he said, pointing at Forbes. "Not you," he snarled turning his gaze back on Julie.

He wanted Julie on film explaining the dire conditions the country faced. Americans were soft for women. He knew that. Gurnov smiled maniacally and left the stateroom. He locked the door behind him and marched down the companionway.

For several days the *Stashinsky* shook bow to stern as the Cossacks pushed the ship full speed into a gale. The black bow plunged forward into deep troughs, smashing spray out to windward. Then as the next comber rolled beneath her, she rocked, pitched, shuddered in protest, and shed her foam of white water, only to plunge into another huge wave. The sound and fury of enormous seas transmitted their immense power through her frame, causing the decks to vibrate with raw energy. Racing up the South China Sea at twenty knots, she put the foul weather behind her for the calm of deep Pacific blue. Then she ran with the trades on a great circle route directly for Johnston Atoll. For several more days she steamed full speed cutting through smooth seas.

They had discussed their situation several times. Locked in the first mate's cabin, they strained their ears to hear conversation outside their prison, even though they couldn't understand a word of Russian. Sleeping and talking passed the time of day.

"What do you think they are up to, Julie?" Forbes asked, sipping the morning tea the steward had just delivered.

"Extortion," Julie replied, flatly.

Neither of them had wanted to say the word.

"That would be my take," Forbes agreed. "I recognized one of the words on the boxes they were loading on board the ship."

"And?" Julie asked. She was feeling better and trying to come up with a plan of escape or some way of fighting back.

"Semtec."

"What's that?" she asked.

Forbes looked at her with a deadly serious expression on his face. She had a huge black eye and one cheek was distorted by swelling.

"Soviet explosives. There must be ten thousand pounds on board this ship."

"The major said Hawaii was in big trouble. Maybe they are going to rig the ship with explosives and run her aground on Waikiki?" Julie suggested.

"That would be a good guess. But why Hawaii?"

"It's close to the ship's destination. No one looking down from a satellite will get the wiser until she sails right by Johnston Atoll. By then it will be too late."

"Sounds like a plan to me," Forbes agreed.

"Lee told me the government is really worried that terrorists will seize a ship loaded with natural gas and explode it in a major U.S. harbor."

"Why not an oil tanker?" Forbes asked.

"That too. The oil would cause an environmental disaster. But a ship filled with natural gas would kill thousands, perhaps millions if it exploded near Boston or

New York, or San Francisco. The reason they are so concerned about LNG ships is because natural gas is heavier than air. To use Lee's words, a cloud of gas would roll over the city burning on the edges as it consumed the oxygen in the atmosphere around it. Depending on the wind, millions could die. Analysts have estimated that such an explosion could be worse than an atomic bomb."

"If this ship is carrying what we think it is then everyone in the Hawaiian Islands is at risk," Forbes suggested.

"Exactly. Anyone down wind. The question is, what can we do to stop them?" Julie asked.

"Not a damn thing. This is a Russian ship and we're locked inside a steel compartment. Another point Julie, if we don't do exactly what that maniac bastard says to do he'll throw us overboard. This is the high sea, Julie and there are no friendly SEALs out here to rescue us."

"Sharks might be the easy way out, Gordy. Did you see the look in his eye when he told me he would throw me overboard?"

"Yeah. He's a stone cold killer, all right. No doubt about that. Our best bet is to play along and try to jump overboard if we get near land."

"First we have to figure out how to get out of this coffin," Julie agreed.

"I've been practicing lock pickin'," Forbes grinned.

"Any luck?" Julie asked.

"No. Not yet. But I'm workin' on it."

Julie was correct in her assessment of the situation. Baranov had used the calm weather to rig and wire the ship with explosives. Using twelve thousand pounds of semtec, he had turned the *Stashinsky* into a huge chemical bomb. When the job was completed, the Cossacks had celebrated. They even allowed their captives extra rations, one last good meal. They didn't intend to allow anyone to survive. Witnesses could identify them.

Locked within metal compartments behind thick steel hatches, unnecessary crewmen and Gurnov's chemical troops were powerless to escape. When the cook provided the captives with food and water, Baranov stood guard with an assault rifle. And with the ship rigged with booby traps, the small number of crewmen they selected to help sail the vessel lived in fear for their lives. From time to time Gurnov would kill a crewman at the least provocation just to incite fear. Standing port and starboard duty on the bridge, Baranov and Gurnov took turns carrying an RFD, a radio firing device, which they explained would cause the ship to be flooded with poisonous gas.

"The Russians have always been ahead of the rest of the world in poison warfare," Julie said. "It's in keeping with their paranoid culture. Their first generation weapons were blister agents, then came nerve gas, with all its attendant horrors, and now bio-weapons."

"What do you think is on this ship?" Forbes asked.

"A third generation poison, a biotoxin. While the U.S. developed safer-to-handle binary chemical weapons, the Russians pressed on with the development of biological toxins. Whatever it is, it's new to Western science. There is one thing we can be sure of."

"What's that?" Forbes asked.

"What it does to human beings."

They were both visualizing the blackened corpses of the fishermen when keys rattled outside the room.

Gurnov kicked the door open and grunted, "Bring camera."

Forbes pickup his camera and nodded for Julie to follow him. Across the companionway, Gurnov open the door and motioned for them to enter the captain's stateroom. He watched them closely with hawk-like eyes. He closed the door behind them, locked it, and went directly to the Captain's desk. Picking up a note pad, he handed it to Julie.

"Read this," he ordered. "You vill take pictures," he snarled at Forbes.

Julie scanned it. "It's not good English."

"*Fix it!*" Gurnov boomed.

Julie flinched. The man had been drinking heavily. She could smell it on his breath. She quickly scribbled a few corrections between the lines, tore off the sheet, and handed it to him. He gave it a cursory glance and gave it back to her. Then, using the Captain's VCR, he ran the videotape Forbes had taken of the *Stashinsky* until the helicopter crashed on deck. The part focusing on Yuri Baranov had been erased. He removed it from the VCR and handed it to Forbes.

"Film her. Read demands," he ordered.

Forbes inserted the video into his camera and focused in on Julie's face.

"*Read!*" Gurnov shouted.

"Okay. Okay," Julie said. She cleared her throat and looked into the camera. "This is Julie Jennings reporting from the Russian ship, the Bogdan Stashinsky," she said without looking at the paper. "This message is for President Clinton." Glancing down at the paper, she read, "I quote: President Clinton, you will immediately give orders to transfer one hundred million dollars to the bank of Estonia, account number zero-zero-zero-six-four-seven-eight-nine-two or we will explode this ship. As you will see in this video, the *Stashinsky* is loaded with chemical and biological toxins, and booby-trapped with

251

tons of explosives that we can detonate remotely. You will transfer the money within twenty-four hours or we will explode a chemical bomb in Honolulu. If we do not receive the money within twelve hours of the delivery of this videotape, copies will be sent to all major news organizations showing the people of your country that it was you who made the decision to kill the people of Hawaii. If this transaction is accomplished in less than twelve hours, no one will know you paid us the money. End quote."

Julie stood there in front of the camera with her bruised and battered face.

"Enough," Gurnov growled.

"Clever. Very clever," she sassed.

"I don't care what you think, woman. *Out!*" he shouted, causing Julie to flinch.

Gurnov opened the door and gestured for them to cross the companionway to their prison.

"Not you," he said to Forbes.

A shiver of fear surged through Gordon's body.

Gurnov locked Julie in the stateroom and made Forbes walk ahead of him through the empty corridors of the *Stashinsky*.

"Where are we going?" Forbes asked.

Gurnov ignored the question.

"*Stoi!*" he yelled. Forbes froze, expecting to catch a bullet in the back of the head. "That way," Gurnov ordered, motioning with the barrel of his pistol when Forbes turned to look. From passageway to passageway, ladder to ladder, he directed Forbes down into the bowels of the ship. When he reached the holds he directed Forbes to stand off at a distance while he removed a large pad lock and opened the hatch. It was black and silent inside. A blast of stale air that reeked of a strange odor hit them in the face.

Gurnov switched on the beam of a powerful flashlight and carefully stepped inside. Forbes thought about running. But there was no place to go. The ship was far from land and the Russian was armed. He thought about jumping the hardened warrior and concluded that his efforts would only end in his death. The Russian was a careful man, powerfully built, and he maintained a distance just beyond the range of any prudent heroic attempt. Gurnov flipped a switch and the lights inside the cargo hold came on. It wasn't a huge open bay like Forbes expected. Directly in front of him was another bulkhead. Motioning Forbes inside, Gurnov closed the hatch behind them and directed him down the passageway to the third compartment.

"*Stoi*," he growled.

There the Russian opened another hatch and shoved the anxious cameraman inside. Forbes was sure he was going to be murdered when he saw the pistol in the Russian's hand. Using the weapon, Gurnov motioned for him to step back so he could peek through a small porthole.

Seeing the rabbits were still alive, he opened the inner hatch and turned to face Forbes.

"Inside," he growled. "Take pictures of explosives. Take pictures of bombs. Take pictures of everything. Everywhere," he shouted. "I want Clinton to see what vill happen if he not give us money," Gurnov growled. "Do not take picture of me," he said, shaking the gun in his face, "or I vill kill you and take pictures myself."

Forbes knew the Russian couldn't operate the complicated camera but he didn't want to get shot proving it. Seeing rabbits hopping about inside their cages he went to work. Explosives were strategically placed all over the hold. Some were rigged to the overhead to blow off the huge steel hatch covers that opened the hold for loading by crane. Other haversacks were placed under pallets of chemical munitions to blow them skyward. Forbes shot the compartment from every angle until Gurnov ordered him to stop.

"Enough," he snapped. "We go."

He directed Forbes to hold number four, checked the air lock, and opened it. When Forbes saw all the dried blood and fingers on the deck his heart jumped into his throat. The man the *Sirius* had recovered from the *Stashinky's* wake had been murdered right where he was standing. Gurnov peeked through the porthole into the huge cargo compartment then back at Forbes.

"Can you take pictures through window?" he asked, gesturing at the porthole with his pistol.

Forbes looked through the porthole to judge the light conditions. Inside, next to the rabbit cage, he saw a man, strapped to the gripes that held down the pallets of munitions. He was naked and shackled spread eagle to the chains.

"What are you going to do?" pleaded Forbes, his mind racing with fear.

Gurnov pointed the pistol at him and sighted down the barrel. His cheek twitched with hate as he eyed the Southern California yuppie.

"Can you take picture through window?" he demanded.

When Forbes didn't answer, Gurnov place his finger on the trigger.

"Okay-okay. Yes. I can do it," Forbes blurted.

"Step back."

There wasn't much room to step back in the tiny airlock but Gordon got out of Gurnov's way and readied his camera. When Gurnov opened the inner hatch the man strapped to the pallets looked up with crazed fear. He began begging in Russian.

"*Major Gurnov?  Major Gurnov, please*," Lieutenant Romanovsky begged.

"Fuck you, *schoolboy*," Gurnov snarled.

Forbes couldn't understand the words, but he understood.  The Major picked up a glass bottle he had placed just inside the hatch, tossed it in the air, and slammed the hatch closed.  The small bottle came down on the steel deck and shattered.

"Take pictures," he ordered.

Forbes placed the camera up to the porthole and focused on the naked soldier.  At first nothing happened.  Then the man began struggling to free himself as the toxin spread about the sealed compartment.  In agony as if his body was on fire, he screamed at the top of his lungs.  Then he began to gag and foam at the mouth.  Forbes stared through his viewfinder, aghast, as the soldier convulsed, vomited, and fouled the deck with uncontrollable bowel movements.  Then the foam at his mouth turned pink and frothy and his eyes bugged out.  When blood filled the man's eye sockets, Forges could take no more. He stepped back against the bulkhead and began retching.  Gurnov peeked through the porthole, turned, and yelled at him.

"*Take pictures!  Take pictures now!  Or I shoot you!*"

He slammed Forbes back against the bulkhead and forced him to raise the camera up from where it was dangling at his side.  When Forbes refocused on the man inside the hold, the soldier's skin was turning blue and his body was limp and quivering in rhythmic spasms like shaken jello.  Blood was dripping from his nose.  Then he focused on the rabbits. They were dead.

# Chapter
# 19

The previous two hours had been extremely tense for the men of Charlie Platoon and the four DELTA soldiers who had joined them for the operation. In a rush they had deployed from Ford Island to an aircraft carrier steaming sixty miles off the coast. Weapons at the ready, they waited aboard three Blackhawks turning on the deck for orders to assault the target. Over the roaring sound of turbine engines at low power the steady *whump whump whump* of the rotor blades marked out the pace of Lee Sanz's life.

He looked over the pilot's shoulder. There were switches and indicators all over the cockpit, illuminated by a dim orange-red glow. Through the canopy he saw a lone sailor standing on the flight deck in front of them, infrared batons in hand. The pilots were using Night Vision Goggles but they were not necessary. The moon was bright enough to see men on the flight deck and the sea beyond. In the distance silvery light reflected off eight-foot wave crests.

The pilot increased the RPMs a tad and teased the cyclic in all directions. Sanz could feel the helicopter's instant response.

*He's getting ready to takeoff*, Sanz thought.

He glanced back at Ears Fellars seated near the open cargo door on the right side of the aircraft. A green thick-braided nylon rope lay coiled at his feet, hooked to the hoist. Beside Fellars sat an army sergeant with a big wad of tobacco in one cheek. He grinned and gave Sanz a thumbs up.  Lee nodded and continued his visual check of the compartment.

*Men, equipment, time schedule*, he said to himself.

He counted the men for the fifth time, their weapons, radios, and other gear.  Inventory complete, he looked forward through the canopy just as two 500MDs lifted off the deck.  They hovered at sixty feet, then pitched forward and disappeared to the starboard side of the carrier.  Out on the flight deck a crewman raised both his arms in the air above his head in a deliberate signal.  The pilot increased power and the Blackhawk lifted off the deck on uncertain legs.

In the days following exercise *Freedom Express* Colonel Ardison had ordered several missions for each assault unit to make use of all the assets programmed into the exercise.  Without the interference of VIPs the men were able to concentrate on tactics.  Each team, with exception of Charlie Platoon, received a submarine infiltration mission.  Sanz had sent Master Chief Blaze and Petty Officer Carroll with each of the army units using the *USS Aspro* to teach them the most efficient ways of employing the boat.

Six days after the seizure of the *Alliance*, Charlie Platoon received its second mission; rescue a dozen hostages held by eight terrorists in a building located on Hickam Air Force Base.  Reciprocating for the submarine assistance, DELTA soldiers joined the platoon to help them plan and execute the mission.

The Blackhawks circled the ship and joined with the waiting little birds before heading off toward land.  Skimming the surface at fifty feet, the five helicopters flew in formation until they went *feet dry* over land.  There, the two smaller helicopters flanked right and left and circled out to approach the target from opposite sides.

On the ground, barely visible patches of night air

seemed to coalesce and float across the hot tarmac. Under the command of Lieutenant Junior Grade Thomas, the patches took shape almost surrounding the building. The target was a medium size single story structure used to store old equipment. Inside, huddled in the middle of the largest room, twelve soldiers and sailors complained and argued about their assignment as hostages. Half a dozen controllers with white armbands kept close watch over the terrorists and the hostages. Tangos were stationed strategically around the interior of the building hidden behind whatever cover was at hand. Two terrorists were hidden behind the main door ready to ambush the rescue party. They were the first to hear the helicopters.

"*Here they come!*" one of the OPFOR yelled.

The clacking of receivers sliding home followed the warning. The opposition force was armed with MP-5s loaded with simunition paint rounds. They checked their gear, put on their protective face shields, and hunkered down behind cover.

The sharp shooters in the 500MDs were the first to arrive. The little helicopters hovered in positions where the shooters had the best firing angles on the main doors. A few seconds after their arrival, the first Blackhawk appeared. The pilot made his approach at ninety knots and at the last second hauled back on the cyclic to blast the tarmac with a windstorm.

Ears Fellars threw the rope out before the helicopter reached hover at thirty feet.

"*Go!*" he yelled, when it was safe to exit the aircraft.

Shorty Moore was first out the door. Wearing thick welder's gloves, he grabbed the rope with both hands and leapt out into the night. With his legs spread wide apart, he let himself fall until he was fifteen feet above the ground. Then he gripped the rope tightly with both hands to slow his descent. He landed on his feet and dashed away from the landing zone far enough to clear the area for the next commando. While on the move, he saw the door to the building burst open and two men open up from inside. Dropping to one knee, he brought his weapon to bear. But the terrorists had the advantage. Weapons blazing with deadly accurate fire, they mauled him and the DELTA sergeant that followed him down the rope. In the exchange that followed, Moore was hit with five rounds that peppered his upper torso with big red blotches. The sergeant was hit with three rounds later judged to be fatal. Lieutenant Sanz, the third man down the rope, was struck twice in the back.

The snipers in the little birds, along with the SEALs in the ground force, eliminated the two terrorists behind the doorway, but the two men hidden behind the open window continued the firefight. The exposed commandos were pummeled as they slid down the rope and ran for the open door.

On the opposite side of the building, Master Chief Blaze and his men fared much better. Their helo encountered no opposition. They slid down the rope like firemen on a call and scurried across the tarmac weapons at shoulder ready. The point man burst through the back door with a front thrusting kick, tossed in a concussion grenade, and took cover behind the door jam. The explosion rattled the entire building. Rushing through the smoke, the commandos peeled right and left to clear the fatal funnel.

*"Get down! Get down! Get down! Everybody down!"* they yelled.

The controllers wearing white armbands stood their ground grading the entry. Terrorists, wearing black armbands engaged the men in a firefight.

Another explosion shook the building as a well-placed concussion grenade preceded the men into the second room, followed by shots as the terrorists fought back.

*"Clear right!"*

*"Clear left!"*

*"All clear!"*

*"Next room!"* Blaze yelled, watching the room clearance from the corridor.

The squad moved from room to room with deadly efficiency.

Dan Carroll and his crew hit the ground a few seconds after the first two squads. They maneuvered to a shuttered window and blew it in with a water charge. Scrambling inside, they headed directly for the room where the hostages were being held. Hearing the rescue party's approach, a terrorist began shooting hostages one at a time.

*"Goddammit!"* one of the prisoners yelled. *"Watch where the hell you place your rounds!"*

The soldier didn't like playing the part of a hostage and he didn't like being shot in the back, even if was a paint round. All of the hostages were complaining like a bunch of old women when Carroll and his men burst through the door and tossed in a concussion grenade. The grenades were down loaded so they didn't pack much of a punch but they were noisy and created a lot of smoke. The SEALs followed the explosion through the smoke and cordite, weapons at shoulder ready.

*"Get down! Get down! Get down! Everybody down!"* they yelled, as they peeled right and left into the room.

*"Yeah, yeah, yeah, Hollywood!"* one of the hostages yelled. *"Shit-for-brains has already capped us!"*

The ungrateful hostage was on his knees bent over into a ball to protect his face and privates. A terrorist had placed two rounds in the center of his back. Carroll blasted the tango before he could regain his senses from the flash bang.

*"Clear right!"*

*"Clear left!"*

*"All clear!"*

"You Hollywood dudes are always late," one of the men complained. "You stop to sign autographs?"

*"Cuff 'em!"* Carroll ordered, ignoring the sarcasm. *"Let's get 'em outta here!"* he said, watching the corridor from just inside the door jam. He saw Blaze moving down the passageway and signed him with a hand signal.

*"Coming in!"* Blaze yelled.

The two squads linked up and while Carroll and his men prepared the hostages for transfer, Blaze finished clearing the building. He surprised the two tangos pinning down Sanz's fire team and capped them both before they knew he was behind them.

Communicating with Lieutenant Thomas on his inner squad radio, Blaze coordinated link up with the ground force. Thomas, now in charge of the operation, double-checked the building and the adjacent grounds while Blaze and Carroll escorted the hostages to two HH-53's helicopters turning on the tarmac. Medics immediately began treating the wounded. Five minutes after landing, the big choppers thundered off toward the carrier with the wounded, the dead, and the hostages. Sanz was among the dead. Accounting for all hands, Thomas ordered his remaining men aboard the waiting Blackhawks and headed back to sea.

The day following the assault, the platoon stood down for debriefing and crew rest. At zero nine hundred they mustered in the briefing theater. Sanz knew that it was going to be a bad day when he entered the room. Major Verduchi was seated in the back chatting with some of the controllers. He flashed Lee a fake smile. The evolution was called an After Action Review or AAR and its intent was to improve performance. Criticism was supposed to be constructive in nature. But it was not to be in this AAR and Sanz knew it.

Carroll mustered the platoon and the men took their seats. A few minutes later Colonel Ardison entered the briefing theater and AAR commenced. For the next hour the controller staff walked them step-by-step through the mission from warning order to execution. At each stage the controller in charge of the phase read of a list errors long enough to bore a saint. From noise and light discipline to gun handling, Charlie took a hit. Several times during the meeting Colonel Ardison stopped the briefer to ask a pointed question. The nature and tone of the AAR sent up his antenna. Neither Sanz nor Blaze attempted to counter the charges of incompetence. They knew the deck was stacked against them because of the large number of casualties they had sustained during the operation. Finally one of the Delta sergeants that had gone with them on the mission spoke up in the Platoon's defense. He opined that the helicopters had been restricted in their approach. He told the Colonel that Lieutenant Sanz had wanted to fast rope onto the roof of the building but the controller staff had restricted them to an LZ directly in front of the main doors.

At the conclusion of the AAR Charlie Platoon was given an unsatisfactory grade. Colonel Ardison thanked the men for their hard work and went about his busy schedule. To the men of Charlie Platoon the AAR was slap in the face and a source of great disappointment. As Sanz got up to leave the theater he eyed Verduchi. The bucktoothed Major lifted his chin in the air and smirked.

The next day Charlie Platoon resumed a routine training schedule. A typical day at the hangar when not assigned a mission consisted of reveille at 05:00 a.m., followed by calisthenics and a run. After PT Sanz, Thomas, and Blaze watched the morning news on CNN and read the message traffic that had come in during the night. With the assistance of staff communications personnel, they tracked items of interest that pertained to SEAL Team FIVE.

"*Outstanding!*" Sanz exclaimed, as he read the message board. We've got another mission."

"When?" Thomas asked.

"The day after tomorrow," Sanz replied.

He passed the message to Thomas and the copy to Master Chief Blaze.

The Master Chief's brow furrowed as he read the mission order.

"You know, L.T., even with HRT we don't have enough men to take down a vessel the size of the *Independence*," he scowled.

Their orders were to board and seize the *Independence* by means of boat and pier assault in concert with the FBI Hostage Rescue Team.

"It'll be good training," Sanz replied.

"I don't like it," Blaze grumbled. "We need seventy men for this op."

"Mike."

"Yes, sir," Thomas replied.

"Get with HRT and set up a mission planning schedule. Master, have Petty Officer Carroll prepare the gear."

"Roger," Blaze growled. "But I don't like it. We looked like shit on the last op and now the bastards are setting us up for the big fall. Lieutenant, there is no way in hell we can do this mission with less than seventy men."

"Let's study it, Master," Sanz said. "It might be easier than it looks."

"Right," Blaze replied, ironically. "Later." He left the TOC in an angry mood.

Sanz knew the *Independence* operation would be their last graded mission during the deployment, and he wanted to look good for Team FIVE, but there was nothing he could do to change the mission order. He didn't want to whimper that he didn't have enough men for fear Major Verduchi would be assigned to assist. To relax and take his mind off the problem he decided to bust a few caps. Outside the hangar the staff had set up two shooting vans, large semi truck size containers outfitted as indoor shooting ranges. He checked out his MP-5 and nine-millimeter pistol from Petty Officer Johnson and mustered at one of the van doors.

When it came his turn the old sergeant inside spit a gob of tobacco juice in a Styrofoam cup he was holding in his hand and said, "You back for more, Lieutenant. Damn if you ain't gonna wear me out."

"I got something for you, Buckshot," Sanz said.

"What?"

"My trident," Lee replied.

Sanz took a golden SEAL breast insignia out of his pants pocket and handed it to the battle-hardened sergeant.

"Damn if that ain't the prettiest thing. I'm gonna ask the Colonel for orders to BUD/S so I can earn me one to wear on my class 'As'. You think I could make it through SEAL training, Lieutenant?"

"Hell, Buckshot, you've done everything else from the Rangers to the SF. You'd find a way to hack it."

"Damn straight I would," the grizzly old sergeant growled. "Now, tell me again what all this stuff means."

*"How about hurrying up in there!"* someone yelled from outside the van.

*"Take a hike!"* Buckshot hollered back.

He hung a sign on the door and shut the van down, leaving two soldiers standing in the sun. Then he held the shiny device in his hand and beamed.

"My son is gonna love this one," he grinned.

Buckshot Martin had collected nearly every patch and warfare insignia in the world. Each item in his collection had come from a man who had earned it.

The acronym SEAL was derived from the words, sea, air, and land, and was a play on the word referring to the sea animal that is more at home in water than on the land. The SEALs called it a trident because of the scepter that crossed through the heart of the device. The symbolism had been carefully chosen by men of action to represent the media in which SEALs operated. Sanz explained.

"The anchor stands for the Navy," he said. "A swab can't get too far away from his moorings, you know. This eagle here," he continued pointing out the lines of the device, "with its wings outstretched, represents strength and courage as well as our ability to infiltrate by air. One of the talons is holding a trident. See?"

"Yeah," Buckshot said, studying the insignia.

"The scepter is the symbol of the Roman god of the sea. It's our primary method of infiltration. You see the other talon?"

"Yeah. He's holding an old flintlock pistol," Buckshot said. "I wish I had one of those in my collection."

"A cocked flintlock, sarg. That indicates our readiness to fight on land."

"That is way cool," the gnarly old sergeant beamed. "Here," he said, handing Sanz a well-worn SF insignia. "I smoked a gomer wearing that insignia," he grinned.

"Had it pinned inside my camies."

The badge consisted of crossed arrows over a dagger with the words, *DE OPPRESSO LIBER*, curved around the bottom.

"Now that's what I call way cool," Sanz grinned. "I've never been in a real firefight."

"Stick around this business son and you'll get more than you bargained for. Okay, what'll it be?" Buckshot growled.

"Something new, sarg. I'm bored shitless."

"I got just the program for you, lady killer," Martin grinned. He poked his keyboard with a stubby finger and the screen at the far end of the trailer illuminated.

The last time Sanz had gone through the van, Buckshot had used a program that projected friendly female hostages and terrorist women. Sanz had shot one of the hostages, a mistake that guaranteed a bit of ribbing.

As Sanz prepared himself, Buckshot coached him. "The last time you ran the range, you were shooting a skooch too high and a bit to the right. Compensate by shooting the lower left quadrant of the target. Remember, *squeeeze* your trigger gently, like your old lady's tit."

"I'm ready," Sanz reported.

Reacting to the images projected in front of him as if he were moving through a hotel corridor, Lee engaged target after target. He used half the rounds in his MP-5, pretended to have a malfunction then drew his pistol.

For half an hour Buckshot coached him. Finally, the old sergeant ran him off so other shooters could use the range.

"You've mastered this one too, lady-killer," he growled. "You best go choke your chicken to relieve the sexual frustration that's driving you like a demon."

Sanz reluctantly unloaded his weapons and headed

for the door.

"Hey," Buckshot said.

Lee paused and looked back at him.

"I got an old buddy over in the OPFOR. They're gunnin' for you son. Settin' you up," he cautioned. "Don't tell nobody that I warned you." Then he went back to kidding. "Tell Blaze if he wants to *learn how to shoot* to stop by for a visit."

"Thanks, Buckshot. Thanks a million for the lesson and the heads-up."

On the way back to the hangar Lee stopped and stared at the western sky. The clouds were backlit with red and salmon colors.

*I wonder what Julie's doing?* he thought. *I wonder where she is?*

Koshkin watched the activity on Ford Island with growing apprehension. It was almost sundown and the Pacific Ocean in the west had turned to gold, reflecting the last rays of the huge bright orange orb like a mirror. Helicopters had been coming and going all day. Special high-speed boats had been buzzing about the harbor running up alongside a large civilian cruise ship tied up at the largest dock in Pearl Harbor. From his vantage point in the hills above Pacific Palisades he could see men walking to and from the hangar. If he had sighted his telescope on the shooting van he could have read the expression on Lee Sanz's face.

*If this is an exercise they would have left by now*, he worried. *This has gone on way too long. What if they know? Maybe Alex is right about Markov. I need an alternate plan in case they hit the ship before it reaches Hawaii.*

Out of habit Koshkin counted the security guards on patrol around the perimeter and mentally noted the shift change. He drank the last of the vodka and took a deep drag off his Camel.

*The Stashinsky should be near Johnston Atoll. If they're on to us, they'll hit the ship within the next twenty-four hours, before she gets too close to land.*

"Boss," Blaze shouted, as Sanz ambled through the open hangar doors. He was standing with a senior army sergeant.

"What's up, Master Chief?" Sanz asked.

"Dildo Dodd, here, and his men are bored shitless. They've finished their last mission and they'd like to help us take down the *Independence.*"

Dodd was slim and lithe and didn't look old enough to be an E-9. He was at least ten years younger than Blaze, immaculately groomed, and his BDUs were neatly pressed, unusual in the tropical heat of the hangar. Distrust crossed Lee's face and the sergeant read it clearly.

"Sir, we've never had the pleasure of taking down a ship and the Major thought you might need some help, seeing as how SIX used more than a hundred men to do the job. He told me to tell you that if you allowed us to tag along, he'd tote your ruck for ya like a buck private."

The major in charge of the army unit out ranked Sanz by a grade. As Lee studied the sergeant's face, Buckshot Martin's warning came back to him. He looked at the twinkle in Blaze's eyes and knew what the Master Chief was thinking. They wouldn't be alone at the debrief. The Opposition Force wouldn't dare smear DELTA.

"How many of your men want to play, Top?" Sanz

asked.

"Oh, about twenty-five," Dodd replied.

"Any snipers?"

"Damn near all of them are sniper qualified."

"Perfect," Sanz replied. "Let's go get your Major and design a new assault plan."

"Lieutenant. One more thing," said Dodd.

"Shoot."

"The Boss said to tell you that he don't much cotton to what Major Verduchi is up to."

"Let's go see him."

"This way sir," Dodd said, gesturing the way with a hand signal.

Blaze grinned and winked at Lee as they walked off toward the back of the hangar.

The term *intelligence* as used by the U.S. Military is not defined in Webster's Dictionary. Information becomes intelligence only after it has been processed. It must be collated with other reports, analyzed, interpreted, and disseminated. The sources of information vary widely, from spies to satellite imagery, and the more sophisticated the source, the higher the level of classification placed on the information derived from it. The more widely known classifications such as secret and top secret are used as appropriate, but some sources are so sensitive that they are given additional *code word* classification. Only people with a need to know have access, and if cleared for access, they are forbidden from even revealing the existence of the code word, to say nothing of the subject or the means of collection. This divides the U.S. Military into two groups; the vast majority ignorant of code word intelligence, and a tiny minority with access to extremely sensitive information.

As Sanz planned the mock counter terrorist mission for the *SS Independence,* the code word intelligence that would have tipped him off that something was seriously wrong with the voyage of the *Bogdan Stashinsky* was only paces away. But he didn't have access, nor did his counterparts. General Carlson and Colonel Ardison did, but the bits and pieces were too scattered to have meaning. Communications intercepts of Russian message traffic, reported that the Russians were concerned about a loss of communications with the *Stashinsky*. That alone didn't raise a red flag. The ship's communications equipment could have malfunctioned. State Department messages reported that Julie Jennings, Gordon Forbes, and William Overton were missing off the coast of Malaysia and that a search was in progress. But neither the General nor the Colonel knew Jennings, Forbes, or Overton. There was even a CIA message reporting a large shipment of explosives leaving Burma under mysterious circumstances. Under another code word there was a message reporting rumors that a Burmese drug lord had acquired a large stockpile of chemical munitions. The NRO even had an image of the *Stashinsky*, but its position near Johnston Atoll was accurate enough for government work. Only Lee Sanz could have raised an alarm, if he'd had access to all the appropriate code words.

A flood of information deluged the tactical operations center, both real and contrived, as Sanz worked with his counterparts to plan the *Independence* mission. There was so much information that no one person could possibly read it all on a daily basis. Sanz used the appropriate assets of the TOC; mock agent reports of observations of the *Independence*, ship's blueprints, overhead imagery, signals intelligence, etc., to rework his assault plan. The result was a three-pronged attack. The FBI HRT mission consisted of storming the pier and gangway under cover fire provided by army sniper units.

Using Charlie Platoon and a DELTA team to climb the outboard side of the vessel fore and aft, he planned to marshal sufficient firepower to control the weather decks before clearing it compartment by compartment. He knew that loses would be heavy and criticism loud and vocal. But SEAL Team FIVE wouldn't be alone in the briefing theater.

The next day the teams rehearsed climbing, shooting, and tactics. They studied cut-away models of the vessel and practiced room clearance inside the hangar. Unlike SIX, they weren't afforded the opportunity of boarding and practicing on the ship before the assault. By sundown all of the men were tired of walk-throughs and were ready for action.

The first unit to leave Ford Island was the HRT. The FBI men crossed the bay by ferry in cars and trucks, and took up positions so that they could quickly storm the pier and rush up the gangway. The next units to launch were army dive teams consisting of six crack snipers and their spotters. Sanz watched as they slipped below the surface of the water for the short swim across the bay. Once in position they would begin relaying intelligence to the TOC. The telescopes on their rifles were perfect for surveillance.

The hum of powerful engines reverberated off the ferry landing as the two fast boats prepared for launch.

*So much for the element of surprise*, Sanz thought, looking across the bay at the *Independence*.

Armed terrorists were patrolling the weather decks in

plain view of the SOC boats. Sanz waited for the army dive teams to clear the area and then motioned to Petty Officer Carroll to get the men on board.

"Okay guys, all aboard," Carroll bellowed. "Tie everything down. Quickly, quickly. Then strap your asses down tight. This is gonna be rough ride."

Carroll had just finished an equipment check on the pier but once the men were aboard he double-checked to ensure that no one had left any gear behind. He gave the Master Chief a thumbs up, then the Lieutenant, and took his seat.

While the men were loading the gear and buckling up, Sanz ran a com-check with the TOC and his sister boat. When he was satisfied with their connectivity, he positioned himself behind the two coxswains, hooked in his harness, and cinched it up tight.

"Let's go do it," he ordered.

"Aye-aye, sir," the senior sailor in charge of the boat replied.

He spun the wheel in the direction of the pier and goosed the engine a couple up times to swing out the stern. Then he reversed the wheel and backed down hard to clear the landing. Easing the boat into forward, he idled slowly down Battleship Row and out the channel past Hospital Point. When they reached open water the coxswains shoved their throttles down and rocketed across the sea at fifty miles per hour, giving their passengers bone jarring, kidney bruising rides straight out of Miami Vice.

# Chapter 20

Yuri Baranov patrolled through the empty corridors of the *Bogdan Stashinsky,* stopping from time to time to tie in the booby traps he had rigged at strategic locations. Beneath the galley he paused at an interior ladder way leading up to the 02 level.

*A perfect place for a pull release*, he thought.

He placed his bag on the deck and took out the tools and supplies he needed to build another booby trap: Detonation cord, tape, blasting cap, crimpers, a firing device, and wire. He carefully laid his materials out in a neat line then studied the ladder well.

*I'll run the trip wire across the third step*, he thought.

On the long haul across the Pacific, he had constructed the components of the largest chemical weapon ever devised by mankind. The holds and fuel tanks were rigged with explosives. All exterior hatches, with exception of those on the bridge, were booby trapped and tied into trunk lines that ran throughout the ship. A radio fire device was hooked into the ship's antenna. It was ready for easy attachment to the explosive field. To assemble the massive bomb all Baranov needed to do was tie the components together with a few simple knots.

Det-cord consists of a vein of explosives bound inside a textile tube coated with a thin layer of plastic. It is about the diameter of a pencil and it will transmit an explosive wave from one point to another at twenty-one thousand feet per second, even underwater. Lengths of the cord can be tied together with square or right-angle knots to create an explosive field for simultaneous detonation. Wearing a protective suit, Baranov had placed thousands of pounds of explosives in the holds containing the chemical munitions. With the touch of a master craftsman, he had carefully drilled through the bulkheads of the airtight compartments. Through these holes he passed the explosive cord that linked the charges together for simultaneous detonation. To disguise his work he had sealed the trunk lines with caulk and painted the visible parts to look like ship's wiring. To conceal the five main trunk lines that ran from bow to stern, he ran them along the overhead above cables and pipes with other ship's wiring.

*I'll tie this one in after I've moved the woman*, he thought.

He picked up the fire device and removed it from its cardboard box. In keeping with his nature he carefully examined it for defects.

"Good," he mumbled. "Czechoslovakian. Excellent craftsmanship."

A thin wire, almost invisible in the dim light of the passageway, was attached to one end of the olive green device. He tied it to one side of the ladder and ran it across the step so that anyone climbing the stairs would disturb it. Then he worked his way behind the stairwell. Squatting down, he ran the tripwire behind the steps and attached the business end of the booby trap to a pipe with a piece of wire. He secured it with tape as an extra precaution before winching the tripwire taut. The device was designed to fire if anyone stepped on the wire or cut it. Either way, pull or release, it fired a tiny explosive charge, a base coupling, designed to initiate a blasting cap. He adjusted the tension several time before pulling the firing pins.

When the base coupling didn't pop, he replaced the firing pins. With proficiency born of experience he taped a non-electric blasting cap to a bite in a twelve-foot length of det-cord then secluded the cord with duct tape to the backside of the metal ladder. He ran the explosive cord up to the overhead where he had hidden his trunk lines in the ship's plumbing. But he didn't tie it in. Instead, he taped the cord near the trunk line so he could quickly tie it later with a right angle knot without disturbing the booby trap down below.

"Easy does it, Yuri," he said to himself. "One step at a time."

Carefully, ever so gently, he crimped the blasting cap and det-cord on to the base coupling of the firing device. As he did so he turned his face away and the meaty parts of his body toward the blasting cap so that if it exploded the metal fragmentation would hit him in the buttocks.

"Okay. Now for the big test," he mumbled.

Glancing over his shoulder, he grasped one of the safety pins, looked away, and pulled it, arming the release function of the mechanism.

"Excellent. No boom-boom."

He checked the tension again before pulling the other pin in the same manner.

Satisfied with his work he continued his patrol from hatch to hatch, ladder way to ladder way, deck to deck. Some booby traps he rigged so that he could quickly tie them into his fore and aft trunk lines, others he fastened to grenades or blocks of plastic explosives that were independent of the explosive field. When he was finished with the 04 level he unlocked the first officer's cabin and motioned for Julie to follow him.

"Come. Come," he grunted, like a boar hog being stalked by a lion.

Julie rolled off the bed and shuffled obediently across

the deck to the companionway.

"Where is my cameraman?" she demanded.

She hadn't seen Forbes since Gurnov had taken him away more than a week ago.

"You come. Now!" Baranov growled.

He yanked her by the arm. Julie's ribs were still sore. Wincing in pain, she cried, "*Okay! Okay! I'm coming!*"

He shoved her down the companionway keeping her at arm's length. At the ladder leading up to the bridge he grabbed her by the hair and yanked her to a stop. Crying out in pain Julie cursed him.

"*Stop it, asshole!*"

"Look," he grunted, shining his flashlight on a booby trap he had concealed across a step. "Booby trap everywhere on *Stashinsky. Everywhere!* You tell Clinton. If anyone come on *Stashinsky*, whole ship explode."

Julie stared at the device trying to memorize every detail.

"Understand?"

"*Yes!*" she sassed. "I understand. You're a fuckin' maniac."

"You go now," he bellowed.

"Where?" Julie demanded.

Baranov shoved her down the passageway to an open compartment on the starboard side of the ship. The hatch was made of heavy steel like those that sealed the weather deck.

"Inside," he grunted.

When Julie stepped into the tiny space he slammed the hatch shut and locked it from the outside.

Finished with his chores below decks, Baranov climbed the ladder to the bridge, taking care to avoid the trip wires he had place along the way. For a few minutes he stood in the darkness inside the light locker, letting his eyes adjust. Then he crept out from behind the blackout curtain and stood at the back of the bridge. Gurnov was on watch, smoking a cigarette, guarding the helmsman and Lieutenant Zhukov.

It was pitch black. The sky, the land, and the water merged at indistinct places on the horizon. The flashing channel buoys emitted sharp pricks of red, green, and white lights in the distance. They were the only visual features that could be trusted to navigate the ship. Beyond, the lights of Oahu, which had just been a bright glow on the northern horizon when he had gone below, had resolved to thousands of twinkling points spilling out from shore to mountain.

"Captain Gurnov," Baranov shouted.

Gurnov jumped at the sound of his voice. His hand reached down for his pistol.

"Easy, my friend. Easy. In a couple of hours we'll be drinking a toast with Nickoli."

"Call him," Gurnov blurted, his nerves raw with anxiety. "Your English is better than mine," he said handing Baranov the cell phone Koshkin had provided them.

Baranov replied calmly. "Certainly."

One had to be calm to set booby traps. He took the phone and dialed the number the KGB agent had instructed them to use when they were close to land.

"Hello," Koshkin answered, betraying none of the anxiety he felt inside. He was seated on the bank fishing in the channel just to the south of the Hickam Officer's Club.

"Can you give us ride, my friend?" Baranov asked, evasively.

"When?" Koshkin asked.

"How long till we go ashore, Alex?" Baranov asked, holding his hand over the receiver.

"Thirty minutes," Gurnov snapped.

"Thirty minutes," Baranov repeated into the telephone.

"I am waiting for you," Koshkin replied.

"Excellent. See you soon." Baranov terminated the connection.

"Ahh, the wonders of modern communication," he said in Russian. He handed the tiny wireless telephone back to Gurnov. "If Stalin had had such a system, he would have conquered the world."

"*Da*," Gurnov agreed, as he scanned the channel ahead of them with binoculars.

"This ship is ready for sale. All I have to do is tie in the trunk lines. When I do, I want to put some distance between us and this bomb," Baranov worried.

Hearing the anxiety in his voice Gurnov turned and faced him in the dark.

"Worried about your work, Yuri?" Gurnov asked.

"No. Stray electronic emissions. We are parking this ship on the largest naval base in the Pacific, you know," he explained, concerned that the remote firing device might be triggered by U.S. Military communications signals.

"Yuri, surely Nickoli checked the system before he sent it to us," Gurnov argued, without conviction.

"You'd better hope so, *Zakuski*. There's enough explosives in this boat to blow the hatch covers all the way up to MIR."

"Why you tell me this now?" Gurnov complained.

"I just thought of it," Baranov roared back.

"Okay-okay. Stop thinking of bad shit. You make me nervous," Gurnov griped.

"Alright, alright. Then, I'll tell you a joke."

Baranov wanted to calm Gurnov's nerves, as well as his own. Working with explosives was nerve racking.

"You see, there was this communist train that broke down outside Moscow station and Stalin, Khrushchev, and Brezhnev were on it. Stalin got angry when the train did not go so he ordered the crew to be taken out and shot. But that did not make the train move. What do you think Khrushchev did?"

"I don't know," Gurnov grumbled, not in the moody for humor.

"He ordered the crew rehabilitated posthumously. But still the train didn't move. So both men turned to Brezhnev. What do you think he did, *Zakuski?*" Baranov asked.

"Ordered the Army to push it," Gurnov supposed.

"No. No. No. He pulled down the shades, took a big swig of vodka, and said, 'Let's pretend the train is moving.'"

Gurnov chuckled. "Do you know what Yeltsin would have done?" Gurnov asked.

"No. But I have a feeling that I am going to find out."

"He would have privatized the damn thing and sold it to the Americans. They can make it run on time, but no damn Russian could afford to ride on it," he grumbled.

"*Da.* Clever, Alex. Very clever. You're back to your old self," Baranov praised.

"Yuri?"

"Yes," Baranov answered.

"Let's privatize this damn garbage scowl and sell it to the Americans. What do you think?" he asked, glibly.

"How about one hundred million," Baranov replied, with a broad smile.

"*Da.*"

"Tango Juliet, Tango Juliet, this is Tango Alpha, over?"

"This is Tango Juliet, roger, over," the radioman on the SOC boat replied.

The two fast movers were skimming along at fifty knots heading north for the channel into Pearl Harbor. Spray was drenching the men and the pounding of the boat on the sea was brutal. As Sanz listened to the radio traffic, he steadied himself with one hand and wiped his face with the other. Checking their position by the buoys leading into the channel, he mentally fixed their location and the timing of their approach. He glanced back behind the boat searching the bioluminescence for their sister craft. The other boat was running off his port quarter at a hundred meters, kicking up a rooster tail ten feet in the air.

"Tango Juliet, be advised there is a ship entering the channel. Do you have a visual?" the radioman asked from the circling Hawkeye. The aircraft was orbiting at twelve thousand feet above them.

Sanz scanned the entrance to Pearl Harbor. A couple of miles ahead he spotted a dim stern light, flanked by red and green running lights.

"Negative, Tango Alpha," the SOC boat radio operator replied. He served two functions; copilot and communicator.

"Tango Juliet, vessel is four thousand yards dead ahead of you, bearing three-five-six degrees true. How copy, over?"

"Good copy, Tango Alpha."

Sanz tapped the coxswain on the shoulder and pointed out the black void blocking the shore lights.

"Got it, sir," the coxswain shouted over the *woosh* of wind and water rushing by them.

"Tango Juliet, recommend you bear left three degrees

and pass her to her port," suggested the man in the airplane.

"Roger, Tango Alpha. Good copy. We have a visual."

The radioman notified the other assault craft zipping along behind them and the coxswain altered course slightly to give the ship a wider berth. They were a hundred yards behind the freighter when the lead boat smashed into the ship's wake and went airborne for a few seconds. Its engines shrieked as the RPMs increased to red line. Sanz braced himself for impact but kept an eye on the channel. The sleek assault boat cut into the sea like a knife and raced on through the dark water at amazing speed.

Gurnov saw the blips on the radarscope and rushed to the bridge wing with his binoculars.

"Look," he wailed, concerned by the fast moving speedboats.

Baranov calmly evaluated their situation, mentally going over the weapons and ammunition readily available to him. Glancing back over his shoulder, he kept one eye on Lieutenant Zhukov, tied in the captain's chair, and the helmsman, free to run if given the opportunity. Gurnov had chosen a man who couldn't swim, just in case the sailor was tempted to jump overboard when the ship was near shore. Zhukov, he needed for advice in sailing the vessel.

"Calm down, *Zakuski*" Baranov said. "If the Americans knew of our plan they would have boarded this vessel long ago. Two aircraft carriers would have steamed up our wake, not two pissy little speedboats," he reasoned.

"They are going to pass us," Gurnov said, putting down his binoculars.

"Of course they are," Baranov snapped. "No one knows we are here except Nickoli. Now is the time for calm deliberate action, my friend, just as we've planned for so many months."

Sanz and his two boats blew by the *Stashinsky* like an ill wind three hundred yards to port. As the young officer surveyed the ship's black hull a shiver ran down his spine. He was drenched with seawater and the wind across the deck had chilled his wet body. He was cold but what he felt inside was a different kind of chill, as if some ominous menacing evil was lurking nearby. Thoughts of Julie Jennings briefly crossed his mind but in his worst nightmare he could not have imagined she was three hundred yards away locked inside a steel compartment without portholes. Turning his thoughts to his mission, he continued up the channel at top speed.

"Call Nickoli!" Gurnov ordered. "Call Nickoli!"

The experienced spetznaz took the cell phone and dialed Koshkin.

"Hello," the KGB man graveled.

"We need ride, my friend," Baranov said, evasively.

"I am waiting for you," Koshkin replied.

Baranov listened anxiously on the phone. In the background he heard the two boats rumble by Koshkin's location. Wave restrictions in the harbor prevented a full speed approach to the *Independence* so before entering the main body of the harbor, the Hawkeye circling above ordered the boats to reduce speed to eight knots.

"Any problems?" Baranov asked in poor English.

"No. Standing by."

The change of speed came just as the boats passed Koshkin's location. Adrenaline and panic surged through his body when he saw the boats fall off step.

"Nothing to worry about," Koshkin said, not fully convinced that they weren't sailing into a trap. Distressed, he watched the boats motor by up the channel. He was worried but he didn't want to alarm Baranov and Gurnov. There was nothing they could do to stop the ship entering the channel. They were committed.

"See you in a few minutes," Baranov said before terminating the connection.

He reported the results to Gurnov. "The boats went by him. I could hear them," he said.

"All stop," Gurnov shouted to the helmsman.

"Aye, sir," the sailor replied.

"But Alex, we are still a very long way from Nickoli," Baranov protested.

"It will take this ship a mile to stop, Yuri."

On the bow the anchor was set. All Gurnov had to do was hit a chain block with a sledge to release it.

"All back one third," Gurnov ordered.

The helmsman sent the signal down to the engine room without protest. When the engineer reversed the screw, the ship began to shudder, protesting its forward speed. Cups rattled on the chart table and a dog-eared logbook fell off onto the deck.

"You will feel the anchor pay out, Yuri," Gurnov said.

"*Daaa*," Baranov snarled. "Go. Quickly. I know what to do."

They had gone over the procedure four times but

Baranov couldn't seem to get it through his head that the ship was going to plough forward through the water for several minutes.

"When you feel the anchor chain run out, stop the engines," he reminded Baranov as he walked toward the starboard hatch.

"I remember. I remember," Baranov grumbled.

Gurnov stepped out of the pilothouse and climbed down the ladders to the main deck. When he got to the foscle he checked his GPS. For what seemed like an eternity, the momentum of the big freighter carried her forward into the narrow channel. She was still moving when Gurnov let loose the anchor.

Baranov felt the rumbling of the heavy chain on the deck as it paid out.

"Stop engines!" he ordered.

He waited until the ship stopped shuddering then shot Lieutenant Zhukov in the back of the head at point blank range. When the helmsman turned to look in the direction of the report, he murdered him with two rapid-fire shots to the chest. The heavy caliber bullets hammered the seaman backwards, sprawling him out on the deck with a thud. As planned, Baranov turned off the ship's air circulation system and rushed down through the dark corridors to engineering. There, he unlocked the steel hatch that separated the engineering spaces from the rest of the ship and tossed in two chemical bombs he had secreted outside in the passageway.

Gurnov was concerned that the engineers would find a way to free themselves with tools hidden inside the engineering spaces. So they had to be eliminated. But he didn't want to kill everyone immediately. He wanted the girl alive as proof to the Americans of good faith.

Bolting the hatched shut, Baranov reversed his trek, tying in det-cord leads along the way. When he reached the radio shack below the bridge he tied in the radio firing device with a reef knot and stuffed the det-cord behind the radioman's console. He set the booby trap he had affixed to the door then he rushed up to the bridge. As fast as he could, he rigged the port hatch with a hand grenade, planted a fake booby trap on the starboard hatch, and dashed down to the main deck.

Gurnov was waiting for him at the side of the ship. He had lowered a small rubber boat and loaded it with two boxes of special chemical munitions and supplies.

Locked within her tiny cell Julie felt the ship shudder as the engines reversed. When she felt the vibrations of the chain running out she knew what was happening.

*We're anchored*, she thought. *They're really going to do it. But where are we? The ship's not moving. No waves. Oh, my God. They've anchored in Honolulu Harbor. I've got to get out of here.* There was no food or water, nor place to lie down like there had been in the first officer's cabin. There was no door with a lock to pick, just four gray metal walls enclosed by a steel ceiling and a metal floor. She may as well have been locked inside a bank vault.

*Why the candles? The matches? The tools?* she thought.

She sorted through the tools to see if there was something she could use on the hatch to open it.

"*Pozhaluista, Yuri. Bystro!*" Gurnov hissed.

As fast as he could, Baranov climbed down the side of the ship on a narrow chain ladder. As soon as he was in the rubber boat, they shoved off and began paddling like crazy. The noise of the anchor chain running out and the ship swing about had drawn the attention of people all along the channel. As they paddled the short distance to shore, people standing on the terrace of the club gawked at the vessel standing in the passage. "Over here," Koshkin shouted.

He flashed a small pen light at them as a signal. Pumped up on adrenaline the two soldiers stroked with all their might blade-ing the water like turbines. Koshkin met them at the bank. They bounded out like two Olympic athletes in a race for gold.

"There are people everywhere," Gurnov whispered, high on adrenaline and vodka.

"*Let's go,*" Koshkin gasped. "*Quickly. Quickly.*"

The spot he had chosen for them to make landfall was dark and provided good cover, but as they made their way the short distance to his car a couple of men from the Officer's Club walked toward them on an intercept course.

"*Hey!*" one of the men yelled. "You need any help?"

"*No!*" Koshkin shouted, in perfect English.

The men looked at the ship moored cross-wise in the channel, then marched over to the Cossack's car. They had just finished loading the trunk with munitions when the gentlemen walked up dressed in Hawaiian formal.

"What the heck is going on?" the older of the two men asked. He was a retired Air Force general and he was used to getting his way. He looked at the three Cossacks curiously, dumbfounded by the ship blocking the channel into Pearl Harbor.

"We don't know," Koshkin replied. "We were fishing in the channel when that ship dropped anchor."

"Bullshit," the general said. "These two men climbed down the side of that ship."

Baranov and Gurnov raised their pistols at the same time and fired two quick shots each in rapid-fire succession. Both men fell dead.

"*Quickly. Quickly*," Koshkin shouted. "*In the car*."

The three Cossacks jumped in and sped away with a screech of tires. Koshkin slowed down a half mile from the officer's club and motored through the base at the speed limit so as not to drawing attention. In route to the safe house he stopped long enough at a pay phone to call the FBI.

The single bare light bulb illuminating the gray bulkheads cast gloomy shadows. For several minutes after being thrown into the room she had studied the entry hatch before conceding that there was no way to use the tools to open it. Like a rat in a maze, she poked around her cell until the realization occurred to her that the wrenches fit the nuts on a half inch steel plate bolted on to one of the bulkheads. It was the size and shape of a hatch, as if some workman had cut a hole in the bulkhead to install a hatch and his foreman had come along and made him patch it up. She had only managed to get two of the twenty bolts out when the ventilator stopped blowing fresh air. When the light went out she knew what the candles were for. Not one ray of light seeped around the hatch or into the compartment around the pipes and wires that passed through the space. Nothing. Only inky blackness surrounded her, like the inside of a coffin buried deep underground.

"Dear God. Don't let them do this," she prayed. "Help me."

The ship was silent, motionless, and lifeless, as she felt for the matches that Baranov had left her. Striking one, a flicking orange light illuminated her tiny world and gave her a glimmer of hope. She lit one of the candles, stuck it to the deck with melted wax, and grabbed the wrench.

*Why did he show me the booby trap?* she thought, as she twisted down on another bolt.

It squeaked and complained with a terrible groan that filled the compartment.

*There's a way out and this has to be it. They want me to tell the President the ship is booby-trapped. They want the government to know that someone is alive on this ship.*


Charlie Platoon was still engaged on the *SS Independence* when FBI agents, Hawaii Five-Oh, and the base police placed a cordon around the *Stashinsky*. If Sanz had planned a time on target for 2300 hundred hours instead of 2200, the SOC boats would have had trouble maneuvering around the Russian freighter resting cross-channel at the entrance to Pearl Harbor.

With the aid of a helicopter for diversion, Sanz and his crew assaulted the *Independence*. The FBI Hostage Rescue Team screeched up to the side of the cruise liner right underneath the helicopter. Using their vehicles for cover, they began maneuvering to take the gangway. When the opposition force took them under fire, DELTA snipers opened up from several strategic locations around the ship. Using laser devices on their sniper rifles to score hits, they easily picked off the OPFOR holding the weather decks. With the troops engaged on the starboard side, Charlie Platoon climbed the ship portside aft while DELTA troops scrambled aboard portside forward. It took several hours to search the big ship thoroughly and in the process a large number of the hostages were killed, as well as several men on the assault force. But by sunrise JSOC was in control. The mission from hell was over but the nightmare had only just begun.

# Chapter 21

At the safe house Koshkin previewed the videotape Gordon Forbes had made on board the *Stashinsky*. His mouth fell open and his stomach churned when he reached the part where the Russian soldier turned into a massive quivering hemorrhage.

He stopped the VCR before the end of the tape and asked, "Is the ship full of that shit?"

"Just one hold," Gurnov replied. "But that's enough," he sneered.

"Most compelling," Koshkin said, sick to his stomach. "This will get their attention."

"You damned straight it will," Gurnov declared. "When Clinton sees what happened to that asshole schoolboy, he'll transfer the money quicker than he can undo his zipper."

Lieutenant Romanovsky had been the third officer in charge of Gurnov's chemical troop, a school educated officer that Gurnov had detested from the first moment he had laid eyes upon him.

"That's what's going to happen to the people on this island, Nickoli," he continued.

Gurnov was lying on the sofa. His eyes had a vacant stare as if he was looking through the ceiling.

Koshkin rewound the videotape. Wearing cotton gloves, he took it out of the machine and wiped it clean of prints. Then he slipped it into a Priority Mail envelope, sealed it with its self-adhesive strip, and put the envelope in a plain shopping bag.

"I'll deliver this to the FBI tonight," he said, still unnerved by the images he had seen.

Retrieving two folders from his coffee table he handed one to Gurnov and the other to Baranov.

"I had the best cobbler in Central America make your passports," he said.

Gurnov looked at his new identity. "Polish?" he complained. "Me, a fuckin' Polack?" he chuckled.

"I'm a Czech," Baranov exclaimed. "Would you believe it? A spotted assed Czech."

"I constructed legends which correspond to your lives. Alex, you served in Poland. You speak Polish very well. Yuri, you speak several Slavic languages. With those passports you'll have no trouble with immigration or customs anywhere in Asia. Just memorize the information I've listed on the paper inside your folders. Then destroy it. I'll take you to the airport in the morning and you'll be in Burma getting laid before the Americans have time to organize."

"No," Gurnov snapped.

"What?" Koshkin questioned, surprised by Gurnov's response to his meticulous evasion plan.

"I'm not leaving until the money is in the accounts," he said.

"But you must get off this island, Alex," Koshkin insisted. "I fit in here. You do not."

"Alex doesn't believe you will explode the ship, Nickoli," Baranov explained.

"But we, we don't need to explode the ship," Koshkin stammered.

"You don't. We do," Gurnov growled.

"But why? They'll give us the money. If we explode the ship thousands of people will die," Koshkin argued, in a pleading voice.

"Millions," Gurnov corrected. "And if we don't blow

up the ship the crew will identify us. But not you, Nickoli. Even if we had killed everyone before we abandon the ship, when they sort the dead they would begin looking for me. But not you, Nickoli. You are KGB. A secret agent man," Gurnov sassed, with a tone of derision in his voice.

"We all have new identities, Alex. New lives," Koshkin implored.

"I told you, Yuri," Gurnov barked. "He can't do it. You two will leave tomorrow. I'll be the sweeper of this house."

"Alex, if you explode that ship the Americans will not rest until we are all hanged by the neck," Koshkin warned.

"Fuck the Americans. After I explode that garbage scowl it will take them ten years just to bury the bodies." He glared at Koshkin. "You leave tomorrow, Nickoli. I'll do what has to be done."

"Alright," Koshkin conceded, pleased for the opportunity to escape the frag-zone. "In a field of wheat, only the stalk whose head is empty of grain stands above the rest."

"If you are going to quote Old Russian proverbs Nickoli, remember that when you cut down trees, chips are going to fly," Gurnov smirked.

He sat up just long enough to take a big swig of vodka then reclined back on the sofa. Taking a deep drag off his *papiroska*, he blew a smoke ring and stared at the ceiling. There was no peeling paint to stimulate his imagination or shadows to haunt him, just dreams of Oriental earmuffs and Mekong Whiskey.

Koshkin looked Baranov in the eyes and shook his head. "I'll be back in two hours. Don't leave this house," he warned, with a deadly serious expression. "When I get back I'll teach you how to avoid drawing attention to yourself in this country. It's an art and a science."

"Very well secret agent man," Gurnov said sarcastically. "We're up for a lesson in American decadence."

Koshkin out ranked Gurnov by two grades but not in the lessons of life and not in the category of ruthlessness.

"There is something I want you to get me, Nick," Baranov said.

"What?" Koshkin asked, wondering what on earth Baranov could want at such a time.

"An American pizza," he grinned. He flipped on the TV and eased back in an easy chair. Koshkin smiled and shook his head.

"You got it, Yuri. I'll be back as soon as I can."


Koshkin left the safe house and drove slowly to Honolulu via H-1 and Nimitz Boulevard. At Fort De Russy, he parked his car in the military lot a hundred yards from the Hawaiian Hilton where Julie Jennings and her crew had stayed before stalking the *Stashinsky*. Before getting out he checked his shopping bag that contained the bombs Baranov had constructed and the videotape. The parking lot was poorly lit and the contract security guard on duty was half-asleep. He waited until the man was occupied inside his kiosk before crossing the lot in the direction of Ala Moana Boulevard.

When he reached the street, he walked deliberately to the busiest section of Waikiki. At one o'clock in the morning the resort was still teaming with people out for a good time. Music blared from bars and night owls chattered in crowded sidewalk cafes. Blending with a group of tourists, Koshkin ambled down the street to the International Market Place. There he planted the bomb where no one was likely to discover it for days, in a location where the prevailing wind would carry the noxious gas into the surrounding buildings during business hours. Knowing that there might be surveillance cameras about, he concealed his face by moving in shadows and by keeping his head bent forward and his eyes down cast. When he cleared the market area, he walked briskly to the Federal Building to see if there was any activity. At one thirty in the morning it should have been dark and unoccupied. But it wasn't. There were people coming and going like an emergency room at a hospital.

*When they see this videotape,* he thought, *they will shut down all access to this island. For now they are in a complete state of confusion. But when they get organized they'll quarantine this island. By the time they do I've got to be on my way to Korea. But not Gurnov. He won't be able to get off the island and if they catch him, they'll catch me,* he worried. *Perhaps I should kill them.*

For a few seconds he thought about killing his partners to cover his trail. He didn't have enough money in the bank to sustain himself and Yong-Sook on the lamb, especially if the U.S. Government was actively searching for him. Indecision racked his brain until he visualized Yong-Sook's gorgeous face. Then he forged ahead with the plan.

He selected a trash container near the Federal Building, and using techniques he had learned as a spy, casually deposited the envelope as he strolled by. A quarter mile down the street he used a public telephone to call the FBI. It was in line of sight with the Federal Building so he could see what was happening. When he made connection he delivered a short message in a contrived gruff voice telling the operator where to find the videotape. Then he hung up. Strolling slowly down the street, he paused from time to time to glance back at the Federal Building. When he saw a swarm of agents rush out and comb the area, he picked up his pace and hurried back to his car for two more bombs.

He planted the second gas bomb outside a steak house directly across the street from Fort De Russy where people often stood in long lines to get a table. Shopping bag in hand, he nonchalantly stopped on the sidewalk in front of the restaurant and pretended to check the bottom of his shoe while searching the street in both directions. When it was clear he pulled the packaged out of his bag and quickly shoved it up into the thick hedges that fronted the building.

*Hide it in plain sight and they will not see it*, he thought as he continued down the street to the pedestrian crossing.

Directly across Ala Moana Boulevard the Hawaiian Hilton eclipsed Waikiki beach with a maze of high-rise towers. Koshkin waited for the traffic light, crossed the street and entered the complex like a tourist. He selected a stool at the open-air bar near the swimming pool and ordered a Coke. The resort hotel was full of people from all over the world and it was still bustling with activity at two o'clock in the morning. Tourists, making the most of their vacations in paradise, lounged around the bar drinking and chatting. Down near the beach Koshkin spotted a group of hula dancers performing under fire torches. A small crowd had gathered to watch the show.

*An excellent distraction*, he thought.

For several minutes he furtively studied the people at the bar. Near him two men were putting the make on a lovely young lady who spoke with a New York accent. Both men were wearing wedding rings and nametags identifying them as members of a business conference.

*No one believes in anything anymore*, he thought. *To*

*hold clear vision of honorable values is to tear yourself apart inside, to let the things you believe in and the things you want gnaw at each other until they open secret wounds. The Soviet Union is no more and Russia is in chaos. All that remains for us is the journey into exile. Etap,* he thought.

For Russians the journey into exile to the fetid prisons of the gulag archipelago was known by the innocent word *etap*, which means transport or stage. It is a word that struck terror in his heart. Koshkin repeated the word several times. Then he thought of the words to an old Cossack song that Gurnov was fond of singing. *'Tis not easy, brother mine, in a foreign land to live.' Bullshit*, he thought, appreciating the beauty surrounding him. *Twenty-five million dollars will ease the pain.* He smiled inwardly at the thought.

After a decent interval, he took his drink and moseyed around the pool to an area overflowing with lush tropical plants. There he sat down on the concrete wall and placed his shopping bag beside him. When the hula dancers walked by after their performance, he slipped the package out of the bag and slid it into the foliage behind him using his body for cover. While the tourists eyed the half-naked women, he secreted his third bomb. He knew the resort's gardener would eventually find it but with any luck it would be there for days. By the time the bomb was discovered, he planned to be a half a world away making love to Yong-Sook. Mission complete, he returned to the safe house. He arrived at three o'clock in the morning with four large pizzas to find Gurnov and Baranov fast asleep, potted by vodka.


After viewing the videotape, FBI and local police

officials went into overwhelm. Koshkin's first telephone call, made just after the *Stashinsky* dropped anchor, had warned them not to let anyone go aboard the ship. He had informed them that the vessel was booby trapped with explosives and full of chemical weapons. The videotape confirmed the warning and the fact that Americans were imprisoned on board the freighter. With two dead bodies just a few feet from the channel and a Russian ship blocking the entrance to Pearl Harbor, local officials realized that the situation was potentially cataclysmic. Military police began quietly evacuating Hickam Air Force Base and Pearl Harbor Navy Base.

General Carlson, who was staying in VIP quarters within sight of the *Stashinsky*, was notified at five in the morning. He immediately showered, shaved, put on his best uniform, and was driven directly to TOC headquarters on Ford Island where Colonel Ardison briefed him on the situation. He was discussing the matter on the telephone with senior officers in the tank when news of the videotape was delivered to the Joint Chiefs of Staff in Washington, D.C. An hour later, an FBI agent from the Honolulu office delivered a copy to the General. He watched it with Colonel Ardison and the commander of the FBI Hostage Rescue Team. When the tape ended the three men were at a loss for words.

Carlson called in an expert on explosives and showed him only the part of the video Forbes had shot inside the first cargo hold. The EOD specialist confirmed his worst fears. The explosives were positioned to blow the top hatch cover and catapult the chemical munitions into the air. Then he called in a climatologist for a briefing on prevailing weather patterns. As he suspected the trade winds blowing over the island were generally from west to east, which would carry the poison over Honolulu and on to the other islands of Molokai, Lanai, and Maui.

"Thank you," Carlson said dismissing the weather guesser. He hit a buzzer that called in the sentry. The corporal reported with a snappy salute.

"Ask Captain Watson and Colonel Boyd to come in, please."

"Yes, sir," the sentry replied.

"General, I just finished taking down the *Independence* with Lieutenant Sanz and Master Chief Blaze," the FBI agent said. "They are about the best I've seen in this business. I recommend they be read into the situation."

"Wait," Carlson ordered.

The sentry paused at the door, braced, and stood at attention. Carlson wasn't interested in Lieutenant Sanz, an inexperienced junior officer, but Blaze was a different matter. He knew Blaze was a Ph.D. candidate. He had recently read his draft thesis on international terrorism and had been impressed.

"Get Master Chief Blaze also, and his Lieutenant."

"Yes, sir," the sentry bugled.


When Boyd, Watson, Sanz, and Blaze were seated around the table, Ardison's deputy, Lieutenant Colonel Houston, briefed them on the code word encompassing the situation and asked them to sign disclosure forms. Then he showed them the videotape. Sanz nearly lost his mind when Julie's bruised and battered face filled the television monitor.

"You know that woman?" Carlson asked, caught off guard.

*"General, that's my fiancé!* We would have been married two weeks ago if not for this exercise."

"Stop the tape," Carlson ordered.

Lieutenant Colonel Houston pressed the stop button on the VCR.

"I'm sorry, Lieutenant, but I'll have to ask you to leave the SCIF," he ordered.

"*But General!*" Sanz blurted, his eyes begging.

"General Carlson, sir," Blaze interrupted. "I most strongly recommend you reconsider. Lieutenant Sanz's knowledge of the girl and the cameraman may prove useful."

Carlson glared at the Master Chief but Blaze held his stare without blinking.

"In what way?" Carlson demanded.

"The Lieutenant knows the project Ms. Jennings was working on. He spoke with her just before we went into isolation. He also knows the cameraman. If either person was able to incorporate a veiled message into the videotape, he is the most likely person to pick up on it," Blaze explained. "Besides, he can handle it."

"Very well. Get a grip on yourself, son. The end of this tape is hard to watch. Continue," he ordered.

Houston pressed a button and Julie's face filled the TV screen.

*"This is Julie Jennings reporting from the Russian ship, Bogdan Stashinsky," she said without looking at the paper. "This message is for President Clinton." Glancing down at the paper, she read, "I quote: President Clinton, you will immediately give orders to transfer one hundred million dollars to the bank of Estonia, account number zero-zero-zero-six-four-seven-eight-nine-two or we will explode this ship. As you will see in this video, the Stashinsky is loaded with chemical and biological toxins, and booby-trapped with tons of explosives that we can detonate remotely. You will transfer the money within twenty-four hours or we will explode a chemical bomb in*

*Honolulu. If we do not receive the money within twelve hours of the delivery of this videotape, copies will be sent to all major news organizations showing the people of your country that it was you who made the decision to kill the people of Hawaii. If this transaction is accomplished in less than twelve hours, no one will know you paid us the money. End quote."*

Sanz viewed the video from beginning to end, but even when he saw the Russian soldier die in agony, Julie consumed his thoughts.

When the screen when blank Carlson asked, "Lieutenant, what sort of project was Ms. Jennings working on?"

Stuttering and stammering, Lee told the General about the fishermen who had died of mysterious causes and about Greenpeace's assertion that the Russians were dumping toxic waste at sea. He explained that she was making a documentary with the aid of the environmentalists and had gone to Malaysia to film the ship in transit to Johnston Atoll in hopes of catching the Russians on videotape dumping toxins at sea.

"Houston, get the Coroner in here right away," Carlson ordered. "I want a thorough briefing on his findings. Use a helo. And get in touch with Greenpeace. I want to speak with whoever's in charge of the organization."

Houston rushed out of the SCIF like buckshot coyote.

"Any ideas?" Carlson asked, looking from man to man.

Blaze was the first to speak. "General, I recommend we plant listening devices on the ship's hull. We may be able to set up communications with the people inside by means of Morse code."

"Next," Carlson said, as if he disliked the suggestion. He had already ordered the mission.

Blaze was taken aback by the General's abruptness but continued. "Can we prevent all radio frequencies, all RF emissions from reaching the ship? Is there any way to block the full RF spectrum?" Blaze asked.

Carlson's exhaled heavily but his eyes brightened slightly in his worried face. "I sent off a message an hour ago asking the same question. We'll have an answer soon."

"Maybe they are using cell phones to communicate," Blaze suggested. "Perhaps we should shut down the entire system until this is over?"

A slight smile parted Carlson's lips. "You're staying in here with me, old man," Carlson said, pointing his finger at Blaze. "The rest of you go find out everything you can about that ship. And Charlie," he said to Ardison, "Talk to the CIA personally. Stress the fact that we need the Russian's help on this. We've got to know who sailed on that vessel and what she is transporting. Have someone analyze the cellular phone system in this area. Figure out what we have to do to shut it down. But take no action."

"Yes, sir. I'll get right on it," Ardison replied.

As the others stood to leave Blaze piped up again.

"Sir, I recommend we prepare for an underwater assault with cutting torches. It's a long shot but we might get the chance to cut the anchor chain and tow the vessel out to sea. We might even be able to clandestinely cut a hole in the bottom of the ship and enter underwater."

"Why did you say, it is long shot, Master Chief?" Carlson asked.

"Well, the area on the west bank of the channel is uninhabited. No lights. Hickam and Pearl are on the east bank. If we turn out all the lights on the bases it will be pitch dark around the ship. And if we're lucky and a rainsquall happens to pass through, we might have time to cut her loose and scuttle her at sea. Once she's underwater, the threat is substantially reduced."

"Excellent idea. But what if the crooks aren't watching from the mountains, Master Chief? What if they're on Hickam or Pearl or have a look out at the international airport?" Carlson asked.

Blaze hunched up his shoulders and raised his eyebrows. "We ought to be ready for all contingencies, General," he replied.

"Agreed. Charlie," Carlson said.

"Yes, sir," Ardison answered.

"Get a team of men on it. Get an expert in here on tugboat operations. But play this whole thing out as if it's a part of exercise *Freedom Express*. Understand?"

"Yes, sir," Ardison replied.

"General?" Sanz said.

"Yes, Lieutenant."

"I volunteer to board the ship," Lee said, worry written all over his face.

Carlson thought, *Trouble*. He said, "The very last thing I need is a volunteer who is emotionally involved, Lieutenant. Dismissed."

Outside the specially constructed room, in the main part of the TOC, Houston briefed Watson, Boyd, and Sanz into several code words and gave them access to the files and data banks.

While they studied the problem two television sets located in the corner provided continuous news coverage. When the regional news came on, a female intelligence officer turned down the volume of CNN so they could hear the local channel. Lee recognized the reporter as the same man that had exposed *Freedom Express*. He introduced Captain Bowers, the CINCPAC PAO, and asked him about the ship blocking the channel into Pearl Harbor. To Lee's amazement Captain Bowers explained the presence of the *Stashinsky* as part of exercise *Freedom Express*.

*He's lying and doesn't know it*, Sanz thought. *This whole island is about to explode and he's lying.* Then he thought. *But what else can we do? If he tells the truth there will be complete chaos. There's no place to go. We can't evacuate this island.* Then he thought of Julie. *I've got to get Julie off that ship. But how?*

Using all of the assets available to the TOC he set his mind to the task.

It was late in the evening when Master Chief Blaze placed a hand on his shoulder and said, "Take a break, sir. Go get a bite to eat. I'll get word to you if anything comes up."

"I'm not hungry," Lee replied.

"You know, if you don't take care of your body sir, your body will not be able to perform when the call comes."

Sanz eyed the pugnacious Master Chief for a few seconds then nodded agreement. He stacked up his folders and shuffled out of the TOC with his mind still on the problem. He was halfway to the chow hall when Major Verduchi spotted him with his hands in his pockets.

"*Stand at attention, Hollywood!*" he yelled, loud enough that anyone within a hundred feet could hear his command.

Lee stopped in his tracks and gritted his teeth. He pulled his hands out of his pockets and rubbed his temples between his thumb and forefinger.

"You just don't get it, do you boy?"

"Get what?"

"Discipline. I heard you fucked up another take down," Verduchi snarled.

"You have anything to do with that?" Lee demanded.

Verduchi smiled. He shook his finger in Lee's face.

"Don't talk when a senior officer is addressing you, Lieutenant."

Lee had had enough. He balled up his fist and was about to knock Verduchi unconscious when a voice boomed out of the darkness.

"What's going here?"

Colonel Ardison stepped out of the shadow of a stack of pallets.

"I was just correcting the Lieutenant's bearing and comportment, sir. He can't seem to keep his hands out of his pockets. He is setting a bad example for the men, sir," Verduchi said.

"I see. Lieutenant?"

"The Major is correct, sir. I had my hands in my pockets," Lee said.

Verduchi smirked just a little. Wrinkles and shadows cracked Colonel Ardison's weather worn face.

"Major Verduchi," he said in a tired voice, "did you have any contact with the Controller Cell prior to the *Independence* mission assigned to SEAL Team FIVE?"

"No, Sir."

"*Stand at attention, Major!*" he roared.

He looked at Sanz and said, "Dismissed, Lieutenant."

Lee did an about face and as he walked away he heard Ardison growling like a junkyard dog, *"I hate liars. And I hate men who hide behind their rank. Pack your bags, Major. You're outta here!"*

# Chapter
# 22

It was late morning when an olive drab army truck, one of those cubical bread truck designs, pulled up next to the old warehouse at the south end of Ford Island. The driver backed up next to the seawall, got out, and walked coolly to the rear and opened the back doors. The six SEALs concealed in the back of the truck were dressed in wetsuits. On their chests they wore closed circuit oxygen rebreathers. Beads of sweat formed on their brows and faces, not from stress but from the heat in the closed metal compartment. The team leader looked over his men carefully. None of them were armed. The devices they carried were electronic.

"Okay, guys. Gear up," he ordered.

They slipped on their swim fins and tightened up the cinches on their rebreathers.

"Purge," he ordered.

They spit in their masks, rubbed the saliva around with a finger, and rinsed them in a bucket of seawater setting in the middle of the truck. Frogmen had learned from experience that saliva prevented their masks from fogging underwater.

The commander donned his own mask, opened the value on his oxygen bottle, and placed his mouthpiece between his teeth. Breathing deeply by mouth, he exhaled through his noses, allowing the air to leak out around the seal of his mask. When the breathing loop was dry he filled it with fresh oxygen by pushing on a button in the middle of the scuba. As he purged his scuba of nitrogen he watched his men repeat the procedure until the only gas remaining in their scubas was pure oxygen.

When all of the troops were ready, the commander slipped out the back and over the seawall into the bay. With his breathing loop near empty he sank to the bottom and made way for his teammates to join him. The others followed, one at a time, gathering like a pod of orcas.

The confusion of entry quickly cleared. The SEALs paired off and checked each other's scuba for leaks. They signaled the team leader with *okay-signs* then set off on a southerly course toward the *Stashinsky,* periodically clearing their ears as they increased depth. Holding on to a line tied to the navigator's web belt, they crawled the bottom to deeper water. They swam quickly with strong kicks of their wide duckfeet fins hugging the sandy bottom until it dropped off too deep for oxygen scuba. Using a depth gauge, the navigator maintained a depth of twenty-five feet and steadied on his preplanned course. Above them the reflecting surface of the bay gave no hint of their presence below because their scubas did not emit bubbles.

Tiny bright, multicolored fish of all shapes and descriptions gently lazed around patches of broken coral below their flight path. A green turtle flew by them through its blue liquid atmosphere and disappeared into the fog at the outer limit of visibility. Kicking on, they passed a huge jellyfish undulating rhythmically through the water in slow, pulsating motions.

In mid channel, the bottom gave way to a desert of sand and silt gliding by below. Kicking with powerful strokes developed by intensive training, they followed a precise course that led them directly to the hull of the Russian ship. As they neared the vessel the noise of shrimp and fish was joined by the sound of people pinging on the hull with metal objects. Up above, the surface took on a fluid pattern downstream of the *Stashinsky's* black hulk.

At the keel the SEALs separated into three swim pairs. Each team swam to a different part of the ship and removed electronic listening devices from their backpack containers. As swim buddies, one man paid out a long line from deeper water. Using the line as an anchor to prevent breaking the surface, the implant man ascended the curve of the hull to just a few feet below the surface. Below the waterline each team attached two magnetic limpets. From each, a slender stiff wire antenna protruded a few feet above the surface of the bay and began transmitting data to the TOC at Ford Island. Mission accomplished, the SEALs regrouped at the keel and returned to base.

"Alex, soon the Americans will close this airport," Koshkin said, in a low voice. "When the time is near there will be no flights in or off the island."

"Then I will take a ferry to another island," Gurnov replied.

"No. No. You do not understand. This is the international terminal. When it shuts down there will be chaos. All other means of transportation will be flooded."

"I'll find a way off this island," Gurnov snapped.

Koshkin had taken his partners on a windshield tour of Honolulu before driving to the airport. Along the route he had pointed out the locations of the bombs he had planted and the best sites to use the radio firing devices to activate them. He had also shown Gurnov the freighters he had booked passage on. Over drinks at the airport, he was trying to coach him but Gurnov was not in the receive-mode. He gulped down his drink and ordered another.

"Alex, you must not drink too much. The policemen in this country are trained to catch intoxicated drivers. Flow with the traffic, obey all the traffic rules, and do nothing to draw attention to yourself. If you are stopped for any reason, say nothing. Smile and give them the papers I showed you, the ones in the glove compartment."

"*Da, da,*" Gurnov acknowledged in a testy mood.

Koshkin had sterilized the house but he couldn't be sure he hadn't left behind a fingerprint, a stray hair, or DNA evidence that might tie him or his Korean beauty to the crime. With Baranov's assistance he had even rigged the place with a time delayed incendiary. But if Gurnov was arrested, the trail would lead directly to him. He shook his finger at his tortured colleague.

"If you are smart you will stay inside the safe house until Markov calls with word that the money is in the bank. Then set the timer and leave this island by the first available means. I'll call you from Hong Kong in about fourteen hours. If necessary I will negotiate with the FBI from there."

"There will be no negotiation," Gurnov roared, too loudly.

"*Shooo!*" Baranov hissed. "Nickoli is right. Don't draw attention. You will get us all caught, *Zakuski.*" Both he and Koshkin looked around the bar nervously.

"There is always negotiation. The first thing the Americans will try to do is negotiate," Koshkin argued. "That is their modus operandi. It is not in their nature to transfer the money until their hand is forced."

"Then I will force their hand. I will blow up one of the bombs when I leave here," Gurnov said, determination written on his face.

"No. No," Koshkin hushed. "Timing is everything. Don't be so fuckin' hard headed. You are going to fuck us all. Follow the plan! Wait until tomorrow when the streets are busy," he said, face serious and grave. "Alex?"

"*Da.*"

"Listen to me. No one knows about the safe house. And no one knows about your legend. Moreover, there are many foreigners on this island. Keep a low profile and follow the plan. And Alex, do not blow up the ship," Koshkin begged. "They will pay the money if you handle this right," he argued in a pleading voice. "Your legend is perfect. Use it. When we have the money, live and let live."

"Nickoli is right, Alex," Baranov butted in. "They are excellent papers. When the Blue-X goes off they will pay the money like frightened schoolgirls. Live and let live. What do you say, Alex?" Baranov asked in a pleading voice.

Gurnov shook his head in reluctant agreement. "Okay. Perhaps you are right, Nickoli. I should be getting on the plane and you should be handling the details. But it's too late to change now. Call me from Hong Kong."

"Good decision, Alex," Koshkin gushed, relieved by his acquiescence.

"I will see Yuri to his gate and then go to mine. See you in Asia, Alex," he said, holding out his hand.

Gurnov shook it vigorously and said. "Don't worry. I will follow the plan."

In his mind's eye he saw the *Stashinsky* explode and a huge cloud of noxious gas spread over the island.

"*Do svidaniya*, my friends," Koshkin whispered as he stood up to leave for his gate.

He dug a generous tip out of his pocket for the

waitress and placed it on the table.

"*Do svidaniya*, Alex," Baranov said. "I will see you in Burma in a couple of weeks. If you don't show," he grinned, "I'm going to screw your woman."

"You can have her, Yuri. I'm going to buy some fresh ones because I know you fucked her every time your woman was away," Gurnov replied.

Baranov chuckled and shook his head no. They walked together in silence to the departure corridor, all three men wearing smart business suits Koshkin had provided. At the security check they gave each other a traditional hug then Gurnov watched as his comrades passed through the metal detector and cleared airport security. Fear consumed him as he watched his comrades walk down the corridor to freedom. Intense fear he had not felt before.

*They are all looking at me*, he thought. *Why are these people staring at me?*

He wheeled about and left the terminal as fast as he could walk.

Following Koshkin's advice, Gurnov drove carefully back to the safe house and assumed the watch. Sipping on iced vodka he relaxed and observed the activity on the bases below. The *Stashinsky* lay in the channel like a ghost ship, black and foreboding. Helicopters were coming and going from Ford Island but the streets of Pearl and Hickam were deserted.

*That's where their operations center is located*, he thought, focusing on Ford Island. *Excellent. The building is run down and the base is remote. Good cover.*

He put the binoculars down and used the telescope to zoom in on the men arriving by helicopter. For a second his mind stopped, as if his heart skipped a beat.

*Chinese. What are they doing here?* he wondered.

Then he remembered that there were lots of Oriental

people in Hawaii. As he watched Coroner Chang and his staff walk across the tarmac, he remembered Vietnam, but not the Vietnam of the Americans. He recalled the Vietnam experience of the Russians. In his mind's eye he saw an armed conflict between the Chinese and his Vietnamese allies.

The fissure in Sino-Soviet relations had begun long before Yuri Baranov molested a Chinese official's daughter in the hot surf off Hodeida, Yemen. It began in a lake in the middle of Peking. During a visit to China, Stalin and Mao had gone for a swim together. When they were alone, dog paddling in the middle of the pond, Stalin urged Mao to use nuclear weapons on American forces fighting in Korea. When Mao refused, knowing that to do so would result in a nuclear war he could not win, Stalin became angry and insulted him. Mao knew that the Americans would level every city in China while Stalin was busy seizing France and Britain. He also knew that Stalin had ordered Kim IL Sung, the North Korean leader, to invade South Korea, and that he was positioning himself to conquer the world. He refused Stalin's order, and unbeknownst to the West, the great Sino-Soviet bloc fractured like glass. Mao recounted the momentous conversation to his deputy in the presence of several functionaries. Unfortunately word of the fissure didn't filter out to the Western world until decades later.

*Vietnam wasn't a war, you fools*, Gurnov thought as he stared out over Pearl Harbor. "It was a shitty little battle in a world war, a little skirmish," he mumbled, studying the military facilities down below with an expert's eye.

Gurnov, Koshkin, and Baranov had fought numerous battles in the latter part of the Cold War including several tours of duty in Vietnam. Baranov had taught guerrilla warfare and terrorist tactics. Koshkin had been an advisor to Vietcong leaders. Gurnov had taught tactics and advised senior NVA officers in the north.

The principle preoccupation of U.S. Military planners and senior politicians during the late 1940's, 50's, and 60's was nuclear war. With both China and the Soviet Union in possession of the hydrogen bomb, the fear of nuclear holocaust consumed Western leaders. But in the communist world, a strategy developed which subordinated the military to prolonged economic, psychological, and political confrontation. Stalin directly challenged the West with the Iron Curtain, the Berlin Wall, and the Korean War. Khrushchev continued the confrontation with Cuba and *Wars of National Liberation,* which threatened existing governments in a startling number of countries around the world, most of them in the underdeveloped areas of Africa, Latin America, and Asia. The French called them *Revolutionary Wars*. Americans, reluctant to attach any phraseology remotely related to the *Spirit of '76*, called them insurgency. The three Cossacks who had been involved in most of the conflicts, called them encounters.

The engagements varied in detail from place to place, but they all shared three important characteristics. First, they were basically indigenous. Second, they were rooted in deep dissatisfaction with existing forms of government, and in some cases in the sheer misery of native peoples. Third, they were sponsored and supported by the Soviet Union for the purpose of confronting the West.

Facing what appeared to be a unified monolithic Sino-Soviet communist bloc, which possessed enormous quantities of chemical, nuclear, and biological weapons of mass destruction and massive numbers of troops in arms, the United States drew a *line-in-the-sand* in the *Wars of National Liberation*. It was drawn at the fifty-second parallel in Vietnam. But neither the Eisenhower administration, nor the Kennedy and Johnson administrations that followed really understood the dimensions of the struggle.

*The Americans are not as good as they think they are*, Gurnov thought, as he surveyed Pearl Harbor. *They failed on all accounts in Vietnam. They blindly followed in the footsteps of their French whores in support of a corrupt and worthless government detested by the Vietnamese people. Their proclivity to see all problems and solutions in their own terms, and to grow impatient when the struggle drags on, are fatal flaws in their national character. I can wait them out here too.*

With instructors like Yuri Baranov, the VC were able to make highly effective use of terrorism. Koshkin had helped direct kidnappings, assassinations, and terrorism against South Vietnamese officials from bases in Cambodia. Recognizing the value of such guerrilla warfare, the KGB had set up special schools for terrorists in Czechoslovakia, Cuba, and North Korea. They trained thousands of third world terrorists. The three Cossacks had taught at the schools at various times during their careers.

"A guerrilla is of the land and of the people and therefore has ready information and intelligence," Gurnov recited, from one of his lectures. "He can strike or not strike, when, where, and how he chooses, withholding action until the odds are in his favor. He can destroy and terrorize with little concern or responsibility, because he has no need to defend, protect, or secure territory. His effectiveness depends upon his ability to exploit these strengths to offset his enemies' strategic advantage. I am not of this land, nor of these people, but they don't know that. They can't tell I'm a fucking Cossack by the look in my eye."

Then he thought, *a guerrilla must have the support, or at least the passive indifference of the population. He must have outside logistical help and a cause to rally around. I am alone and my only cause is money. But at least I'm not like the Boyars selling out my homeland.*

"A guerrilla's enemies succeed or fail, not on the basis of their physical numbers and technological strengths, but according to their abilities to separate him from the people. The enemy must cut off his outside assistance, cast doubt on the validity of his cause, and convince the people of the worthiness of the government," he recited out loud in an almost psychotic breakdown of his reality.

*I'll stay in this safe house until it is time to strike. Then I will blend with the people and strike without warning. When I achieve my goal I will blow up the ship to cover my trail and disappear.*

In the mid 1960's, the CIA had countered the KGB in Vietnam with *Counter Terror Units*, a South Vietnamese program, funded and coordinated by the Agency. Its objectives were to identify, capture and kill members of the Vietcong infrastructure living undercover in South Vietnam. When the U.S. Military took over the program they code-named it *Operation Phoenix.* They also wrestled control out of Vietnamese hands, largely because of the torture tactics used by the South Vietnamese. Without brutality to counter brutality, *Operation Phoenix* lost its effectiveness and died a lingering death, like the U.S. effort in Vietnam. Master Chief Tom Blaze had been one of the most effective advisors in the Delta. On one mission he had come within a hair's breadth of killing Alexander Gurnov deep in the jungles of Cambodia.

*How did they do it?* Gurnov thought. *Despite a lack of vision on the part of their leaders, despite their ineptitude, despite the support of the American counter-culture, they won the damn war. We won the battles and they won the war. We didn't defeat them in Vietnam. They simply re-deployed and out of vengeance broke our back in the marketplace.*

Gurnov hated the Americans with a passion for what they had done to the Red Army.

"Now they are destroying the Motherland," he mumbled. "They, and the lousy Chinese."

Coroner Chang had reminded him of a different war, one absent of Americans. In February 1979, the Chinese had invaded Vietnam to punish Hanoi for seizing Cambodia, for mistreating the Chinese who were living in Vietnam, and for forcing more than fifty thousand ethnic Chinese to flee overland back into China. By the time Gurnov arrived in North Vietnam the People's Liberation Army had penetrated ten miles into Vietnamese territory with more than thirty thousand soldiers. His job was to advise the Vietnamese general responsible for leading the counter offensive on the employment of chemical weaponry provided by the Soviet Union.

As Gurnov watched Chang and his subordinates hurry into the hangar, it all came back to him in a kaleidoscope of images. From the lush green hills above the battlefield he had seen an entire Chinese battalion wriggling and squirming in a death dance, wiped out by chemical munitions. Those that survived withdrew from Vietnamese territory like scalded dogs. Peking never registered a complaint at the United Nations, knowing that Russian troops were massed on their northern frontier with nuclear, biological, and chemical weapons. While the Americans fretted over Nicaragua and El Salvador in 1979, mankind was on the brink of biological, nuclear and chemical warfare in Asia.

"It's my turn, you assholes," he mumbled, visualizing the *Stashinsky* exploding in a great inferno.  He picked up the remote firing device and with hate boiling in his brain was tempted to push the button.

"*Nyet.  Nyet.  Yeb vas veruyushchii! -- No.  No.  Fuck you God believers!*  You'll get yours after I get mine," he mumbled, thinking of ten lovely Oriental girls serving his every wish.

# Chapter
# 23

Julie lit her last candle and cemented it to the deck with a little melted wax. She was wet with sweat and exhausted. It had taken her what seemed like hours to figure out a method of removing the huge nuts. Then driven by fear and determination, she had worked feverously to escape her prison while she still had candlelight to work by.

*Just one more*, she thought, returning to the struggle.

She placed the boxed-end of a huge wrench on the last nut holding the steel plate to the bulkhead and slipped a length of pipe over the end of the tool to add leverage. Groaning in pain from her injuries, she pushed down with all her body weight and felt it break loose. All the bolts had been exercised recently and once broken loose were easy to unthread.

*Oh thank you, God*, she prayed silently. *Thank you.*

The nut complained with a loud creak that reverberated through the compartment, then unthreaded easily by hand. She dropped it on the deck and using the wrench as a hammer pounded on the steel plate to no avail.

*The screwdriver*, she thought. *They left it for me to use as a pry bar.*

She picked up the over-sized screwdriver and scratched around the edges of the plate to break the paint seal. Then using the wrench as a hammer she pounded on the butt of the screwdriver until she was able to pry the plate off the bulkhead. It fell on the deck with a clatter that rattled the whole compartment.

Taking what was left of her candle, she stepped through the opening. The compartment was similar to the one she had just escaped. She hurried to the hatch and tried to open it. It too was locked from the outside.

*"Damn!"* she cursed.

Struggling with all her might, she yanked on the locking bar until she was exhausted. Giving up she slumped to the deck and began sobbing like a little girl.

"Why? Why? Why?" she cried. *"There has to be a reason."*

When she regained her composure she surveyed the room by holding the candle up at arm's length. In the far corner of the compartment she spotted another stack of candles and a small black object.

*"A phone! A cell phone!"* she gasped.

She crawled across the deck and examined it with wide eyes.

*The battery is good.*

She dialed the operator and pushed the send button.

*"Nothing!"* she screamed.

*"You sick bastards!"* she yelled in frustration, realizing that a cell phone wouldn't transmit from inside the steel compartment. *"That's one hell of a cruel joke!"* she shouted. *Maybe they're so damn ignorant they don't know it won't work from inside the ship*, she reasoned.

Shaking with anger, she lit another candle. It was then that she noticed the sheet of paper lying under the candles. She jerked it out from beneath the pile and read the words Baranov had written in block letters: *Tell Clinton if anyone come on ship we blow it up.*

Underneath the message he had drawn a crude diagram. It was a telephone attached to a cord. At first she thought the wire represented a telephone line.

"What are you trying to tell me, you ugly brute?" she

mumbled.

Searching the walls and overhead with the dim light of the candle, she spotted it. There in front of her was a loose wire hanging down the side of the bulkhead.

"*An antennae,*" she gasped.

Struggling to her feet, she hooked the wire to the antenna on the cell phone and started to dial a number.

"*No!*" she cried. *What if it's hooked to explosives?* she thought. *What if I'm the trigger? No. They wouldn't take the chance of me detonating the ship before they get their blood money.*

For several minutes she agonized over the decision. With her strength gone and down to just a few hours of candlelight remaining, she decided to use the phone.

"You want me to tell the President not to let anyone aboard this ship. Okay," she murmured. "Then that's what I'll do."

She dialed the operator and waited for the explosion.

"Island Cellular, may I help you," came a young feminine voice.

"Yes," Julie cried, with a great gush of relief. "Please connect me with the FBI. Immediately."

"General Carlson, I will not accede to extortion under any circumstance. To do so would only invite further criminal acts against this country," the confident voice on the other end of the line boomed.

"Mister President," Carlson replied. "There are two realities to any emergency of this nature. The first is what is happening or what has actually happened. The second is, what the public thinks is happening, or has happened. Two very different realities, sir," Carlson argued. "I think we,"

The President interrupted him. "I will not be a party to the deception of the American people," he roared into the receiver. "Is that clear? Find another way, General. Why can't you sink the ship?"

"Sir, the channel is too shallow to sink the vessel in situ and if we try to tow it out to deep water there is a high probability the extortionists will detonate the explosives and contaminate this entire island. Mister President, the magnitude of the threat is so great we must accede to their demands," Carlson insisted.

"No. To do so sets a precedence that will result in more extortion. There has to be another way, General. *Find it!*" the President demanded.

"Sir, if you'll just hear me out. What I am recommending is a third party, a private party. With your permission I will ask a personal friend to transfer the money to the specified account. No one need know we had this conversation, that you gave me permission to meet the extortion demand by means of a private party. But I need authorization from you, between the two of us, so we don't muddle this up with conflicting solutions. We can deal with the criminals and retrieving the money later, after we have eliminated the threat," Carlson argued.

For a long time there was silence on the line.

"Taken under consideration, General Carlson. In the meantime, explore all options."

The line went dead, leaving Carlson in despair. The twenty-four hour deadline stipulated in the videotape was fast approaching and not two miles from where he was seated was a ship loaded with the most ghastly war poisons ever created by mankind. And it was rigged to explode on command. He couldn't sink it, he couldn't tow it to deep water, and he dared not put anyone aboard it for fear they would be seen or trip a booby trap and explode the vessel.

*If they blow up the ship they have no leverage*, he thought. *They know that. That's why they planted bombs in Honolulu, to get our attention. Maybe the cops will find them before the deadline and buy a little time. But then what? They'll just make their demands public and we'll be forced to act. Then the world will know that this country gave in to extortion. I've got to do something and fast. But what?*

Carlson pushed a button that illuminated a light outside the SCIF in the TOC. Shortly the sentry appeared.

"Ask Colonel Ardison to step in please."

"Yes, sir."

When Ardison reported he gave him a secret mission.

"Charlie, I want the fastest bird in Hawaii to take Lieutenant Colonel Houston to Dallas. Ask him to come in for a private conversation. I have a top secret priority mission for him."

Ardison nodded and left the room. When the door closed Carlson placed a long distance telephone call to Texas, spoke briefly then signaled for Houston to enter the SCIF.

Master Chief Blaze was seated outside in the TOC working over a pile of intelligence documents when he saw Houston enter the SCIF and rush out a few minutes later like a transplant surgeon carrying a newly extracted heart.

"Something's up," he said to Sanz, cutting his eyes at the Lieutenant Colonel rushing out of the TOC.

"What do you think it is?" Sanz asked.

"No telling. General Carlson is genius. He'll figure something out," Blaze replied.

"Master Chief? You remember that feeling I told you about on our way to Hawaii?"

"Yes sir, I do," Blaze replied.

Sanz stared at him, studying his face. "Do you think the Russians are behind this?" he asked.

"No."

"Neither do I. But I believe that there are people in the Russian military that know what's on board that ship. They are not going to tell us that there are super poisons on board that vessel. The Russians are no more in control than we are," Sanz said.

Blaze nodded his head in agreement. "What's your point?"

"Do you think the men behind this are part of the ship's crew?" Sanz asked.

Blaze raised one eyebrow and said, "It's most likely an inside job, with accomplices here in Hawaii. Witnesses reported seeing two men row ashore and three men drive away."

"The question is, will they explode the ship?" Sanz asked.

"I don't know," Blaze answered, shaking his head. "I wish I could reduce this to a mathematical probability like the General, but I can't. I just try to read the facts and see them in terms of human nature."

"Me too. They're going to blow up the ship when they get the money," Sanz continued, in a somber voice.

Blaze looked deep into his boss's eyes. "How do you figure that, Lieutenant?"

"To cover their trail. I have a feeling, Master Chief. A real bad feeling."

For a long time, Blaze stared at him with unblinking eyes. Thinking. *If I were a tango I'd blow the ship up as soon as I had the money. The carnage would cover my exodus and hide my identity.* "Let's not start that *bad-feeling-shit again,* okay? I'm not a superstitious man and I don't believe in ESP. No one would kill a half a million people for a hundred million dollars."

"Yes they would. Just as surely as they killed one of their own," Sanz insisted.

Blaze looked away, concerned that his agreement with Sanz's assertion would show on his face. Images of the young Russian dying in the cargo hold of the *Stashinsky* filled his thoughts.

"Master Chief Blaze?" the sentry said.

"Yes."

"Please report to General Carlson."

"Aye," Blaze grunted, as he stood up from the table.

"I have to get her off that ship, Master Chief," Sanz said, his eyes boring into Blaze's skull.

"You can't do that, son," he said in a fatherly voice. "You don't know what we're up against."

"I know I have to do something or I won't be able to live with myself," Sanz insisted.

"Don't do anything rash," Blaze cautioned. "We'll talk about it later. Maybe General Carlson has figured something out. Okay?" he said.

Sanz nodded. Blaze eyed him for a few seconds before heading for the security door to the SCIF.

Inside the electronically sealed space Carlson sat at a table piled high with data. For hours he, the head of Hawaii Five Zero, and the regional director of the FBI had received numerous briefings from experts on weather, currents, the ship's configuration, Soviet bloc explosives, the chemical weapons manifested on board the ship, and a dozen other subjects. The only part of the puzzle that he was missing was who was behind the extortion. The Russians had agreed to provide pictures and personality profiles of the crew but Carlson hadn't yet received the information.

Blaze entered the room quietly and spoke softly. "General?"

Carlson's head was down and when he looked up Blaze noticed how tired his eyes were. Worry cracked his face with heavy lines.

"Have a seat, Tom," he gestured to the chair across the table.

Blaze sat down and was quiet until the General spoke.

"Tom, why haven't you accepted a commission?" he asked, off the wall.

Blaze sat dumbfounded, baffled by such a question at this dark hour.

"I know you have a master's degree," Carlson continued, "and that you are working on a Ph.D. Your thesis is the best piece of writing I've ever read on terrorism. Hell, you are going to get your Ph.D. before I get mine. Then how will I address you, old friend? Doctor Master Chief Tom Blaze? Why did you leave SIX, Tom?" he asked.

"Simple question, General. It deserves a simple answer. It was time to go. We can't hope to combat this new face of warfare by concentrating our efforts in just a few commands on the East Coast. It was time to spread the experience and tactics. Besides, all CT commands are too close to Washington for my comfort zone," Blaze said with a stern expression on his face.

"I know what you mean," the General replied. He took a deep breath and exhaled slowly. "In your thesis you had some very profound things to say about this business," Carlson continued, as he studied Blaze's face like a book. "You wrote, and I quote, the public must be prepared for the loss of innocent life to terrorists, unquote. You also expressed the point of view that the public must be informed, that the government must sometimes act on limited data, before all the facts are known. I believe you expressed most appropriately that SOF can't afford to wait for opinion polls."

"In this case do you think our political leaders will wait for an opinion poll?" Blaze asked.

Carlson ignored the question and asked, "In your thesis you stated that counterterrorism operations are reactive, like firemen called to the scene of a disaster after a building on fire and that in the era of weapons of mass destruction CT would be too little, too late. You recommended aggressive antiterrorism measures in hardening targets, tightening up the border and immigration policies, and most importantly, integrating and enhancing intelligence efforts focused on terrorism. But, one aspect of your thesis particularly intrigues me at this late hour. You called it the devil's dilemma, the decision of whether to act, or not to act, when hundreds of thousands of lives are at risk. In your opinion Tom, is there any way to get aboard that ship and defuse it?"

"There is always a way, General." Blaze took a deep breath and exhaled slowly. The scars on his face appeared to deepen. Carlson read them like a roadmap, seeing the wisdom and experience they bequeathed. "In the videotape I noticed that the explosive were rigged with Communist block det-cord in a standard military field. The master blaster who did the job used overhand, reef, and right angle knots to tie in his charges into the field just like we do. The placement of the explosives and the way they were tied into the trunk lines suggest he used delays. I would use delays to blast the hatches first then project the chemicals into the air for maximum dispersion. Those trunk lines however, have to exit the holds somewhere and they have to run up to a receiver. That receiver has to be tied into one of the ship's antennae, either on the bridge or in the radio room. Maybe both. If you ask me to go aboard that vessel, I'll be steppin' lightly looking for booby traps, and every place I see a length of det-cord, I'll cut it, hoping to get them all. Once the receiver is isolated from the system, or the holds are cut off from the receiver, the crooks lose their leverage, sort of like defanging a cobra. But even a careful man can get bitten by a snake in the dark."

"But you're telling me it could be done?" Carlson pressed.

"The biggest problem will be getting into the ship without setting off a booby trap."

"Is there a way?" Carlson demanded.

"Of course. There is always a way, General."

"How?"

"The bridge has glass windows. Glass breaks. That's one way."

"What if there's a motion detector or a tremble switch?" Carlson suggested.

"That is certainly a possibility but I doubt the master blaster used any sensitive switches. He had to rig the explosives while the ship was underway. When they dropped anchor the whole damned ship vibrated like a truck going down a gravel road. Tremble or mercury switches aren't a good idea under such conditions. Even IR motion detectors present a problem to the master blaster in this condition. Birds or rats, for example could prematurely trigger the system."

"What about the underwater business? Can we enter the vessel underwater without being detected?"

"Yes. But it would be a messy job. We could cut a hole in the bottom of the ship into a compartment that is likely to be sealed. We could use it like an airlock. Once inside, we could plug up the hole behind us and cut our way through the hatch."

"Tom, can you defuse that bomb?" Carlson growled.

Blaze stared at him without blinking. "It would be the biggest gamble of our lives, General."

"It's the devil's dilemma, isn't it?"

"There's another problem, sir," Blaze said.

"What's that?"

"What if they flooded the ship with nerve gas? Anyone attempting to render safe the ship would be killed or have to work from the safety of MOP gear. Everyone on that ship may already be dead."

"They are alive," Carlson said. "I had eavesdropping equipment planted on the hull straight away. And Ms. Jennings is still alive. She called the FBI on a cell phone from inside the ship. Here's a transcript of the conversation," he said, sliding a few sheets of paper across the table.

As Blaze scanned it, Carlson summarized the information.

"Her battery must have been low. She wasn't able to talk very long. She described three Russians, one of whom she took to be a steward following orders. Hawaii Five-Oh has an APB out. They're checking all Slavic looking individuals. Just before the ship anchored one of the Russians showed her a booby trap and told her to tell Clinton that if anybody boarded the vessel they would blow it up."

Blaze exhaled heavily. "Hummm. Did she describe the device?"

"No. Keep this conversation in this room. I've asked Ross Perot to deposit the money. A third party payment means that the U.S Government will not be giving in to extortion," he said gravely.

"Has the money been transferred?" Blaze blurted out, concerned by the revelation.

"No. Not yet. I'm waiting to see what the President decides to do."

"Don't pay the money, General! They'll blow the ship to cover their trail?" Blaze opined. "If it was me, the second I had the money I would blow her to hell."

Carlson stared at him.

"*Goddammit!*" he shouted in frustration. "I'm in command of the most powerful military force mankind has ever created and I am powerless."

He held both fists in the air and shook them in frustration.

"Sir, the weapons of war have changed throughout history, from fire to atomic bombs, clubs to AKs, but not mankind's basic nature. We have developed technologically much faster than we have socially. Terrorism, blackmail, and extortion are Stone Age tactics that render our most sophisticated weaponry impotent. There are no easy decisions here."

"The Russians are sending a crack unit of spetznaz to communicate with the crewmen trapped inside the ship. Maybe they can acquire the intel we need to board the vessel," Carlson said.

"We're running out of time, sir. We're dealing with a ticking bomb. I can almost hear it ticking. In a couple of hours we'll know if there's a get-your-attention bomb in Honolulu. If the cops don't find it, it'll find us."

"Study that ship, Master Chief. Every damn inch of it, every compartment, every wire, every pipe, and pray to God I don't have to ask you to board her. And if I do it may be a non sanctioned mission."

"General, what do your instincts tell you to do?" Blaze asked.

"Board her before they blow the thing to hell and kill a hundred thousand people. Tow her black carcass to sea and scuttle her in deep water."

"Sir, I learned from my study of *bushido* that a warrior must follow his instincts, that martial ferocity must be tempered by an exquisite sense of courtesy, loyalty, honor, and justice. The spirit of the warrior is bound to the service of his nation, to the people of his nation. Ultimately, his bond is with the people that he serves."

"What's your point?"

"The people on this island don't know what's happening. They haven't been given a choice."

"Neither have I. It's not my call, goddammit," Carlson snapped. "The devil's dilemma is the President's dilemma."

"Do you have confidence in the White House, General?" Blaze asked.

"I'll not answer that question," Carlson roared, leaving little doubt as to his true feelings. "And you sir, are dismissed," he growled like a junkyard dog prodded with a stick.

"General, the devil's dilemma is your dilemma. It's also my dilemma. It's every warrior's dilemma at some point in his life."

Blaze looked at the General without blinking for the longest time. His body language was saying, "If you don't make this decision, I will."

Blaze took his leave but as he opened the door to the SCIF he looked back at General Carlson. His head was in his hands in a soldier's prayer. He was asking God for guidance.

The phone rang causing Gurnov to jump, as if an enemy soldier had tossed a hand grenade into the room. He calmed himself by taking a deep breath before picking up the receiver.

"Hello," he said in his best English.

"I just spoke with our mutual friend," Koshkin reported from Hong Kong. "Our account is very low on funds. You should take appropriate action to speed up things on your end. I will call you in six hours to check on your progress."

"Understood," Gurnov replied.

The line went dead, leaving him with his thoughts. *Okay assholes. I'll strike without warning at a time of my choosing.*

Gurnov took a shower, put on fresh clothes, and drove to town on H-1, blending with traffic as Koshkin had warned him to do. Taking the Nimitz exit, he motored to Ala Moana Boulevard and parked the car at Kakaako Park. From there he hiked the short distance to Waikiki. Near the spot Koshkin had recommended, he reached down into his shopping bag and raised the antenna on his sending unit. Pushing the button, he watched the street ahead, looking for a blue cloud of smoke issuing from the International Market Place. At first nothing happened.

*Damn*, he thought. *They must have found it.*

Then he saw a man run into the street waving his arms wildly. He bent over at the waist and heaved on the road. A bluish cloud of smoke engulfed the front of the building. By nature, Gurnov couldn't resist going closer. He walked to within a block of the scene and with a group of spectators watched as people staggered into the street, gagging and vomiting. Good Samaritans rushed into the smoke in vain attempts to rescue victims, only to succumb to the incapacitant.

"What's going on?" a pedestrian asked, alarmed by the commotion.

Gurnov hunched up his shoulder and shook his head with a look of concern. He didn't vocalize a response for fear his accent would give him away.

"Fire," said a woman standing nearby. "See the smoke."

Gurnov wheeled about and walked briskly back to the car. He was sweating profusely when he reached the park and his hands were shaking so much he had trouble unlocking the car door. Climbing inside, the hot air hit him like a blast furnace.

*Gurnov, you son of a drunken whore. No one knows you are here. Get a grip. Drive slowly. Be one of the people*, he thought.

He fired up the engine and sat in the luxury of the air conditioning to calm his nerves. When he regained his composure, he drove back to the safe house and locked himself inside. He gulped down a slug of vodka straight from the bottle and collapsed on the sofa.

*News. Watch the news,* he thought. *But first check the ship.*

He lit a cigarette and studied the ceiling until he was in complete control of his emotions, then he went outside and used the telescope to examine the *Stashinsky.* The area around Hospital Point was devoid of activity.

*They dare not go near her*, he thought. *Even Americans are not that stupid.*

Feeling confident, he went back inside, turned on the television, and raided Koshkin's well-stocked refrigerator. While he was working on the makings of his sandwich, he sang a verse from Vysotsky's *Wonderland*.

*There is much unclear in this strange land
You can get confused and lost,
It even makes you feel creepy all over,
If you imagine what can happen.
Suddenly, a precipice, you need to jump,
Will you be a coward, or will you leap bravely?
Ah? Eh? Just so, my friend,
That's the main point.*

Before he finished preparing his food a news bulletin interrupted the scheduled programming to report a fire in the International Market Place.

"Ha. Fire my ass," he said with glee.

# Chapter 24

The troops in the TOC stopped what they were doing when the local television station interrupted with a special news bulletin. The guard informed General Carlson. He got up from the conference table in the SCIF where he was conversing with his experts and walked out into the TOC to view the report. He had a tired man's walk, like some burnt out grunt on one more useless patrol. He took a seat in the operations center just as a camera crew in downtown Honolulu began reporting a fire in Waikiki. Police quickly cordoned off the area and pushed the news team back, but not before they filmed hundreds of sick and unconscious people lying in the street.

Blaze knew by the look on the General's face that he had made up his mind. First he would call the Pentagon, then the NCA, and finally, he would discuss the options they had worked out with the President. He knew he was one of those options and he was mentally and physically prepared for the challenge. He felt as if his whole life had prepared him for the moment. The SEALs, Ranger School, SFQC, Jungle Warfare, Explosive Ordnance Disposal School, and a hundred other training courses uniquely qualified him for the hour of his nation's greatest need.

*If our society is going to have people in whom we give the job of risking their lives, and if necessary taking the lives of other human beings, how are we to deal with them in times of peace? How are we to think about them? In wartime it's easy. But in this murky world of low intensity conflict it's all confused.*

The General watched the news bulletin then disappeared into the SCIF without uttering a word. For several hours Blaze studied the blueprints of the *Stashinsky.* He memorized every compartment, passageway, and hatch. Closing his eyes, he mentally boarded the vessel and walked its passageways, over and over, and when in doubt, checked the blueprints and visualized doing it again, each time picturing himself inside the ship. The mental exercise was exhausting but it took his mind off the horrendous task before them.

*I wish I had one of those virtual reality games,* he thought.

As Lieutenant Sanz struggled with his inner feelings, Blaze tried to read his face as a diversion to relax his own mind.

*We are no different than the Massai or the Yanomami,* he thought. *Our weapons are just more powerful. Like all tribes we need men and women who live by the unspoken warrior's code. Policemen too,* he thought, looking at the FBI men sharing the TOC. *Such men and women are all around us. They don't deserve to be represented as super heroes like Rambo and GI Jane. That's not what it's all about. That's just so much Hollywood celluloid. They deserve to be acknowledged and appreciated for what they are, and for what they are willing to do when called upon. It's not about winning or losing or killing. It is putting one's life on the line for the sake of one's society when necessary.*

The words of the warrior came to him.

*A warrior is not one who goes to war to kill people, but rather one who exhibits integrity in his actions and control over his life. The spirit of the warrior is his commitment to the people he serves. The General wants to order me to defuse the ship. But it's not his call. It's not my call either. God help us. It's a politician's call, a man that earned his station in life by prevarication, obfuscation and inveigling.*

To Tom Blaze the word politician was synonymous with words like unscrupulous, dishonorable, and usurious.

For the rest of the afternoon and into the evening he waited for General Carlson to call him in and order him to board the vessel. When the call didn't come, he went to dinner in the mess hall. When he returned, Lieutenant Sanz was gone.

Sanz checked out his operational gear and laid it out on the concrete deck of the hangar next to his rack. The troops had arranged pallets of gear to create sleeping areas that offered a slight degree of privacy. As the senior officer in the platoon, Lee had the best spot, complete with a folding cot, a field desk, and poncho liners for privacy curtains. Inside his private space he cleaned his pistol and his rifle and set them on his cot alongside his knife and climbing gear. Before turning his attention to his Draeger oxygen scuba, he went to the washroom and cleaned his hands of gun oil. Pure oxygen and oil are an explosive combination, so he washed his hands thoroughly.

On the way back to his corner of the hangar, he looked for Petty Officer Carroll in a crowd of men and women watching a movie projected on a makeshift canvas screen erected on the side of the hangar. Carroll was seated next to Sergeant Smith. On several occasion he had seen them sneak off together after the movie. Lee checked his watch and went back to his chores.

He completed the maintenance on his scuba and lay down on his cot.

*I have to do something,* he thought.

He focused his mind and visualized boarding the Russian ship. Like Blaze, he was prepared to do the unthinkable. He rehearsed the mission step by step.

When the movie ended, he waited for the crowd to disperse then put on his operational gear and slipped out of the hangar. Outside he kept to the shadows until he was clear of the men having a smoke near the front of the building then scurried from shadow to shadow allowing the darkness to swallow him up like pools of bunker oil. Near the fence line he prowled alongside a rundown building and up behind the kiosk commanding the back gate to the isolation area. He lifted the tape on his watch face and checked the time. It was five minutes to midnight.

At twenty-four hundred hours, Sergeant Smith walked up and relieved the guard on duty for MIDRATs. Sanz listened from behind the kiosk as the soldiers exchanged a few words. Shortly, the man on duty marched off toward the hangar leaving Smith in the kiosk. Before he reached the building Carroll joined Smith in the booth. Sanz stood silently listening for sound from inside the kiosk. When Smith started moaning he made his move. As quietly as a jewel thief he slipped out the pedestrian gate and disappeared into the shadows.

Lee made his way the short distance to the bay and hid in a secluded area just south of Battleship Row. The *Stashinsky* was anchored within sight less than a mile up the narrow channel. Black and devoid of lights, she was visible only by moonlight. He put on his swim fins then spit in his facemask. While rinsing it out, he heard a noise behind him, the sound of a man clearing his throat.

Startled, and expecting a JSOC security guard, he turned to see Master Chief Blaze standing over him.

"And just where are you going, L.T.," he asked in a hushed voice.

"I'm going to get Julie off that ship," Sanz replied.

It was dark but the moonlight playing on the bay illuminated the determination written on his face.

"You're going to get yourself killed. Maybe half the people on this island too," Blaze opined.

"You don't know that."

"I know one thing for sure," Blaze growled.

"What's that?" Sanz snapped.

"If you survive, you'll be court martialed," Blaze said.

"Then so be it. I'll be court martialed."

For a few seconds both men were silent. Sanz finished rinsing out his facemask and preparing his swim gear.

Finally Blaze spoke, "What are you packing?"

"MP-5. Ninety rounds."

"You won't need a gun, son," Blaze said, matter of factly. He sat down in the shallow water beside Sanz. "There aren't any bad guys on board that ship. Just lots of booby traps set for fools like us."

Blaze placed his scuba in the bay between his legs. Pushing it underwater, he checked the breathing loop for leaks.

"What are you doing?" Sanz asked.

"I'm going to render safe a big bomb," he replied, occupied with his gear.

"I can't let you do that, Master Chief," Sanz argued.

"You can't stop me," Blaze growled. "What are you going to do? Call Sergeant Smith. She's back there in the kiosk getting laid," he smiled.

Sanz glared at him.

"You've been watching me."

"Did you actually think Dan Carroll wouldn't tell me what you're up to? That Shifty King wouldn't tell me you snagged a Draeger? That Johnson wouldn't tell me that you checked out your weapons. I've been a SEAL since Christ was a mess cook and my job is to turn junior officers in senior officers. If I can't do that, I'll settle for second best."

"And what's that?" Sanz asked.

"Keeping your ass alive long enough to witness at your court martial. Now, let's you and me go back to the hangar and talk this over with the old man?"

Sanz ignored him and adjusted the Draeger on his chest. He turned on the oxygen and began filling his breathing bag.

A Draeger is a close circuit scuba that filters the diver's exhaled breath of carbon dioxide and re-circulates the oxygen. The SEALs use closed circuit scuba because no bubbles escaped to give away the diver's presence underwater. By re-circulating the oxygen, a small bottle is good for a six-hour mission. It is a shallow water scuba designed for long underwater swims just below the surface.

"How are you planning to get aboard?" Blaze asked.

"Anchor chain," Sanz replied.

"Bad idea. First it's in plain view of the base and the hills. With NVGs anyone can see it from here. You can bet the General has a dozen eyes on it," Blaze argued, looking at the *Stashinsky's* black shape. "And to make matters worse there are probably a couple of booby traps on the focsle. And, there is a lot of distance to cover to get to the pilothouse."

Blaze placed his waterproof bag in the bay and checked its buoyancy.

"What's in there?" Sanz asked.

"Tools of the trade. NVG's, a can of spray paint, a

thin piece of wooden dowel to feel for trip wires, tooth picks, a couple of rolls of friction tape, crimpers, wire cutters, zipcuffs, stuff like that. Got anything like that in your bag?"

Sanz looked him in the eye but didn't answer the question.

"Here," he said, handing Sanz an old painter's pole. "I'll carry the caving ladder. I noticed in one of the surveillance videos that there are a lot of seagulls hanging out on the stern. Birds are creatures of habit, you know," he said, looking at Sanz as if to say so are men. "That's where the mess cooks throw over table scraps. If there were any sensitive booby traps in that area the birds would have set them off by now."

Sanz stared at the seasoned warrior. The few lights still on at Pearl Harbor across the bay didn't illuminate his face enough to see his eyes but he could read his body posture. Sanz nodded agreement.

*The man is a genius*, he thought, a *warrior genius.*

"Before we do this I want to tell you something," Blaze said.

"What's that?" Sanz asked.

"You're the best officer I've ever worked for. But you're not a true warrior, at least not yet. You've got all the right stuff, but you're not there yet. Words like loyalty, integrity, patience, intensity, calmness in the face of danger, compassion, and tenacity of purpose all come to mind. All those things you have in great measure. But a true warrior knows himself and knows his limitations. He has self-mastery."

"I know my limitations," Sanz argued.

"No you don't!" Blaze cut. "If you did you would pick up your gear and go back to the hangar."

"I have to do something," Sanz argued.

"Killing yourself and the people on this island is a

real bad move. If you were an enlisted man, in about ten years you might attain sufficient mastery of the skills necessary to board that vessel and survive. What do you know about booby traps?" Blaze asked.

"What's your point?" Sanz snapped.

"There are dozens on that ship. That's my point. How about teamwork or is it just another bullshit word for you? Can you follow my every step without error, my precise directions? Cause if you can't, I'm going to leave you here.... one way or the other."

"I know my limitations."

"We just covered that ground, Lieutenant! You don't. You don't know how to defuse that bomb," he said, pointing toward the *Stashinsky*.

"I know when to lead and I know when to follow, Master Chief. I'll take the point until we get to the ship. Then I will follow your lead."

"So be it. You know, Lieutenant, the Massai believe that only by killing a lion with a spear and facing down an elephant, can one truly master fear. Do you think they are right?"

"Yes I do. That's why we jump out of perfectly good airplanes and lock out of underway submarines."

"So you are ready to face this elephant square on without flinching?"

"Yes."

"One mistake and a half million people die. Does that frighten you, Lieutenant Sanz?"

"Yes, Master Chief, it does. It frightens me more than losin' my own life."

"A right-thinking answer," Blaze complimented. "You're still determined to do this?"

"Yes. One way or the other, if I have to leave you here unconscious," Sanz replied.

"A right-thinking answer, Lieutenant. Confident and

determined. So let's do it, as a team, calmly, deliberately, with every footstep planned in advance."

"I roger that, Master Chief," Sanz agreed.

"Okay."

"Master Chief?"

"Yeah."

"I know that if I don't do something that ship is going to explode."

"And just how do you know that, Lieutenant?" Blaze asked, quietly.

Sanz didn't answer. He checked his attack board and set the compass course. Finally he said, "That is what I would do if I was the evil son-of-a-bitch that planned this crime."

"I agree with your logic. And since we are the only two men crazy enough and talented enough to pull this off, let's go do it."

Blaze slipped on his swim fins and then they both put on their facemasks so they could purge the nitrogen from their Draeger scubas. When all that remained was pure oxygen, they eased silently into the water up to their necks. They checked each other's scuba for leaks. Blaze gave Sanz an okay-sign when he was ready then grasped one of his chest straps to maintain contact with him underwater. He shook it vigorously indicating he was ready to dive and then slipped silently beneath the surface. Head still above water, Sanz took one last bearing to check his compass. With course set, he blew a little oxygen out through his nose like a submarine blowing ballast. The life giving gas leaked out around the seal of his facemask as he squatted down underwater. He began kicking slowly, watching the instruments on his attack board. Following the bottom, with an outgoing tide, they swam with strong, steady flutter kicks toward the Russian ship.

The phone rang causing Gurnov to jump out of his skin. He put out his cigarette and answered.

"Hello."

"It seems we have been paid a bonus, my friend. Twice the amount we requested has been deposited in our account," Koshkin said.

Gurnov couldn't believe his ears.

"Business is good," Koshkin continued. "You have been working too hard. Take a vacation, my friend, as soon as you can. See you soon."

The line went dead.

*Gurnov, you son of a drunken whore. You did it. Now you American bastards are going to pay for what you've done to the Motherland.*

He rushed outside and used the binoculars to examine the *Stashinsky*. She was standing in the dark channel, lifeless. It took all his will power not to blow the ship up from the terrace. Then he focused on the airport. Koshkin had been wrong. They hadn't shut it down. Flights were still coming and going at midnight.

Hurrying back inside, he checked the tickets the KGB agent had purchased for him.

*I could leave in the morning*, he thought. *Northwest Orient to Japan. No. They'll be watching the airport like the Mossad. I'll leave by ship. And when I clear the harbor I'll blow that garbage scowl to hell.*

He checked his list and saw that he had passage on a ship leaving for Singapore at six in the morning.

*Da*, he thought. *When the ship clears the harbor I'll blow the goddamned thing sky high.*

He rushed around the house gathering up the few things Koshkin had provided for his comfort. He packed a small bag with clothes, money, and several vials of toxin before turning to a bottle of liquid courage. Vodka steadied his nerves. Crashing on the sofa he rested, examining the ceiling in detail for images of the past.

# Chapter 25

Following the compass on his attack board, Sanz swam toward the *Stashinsky* with Master Chief Blaze looking over his shoulder. He hugged the bottom until his depth gage read twenty feet, then maintained course and depth. Small fish and crabs darted about in flashes of bioluminescence until the bottom disappeared beneath them, leaving them in a weightless inky black void. The light of the attack board was their only connection to the world above and their direction of travel.

Estimating distance by the number of kicks of his swim fins, he swam out the channel with Blaze holding on like a remora. When he finally took a peek at the world above it was only for an instant, like a fish momentarily breaking the surface then slipping back beneath the water. The *Stashinsky* was directly in front of them just a few yards away. He continued on his compass course until they made contact at the bow then swam down the port side to the screws. They surfaced under the stern just aft of the rudderpost.

Without a word, Sanz extended the painter's pole, reached up, and hooked a caving ladder to the railing twenty-five feet above. The ladder was constructed of thin cables with six-inch rungs just wide enough for a diver's bootied foot. Using the ladder for a mooring, they took off their swim gear and tied it off underwater. Blaze was the first to climb. Sanz assisted by pulling down on the bottom of ladder. The Master Chief shimmied up with relative ease and slipped on deck. While still on his belly he checked every inch of his landing then signaled Sanz by yanking twice on a line he had tied off to his web belt. Sanz signaled back with yank and paid out the line as Blaze pulled on the tether until his gear bag appeared. Attached to his bag was Sanz's tether line. He continued pulling on the line until the Lieutenant's gear slid on deck. By the time Sanz climbed aboard, Blaze was ready for action.

While Sanz pulled up the caving ladder and prepared his gear, Blaze used his NVG's to search the stern of the ship for infrared beams.

"Clear of infrared," he whispered.

"Roger," Sanz replied.

Blaze didn't expect to find any beams outside the skin of the ship because of the large numbers of seagulls he had seen on surveillance tapes. It was just in his nature to be thorough. Using a wooden dowel to feel his way across the deck, he led the way to the nearest hatch into the superstructure. The metal lever was in the secured position, so he passed the hatch and slowly patrolled around the main deck looking for trip wires, an unsecured hatch, or an infrared beam. It took him twenty minutes just to check the 01 level around the superstructure. It was two o'clock in the morning when they reached the ship's bridge five decks above.

Using an infrared flashlight and NVGs, he searched the interior of the pilothouse by shining the invisible light through the bridge windows.

"Sweet Jesus," Blaze gasped. The first thing that caught his eye was Lieutenant Zhukov, mouth open in a death stare. His skull was shattered and his face was distorted. Still tied in the captain's chair, his head was bent sideways at an awkward angle.

"What is it?" Sanz whispered, straining his naked eyes. His stomach jumped into his throat when his brain made sense of the gruesome scene inside the bridge.

"Bullet to the back of the head," Blaze whispered. "No sign of the gas that killed the soldier in the hold."

Then Blaze saw the helmsman sprawled out on the deck. He swallowed hard and continued his search by shining the invisible light methodically all around the interior of the compartment. The NVGs allowed him to see the booby trap Baranov had rigged to the lever on the starboard hatch on the opposite side of the bridge. Using his wooden dowel he carefully felt his way to the other side of the ship and checked the port hatch. Seeing the fake booby trap on the inside of the starboard hatch, he turned off his IR flashlight and searched the interior of the bridge for motion detectors and infrared beams. It took him ten minutes of meticulous study to satisfy himself that is was safe to open one of the windows. He chose a window on the starboard side, aft of the bridge wing hatch. A chart table was located underneath it. Using a glasscutter, he etched the glass, broke it, and removed an eight-inch circle with a rubber suction cup.

"Here goes," he said in a hushed voice.

Reaching inside, he unlocked the window then pulled it out on its hinges. The opening was only three feet square but it allowed easy access.

"Give me a hand," he said in a hushed voice.

With the Lieutenant's assistance Blaze eased his body through the opening and lay on the chart table. The copper smell of blood and death filled his nostrils.

"Pass me my gear," he said to Sanz.

Lee handed him his NVG's, IR flashlight, and gear bag. From the chart table Blaze thoroughly studied the interior of the compartment again. The glint of a trip wire caused as surge of adrenaline to course through this body.

*Simple pull-release*, he thought, as he studied the

device from above.

Easing off the table he covered the short distance to the hatch like a man walking on eggshells. He examined the booby trap from every angle before taping up the spoon on the grenade. He inserted two toothpicks to serve as temporary safety pins and cut the tripwire with his crimper.

He opened the hatch and whispered, "Step only were I step."

"You can count on that, Mater Chief," Sanz said, gaping at the helmsman lying below the ship's wheel in a pool of congealed blood.

For ten minutes they searched the bridge for detonating cord or anything resembling an RF receiver. When Blaze was satisfied there was nothing more he could do on the bridge he turned his attention to the light locker at the back of the pilothouse. Slowly, cautiously, at a snail's pace, he carefully felt his way through the light locker and down the ladder one step at a time. His heart skipped a beat when he felt a tripwire on the third step from the bottom of the ladder.

"Stay where you are," he said to Sanz.

"What is it?" Lee asked.

"A tripwire. It's rigged across the ladder."

Blaze studied the area around the booby trap for a few minutes. Using a regular flashlight he followed the wire in both directions until he located the fire device behind the stairwell. Then he searched the deck below the ladder in both directions for additional booby traps.

"Hold the beam here," he said, illuminating the tripwire.

Sanz climbed down the steps far enough to hold the flashlight and Blaze carefully stepped over the tripwire. On deck, he checked both directions of the passageway with his dowel rod.

"Hand me my bag," he ordered when he had completed the task.

In silence Sanz complied being careful not to let anything fall on the tripwire.

Blaze flipped down his NVG's. "Turn off the flashlight," he ordered. "I need to double-check the passageway for IR."

When Lee turned off the light they were thrown into total darkness. Sanz felt his heart beating and his breath come in shallow puffs as if to breathe too deeply would cause the ship to explode.

Standing in place Blaze searched the corridor for infrared beams a second time to ensure he hadn't missed anything looking down from the top of the ladder.

"Light," he ordered.

Lee turned on the flashlight and shined it on the booby trap.

"This is a pull release. If I cut the wire or pull it, it'll go off."

"It looks a lot like our M-Three," Sanz commented.

"Hey," Blaze said, pleasantly. "You're pretty smart for a cake-eater. What we have here is a cloned M-Three pull-release firing device, blasting cap, with a taped det-cord lead, crimped to a base coupling. Simple enough. What should I do to defuse it, Lieutenant?" he asked, like an instructor at EOD School.

Inside the ship they were free to talk openly but both men spoke in hushed tones as if their voices might disturb some monster lurking in the darkness.

"In your bag you have a box of tooth picks. Use them as safety pins."

"Right on."

Blaze took two heavy round toothpicks out of his gear bag and carefully slipped them into the holes at each end of the device.

"Now what?" Blaze asked.

"Crimpers," Sanz replied. "Cut the det-cord. Isolate the device."

"You should have gone to EOD School Lieutenant," Blaze praised.

"I did. Short course," Sanz replied. "It was a turning point in my life."

"How so?" Blaze asked, making conversation to keep calm.

"Every IED on the range killed me. I decided EOD wasn't for me."

IED was short-talk for improvised explosive device. The EOD School at Indianhead, Maryland had a special training course in IEDs where they taught technicians how to render safe the most devious bombs terrorists could conceive. Unlike real bombs, the dummy devices didn't explode. They were rigged with lights, sound, or firecrackers to apprise students of errors in their render safe procedures.

"Perhaps I shouldn't confess at a time like this, but most of them got me too." Blaze cut the explosive cord and followed it to the trunk line running along the overhead plumbing.

"Damn," he said, seeing the lines. "The master blaster built in a lot of redundancy into the field. There are four trunk lines up here."

"Cut 'em all," Sanz urged.

"Right again."

Blaze cut all four trunk lines by removing a short section from each then he followed the explosive cord to where it passed through the bulkhead. There he cut them again. Then, using a can of international orange spray paint, he marked the deck, the overhead, and bulkhead where he had made his cuts.

"We've got to work our way to the business end of

this ship," he said. "If we can cut all the trunk lines leading into the cargo holds, we can defang this monster."

"What about Julie and Forbes?" Sanz asked.

"You know the answer to that question, LT. First things first, and first we've got to defuse this bomb. Your woman will just have to wait a few more hours," he explained.

"Let's do it," Sanz agreed.


At four o'clock in the morning Gurnov got up off the sofa and made a pot of coffee. He hadn't slept a wink for fear ghosts would haunt him. To occupy the time he showered, shaved, and ate breakfast. At a quarter till five he could take no more. He set the timer on the incendiary and left the safe house.

Blending with early morning traffic he motored slowly toward Honolulu. Driving down the upper deck of H-1, he spotted a police car speeding up behind him and nearly panicked. He reached for the comfort of his Tokarev lying underneath his bag and swerved slightly to the right. The police car, lights flashing, sped by.

*Get a grip Gurnov, you son of a drunken whore. Paranoia will get you caught. Be one with the people.*

Flowing with the morning traffic he drove directly to Kakaako Park and abandoned the car. Like a tourist he strolled the short distance to the harbor and marched up the pier to his ship. As he climbed up the gangway, a Filipino sailor in scruffy clothes yelled at him and asked him what he wanted.

"Passage," he shouted, showing the sailor the paper the ship's captain had given Koshkin.

"*Salamat!* Please come," the sailor said, leading the

way.

He led Gurnov to a small cabin in the aft superstructure and opened the door.

"This is your room," he said, holding the door open.

The smell of oil and diesel poured from the room.

"Thank you," Gurnov replied.

He tipped the mate generously and received a big toothy grin. Once inside the room, Gurnov locked the door and unpacked his bag. The first thing he took out was his pistol. The second was a full bottle of vodka. He took a slug straight from the bottle and wiped his lips with the back of his sleeve.

*Yeb vas veruyushchii! -- fuck you God believers. You'll get yours in couple of hours.*

He looked at his watch. It was a quarter till six.

For hours the two SEALs carefully patrolled the passageways of the *Stashinsky*, rendering safe booby traps and cutting detonation cord wherever it passed through bulkheads and decks. As Blaze followed the explosive trail downward through the superstructure of the ship he learned more and more about the man who had rigged the vessel. Studying the knots and the care the man had taken to conceal his work, Blaze tried to get inside the blaster's head.

Below the main deck they heard muffled voices inside a closed steel compartment. They stopped and listened, ear up against the hatch.

"Russian," Sanz whispered.

Blaze nodded agreement and marked the door with paint before silently probing his way forward toward the cargo hold. At the main hatch leading into the hold he stopped to relax before tackling the monster in the belly of the ship.

"This hatch is booby trapped from inside," he said, slumping to the deck for a break.

"How do you know that?" Sanz asked, searching the seal around the entry with his flashlight.

"Educated guess," Blaze replied. "See the lever? It's not pulled all the way down. That's the only hatch we've come across that's not locked down tight."

"Look," Sanz said, shining his flashlight in the corner below the entryway. "Metal shavings."

"Yeah. I expected that. The cargo hold is a watertight space. He had to drill through this bulkhead for his trunk lines." Blaze got up and searched the overhead for det-cord. "There they are," he said, shining his flashlight on the four trunk lines they had been following. Baranov had taken care to caulk around the explosive cords and had paint them the same color as the other cables and pipes passing through the steel wall.

"Five holes," Blaze muttered. "He drilled five holes."

Five evenly spaced holes had been drilled through the steel but only four trunk lines passed through the bulkhead. The fifth hole was neatly plugged and painted over.

*Why*, Blaze thought. Then it hit him. "He changed his mind. There are five trunk lines," he said. "The fifth is a loner. Come. We've got to find the trigger to this beast."

"Where?" Sanz asked.

"The radio shack. Oh-four level."

From his study of the ship's blueprints he knew exactly where the radio room was located. He had spotted the international symbol on the door when they had cleared the deck but he had passed the space by because the door was locked. Following the route he had

352

painted on the deck, they quickly backtracked up to the 04 level.

Using a locksmith's kit, Blaze unlocked the door and opened it just a crack. With a dentist's mirror and flashlight he searched the backside of the door through the crack. The glint of a tripwire told him he had found what he was looking for. It was rigged behind the door just far enough for a large man to squeeze by. Being a big man, Baranov had given himself plenty of clearance to get out of the room.

"The door is rigged," Blaze said. "What time is it?"

Sanz looked at his watch with the flashlight. "Almost seven."

Morning light was seeping around the light locker at the top of the ladder way behind the bridge. Inside the ship it was as dark as a cave. Using the mirror and flashlight Blaze studied the entire room until he was sure of the booby traps construction. First he inspected behind the door and then above and around it. For several minutes he poked and probed through the crack with his wooden dowel. Finally satisfied, he took a deep breath, eased the door open just wide enough to slip by, and stepped inside. He checked the room with his NVGs, and seeing no infrared beams, used his wooden dowel rod to search for tripwires. Before disarming the simple pull-release booby trap Baranov had rigged across the room, he studied it carefully. Using toothpicks that Sanz passed to him from outside the room, he disarmed the booby trap and cut the det-cord leading out of the device. Then he cut the tripwire and opened the door wider so Sanz could more easily assist him from the passageway.

Less than ten miles from the *Stashinsky,* the merchant

vessel *Eva Luna*, cleared Honolulu Harbor with the assistance of a tug. Once clear of the breakwater, the harbor pilot bid the captain farewell and the *Eva Luna* set sail for Singapore. Gurnov stayed in his cabin until he felt the ship move under her own power. When he came out on deck the Rainbow Tower of the Hawaiian Hilton was clearly visible less than a mile to stern. He lit a cigarette and stood at the railing for a few minutes taking in the sea breeze and a magnificent view of Oahu.

"Tis not easy brother mine, in a foreign land to live," he mumbled, as he watched the land slowly receded behind him. "Bullshit!" he exclaimed, not wanting the leave the Islands without exploring them as a tourist.

He finished his cigarette, checked the deck fore and aft for crewmen then removed the RF sending unit from his pants pocket. It was no larger than a pack of cigarettes. He extended the antenna and without a second thought pushed the button twice. He changed the channel on the unit then fired off a second signal. The first radio wave activated the gas bomb hidden near the swimming pool, the second the one in the hedges outside the steak house.

Gurnov couldn't see it but a cloud of noxious gas billowed up between the towers of the Hawaiian Hilton. It engulfed tourists lazing around the pool and entered the buildings through open balcony doors. Panic ensued.

The second signal bounced off the towers of the hotel and initiated the bomb planted outside the restaurant. Bluish-brown gas, carried by a gentle tropical breeze, seeped into the apartments and hotels lining the street. Complete and utter bedlam ensued.

He tossed the RF unit in the water, lit another cigarette and checked his watch.

"Seven fifteen," he mumbled.

The *Eva Luna* was running behind schedule. It took

another ten minutes for her to clear land far enough for Gurnov to see the airport.

He checked the wind with a wet finger and mumbled like a madman. *"Yeb vas veruyushchii!"*

The wind was blowing from sea to land so he was safe. He searched the deck for crewmen then removed an RF sending unit from his pocket. It was larger than the last but still small enough to conceal in a man's pants pocket.

The *Stashinsky* was clearly visible off the starboard side when he dialed in the frequency and pulled up the antenna. With his finger poised on the button, he stared blurry eyed at the black ship. He was about to push the button when he heard a noise behind him. The crewman who had shown him to his room cleared his throat. Gurnov quickly secreted the RF device in his shirt pocket as if fishing for a cigarette.

"Room okay?" the Filipino asked.

"Yes," Gurnov growled annoyed by the interruption.

The sailor bummed a cigarette and tried to make conversation while he smoked it. But Gurnov kept grunting and glaring at each toothy grin until he discouraged any meaningful conversation. Five miles north of the *Eva Luna*, Master Chief Blaze racked his brains to make sense of Baranov's detonator.

"Master Chief," Sanz said. "I think there's a trunk line running along inside this bundle of cables." Lee was six inches taller than Blaze and it gave him a better angle to see the detonation cord.

Blaze stepped out of the radio shack. "Where?" he asked.

"Right here," Lee said, using his flashlight to point

out the detonating cord from other cables.

"Bingo," Blaze exclaimed. "Number five."

He stepped back inside and followed the bundle of wires with his flashlight until they ran down the wall to the backside of the radio console. He looked for a location where he could get a bite, then reached back and cut the det-cord with his crimpers. Stepping back out of the room, he cut the trunk line were it turned and ran athawartships with a bundle of wires. He was pulling a section clear when Gurnov pressed the button on the RF sending unit. The blasting cap behind the console exploded, detonating the length of explosive cord behind the radio and the section buried up inside the cables. The shock wave, contained inside the radio shack was deafening. Both Blaze and Sanz nearly died from heart failure.

"*Goddammit, I hate it when that happens!*" Blaze exclaimed.

"*What happened?*" Sanz gasped. His pupils were dilated and his mouth was open in shock.

Blaze opened the door to the radio shack and shined his flashlight into the room. It was full of acrid smoke. He located the point where he had cut the det-cord and followed the trail of destruction back to the radio console. Behind a rack of equipment he saw what was left of the RF receiver hanging from a smoking antenna cable.

"Someone just tied to kill a half a million people," he mumbled, not believing his eyes.


From sea, Gurnov could clearly see the *Stashinsky*. He pushed the button over and over again. When the ship failed to explode he flew into a mad rage and tossed the sending unit into the ocean.

*I wonder if Nickoli sabotaged it?* he thought. "I have something special for you, asshole, something that will turn you into a fucking hemorrhage."

# Chapter
# 26

"Let's find Julie and get off this tub," Sanz exclaimed.

His heart was racing and his ears were ringing from the concussion of the detonation cord. Smoke and cordite from the radio shack was billowing into the passageway. Over the ringing in their ears they could hear muffled voices through the air ducts. People began banging on the bulkheads and pipes with metal objects.

"No, no," Blaze replied. "The first priority is the safety of the people on Oahu. There may be more surprises on board this crate. Before we start opening up compartments we've got to move her out to sea."

"How?" Sanz asked.

"Tugs. It's time to face the music, Lieutenant."

"The General?" Sanz asked.

"Yes."

"The radio on the bridge?" Sanz asked, more as a statement than a question.

"Partially right. It's not likely the ship's radios will work," he said, eyeing the smoke and mess behind the console. But I got a brick in my bag."

"You think of everything," Sanz said.

"You'd better hope so. One wrong move and we're dead. Now, let's slow down and do this by the numbers. Walk only where we've walked. Step only where we've stepped."

"Roger that," agreed Sanz.

The small handheld radio Blaze packed in his equipment bag didn't have the power to transmit through the ship's hull. They had to return to the bridge. Dowel rod in hand and eyes scanning like radar, Blaze led the way like a point man in a minefield. It was just a few paces to the ladder where he had rendered safe the first booby trap. He stopped at the bottom and used his flashlight to search the area again before climbing the stairs.

Sunlight blinded them when they emerged from the light locker at the back of the bridge. Outside the *Stashinsky* the sun was above the horizon and sunlight shining through the bridge windows illuminated the blood and gore congealed on the deck. When Sanz's eyes adjusted he gaped at the helmsman, mouth and eyes open in death. He looked away only to fixate on a pool of congealed blood below Lieutenant Zhukov, slumped over in the captain's chair. It had taken on the appearance of liver. Sanz shuddered and followed the Master Chief.

Blaze went directly to a window facing the harbor and studied it. When he was satisfied it wasn't booby-trapped he opened it and called the TOC. Using the language of exercise *Freedom Express*, he asked to speak with Delta Tango Oscar Actual, the General. After a few minutes delay Carlson answered using the call signs Blaze had used to establish contact.

"Bright Blaze, this is Three Stars, over?" Carlson queried.

Blaze recognized the General's voice.

"This is Bright Blaze. Phase one accomplished. Be advised the cobra has been defanged. Recommend the carcass be towed to sea for further investigation by men in suits. How copy, over?"

For a minute there was silence as Carlson processed the information. Blaze waited patiently. A hiccup of static broke the silence followed by the General's voice.

"Message understood, Bright Blaze." Carlson's voice

betrayed no emotion as he continued with a string of orders. "Take no further action. UNODIR allow no one to enter or leave without specific guidance from me. Expect tugs your location in twenty minutes. How copy, over?"

"Good copy," the tired SEAL replied.

"Bright Blaze?"

"Bright Blaze aye."

"Outstanding," Carlson said, with a hint of emotion.

"Best damned exercise I've ever been on, Sir!"

Both men realized there were others listening to the conversation. The harbormaster, ham radio operators, and the news media all had access to the frequency. Blaze was throwing curve balls that Carlson knew how to catch. The General smiled a huge smile of relief.

"Three Stars, out," Carlson replied, ending the transmission.

"Colonel Ardison?" he snapped.

"Yes, General."

"Get the tugs out there."

"They are on their way, sir."

"And get that weather guesser in here. I need a forecast right away," he said, issuing orders like a machinegun. "Have the Coast Guard clear all shipping south of Oahu and east of Molokai."

"Roger," answered up a navy commander as Ardison eyed him.

"Deploy a HAZMAT team out to the carrier. I'll discuss their employment personally with SEVENTH FLEET."

"Yes, sir," an army light colonel responded.

"Place my helicopter on standby. As soon as I speak with the Admiral, I'll personally direct tugboat operations from the air."

"WILCO all," Ardison replied. Carlson got up and

walked to the SCIF to confer with the admiral in command of SEVENTH FLEET.

From the bridge of the *Stashinsky,* Sanz watched the operation with anxiety. Three tugs came steaming up the channel at full speed and reversed their screws at the very last second to check their forward speed. Two of the boats began warping the stern of the ship around in the direction of Pearl Harbor. The third disappeared under the bow. Sanz couldn't see what the sailors were doing but he knew they were cutting the anchor chain. On board the tug three men shackled in a hawser while three others cut the heavy chain with an acetylene torch setting the ship adrift. In minutes the three tugs began towing and pushing the *Stashinsky* out the channel and seaward to deep water.

Blaze breathed a sigh of relief when they cleared the breakwater but his anxiety soon returned when the *Stashinsky* began to roll in gentle swells of open water.

*I hope the master blaster didn't rig a dead man,* he worried to himself. *I'll need to cut the trunk lines where they enter the holds. But how do I get access. All the hatches are rigged.* Then he thought, *I'll use a torch to breach a bulkhead. After I cut the trunk lines leading into holds, I'll render safe the booby traps. No,* he thought. *Once we get the hostages off this ship we scuttle her in deep water.*

He looked at Sanz standing behind the helm. The young SEAL was tired and worried. He could see it on his face. His woman was somewhere down below and there was still a high probability the ship would go high order.

A static hiss was followed by the General's voice

blaring from the handheld radio Blaze had placed on the chart table. Hearing rotors in the background, Blaze pointed at the circling helo.

"Blight Blaze, this is Three Stars, over," the General queried.

"He's on that bird," Blaze said as he picked up the brick. "Three Stars, this is Bright Blaze, roger over."

"Anticipate four hour transit to safe area. When we reach the range, lower the accommodation ladder on the port side and take the first boat to the carrier for conference. How copy, over?"

"Good copy. Sir, you said first boat. I assume by that others will be coming aboard?" Blaze asked.

"Correct. A MOP team is standing by to relieve you," Carlson replied. "Major Thompson and his men will assume render safe procedures in appropriate attire."

"Sir, this is no place for bulky suits. The whole ship is one big booby trap. I most strongly recommend that Lieutenant Sanz retain command of this operation."

"Lieutenant Sanz?" Carlson growled.

"Yes, sir. He's been indispensable to this mission. I recommend he lead the team that escorts hostages off the ship, over."

Blaze looked at Sanz and raised his eyebrows. For a few seconds they waited for the General to process the suggestion.

"Very well," Carlson replied in a gruff voice.

"Sir it would be nice if you could rustle up a man who speaks the language."

"Roger," Carlson graveled, giving in to the logic.

"When all of the hostages are safe, Charlie Platoon can scuttle the ship with a couple of small limpet mines. Recommend placement in the vicinity of the forward holds port side," Blaze continued.

"Negative, Bright Blaze. Our orders are to rescue the

362

hostages, render safe the vessel, and examine the cargo."

"But General, one mistake and this ship will go high order."

"You have your orders, Bright Blaze. Three Stars, out."

It was almost noon when the *Stashinsky* reached the designated safe area. The carrier, and several other ships, took station up wind and paralleled the *Stashinsky's* course. Blaze ordered the tug towing the Russian hulk to slowly steam a track that minimized rolling. With the vessel steady on course he and Lieutenant Sanz lowered the accommodation ladder.

Carlson had boats standing by off the starboard beam. They began landing special troops when the accommodation ladder reached the waterline. The soldiers were dressed from head to toe in bulky olive drab suits. They climbed the steps at a trot, packing MP-5s and sidearms, and reported to Lieutenant Sanz for orders.

The Lieutenant put on a protective suit and assumed command of the unit. He posted men at strategic points on the weather decks and then led a squad up to the bridge where he stationed the men in the pilothouse and on each bridge wing. When the ship's exterior was under positive control he took four men inside the ship. Following the lines of passage the Master Chief had painted on the deck, they rendezvoused with Blaze on the 04 level. The Master Chief declined to dress in a protective suit and continued with the mission wearing only his blue and gold and his swim trunks.

Blaze knew where to look for hostages. He knew they would be confined in spaces with heavy watertight doors so they couldn't escape. He began on the 04 level by rapping on a steel hatch with the butt of his diving knife. If he received no response he painted an "E" on the compartment and continued his search. When he was unable to find anyone on the 04 level, he moved down a deck. On the starboard side of the ship he got his first reply, a feeble tapping on the opposite side of the hatch with a metal object.

"Ms. Jennings," he shouted.

"Yes," came a faint reply in a voice near death.

The temperature inside the ship was near one hundred degrees and without the ship's ventilators to circulate fresh air the atmosphere was stifling.

"*Julie!*" Sanz yelled. "*Julie! It's Lee, Honey. We'll get you out of there.*"

She couldn't hear him. Sanz was wearing a gas mask and his voice was trapped inside his protective chemical suit. Blaze had to restrain Lee to keep him from opening the hatch. When the Master Chief had regained control he went back to work as methodically as before.

"Ms. Jennings," he shouted. "Is the door safe to open from your side?"

"Yes," replied a feeble voice.

Using bolt cutters provided by the boarding team, Blaze cut the lock off the hatch and opened it. Julie was slumped against the bulkhead soaked in sweat and near death from heat exhaustion. She shielded her eyes from the beam of Blaze's flashlight, a physical effort that caused her to faint.

Sanz rushed to her aid. With help from the boarding crew, he rushed her outside and down to the 01 level where doctors and corpsmen were standing by to treat the injured and transport them to the carrier. Sanz returned to his duties. By the time he reached the superstructure with another crew, Blaze had rendered safe a booby trap on the port side 04 level, and had opened the ship up for ventilation.

They checked each level of the superstructure, compartment by compartment, looking for hostages. On the 02 level they came across a large group of Russian sailors. The odor of urine and feces assaulted Tom Blaze when he opened up the compartment. It turned his stomach. The men were dehydrated but not in as bad a shape as Julie Jennings. Contained deeper within the interior of the ship their prison cell was not exposed to the direct rays of the sun. Boarding crews escorted the happy Russians off the ship in manageable groups.

For hours Blaze methodically searched the ship liberating soldiers and sailors until most of those manifested on the vessel were accounted for. He came across Gordon Forbes in a small compartment below the main deck just aft of the hatch leading into the main cargo hold. Forbes was full of questions, hungry and thirsty, but otherwise unharmed.

Blaze avoided the main cargo hold that consisted of the forward three fourths of the vessel. When he reached the engineering spaces, he rapped on the hatch and received no response. So he banged on it with a spanner wrench. Reasoning that the extortionist needed the enginemen to sail the vessel into the harbor, and seeing that the hatch was bolted from the outside, he surmised that the engineering crew was locked below and dead. Instinct told him not to open the hatch. Exhausted, he returned to the bridge and discussed his progress with the General. He requested an acetylene torch, and after it arrived, and was set up in the location he planned to breach, he ordered everyone off the ship.

Alone in the black hulk, he cut through the steel bulkhead separating the cargo hold from the rest of the ship, and made his way inside. From hold to hold he carefully made his rounds cutting Baranov's explosive trunk lines.   After three hours of exhausting and meticulous work, he returned to the main hatch leading into the cargo hold and rendered safe the booby trap from inside.   Exhausted, and concerned that he would make an error in judgment, he made his way to the main deck and called for relief.

When a fresh crew arrived, Blaze had the boat ferry him to the carrier.  He was shaking the General's hand at the ship's landing when the *Stashinsky* exploded in the distance.

# Epilogue

The scene was the same, not only in Moscow, but also in Leningrad, Kiev, Tbilisi, and many other provincial capitals. The sea of rural deprivation that stretched across the vast Russian expanse surged in and out of the cities like hordes of hungry locusts. On weekends the trains into and out of the Moscow were always full of country folk coming to the Center to shop. They filled the markets and lengthened the lines for buying red meat, cooking pots, and heavy winter coats. In rough padded vests and scruffy shoes, they darkened the queues like shadows among the brightly colored parkas and trendy boots of Muscovites, who grumbled at them for taking so much of their meat. It was evening and the railroad station was a maze of bundles tied with coarse cloth or wrapped with newspaper and twine. Cardboard totes littered the floors among the women's thick woolen leggings and the men's dirty dun trousers. The people of the Steppes waited for their trains by staring silently and patiently into space. They were going home to another world, one stripped of the thin veneer of modern life.

At the Yaroslavsky station in Moscow, a train screeched to a stop at the platform and an old *babushka* carrying a stringed bag stepped down from the rail car. She was a short, stout grandmother with a square face, a button nose, and dirty gray hair. Dressed more warmly than the others getting off the train, she waddled more than walked. With the crowd pushing and shoving she stumbled into an odd shaped package lying on the platform and nearly fell down.

"Who put things here?  Who put things here?" she complained loudly.

A young soldier in uniform collected the package sheepishly.

"It's mine," he admitted with a shrug.

"Why did you put things there for people to fall over?" she snapped.

The soldier shook his head at the old woman then ignored her like a squabbling hen.

With an angry expression on her face she shuffled out of the station grumbling and waddled down the street to the metro.  At the subway she purchased a ticket for Dzerzhinsky Square and waited for the first car.  When it arrived she struggled on board and stood near the exit. One stop from Red Square she got off.  As she emerged from the escalator at the exit, she noticed the lights were on in an old-fashioned office building across the street.  It had a great number of narrow windows.

"Waste.  Waste," she mumbled, thinking of the oil lamp she used for light at home.

The building was Lubyanka Prison but she knew nothing of such things or the horrors that went on inside its chambers.  She plodded on down the street against a cold wind.  At Khmelintsk Street, she took a narrow public way that was little more than an alley.  People in scruffy clothes were sitting or standing in doorways, drinking and talking in slurred voices.  A few, despite the cold, were sleeping.  It was the gathering place for the alcoholics of Moscow.  She waddled on down the dark alleyway for twenty meters to a heavy door, and pounded on it with her fat little fist.

In Moscow communal apartments were hard to come by.  Most were designed like cheap hotels. They typically had dozens of rooms opening out from a central corridor with four or five people living in each flat.  Few inhabitants bathed, as sometimes they had to wait for half an hour just to urinate in a communal bathroom. The smells and sounds were horrid with people cooking, smoking, drinking, and arguing at all hours. But not on this floor. It was special. A guard looked out a peephole, and seeing the old woman, opened the door.

"Comrade Markov," she squeaked.

Bolting the door behind them, he led her down the hall to the drug dealer's office. The thug knocked a couple of times then opened the door to the luxurious apartment. She had been there before, carrying smaller quantities of heroin. When the door closed behind her, she opened up her string bag and took out two packages the size of cigar boxes. They were wrapped in newspaper and bound with twine. Markov nodded at his lieutenant who gave the old woman a fist full of rubles for her troubles.

"Thank you, Michael," the old *babushka* said in a sweet voice she reserved for children.

Markov ushered her away with the wave of his hand, like shoeing off an old chicken. When the door closed behind the old woman he looked at his henchman.

"The weight is wrong," the goon said. "This box is too light."

"There should only be one box. Open that one," Markov commanded.

A knife appeared in the thug's hand and he cut away the twine in one swift careful motion. He put the blade back in his pocket and tore off the newsprint.

"Cigars," he grinned. "Cuban."

Markov gestured with two fingers for the gangster to give him the box. An envelope was taped to the outside. He opened it and read the greeting card.

*Enjoy.* It was signed, *Your Comrades in Arms.*

He ripped off the cellophane and opened the box.

"Excellent. These are the best cigars in the whole world," he smiled.

He gave one to his lieutenant and they both held the treasures under their noses and breathed deeply, savoring the harsh tobacco aroma.

"Who says crime doesn't pay," Markov laughed.

They lit the cigars and puffed on them vigorously to get them going. Markov's eyes were the first to turn glassy. His pupils dilated and he gasped for breath. He stared at the cigar in complete and utter disbelief knowing that his time on earth had come to an end. His killer was an old poison ladled from an alchemist's cauldron, borrowed from the sewers of the Middle Ages, amalgamed with slime of the newt and the secretions of the frog, chemically engineered by the space age. Markov, Muscovite heroin dealer, gaped at his lieutenant, a sinewy man with dark wiry hair. He was vomiting and fouling his clothes, jerking like an epileptic out of control. He wanted to get up from his desk and flee the gruesome scene but he couldn't control his legs. Then bloody sputum erupted from his own mouth and his body began to tremble in ghastly jerking motions. Gagging and gurgling, he fell out of his chair, joining his bully on the floor. In minutes, both men were reduced to wriggling human hemorrhages. *Yeb vas veruyushchii!*